Saving the Afterlife:
Call to War

By: Kiercy Saméa

This is a work of fiction. Names, characters, places, and incidents are either products of the author's imagination or are used fictitiously. Any resemblance to actual events, locales, or persons, living or dead, is entirely coincidental.

House of Zeerlo

Cover design by **Kiercy Saméa**

ISBN: 979-8-9999266--6

Printed in the United States of America

Dedication:

For my dear friend and editor, **Emma Bascom**—Thank you for believing in this story, and in me, when the fire burned low.

One

Come outside.

She groaned inwardly as she read the text. All she wanted was a quiet night of studying. Naturally, it would be disrupted by the world of Celestials. If she could ignore the text she would. But it wasn't wise to ignore anything that came from Wrath Incarnate. Zeerlo didn't have a non-violent bone in his body. And he did not tolerate being ignored.

"Léana," Elya said looking to her friend. "I think I forgot something in the car, I'll be right back."

"Go ahead, keys are on the counter," Léana said not glancing up from her notes.

Elya nodded taking the keys silently. She'd hate for her friend to catch her in a lie. Especially, when she was one of the few human friends she had. They were a rare commodity for a human who spent far too much time with Celestial beings. Stepping outside, she was met with a tall, muscular man, with dark hair and dark golden eyes. He bore an uncanny resemblance to Satan, only Elya knew Satan always wore a suit. And this man. While dressed in a blazer, was wearing jeans with it. She wasn't even sure the devil knew what jeans were.

Elya staggered back. "You're not Zeerlo."

The man smirked. "No, but I look enough like him and he was *kind* enough to let me *borrow* his phone."

"Gabriel, Satan, Raphael, if any of you can hear me there is a creepy dude that kind of looks like Satan right in front of me." She had no idea if any of them would respond. They usually showed when she was in danger so she wouldn't worry too much. Yet.

"What do you want? Elya asked.

The man chuckled. "You. Out of my way."

"What?"

"You mean far too much to them. It makes them weak."

"Who are you talking about? Who are you?"

The man smirked. "Me? I'm someone you know intimately and someone you don't. A friend, an enemy, a lover who will destroy you."

"Elya!" A voice shouted.

Elya turned to see Zeerlo—the *real* Zeerlo—had arrived. He looked similar to the man, only far younger. Lankier, his eyes unnaturally blue rather than golden, and carrying an intensity only the eldest teenage Son of Satan could. She glanced back to the man only to see he had vanished.

"Dad said you sent out a distress call," Zeerlo said looking around.

"There was a man, he looked like Satan. Only he was wearing jeans."

Zeerlo stilled. "Was he also wearing a white t-shirt, with a sword hung at his waist and a golden pair of wings on his shirt?"

"No," Elya looked to her friend in confusion. "Why?"

"Gramps isn't as creative as he thinks," Zeerlo said.

"Meaning?" Elya shook her head. "You know what never mind, another time. We need to focus on the strange creepy man."

"What did he look like?"

"Your dad, only while he was wearing a blazer he was wearing jeans with it. And his eyes were golden. How didn't you see him?"

"Certain Celestials can make themselves invisible, even to others of Celestial blood." Zeerlo frowned. "I don't—there's nobody in Afterlife that fits that description, Elya."

"Are you sure?"

"In physical appearance sure but not attire. My dad would never wear jeans and a blazer, and the only other person I could think of that looks like my dad would never wear a blazer unless forced into a suit."

"He texted me from your phone," Elya said.

Fires sparked in Zeerlo's gaze. "And here I thought I lost it. Did that man say anything to you, anything at all?"

"Yeah, he said he wanted me out of his way, that I mean too much to them, that I make them weak. But I have no idea whom he was referring to. And then he said he's someone I know intimately and someone I don't. A friend, an enemy, a lover who will destroy me."

"Go inside," Zeerlo said, too quickly. His eyes didn't stop scanning the shadows.

Elya glared. "What?"

"Go inside," Zeerlo tilted his head to the door. "I'm putting a guard on you for the rest of the night."

"What's going on?"

"I'm not sure, but this can't be good," he offered her a smile. "I know you have a final tomorrow. You go on inside, worry about studying, I'll worry about making sure that creep doesn't come back."

"But—"

Zeerlo raised a brow. "Elya, I know nearly every Celestial born in existence. The fact I don't know who you were describing is concerning. You could be in danger. Go. Inside."

Elya frowned. Call it a gut feeling, but she knew he was hiding something from her. The question was what? Still, she made her way to the door, pausing as she went inside glancing back to see Zeerlo was already talking with all four of his brothers.

Zeerlo was the eldest. The shadow they were all measured against.

After him came Fiend—lust—with candy apple red hair, pale skin, and sky-blue eyes. His natural appearance was exotic, but unless someone truly knew him Fiend appeared as what someone found most attractive.

Next in line was Twist—sloth—silver-haired, with eyes to match and his mother's beautiful brown Filipino skin. In plaid purple and red pajamas with a purple shirt that had red accents and the letter Z lined diagonally three times. His life goal was to automate everything to do as little work as possible.

After Twist was Shredder—gluttony—black hair, brown eyes, pointed ears and skin that had a golden sheen to it, half-alien. A master of brewing poisons but when it came to cooking a kitchen fire was guaranteed.

Last was Hellas—greed—fiery red hair, dark brown skin, glowing purple eyes. Twelve years old and he'd successfully stolen from every government on the globe.

Each had weapons in hand. Each a deadly killing machine. The Deadly Sins were efficient if nothing else. Their words were too low to hear, and she did need to study. But she would get answers out of them. *After* she finished her finals.

Closing the door behind her, Elya set the keys down and went back to her notes, trying to concentrate to no avail. She glanced outside the window periodically. Fiend, was stood there with his wings out making him invisible to average human. And the few that could? Well, if not for her habit of tripping into Hell on the daily, she might've thought she was crazy too.

One final. She only needed to study for one final but her eyes glazed over and she found herself reading the same paragraph multiple times. She couldn't stop glancing out the window to her guard of Deadly Sins. Fiend would smirk at her each time. As though he knew she was staring. It was unnerving how still he was.

It was strange to think there was a Celestial being out there that Zeerlo didn't know, especially one that looked like his dad. How many Celestials could God have made that looked exactly like the Devil?

Elya absentmindedly highlighted a few sentences in her textbook that she thought might be important. It was difficult to remember what was important with everything that was on her mind. A strange Celestial showed at her friend's apartment. And they had managed to steal Zeerlo's phone.

Honestly, that terrified her. You had to be either extremely powerful or extremely stupid to steal from Wrath incarnate.

Two

She was cutting it close. Elya wanted to run to get to class for her final, but there was no way she'd risk it. There were too many cracks in the sidewalk, stairs to go up, people riding bikes, cars, and buses to risk it. She'd still get there with a few minutes to spare, but it wasn't ideal. It wouldn't have even been a problem if she hadn't already tripped twice in the last couple of hours. Otherwise, she would've been ready and outside the classroom thirty minutes ago at the latest. She needed those thirty minutes thanks to her mysterious visitor the night before.

She was almost there.

Her phone buzzed. Against her better judgment, she pulled it out. She had two new messages, both from Charlie.

Good luck, you're going to ace it.
And if not, my offer still stands.

> *Thanks!*
> *And don't even think about sending the mafia after my professors.*

She was halfway down the hall when she felt it. Elya sneezed and her entire body tensed for an entirely different reason. The sensation of rushing water surrounded her. Her stomach churned at the all-too-familiar feeling as she hit the ground. Hard.

Elya sat up, taking in her surroundings. The room she was in was clean; the walls were beige and the floors marble. The ceiling seemed never-ending, and a chandelier of fire hung overhead. That would've been intimidating enough by itself, but add the man sitting on the giant throne atop a dais, there was no denying: She had tripped into Hell... again. She stood, brushing the dirt off her arms, and turned to the throne's occupant.

"If you're going to keep dragging me into Hell, the least you could do is pay me." Elya glanced to the grandfather clock situated in the corner. "Not to mention I have a final in five minutes," she crossed her arms. "I'm serious, this can't continue. I'm going to need to get an actual job eventually, and I can't keep disappearing!"

A blur flashed in front of her, but as quickly as it had appeared, it was gone. Now, a dark-haired teen with an ever-present smirk stood next to Satan on his throne. "We could stop, but where would be the fun in that?"

Elya narrowed her gaze, doing her best to appear intimidating. "I need to go back. Now!" The problem was that, while among humans she was formidable, in the world of celestials, she was just the clumsy girl who tripped into Hell daily.

Satan rose from his throne. Most might have found the added height from the dais made him more intimidating—and the first time she met him, Elya would've agreed. At this point, however, she was here so often, she didn't think anything Satan or his children did would faze her. The demons, though, were scary as…. Hell, for lack of a better word.

The Devil stepped down from the dais, stopping mere inches from her face. "I have Fiend currently disguised as you, so there's plenty of time," he grinned. "And better news: You're sure to ace your final!"

She glared. "I'm not going thousands of dollars in debt so *your* son can get a college education."

Zeerlo scoffed. "As though he needs one. Besides, we're doing you a favor."

Elya sighed. She would just have to hope Fiend didn't kill her professor or classmates, like she always had to… The same way she had to hope she wouldn't return to a corpse when Satan replaced her with one of his sons while she was with her boyfriend. If it were Twist, she wouldn't worry, but Fiend concerned her. He loved bloodshed almost as much as Zeerlo. She shuddered at the thought.

"What do you need this time?" Elya asked partially out of curiosity, but mostly out of resignation that there was no way she'd be getting to her final now.

Satan wasn't the worst person in the world, despite his reputation. though she hated that he couldn't just give her everything he needed done the first time around. But Satan operated on his own time frame. Once, he sent Zeerlo to trip her so they could get a female's opinion on what color tie he should wear for a business dinner.

Satan was an opportunist. He sometimes casually made her navigate the fires of Hell's kitchen so she could fix him coffee. A coffee he then wasted by dumping it on Zeerlo.

He grinned devilishly. "Glad you've asked," he gestured for her to follow. "You see, unfortunate as it is, between running an illicit mercenary business for your government – and, of course, all of Hell – I am quite busy. Yet, for some reason, I simply can't escape the paperwork. I've got five reports due to your government tomorrow and one report to my Father that was due three months ago… as well as one due two months ago, last month, and, well, yesterday, but He can wait for the rest."

Elya frowned. "If you're going to keep this up, you have got to start paying me. I feel like I should be getting something out of this."

"Who do you think pays your bills?" Satan asked.

"Raphael pays my bills, and Gabriel sends me money for groceries. Even Kalael drops by once a month to check if I need anything."

Zeerlo scoffed. "We let you leave Hell when you end up here by accident and you get to see my handsome face every time. Not to mention we gave you free security all night yesterday to protect you from a mysterious man we found no evidence of having ever been there. What more do you need?"

"I don't know," Elya snarked, "money? My bank account has $16.32 in it. Or a guarantee I can leave Hell unharmed every time."

"It's Hell," Zeerlo deadpanned. "We couldn't guarantee that if we wanted."

"You could," Elya huffed. "You just choose not to, because what fun would there be in it for you." She raised a brow. "Or am I wrong?"

Satan chuckled. "No, you have him pegged."

She turned her glare onto the Devil. "Don't think I'm not still annoyed with you."

Zeerlo raised a brow. "And what will you do?" He crossed his arms. "I've killed people for breathing too loud. The only reason I haven't killed you is because for some reason, crazy here—" he gestured to his father "—likes you alive."

"Odd," Elya muttered. "I could've sworn it was because we were friends."

Flames erupted around Zeerlo, reflected in his gaze. "I don't have friends!" He crossed his arms, turning his back on her. "The Sons of Satan need nobody." His tone darkened. "Especially me."

"Zeerlo, be nice to Elya," the Devil said.

"How about I just rip her to shreds?" The flames around him grew higher. "Wouldn't that please you? She's making you weak. She's making us *all* weak. She's a hindrance."

If Elya were anyone else, she'd probably have been insulted. But she knew Zeerlo was just acting on his sin. His words were unacceptable, but she understood. He was angry. Elya wasn't blind, she knew there'd been problems in the Lucifer household lately. It was wrong for him to take his rage out on her, but the thing was: Satan never properly taught any of his children how to handle their emotions – well, the few they had. Rage was one of the few things the Sons of Satan could feel, and, being Wrath, Zeerlo felt it in an intensity beyond anything any of them could ever understand.

"Zeerlo!" Satan snapped. "Apologize now!"

"Make me, old man!" Zeerlo snarled.

"Just remember, Satan, it'll all be worth it." The Devil muttered to himself. "He will reach full maturity in a matter of months." He paced. "Hang in there until then. Remember why you have him in the first place." Satan sighed. "Zeerlo will be your perfect weapon; none will stand against him. You've made it this long… you can surely last a few more months."

It was a regular occurrence, Satan muttering to himself trying to give himself a pep-talk about his annoying teenagers. One of these days, maybe he'd believe it. Until then, Elya was prepared for the worst. She had sneezing powder in the smallest pocket of her backpack that she would use in case she needed an escape.

Now, that didn't mean her plans were foolproof. After all, she would be screwed if she landed right back in Hell when she was trying to escape, especially when she could only use that powder in very specific circumstances. In this moment, she'd only be able to use the sneezing powder when an inevitable fight broke out between Satan and his eldest son. That was the only time Satan lost focus on his attempts to trap her there, so she had a very small window of opportunity. Given that he and Zeerlo were both short-tempered, it really was just a matter of time.

While she had never witnessed one of their arguments, she had seen the aftermath. The throne room had been in complete chaos: The chandelier had shattered, the walls themselves were in shambles, and the floors cracked. Satan's throne had turned to a pile of rubble and scorch marks were everywhere… also, there were at least three corpses from demons who had been dumb enough to try and break it up.

Yet, for some unfathomable reason, Satan seemed convinced Zeerlo would turn into his perfect obedient soldier as soon as he reached what Satan called "maturity." Elya got the feeling it wasn't a type of maturity associated with humans. After all, humans all mature differently and at different rates, but Satan had recently been muttering how it was only a few more months… So, whatever it was, it had to be something that automatically set in once Zeerlo reached a certain age. If his personality did a complete 180, it'd be weird, but she wouldn't be entirely opposed to it. She had been on the receiving end of way too many of his 'harmless' pranks. But then, she wasn't going to hold her breath. She wasn't even sure God could change Zeerlo's —well, self.

Elya eyed Satan as she pulled herself out of her over-analytical reverie and noted he was still pacing and muttering to himself. She was a little worried he was descending into insanity. It was his fault, really – she had met his younger four sons. The boys all had their faults, though Zeerlo was the only one who regularly talked back and enjoyed giving the Devil migraines (he was also the only one of them not scared of their father). They all had their ways of driving Satan further into madness. Zeerlo was himself, Fiend had been arrested on more than one occasion, Shredder set Mercenary Mansion on fire daily, Hellas was constantly stealing Satan's wallet… and then there was Twist. To her eternal confusion, the boy who designed and sold weapons to the government was also on their watch list.

She hoped he wasn't going to snap and decide to take his anger out on more than the furniture. She had seen the aftermath of his rage… she didn't need to witness this firsthand.

She glanced at Zeerlo. The fires surrounding him had died down, but they still danced in his gaze. "Should we try to snap him out of it?"

"Nah, he'll be fine," Zeerlo shrugged the flames leaving his gaze. "He spirals at least once a week. Sometimes I push him too far, but he'll be fine in a few minutes." He paused. "Maybe."

"You're sure I shouldn't be worried?" Elya asked.

He grinned. "Have I ever steered you wrong?"

"You want me to trust you?" Elya scoffed. "When you just threatened to kill me? Yeah, I don't think so, bud. And in answer to your question: yes." She crossed her arms. "Constantly. When we met, you convinced me Azrael was going to kill me." Believable, since the entity was the Grim Reaper.

Zeerlo chuckled. "That was a good one." His fangs elongated. "Still can't believe you fell for it, though. I was seven."

"I was eleven and the only exposure to the supernatural I had was your dad and a pair of angels. And do you remember what you were like at seven?"

"Yes. I was the obedient child—" he cocked his head to the side "—crazy over there is dreaming of… Though I did complain about not being allowed to kill people ever."

"You were terrifying," Elya deadpanned.

"Me? Terrifying? Not possible."

"You are the embodiment of terrifying."

"I'm not 'terrifying.' I'm Wrath, in case you didn't notice from everything about me. Remember when I broke your wrist once because you wouldn't share your Skittles? Not to mention, there was the time I hospitalized one of my brothers because he got dirt on my new shoes."

"I remember." She had been fifteen, and he was eleven. Satan had been pissed at Zeerlo for hurting her, but that was nothing compared to the fact that she had to trip fifty-two times afterward before she landed in Heaven to get it fixed. "I also remember having to convince Gabriel he didn't need to come to talk to you and Satan about proper behavior." He sat her down for a long talk about greed and gluttony instead. "I'm surprised he didn't wrap me in bubble wrap. He showed up every day for a year to ensure I hadn't sustained further injury."

"Good times," Zeerlo grinned.

A crash sounded from the other side of the room and Elya hesitated. Slowly, she spared a glance toward Satan. His skin had turned bright red, large black wings speckled with flecks of gray had sprouted from his back, and a set of shiny, black horns stood out from his head. The Devil paced rapidly in front of the debris he caused as dancing flames consumed his entire form. Once again, his throne had been thrown into the wall. (Why he bothered bolting it down was beyond her. They never held when he was in a temper.)

Elya turned back to Zeerlo. "So – this paperwork he wants me to do?"

A stack of papers seemed to appear in his hands. Elya knew better, though. She knew the teen moved at the speed of light. Catching his movements was almost impossible, but she had grown accustomed to his sudden blurred disappearance.

"This should be everything. Reports for the government, reports for Heaven, and the reports on me and my brothers are on top. The reports of the happenings of Hell are obviously on the bottom. Don't rush yourself or anything. Dad never gets his reports in on time, and the ones for Gramps are overdue anyways. One of these days, you might even get to see the report room."

"What's the report room?" How had she, in so many years of tripping here, never seen the report room? Never even heard of it?

"Well, let's see. Dad is supposed to turn in a report once a month on the happenings of Hell. These are the first ones he's done in the entire time he's been down here. So, I'd say—let's just say it's a room filled with boxes upon boxes of incomplete reports. I think the goal for turning these in is to give Gramps a heart attack."

"Can God get heart attacks?"

Zeerlo rolled his eyes. "Why does everyone feel obligated to deify Gramps just because he's immortal?"

She scoffed. "It's hard to go to Hell every day and still be agnostic."

"Whatever. Like I said, don't worry about rushing."

Elya smirked. "If I didn't know better, I'd almost say you cared for my well-being."

Zeerlo gasped. "Perish the thought! How dare you accuse me of ca-" Zeerlo paused, looking deeply uncomfortable. "Ca-" He visibly gagged. "That word?"

Elya laughed. While his tone was exaggerated, to her eternal amazement, he seriously couldn't say caring. Well, not unless it was to emphasize how little he cared. And, she had noticed, the word love made him sneeze; he was literally allergic to the word. He took strange to whole new levels, especially given his inability to be hugged. Not many people had ever dared trying it over the years, but she had witnessed it a couple of times. Apparently, it was a lifelong illness.

"Any chance you'd be willing to take me home?" Elya asked.

"If it gets me away from crazy here, I'll take you wherever." He waved a hand toward Satan. "But Fiend is probably still sitting in on your final, waiting for an appropriate amount of time to pass before turning it in." He shrugged. "Someone might find it suspicious if you return too soon."

"You know what? That's fine. Not like I can just take his place at my final. Could you imagine what'd happen if people saw two of me? My roommates should be gone anyway." At least, Elya hoped her roommates were all gone. She hadn't been gone longer than thirty minutes; she didn't want to explain why she was back already if they weren't. It wasn't like she could say she was done. Also, she hated them.

Zeerlo nodded. "Sounds like a plan."

He gripped her wrist tightly. Elya calmed her breathing, anticipating the rapid movement which resulted from Zeerlo's carelessness. She winced as her arm was yanked and the ground slipped out from under her. Wind rushed past her, her chest tightened, her stomach churned... It was always uncomfortable going anywhere with Zeerlo. He didn't care if he hurt her. She was almost certain that was his goal.

Thankfully, it wasn't long before he roughly released her wrist as they came to a stop at her front porch. Elya winced as she ran into the door. Zeerlo was long gone. She caught her reflection in the mirror, sighing she patted her hair down, trying to make it somewhat presentable. It looked like she had just woken up from a rough night of sleep. Life would be so much easier if she could trip her way out of Hell, or at least control her ability and go where she wanted when she wanted. It'd be nice, but Elya knew it was an impossible dream.

Falling back onto her bed, Elya reached into the drawer of her side table and pulled out a bag of skittles, only to find broken shards of what appeared to be razor blades. It was so mean.

"Damn it, Zeerlo!" Elya tossed the skittles bag in the trash. This was the third time this week he had taken her skittles and replaced them.

The magical transformation of Zeerlo from himself into a mature version of himself who wouldn't pull these cruel tricks on her couldn't come fast enough. After sixteen years, she was done. She had been tripping into Hell since she was six and nobody seemed able to teach her to control it or take the ability away.

Gabriel and Raphael were convinced the only one who could remove her unfortunate ability to trip into Hell was God, and they were under the firm belief she was given the power to trip into Hell for a reason. They said the same thing when she was ten and she broke her arm falling out of a tree. Thankfully that time, she landed in Heaven. Satan would have cracked up laughing and handed her a laundry list of things he wanted her to do, but Gabriel had gently lifted her from the ground while Raphael examined the break. It had splintered and she also managed to shatter her elbow. Then Raphael put his hands on the break and the pain was gone.

That was the day she learned Raphael was the angel of healing. It was the same day two angels accidentally kidnapped her by taking her to Disney World because she was hurt. It was also the tenth time she was reported missing.

Three

Thanks to her talent for tripping Elya found herself back in Hell's throne room before she could even make it to the bathroom the next morning. Not that Satan or his children cared. They allowed her to go to the bathroom and as soon as she exited, she found her clothes forcibly changed by a wave of Satan's hand. One day she'd get it through his thick skull that it was invasive to wave his hand and change her clothes.

Any hope of getting home at a decent time was also quickly dashed as she noted that training dummies and targets had been spread throughout the room. If that weren't enough Elya found a cinnamon roll being shoved at her along with a sword. There was only one thing that Elya could discern from that. Training.

Which was how she found herself sweaty, tired, and hungry because she only got three bites of her cinnamon roll before she found herself dodging fireballs as she attempted to hit the training dummies with a sword that was too heavy for her. But Heaven forbid Satan let her have a sword that she could use.

"Your footwork is sloppy!" Zeerlo called.

Moving swiftly, Elya dodged the fireballs thrown her direction. As though the training they forced her through wasn't bad enough, she had to deal with Zeerlo's commentary too. After their last visit, she'd gladly go without it.

Elya huffed. She swung the sword to strike the practice dummy, only for Zeerlo to appear in front of her, catching the blade in his hand and pulling it from her grip with ease. Elya eyed his skin but, as always, there was no blood. Zeerlo was impenetrable. And if he and Satan were to be believed, in a matter of months, he would be invincible. It was hard to believe sometimes how powerful the Sons of Satan were… but Zeerlo took the power to heightened levels.

"What gives?" Elya asked.

"You're going to hurt yourself." He tossed the sword to Fiend. "Eight years, and your footwork is still sloppy. And you swing the sword like it's a toy."

"I do not!"

Fiend scoffed. "Yes, you do."

"Well maybe if you guys weren't throwing fire at me the whole time!"

Zeerlo sighed. "In a life and death situation, you never know what elements will be thrown at you. Besides, if creepy men are showing up and threatening you it's only fair you be prepared for everything."

"Yes," Elya snarked, "I'm going to want a sword when I'm in a life and death situation. Humanity stopped using them as weapons of war for a reason!"

"Guns are for the weak," Fiend said, balancing his sword in the palm of his hand. "Except our sister. She just likes them."

"Can I try another sword?" Elya asked. "Maybe Fiend's is too heavy for me."

Zeerlo scoffed, crossing his arms, muscles flexing. "You're not using mine."

"Oh, come on! I've tried Fiend's, Twist's, Hellas's, and I've even tried Shredder's. None of their swords have worked over the years. Let me use yours."

"Do you realize you are asking to use a Hell-forged blade?" Zeerlo asked.

"Yes, and I also know you owe me!"

Zeerlo scoffed. "I don't owe you just because I hurt your fragile human emotions."

Fiend handed Elya his sword. "Zeerlo's is also designed to steal souls," he said, defusing the situation. "If something happens, you could lose yours, and I do not want to see who can throw the biggest fit about it when it happens," he grinned. "Now go again."

"No," Satan called. "It's clear Elya won't be satisfactory with the sword. Move onto training her with daggers."

Elya grinned. "Now there's something I can get behind."

Daggers had become her weapon of choice early on. She took to them like Satan's children took to killing. Unfortunately, Satan refused to let her keep the ones she practiced with or give her any. And when she had tried buying some on her own, he sent Shredder of all people to buy them out from underneath her. Honestly, she didn't see the point of training her to use weapons if she couldn't even own any herself. She could hide a dagger in her purse and it would make her feel a lot safer if she was ever walking alone in the dark! Granted, the odds were that if someone tried attacking her, she would run and trip. Then she could sic either Satan, one of his sons, or an angel on her attacker.

Zeerlo pulled two red-hilted daggers from his pendant. "Let's see how well you throw." He pointed to the wall where the targets were set up. "After all, we can't always have throwing knives in dangerous situations."

"No," Satan said.

Elya turned to him. "What?"

"I want to see how well you fight." He stepped forward. "Fiend," he smirked, "fetch me one of the demons. It's time to test what Elya can really do."

Elya gaped. "Whoa, wait what?"

"You heard."

Her eyes widened. "I can't fight a demon!" She staggered back. "They're like three times my size and six times my strength and – can you even cut them with daggers?"

Satan shrugged. "If you hit them in their weak points."

She drew her brows together and shook her head. "What are the weak points?"

"Neck, wrists, inner elbows, abdomen. Hit them anywhere else and you'll only succeed in irritating them," Zeerlo said.

"Yeah, I'm not doing this," Elya tossed the daggers into targets. "I'd rather just go home."

"The chances are, if you find yourself in a dangerous situation, your opponent will be a demon or as powerful as." Satan held his hand out; the daggers flew into his hand. "Do you want to be helpless?"

"Hold up. You control the demons. Why the Hell would I need to fight against one?"

"They only listen so long as I'm near," Satan reminded her, handing her the daggers. "You have to learn to fight back. Why else would we never allow you outside the throne room unescorted?"

Elya scoffed. "You can't just tell them to leave me alone?"

He raised a brow but said nothing.

Elya eyed the daggers in her hands. She wished she had some of her own. She wasn't asking for a Hell-forged dagger, or a custom made one – she just wanted one she could call her own. One that, when she picked it up, felt right in her hand because it was *hers*.

"Alright, I'll do it." She adjusted her hold. "But if I die, none of you are allowed at my funeral. Don't visit my grave either."

Satan rolled his eyes. "I will not allow you to die, and Fiend is more than capable of healing any injuries you might sustain."

Fiend grinned. "Just call me Dr. Fiend Lucifer."

"You don't have a medical license," Zeerlo said.

Fiend waved a dismissive hand. "Details! I'm better than any licensed doctor you'll ever find. The way I see it, doctors can't heal themselves, so they're inferior."

"While I couldn't care less, it is an insult to those humans who actually put in the work and money to become a medical doctor." He smirked. "Also, I hear it's illegal to impersonate a doctor. You know what that means—"

The screeching sound of the throne room doors opening cut him off. Elya turned to the entrance to see a figure about five feet high with rust colored skin. It was leathery with a pair of equally leathery wings protruding from its back. Two small horns poked from the top of its head. The demon knelt as it caught Satan looking at it. Aside from his children, Elya was probably the only person to enter Hell who didn't kneel before its king.

Fiend laughs. "Fifty dollars says Elya can't land a hit on the demon."

Zeerlo grinned. "You're on."

Elya eyed the demon, a little startled that Zeerlo was betting for her, not against her. "I didn't know demons could be so small."

Satan shrugged. "It's a child."

"What?" Elya dropped the daggers. "I am not fighting a kid."

"Suit yourself." The daggers flew into Satan's hand. "But if you refuse to fight the demon because it is a child, then you leave me no choice." He handed the daggers to Zeerlo. "Pick up the sword again, you're to spar Zeerlo."

Elya coughed. "Excuse me? I am not fighting Zeerlo. He'd kill me."

Zeerlo cackled. "What's wrong Elya? Don't you trust me?"

"No."

Satan chuckled. "A wise decision, but I am a man of my word, as are my sons, and you have my word Zeerlo shall not harm you." He glared at Zeerlo. "Will you?"

Zeerlo gasped. "Me? Hurt Elya?" He grinned, that same grin Elya had seen on Satan. "Never on purpose. At least, not without having a good reason, I wouldn't."

Elya scoffed. Zeerlo classified not sharing skittles as a good enough reason to break her wrist when he had been eleven. While Satan had then proceeded to rant and rave about how he wasn't allowed to hurt her, Elya suspected even the slightest thing would be excuse enough for Wrath incarnate. Zeerlo took unprecedented pleasure in injuring others, especially in killing. She had witnessed him at work once long before he was an official mercenary, but once was enough. Regardless of her personal feelings, Elya found a sword thrust into her hands as she stood across from Zeerlo. He pulled his own sword from within his necklace: The hilt was made of silver, encrusted with rubies, and intricate snakes were carved around it. The blade didn't hide its sharpness, appearing shiny and new. His name was engraved into the side of the blade, surrounded with flames.

"Can I just say this is really unfair?" Elya asked.

"We know." All three replied.

Elya gulped as Zeerlo vanished. She turned in vain, finding only a sharp sting in her side. Wrath had drawn first blood and she couldn't even see to fight him. Opponents capable of moving the speed of light should've been outlawed. Elya swung wildly at the air, hoping against hope she'd make contact with Zeerlo. Not that'd it'd cut him. Nothing was capable of penetrating his skin.

Then it happened. A large clump of black hair fell to the ground and Zeerlo suddenly skidded into view. His bangs no longer hung in his face; instead, his hair was choppy in the front. She had somehow managed to cut his hair.

Elya's eyes flashed to Zeerlo.

His gaze was consumed with fire. "How dare you?!" A pair of red feathery wings sprouted from his back. His breathing became heavy. "I will put up with a lot of things." He stepped forward. Flames licked at his feet as the shadows danced around him. "But I will not tolerate this." His fangs were elongated, his face contorted in pure rage. "Nobody touches the hair." He raised his sword.

Elya gulped. "It was an accident."

"An accident?" He seethed. "And somehow that makes it better?"

The sword flew from his hand. "Enough!" Satan caught it in his own. "I shall not have you harming Elya."

Zeerlo didn't look at his father. "She ruined my hair!" He disappeared in a blur. "I won't tolerate it." A flash and then he was behind Elya. "I don't need weapons to kill."

As Satan stepped forward, flames bursting around him, the temperature dropped. His suit ripped and screams sounded in the distance. He seemed to double in size as he went full devil. In one swift movement, Elya was yanked from Zeerlo's grasp. She screamed as she was thrown into Fiend, who thankfully caught her. He pulled her close to him, blocking her view of the two behind her. A crash sounded. The ground shook.

Somehow, all she could think was that the massacre she was about to witness was happening sooner than she predicted.

"Let's get you somewhere safe," Fiend said.

Elya didn't get a chance to protest before Fiend picked her up and the wind rushed past her. Next thing she knew, she was being placed on her bed as Fiend paced in front of her. Agitation radiated from him. His own sky-blue eyes had turned the same candy apple red of his hair. Flames licked at his feet. Sometimes she forgot the other Sons of Satan had power over fire, since not one of them used it the way Zeerlo did. None of them *could* use it the way he did.

"You don't have to stay here, you know," Elya said.

His gaze snapped to her. "I've got orders that say otherwise."

Elya gaped. "Seriously?"

"The last thing we need is you falling into Hell while Zeerlo and my father are duking it out. You'd get killed by a stray fire blast," he shrugged. "Or thrown into a wall, hit by a falling wall – really, there are several ways you could die."

"Zeerlo's going to kill me, isn't he?" Elya asked.

"Not likely." Fiend sat on the floor. "He's pissed, sure, and he will always threaten it, but he'll get his aggression out." He placed an arm over his knee. "That's not to say he won't increase his pranks against you, but he won't outright hurt you."

Elya frowned. "You're sure?"

"You're the one human Zeerlo doesn't see as being worth less than the dirt beneath his feet." Fiend ran a hand through his hair. "If he wanted to hurt you, he would've done it while he had the chance. He's pissed, but he doesn't actually want you hurt."

"Why should I believe you?"

He laughed. "You have my word."

Elya nodded. Satan and his sons had no qualms with lying, but when they gave their word, they never broke it.

The hours ticked by slowly. Elya wasn't sure how long Satan and Zeerlo could possibly fight, but Fiend made no indication he was leaving. Normally, in these situations she'd do homework or study, only now she was done with school.

As it started to get late, she grabbed the sleeping bag and extra pillow she kept for when one of the Lucifer boys—Zeerlo—spent the night after a disagreement with Satan from the closet. From there, she headed into the bathroom to change into her pajamas. When she returned, however, Fiend was gone.

Four

She was exhausted and dressed in only her pjs, but Heaven forbid Satan drag her to his office at a humane hour. The Devil hadn't even given her time to get dressed. She swore if he didn't have a good reason for dragging her to Hell in the middle of the night, she'd tell Gabriel. She didn't know what Gabriel could or would do, but she didn't care, so long as it kept her from more 3:00 am meetings with the Devil. Worse yet, she had been there ten minutes stood in front of Satan and he'd yet to say a word.

She was curious about why she was there. She'd never been good at hiding her curiosity – or keeping it at bay, really. She'd been tripping into Hell from the age of six, but she still knew so little about it. Satan rarely let her out of the throne room, and when he did, she was always escorted.

Somehow, she didn't think he had dragged her there in the middle of the night to regale her with the story of his fall from Heaven or the secrets of Hell. Unfortunately.

Had the mysterious Satan-look-alike with the golden eyes returned? Was he at her apartment? It'd certainly explain why she'd been dragged away in the middle of the night. This wasn't a common occurrence.

"After some careful consideration, I have chosen to pay you," Satan said, suddenly breaking the silence. "You have made valid points in your argument—"

Elya laughed. She wasn't sure if it was her sleep-deprived delirium that made her laugh at the Devil, but she had somehow lost any ability to care. "You sound like Gabriel."

"Well then," his eyes narrowed. "Here I was going to give you a paycheck with a substantial bonus, but now I'm not sure I want to."

"I'm not apologizing." She tapped her foot impatiently as she stared down the Devil, daring him to say something.

"Here," he thrust a check at her. "Not that you deserve it, ungrateful brat."

Elya took the piece of paper in her hand. It was a check made payable to her in the amount of $592,836.17 "Is this for real?"

Worth getting up at three in the morning, though she had no intention of telling him that. If she so much as hinted that she thought it worthwhile, he'd be getting her up at all hours of the night with some meaningless tasks. There was no telling how many late-night pancakes runs she'd have to go make. (All of Afterlife knew that pancakes were essentially the entire composition of Satan's diet. He was lucky he was immortal, because otherwise all those carbs would not work out for him.)

She frowned. The mere fact she was contemplating Satan's diet was a desperate cry for her to get sleep.

"Your next pay won't be as substantial, as you will not have a bonus," Satan said. "The bonus is for all the extra years of work for me in backpay."

Elya grinned. "Dude, this could pay off my student debt and then some!" Her eyes went wide. "I could buy a house!"

"Mortals must have cheap education and housing," he said dismissively.

Elya resisted the urge to scoff and correct him that education and housing were in fact not cheap. Especially housing. Far too many greedy corporations bought out housing and turned them into rental homes for profit rather than allowing the average citizen to buy a home.

"Where do you even get this kind of money?" Elya asked.

"I'm the Devil. I have acquired much wealth over the millennia without much to spend it on." He frowned. "And, between us, my Father still gives me an allowance."

She raised a brow. "Why do any of you need money?"

Satan rolled his eyes. "So when we interact with the mortal world, we have ways of blending in." He crossed his arms. "It's not as though Earth is the only planet we hang around on.

Believe me, the Dyra are *vicious* when they suspect someone is stealing from them."

"The who?" Elya asked.

"The Dyra. Very vindictive people halfway across the universe. Chances are, you'll never meet one, so it's not relevant. Just know they are what humanity would term as an alien and leave it at that."

"But I want to know more!" Elya said.

"I thought it was late?" Satan said.

Elya crossed her arms. "You know I have an endless curiosity, and you're seriously going to dangle that in my face and tell me nothing?"

He smirked. "I'm the Devil. Nothing is ever free. But if you believe you're willing to pay my price for knowledge…"

Elya sighed looking at the check in her hand. "I don't even think my bank can take a check this big."

He shrugged. "Tell them you won a lawsuit."

Elya grinned. "Must have been some lawsuit. Who'd I sue?"

Satan raised a brow. "Does it matter?"

She shrugged. "Might. I mean, if someone asks, they're going to want an answer. And what did I sue over?"

Satan dug into his desk drawers, pulling out a business card. "Here, tell them you sued my security company and won. Tell them we killed your cat or something."

Elya took the card. "Since when do you have a security company?"

"I don't. But I operate a mercenary business that gets contracted by the government a lot. Got to tell people I do something for a living."

"Right." Elya put the card in her pajamas pocket. "I'll figure something out."

Nobody in their right mind would believe she, a college student waiting on her final grades, could possibly sue any size corporation and win. But what did Satan care if she couldn't cash her check?

"Good," Satan said.

She yawned. "Anything else?"

"No," he said.

"Seriously? There's no other reason you dragged me down here in the middle of the night. We need to discuss the importance of sleep," she yawned. "Hasn't Gabriel told you a thousand times it's not nice to disrupt sleep? Especially for humans like me. Believe it or not, we do need sleep. I appreciate the money, but it could've waited."

"Fine. You have me." He crossed his arms. "Because you most certainly will find out and I have nothing to delay you further with. I will simply say that I have it on good authority that it is best that you are not home for the rest of the night. Otherwise, I would've waited until morning. If I've learned anything, it is that women do not like it when they are awoken from their sleep for inconsequential matters."

"What are you—" she yawned "—talking about? Is it the man again?"

"Doesn't matter," he stepped from behind his desk. "The fact of the matter is you cannot return home tonight. But clearly, as you have stated and as is indicated by your persistent need to yawn, you need sleep."

She yawned. "Right. I don't follow."

What could possibly be happening that she couldn't go home? Had there been a fire? Was there going to be a break-in? Satan's brothers were angels and he knew everyone's desires, she wouldn't put it past him to find something like that out. Or was it something elsc? Maybe something more celestial in nature? That man looked a lot like Satan, had it been him again? Or was it something else? But what else could it possibly be? Nobody from Heaven would hurt her, and nobody from Hell would risk pissing off Satan. That was almost a guaranteed way to have the deadly sins sent after you. But if it wasn't because of someone from Heaven or Hell, then who? The only threat they knew of was that man. And the only other celestial she knew was Azrael, and unless she suddenly turned into a squirrel, the Grim Reaper wouldn't hurt her.

"What's going on?" Elya asked.

"Follow me," Satan said.

He was evading the question. Elya was almost certain it had to be the mysterious man with the golden eyes. There was no other logical explanation for why he'd be so evasive to her questions.

"Come along," he said.

Elya didn't bother protesting. She didn't have the energy; she'd just have to interrogate him in the morning. In the meantime, she followed the Devil from his office, through the torch lit halls of his palace, past countless black doors, (most of which had screams coming from within) until he came to a stop in front of one. He pushed the door open, gesturing for her to enter. As soon as she was securely inside, Satan pulled the door shut behind them. A light flicked on. Even in her tired state, Elya noticed how ornate everything was – and surprisingly gothic. Usually, Satan's things gave off the appearance of classy and business tycoon, maybe royalty, but never gothic.

"Where are we?" Elya asked, taking in the dark hardwood floors, black walls, and dark furniture. A black chandelier hung from the ceiling.

"I have a suite down here," he shrugged. "Apartment. Whatever you prefer to call it. There are three bedrooms, each equipped with its own bathroom and closet. As it is not safe to send you home, I'm not letting you where I can't keep you under my protection in Hell. And I'm not so monstrous to deprive you of your sleep. The best I can offer you is one of the spare bedrooms."

"Why would I be in danger if I went home?" Elya asked.

"Don't worry about it." He threw open a door. "Here this is the second largest bedroom – more than suitable for your needs, I'm certain."

Elya stepped into the room, gaping. It was huge, easily bigger than her living room and kitchen combined. Granted those weren't big, but for a bedroom, it was huge… even if it was a little on the side of dreary with the black carpet, black painted walls, intricately carved black furniture, and black candlelit chandelier overhead. And the canopy bed was humongous; it could easily sleep three celestials with their wings out. Or a whole lot of humans. The carpet was soft under her feet, softer than anything she'd ever felt. The furniture was all intricately carved.

"Goodnight," Satan said, shutting the door before Elya could find words.

It was unbelievable. She walked across the carpet and pulled back the comforter. It was soft, it and the sheets felt softer than silk. Maybe a high-count Egyptian cotton? Or was it possible for any kind of cotton to be softer than silk? She only had the vaguest idea when it came to fabrics, and honestly, she was so tired, she didn't care. She could always ask Satan what seemingly magical soft fabric his bedsheets were made from in the morning.

And if he thought putting her in a room and shutting the door would keep her from interrogating him about why she wasn't allowed to go home, he was sorely mistaken. If anything, the sleep would allow her thoughts to be clearer and she'd be able to ask better questions in the morning. And she had full intentions of finding out everything. First thing in the morning. For now, though, she was too tired and too comfortable to worry about those things.

"Sleep well Elya," a voice whispered in the dark.

Normally, she'd be concerned, but given where she was Elya was almost certain it was either just Satan or one of the Deadly Sins, perhaps even a demon trying to mess with her. Snuggling deeper into the blankets she drifted into oblivion.

Five

That night she dreamt of a man with golden eyes. He was dressed as he'd been when they'd met face to face.

"You're beautiful Elya," the man said. *"Join me as my queen."*

"Who are you?" Elya asked.

"I told you once before, I am your enemy and your ally, I can destroy you or I can love you," he smirked. *"For now, I leave the decision to you."*

Her dream shifted from the mysterious man with golden eyes to a more recent memory. Her most recent boyfriend had broken up with her the day before and it replayed in her dreams.

She woke up with the harsh reminder of how much getting dumped sucked. The worst part was that it like every time before had been a result of Fiend and Zeerlo replacing her on her dates. She'd almost forgotten about it in her exhaustion and subsequent excitement and curiosity the previous night, but now that she was awake, the memories came back.

It was irritating, and if she could, she'd kill them and Satan. If they weren't constantly forcing her into Hell, she'd have time for a relationship. It wasn't about the fact they cost her yet another romantic partner – yes, it sucked, but she had learned to deal with it. What bothered her was that they could never just let her date someone. It was like they were trying to sabotage her relationships on purpose, which would be ridiculous if it weren't exactly the type of thing they'd do for laughs.

"You seem frustrated," Satan said.

"I was dumped—" she deadpanned "—because of you guys, again."

"Really?" Satan opened a notebook. "A whole week faster than last time," he grinned. "Well done, boys, at this rate Elya will be single until she's forty."

Elya groaned, flopping down in Zeerlo's beanbag chair to the right of the throne. "I hate all of you so much."

"It's for the best—" Fiend said from his position on the rafters "—the guy was a dick. And he needs to die."

She gaped. "What?"

"Look, we only want what's best for you, and let me tell you, the boy — no. Just no." Fiend jumped from his perch. "You could do so much better."

"I agree," Satan said, standing from his throne. "Honestly, I rather you date a demon than that man. Kakius and Marco even, and those two are — well, rather vicious. Though, once you get past their want for your soul, they're not that bad." He put a hand to his chin. "Marco's not a bad idea at all. Well, he is and he isn't. Kind of a double-edged sword that one."

"And somehow you think it'd be a good idea for me to date him?" Elya asked.

"No. I'm saying I rather you date Marco than that jerk what's his name," he snaped. "In fact, if you want to date so bad, I can have Twist find you someone."

"It's not about wanting a boyfriend or girlfriend—" Elya pointed a finger "—it's about the fact everyone I've ever dated in my life has dumped me because of you guys."

"And?" Zeerlo asked.

He was sat in the center of a pentagram made of candles and skulls. Based on the way he was sat in lotus position, she wanted to say he was meditating. But something about Zeerlo and meditation didn't sound like it'd mix well. Then again, she'd be the first to admit there were still a lot of things she didn't know about Zeerlo. She may have known Satan sixteen years, but she'd only known Zeerlo for eleven, and he was full of surprises.

She huffed. "It's annoying."

"Well, we can't butt out." Satan sat back down. "Best I can offer you is having the boys stalk them prior to you going out and deem whether they're suitable." He steepled his hands. "If a person reminds us of ourselves, they're out, and if they remind us of my brothers, we'll reluctantly allow it. Unless it's Michael. I can only deal with one of him."

Elya frowned. "Hold up Mik-ae-l?" And here she thought it was pronounced the same way every human Michael she ever met pronounced it. Logically, she supposed it made sense.

Satan cringed. "Just pretend I didn't bring him up."

"No, I'm curious." Elya crossed her arms. "Like, he's mentioned in the Bible, but nobody ever talks about him." She leveled her gaze. "I want to know why."

"It's been forbidden by Michael," Satan shrugged. "Normally, I'm against any of his odd rules or decrees, but on this I can agree."

"So, what, he made it a rule that nobody can talk about him?" Elya asked.

Zeerlo chuckled. "No, he made it a rule nobody could mention him in front of, to, or around you."

"But why?" Elya asked.

"I never asked," Satan said. "Point being, nobody who reminds me of Michael."

She hoped that didn't include people named Michael, it was far too common. Like Liam, Ryan, and Noah.

"How weren't you curious?" She sure as Hell wanted to know why he would not want people mentioning him around her. "And why would it be a no if they remind you of him?"

"Three words: God's first creation." He drummed his fingers against his arm. "Sure, I was five minutes behind, but nothing quite like being first at everything." His eyes lightened from dark brown to red. "He was the fastest, the smartest, the strongest, the bravest. I was always second best."

"Got it," Elya said. "Some bitterness going on."

"It's not bitterness," Satan pouted. "One, I can handle. We argue, and then sometimes we get along," a muscle ticked above his eye, "but I refuse to deal with anyone that's a second

Michael. It'd be like dealing with a second me, and not in a fun way."

"Let's just set her up with Michael," Zeerlo suggested.

"Do that, and I kill you all." Satan stood back up. "The last thing we need is him hanging around more." He began pacing. "And that's a no on Gabriel, Raphael, Uriel, Zadkiel, Camael, Raguel, Remiel, Barachiel, Baraqiel, Chamuel, Cassiel, Ananiel, Arakiel, Harut, Marut – definitely not Azazel; he's fallen like myself – Harut and Marut, but he's a right nightmare." He threw his hands up. "Really, just any of my brothers, leave out of it." He turned to Elya. "In fact, don't even make friends with any more of them. Oh, and Lilith. You absolutely are *not* allowed to date that bitch."

"I'm just throwing out ideas," Zeerlo said, eyes closed.

"Yeah, terrible ideas," Fiend said. "Could you imagine if Elya married one of our uncles? That'd make her our aunt, and that takes half the fun out of tripping her." His eyes lit up. "But if you want her to marry in the family, she could always marry you."

"Absolutely not," Satan said.

"We could always hook her up with Thought," Zeerlo suggested.

"The guy's crazy," Fiend said.

"Here's a novel idea," Elya cut in. "All of you could just *butt out of my love life*."

Zeerlo snorted. "Don't be ridiculous."

"Yeah—" Fiend grinned "—why would we do a crazy thing like that?"

"There are all kinds of treacherous, lecherous, and just despicable people in this world," Satan said, pacing. "And I refuse to have any of them involved with someone who's a part of my life." He stopped in front of her. "And since you can't prevent yourself from tripping into Hell, you are most certainly a part of my life. For better or worse."

"Definitely worse," Zeerlo said.

"I would've thought you'd love the treacherous people," Elya said.

Satan scoffed. "Not when they disrupt my life! And I can only imagine how it'd affect your work. Furthermore, I do not tolerate outright dishonesty – you should know that by now."

"You shouldn't waste your time dating," a familiar voice whispered. *"You're meant to be mine."*

Briefly, Elya contemplated whether she should tell the Devil and his sons about the mysterious voice that had been haunting her since her encounter with the strange man with golden eyes. The logical part of her said yes, the part that was annoyed by their antics didn't want them using it as an excuse to butt even further into her life.

"You need better taste in partners," Zeerlo said.

Elya tossed up her hands. "Fine! You guys win! I just won't date anyone."

"There's an idea!" Satan grinned. "Why didn't I think of it?"

"I wasn't serious!"

"Of course you were," Satan said.

She pulled out her cellphone. "I will call Kalael."

Satan held up his hands. "Let's not be rash. There's no need to get Kalael involved. Why don't you put down the phone and we can work this all out."

Elya raised a brow. "Can we?"

"Yes!" Fiend stepped beside his father. "Just put down the phone."

"Will you guys stop interfering with my love life?" Elya asked.

"Yes, just don't call her!" Satan said urgently.

"Cowards," Zeerlo said.

Satan spun on his eldest son. "Excuse me, but do you want Kalael to show up here? You remember her, don't you? Your sister, almost 29 years old, married to Azrael, Princess of Hell, nasty temper, takes offense easily, will shoot you for disrupting her sleep, nearly incinerated both of us when we killed that mortal boy she was fond of? Ringing any bells?"

"Whatever." Zeerlo said. "Now," he said as he turned to Elya, "you have every right to be angry with us. We did violate your privacy, and we probably shouldn't be speculating on your love life," he shrugged, "but getting Kalael involved is going too far. Consider it from our perspective: You've been part of our everyday lives for years. Anyone who you would marry would eventually need to be let in on the whole Heaven-and-Hell-are-actual-places-thing. There'd just be no avoiding it. And despite the gross inaccuracy of deifying Gramps, people would react to that – and they'd most certainly react to meeting Satan, who for some reason has also been deified." He crossed his arms. "There's no need to waste your time with people unsuited to you."

"Ugh fine—" she pocketed her phone "—I won't call Kalael. But we seriously do need to set some boundaries."

"Fine," Satan said. "Name your terms and we'll negotiate."

"No more sabotaging dates," Elya said.

"Done," Satan said.

"All of you will keep your distance." Elya crossed her arms. "You're not going to go stalk or scare off whatever future partners I have."

"Only if we reserve the right to have Twist run background checks," Satan said.

"Done. But if you guys find something that concerns you, bring it to me first and we can discuss it. If it's something I should end a relationship over, allow me to do it on my terms."

"Fair enough." Satan conjured a piece of paper. "I'd have you sign now, but I know you've been around long enough to know better than to sign anything I give you blindly. That said, I'll give you a week to look it over with your lawyers. I would suggest Gabriel and Raguel. You don't even have to ask them. Leave it laying around and I'm certain it'll get to them, and they'll make any changes they deem necessary."

"Yay, problem solved!" Fiend said.

"Kind of ridiculous that it was a problem to begin with," Elya muttered through an unwilling smile.

"We can't help what we are," Satan said.

"Besides, we had valid concerns," Fiend added.

Zeerlo grinned. "I just like ruining your love life."

"At least I have one," Elya said. "When was the last time you went on a date? Never."

Fiend cackled. "She got you there."

"Relationships are pointless endeavors that work toward the carnal desire for sex," Zeerlo said matter-of-factly. "It's a human desire, which I am not. I have no need for such intimacy or barbaric behaviors, just as I have no need for sugary foods. I am a machine bred for greatness."

"Okay, I *so* don't want to have this conversation," Elya said.

She needed to get better friends. Friends that wouldn't insert themselves into areas of her life they didn't need to be in. But that's what she got for befriending Satan, then later his sons. Truthfully, Gabriel and Raphael weren't much better. Sure, they didn't actively work toward ruining her relationships, but she couldn't even begin to count how many lectures she'd received from them on the importance of chastity and purity and waiting for marriage.

Well, okay, so Raphael was kind of lax with his lectures, and Gabriel's were full of him squirming uncomfortably with his face reddened the whole time. On more than one occasion over the years, she had asked blatantly awkward questions just because it was funny. It was mean of her, she knew, but they kind of both deserved it. What made it hilarious wasn't how uncomfortable Gabriel was – no, that actually made his lectures worse – but it was funny seeing just how naïve he was about well everything. Somehow, throughout his existence, Gabriel had managed to maintain a childlike view of the world, with no real idea of what it was like.

"Yeah, that's it. I'm leaving," Elya said.

"What, so soon?" Satan asked.

"Yes. I'm not comfortable with this topic of conversation, and I just want to go home, eat some dinner, and forget it ever happened." She raised a hand. "And no, that is not me saying I'm going to ignore the contract. Send it to Raguel, have him look it over, and when Gabriel or Raphael gives it back to me with the okay to sign, then I will. But not a moment sooner."

Satan huffed. "Very well."

A foot connected with the back of her knee and sent her stumbling forward. As she landed in her bedroom, she could've sworn she still heard Zeerlo's laughter ringing in her ears. Not exactly what she had in mind when she said she was ready to go home. At least she'd be free until she inevitably tripped or was dragged into Hell next, if she made it through to bedtime, that wouldn't be until tomorrow, hopefully, after breakfast later in the day was better.

"Wishful thinking," the voice said.

Elya groaned falling back onto her bed. "I'm going insane."

"Not really," the voice said.

"Really, because I'm hearing a strange voice in my head," Elya paused. "And I'm talking back to it."

Maybe she should see if she couldn't get into the third floor of Wescoe Hall with some of the Grad-Students for some reduced and or free therapy. They'd get their clinical hours, and she could get a nice, padded room for auditory hallucinations. It'd give her a nice break from the celestial world.

"Don't be absurd dear," the voice said. *"Satan and his sons would never allow you to do that. Besides, hallucinations aren't real, which I am."*

Elya chose to ignore the voice, instead heading to the kitchen to fix herself a quick dinner. If she ignored the voice maybe it would go away and she could pretend she was living a normal life. Or as normal as life gets when one tripped daily into Hell.

Six

Elya was having a good day, she'd not only made it past breakfast, but she made it to three in the afternoon, and she hadn't fallen to Hell yet. Naturally, the only thing that could happen because of her being proud of herself for going so long without falling into Hell, was for her to fall into Hell. She had jinxed herself, even if only internally.

As she stood Elya blinked continuously, but the image never changed. Satan sat on his throne speaking with Azrael, who had rose gold hair, periwinkle skin, and shockingly emerald eyes. She'd seen a lot of crazy things from Azrael, but this was a first. She wondered if Kalael had seen it, though that was unlikely, given Pride would take one look at Azrael and – well, she wasn't sure exactly what the princess of Hell would do, but there was no way she'd allow her husband to go out in public like this.

They seemed to be deep in conversation and neither seemed to have noticed her yet.

"Do you have any idea why Elya would be targeted?"

"I have a few theories," Satan said. "But none pressing enough that she'd be targeted at present."

"Well—there must be something, you said It was outside her friend's apartment?"

"Yes," Satan.

Elya frowned. They were talking about the mysterious man with golden eyes. And he's targeting her? Why were they talking about it. And without her. Elya stepped further into the room clearing her throat.

They turned as one. A grin lit Azrael's face whereas a frown marred Satan's.

"Well, hello there," Azrael said. "I don't believe we've met." He disappeared from Satan's side, reappearing in front of her. "Loki, bringer of mischief, incarnate of freedom."

Elya frowned. Was he serious? Was he role playing or something? Or going through some weird phase? She knew he had changed his name before. Was he trying out a new name or was he up to something else?

Though what was weirder was that he had changed his coloring. She didn't even know it was possible for him to turn himself periwinkle. Any other human skin tone, sure. She had seen that plenty, usually when he was disguising himself as someone else or turning into someone to mock them. He could do the same thing with gender as well. (She couldn't begin to count how many times she'd seen him turn himself into an exact replica of Kalael.) Or there was the time when she was eleven that he had one of his clones turn into her eleven-year-old self. That was deeply traumatic. But this was totally different.

"Sin," Satan cut in. "You're Sin incarnate."

"Satan!" Loki rounded on him. "Can you not see I am making conversation with—"

"Leave Elya alone. She's not someone to flirt with, even jokingly," Satan said.

"Yuck," Loki recoiled. "Why didn't you say something sooner?"

Elya frowned. She was so confused. "Okay. What's—"

"This is Loki," Satan said.

That answered who Satan's guest was, but it didn't explain what Satan meant by the comment she wasn't someone Loki should flirt with. Sure, she appreciated it, but it was weird. Weirder yet was Loki's reaction. It was like Satan knew something she didn't, and that one statement to Loki had told him enough of whatever it was.

She hated celestials.

Well, more their ability to keep secrets than anything. And she wouldn't be surprised if there was a whole silent conversation somewhere between Satan's comment and Loki's reaction. Not that they'd tell her what either was about.

"As in the Norse god of Mischief?" She asked.

Satan scoffed. "As in Sin incarnate and Azrael's twin brother."

"Hotter twin brother," Loki said.

"Identical," Satan corrected.

"Azrael has a twin." This was news to her. "Since when?"

"Always." Loki rolled his eyes. "We emerged into existence together in the Garden of Eden, and we were named Sin and Death. Loki and Azrael. And once we met Satan here—" he gestured to said devil "—we formed the greatest friendship the universe has ever known. Even if Azrael was too chicken to join our rebellion."

"Had he fought alongside us rather than against us, we would have won," Satan said confidently.

Elya frowned. "Azrael? I mean, could he have made that big of a difference? Sure, he's powerful being the Grim Reaper and all, but aren't there others who were stronger? How could Azrael have been the difference between victory and defeat?"

"You think as a mortal." Loki shook his head. "The three of us together were practically invincible. Now." He clasped his hands together. "I have a very important question for you," he raised a brow, "Elya, was it?"

"Uh, yeah," she said. There was no need to tell them from what she'd heard, God hadn't even gotten off his throne and left the archangels to handle things. She learned early on sometimes life was easier if she let Satan have his delusions.

"What is your purpose here?" Loki asked.

Well, that was new. She didn't think anyone had ever asked her what her purpose was in Hell, probably because she didn't have one. Sure, Satan put her to work, but that was only because she'd die of boredom otherwise waiting for someone to let her go back to earth. His paperwork was boring, though it did contain interesting surprises on occasion.

She pointed to Satan. "I correct his paperwork for grammar mistakes."

"Intriguing," he frowned. "She's honest. How droll." He turned to Satan. "I miss Eden."

Satan scoffed. "Eden's gone. Nothing left but shambles."

She had so many questions about everything going on, namely why she was just learning Azrael had a twin, and what Satan had meant about Eden being in shambles. Where had Loki been hiding away the last sixteen years? How could Azrael have possibly been so powerful as to make the difference in the rebellion?

Also, if the Loki of Norse myth was real, did that mean other Norse gods were running around as well? Or was it just him? And what about gods from other religions over the millennia? She knew Azrael preferred 'Thanatos,' which was his Greek name. She also knew it was Islamic tradition that gave him the name Azrael, and maybe some Jewish tradition, if the internet was to be believed. She had also read that Satan's original name of Samael was supposed to be a grim reaper, which he most definitely wasn't. But, given the two had a long history of friendship, she wouldn't put it past either to give humanity misinformation. She wouldn't be surprised if there was a time they'd use each other's names either, though that also raised the question of how Loki fit into the mix.

She thought through all of this very quickly.

"I have questions," Elya said.

"Not the time, Elya," Satan said.

"Oh no, let's let the boring mortal speak," Loki grinned. "If I don't like what she has to say, I can think of several dimensions and planets and timelines I could deposit her into."

Satan's eyes flashed gold. "Touch Elya and I'll gut you."

"Now that's interesting," Loki said, his hair turning silver, skin becoming red. "It's not like you to protect others, aside from my lovely wife."

Satan rolled his eyes. "Kalael is Azrael's wife."

Loki raised a brow. "Are you sure about that?"

Satan growled. "Tell me if you really want to continue that claim." Smoke billowed from his nostrils. "Just give me a reason."

Well, that was new. She didn't think she'd ever seen smoke come from Satan's nose before. All around him, sure – usually, it proceeded him either bursting into flames or fire surrounding the entire area he occupied. She wasn't sure what to make of the smoking nose. Would flames come out his nostrils next? Was it a warning that she just never saw him use before? Maybe it was a new trick he learned or one he reserved especially for Loki. The guy had a lot of time on his hands in his lifetime; there was no telling what he could do.

Loki laughed. It was crazed, cold. It was the laugh of someone completely unhinged. "No need to go full devil on me."

"Oh, I'll do more than that," Satan seethed.

Elya huffed, "I'm going to go do my job. Let me know when you finish your petty argument. And if you need me, do me a favor and don't."

"Oh, sassy!" Loki's eyes lit up. "Now that's interesting." He stepped away from Satan and circled her. "If you get tired of him, I'm always looking for people to employ." He crossed his arms. "Usually, I don't make offers to those I can't take to my bed, but you interest me enough that I'm willing to make an exception."

Elya laughed. "You can't afford me."

She ignored the fact that Satan hadn't been paying her until recently, and as much as she had a good skill set, it wasn't as though it was the most difficult. It was grammar, not rocket science. Still, it wasn't like Loki needed to know any of that.

As friendly as he seemed, something about him felt *off*. And not in the same way Satan and his sons felt off. She'd rather not find out what he was capable of. No, she'd be much happier with Satan, who gave her training for years and recently paid her over half a million dollars. She didn't even pause to think about how bizarre that thought was.

He stepped closer. "You think Satan pays well? I can pay you whatever you like. After all, I am the favorite."

Elya scoffed internally. Aside from the—well—everything she knew about Loki so far, it didn't take much to deduce that he was far from the favorite.

"I'm surprised Satan can even pay you. I thought he'd have been cut off long ago."

"I was cut *back*," Satan said. "We all were. Me for leading a rebellion, Michael for his own troublesome behavior over the millennia—"

Loki scoffed. "Troublesome? Is that what they call it? Everyone thought he'd be the one to lead a rebellion – me included."

Satan chuckled. "Yes, well, I fell from grace and my brother rose and proved he had matured. It's not exactly a secret."

That was surprising. Sure, she didn't know much of anything about Michael, but from what she had read in the Bible, he wasn't exactly troublesome. Of course, she knew the Bible was only a small fraction of the story, and, among angels, a problem child was probably someone who refused to eat their vegetables – though she had a shrewd feeling that Loki started plotting from a young age. He had to have gotten a reputation in Norse myth somehow, and being Sin incarnate didn't exactly sound like someone that'd stay out of trouble at any age.

She was curious, though, about just how bad Michael could have been that even Loki thought he'd be the one leading a rebellion. While she didn't think it could have been that bad, Loki was Sin. So, *could* it have been that bad? What had happened in the time leading up to Satan's rebellion? In the parts of Celestial history nobody knew?

She had never met Michael in the sixteen years she tripped into Heaven and Hell, and it was only recently she heard anyone speak of him – and apparently that had something to do with Michael forbidding anyone mentioning him around her, which didn't make sense. Why would he be against her? They'd never even met!

Loki turned his attention back to Elya. "Now that we've established that I have better capabilities of paying you than he ever could, what do you say?"

"Yeah, no." Elya crossed her arms. "I'm sticking with crazy."

Satan gaped. "Excuse me?"

"Do you really have room to talk when you're convinced you're having auditory hallucinations?" The voice asked.

Elya ignored it.

Loki cackled. "She's brilliant." He wiped an imaginary tear from his eye. "If you ever tire of her, I want her."

Elya glared. "I'm not a toy you guys can trade around!" She turned to Satan. "And I'm sorry, but you have to know by now that we all think you're crazy." She glanced to Loki. "Maybe not as crazy as him and Azrael, but definitely crazy."

"And who do you mean by 'we'?" Satan asked.

"Me," Elya counted on her fingers, "your sons, Kalael… probably Gabriel and Raphael as well, except they'd never actually say it aloud."

Loki laughed. "Oh, that's rich. Everyone thinks you're crazy."

Satan raised a brow. "They think you're crazier."

Loki shrugged. "That's just true. In fact, I'd be insulted if they thought you crazier than me. We all know I'm the insane one."

Elya quietly slinked away – there was no need to get further involved in whatever was going on with those two, and she hardly thought they'd notice her absence.

She had no intentions of letting them drive her crazy. *Someone* had to be sane around here, and it certainly wasn't any of the Lucifer family. Zeerlo called his father crazy a lot, but if she was honest, he had no room to talk. He was completely crazy himself. But who knew what differences there could be between the mortal and celestial psyche? And then there were hybrids like Zeerlo and his brothers: half human, half devil, not demon. Apparently, it wasn't the same, and they took the highest offense when she tried to call them cambions. And who was she to argue with five powerful and murderous teenagers? She liked living.

She sat down at the metal black desk Satan had provided for her in the back corner of the throne room and quietly went to work on his paperwork. This had been her designated area for as long as Elya could remember. As soon as Satan realized she'd become a more permanent fixture in Hell he'd taken her, put her at this desk, and handed her a stack of paperwork. She had no guidelines on how or what to do with it. Granted, only Satan would think it a good idea to violate child labor laws and put a 6-year-old to work. Though, she did in part attribute it to why she was reading at a college level in third grade which was also when she first read *"To Kill a Mockingbird."*

Not that she'd ever get him caught up, of course. It'd take an army of personal assistants and secretaries to get Satan caught up on his paperwork. Maybe she should talk to him about seeing how many of those he had residing in Hell? Maybe he could put her in charge of them for a day – with Twist, Fiend or Zeerlo there to ensure nobody hurt her, obviously – and they could play catch-up on Satan's paperwork.

It wasn't a bad idea, she mused. Maybe she'd run it by him later. If she worded it correctly, he'd probably agree. All that paperwork and no pay… it'd *totally* count as a punishment.

If, for some reason, he told her no, she'd implement her automatic plan B for when he denied her requests: She'd go to Kalael and ask her to have him do it. He tended to do anything his daughter asked, and it was a well-known fact that if she asked he'd hand over his throne and return to being the angel of light he was originally created to be. At least it was Saturday, she'd get a small reprieve from Hell soon.

Seven

Sundays were what Elya termed as Heaven Day, every other day of the week she tripped into Hell. But every Sunday like clockwork she tripped into Heaven, once in a blue moon she'd land there on days other than Sunday, but Elya assumed her landing pattern had something to do with Sunday being the designated day of worship.

When Elya fell into Hell, she was greeted by cold, hard floors, and the Devil sat upon a throne. Tripping into Heaven, on the other hand? Well, when she landed in Heaven, the floor was cushioned, despite being marble, and someone was always there to help her to her feet, despite not being the reason she was there.

As Elya sat on the floor, she smiled sheepishly and looked into the warm, brown eyes of the well-dressed angel stood above her. Wordlessly, the blond offered her a hand, and Elya took it, allowing him to pull her to her feet.

"The machinations of my brother, or simple accident?"

Elya sighed. "I *think* it was an accident, but at this rate, I don't know what's because of my own clumsiness and what's because Sat—" a brow rose "—I mean Sam—" he sighed "—okay then your brother—" he nodded. Elya continued. "Anyways, your brother is demanding and seems to think my life revolves around doing his paperwork for him."

"He's far too dramatic," the voice said.

Elya sighed internally. She was growing accustomed to her strange disembodied companion that she hoped was real and not a sign she was falling into madness.

"We're all falling into madness my dear, some just know how to hide their insanity better than others."

Gabriel grinned. "I believe it. Have you eaten anything, or should we make a stop to get you proper nourishment?"

"I haven't eaten yet."

The fact she never left Heaven on an empty stomach was another reason she liked it so much. When Gabriel (or, occasionally, Raphael) greeted her, she was always given some of her favorite foods, from where she considered the best places to get them. (If they knew of a place better, they'd get her a small sample from that location so they'd know for next time.)

If she could live there, she would. Unfortunately, there was a tiny issue of her being both alive and not an angel. Probably didn't help she had a weird friendship with Satan as well. For now, she was content with being one of the only – if not *the* only – human to ever see Heaven while still living. Even if she technically wasn't allowed to be there and had to be escorted everywhere.

"Very well. We shall need to rectify that."

"We have got to work on the way you talk. You sound way too proper."

He chuckled. "It is unnecessary; I seldom leave the kingdom itself, unless, of course, it is to go speak with Azrael on behalf of my Father, which is far more often than I would like."

"You ever wonder if Azrael acts that way on purpose?" Elya asked.

For as long as she could remember, the Grim Reaper had been eccentric and troublesome, always a half second away from exposing Afterlife to humanity, always trying to eradicate the squirrels from existence, and breaking every rule in the book he could think of. How he got away with any of it was attributed to (and she wasn't sure about the validity of it) him being the favorite.

"It is difficult to say," Gabriel said after a minute. "Many believe he simply succumbed to madness, which was brewing for many years, others feel it is genuine, and some, as you asked, believe it is an act."

"Tell me more."

"There is not really anything more to be said. The very nature of Azrael has always made things with him complicated."

Elya frowned. She wondered what he meant by that. "You mean because he's Death?"

"No, I meant — you will have to excuse me. I nearly spoke when I should not. It is not my place to speak of such things."

Not his place? Oh, Gabriel was hiding something big from her. Or was he referring to Loki? As far as she knew, Gabriel wasn't aware she'd met Azrael's twin, and if Loki hung around the Grim Reaper a lot, it'd explain most of the Reaper's oddities. But, once again, she would be left with questions and no answers because Gabriel would never tell another person's secrets – either by accident or on purpose.

Elya huffed. "I hate not having information when I want it. I need to know!"

"Do not whine, it is unbecoming," Gabriel scoffed. "Furthermore, you have no need to know, only your own desire, and I am hardly someone who would cultivate such traits within you."

Elya sighed. She knew he wouldn't tell her, but she really did need to know! Her curiosity was like an itch beneath her skin which wouldn't go away until she had answers. True, it had gotten her into a fair amount of trouble over the years, like the time she was caught eavesdropping on Charlie's dad. Mr. Romano had sent her home immediately, even though she was supposed to be staying for the summer, and it was barely a week in. Her mom then proceeded to ground her for the remainder of the completely miserable summer.

"Now you're being dramatic, as loathe as I am to side with Gabriel, he is right, you don't actually need to know." The voice said.

Maybe she should tell Gabriel about the voice, he was probably the least likely to put her in a padded room. She hoped.

"Don't do that darling," the voice said.

Gabriel pushed open a door that led to easily the biggest kitchen Elya had ever seen, though it never made sense to her why they even had one. She had never once seen any of the angels eat. Well, maybe that wasn't entirely true – she just knew they had no need to eat.

Elya surveyed the granite tabletops, cherry cabinets, and enormous gas stove. "Why do you guys have a kitchen, anyways?"

"It aids in the transition process. When people first arrive, it can sometimes be too overwhelming. Also, it is soothing to cook."

"And yet we usually order me takeout."

Gabriel glanced between Elya and the stove. "Are you asking that I cook you something instead?"

Elya almost said no, but then she saw how Gabriel kept eyeing the stove. He *wanted* to cook. There was no way he'd say it, but she could tell, and she was kind of curious to see what kind of culinary skills he had. Even if he was awful, you couldn't get sick in Heaven, so it wasn't as though she'd have to worry about accidental food poisoning.

"Are you any good?"

"My food is adequate, yes."

Elya sighed. "I can't tell if you're being genuine or if you're underselling your cooking abilities because you're an archangel and refuse to be anything less than humble."

"Alternatively, I could perhaps locate Raphael and we could go to Texas Roadhouse?"

It was a tough decision. She could take a gamble and satiate her curiosity about Gabriel's cooking skills – and she really was curious – or she could go to Texas Roadhouse and get the most delicious dinner rolls in the history of the universe. Guaranteed deliciousness, or test Gabriel's culinary skills? She supposed the real question came down to how curious she was.

"I think I need a second opinion."

The kitchen door opened to reveal another blond, who bore an eerie resemblance to Gabriel – only his features were a bit sharper, and his eyes were a vibrant green, rather than the warm brown belonging to Gabriel. "I thought I had heard voices in here."

"Oh hey, I was just debating whether I should satiate my curiosity and let him cook, or if the three of us should go to Texas Roadhouse."

"I am afraid I would be unable to join you. But, if you want my recommendation, have Gabriel cook," Raphael grinned. "You won't regret it."

"Alright, looks like I get to eat food made by an angel!" Elya grinned. "Oh man, I wish I could tell people about this. You know, this is totally not fair."

"The mortals cannot be given definitive proof of Heaven's existence, as it would defeat the purpose of the faith-based system we operate on," Gabriel said.

"Not necessarily. Zeerlo's the son of your unnamable brother and he's still a deist. Honestly, I'm not even sure how he pulls it off. He's been to Hell – er, I mean, the *other place* – numerous times, Death was his babysitter, and he torments the demons!"

Raphael laughed. "From the few encounters I have had with my nephew, I can confidently say he is very like his father before the fall."

"You mean — never mind. What I was about to say mentioned your brother and had foul language, which I know is a big no with you guys." It was one of the upsides of Hell; there, she could say whatever she wanted. Though, sometimes Satan found what she said amusing, then proceeded to pat her on the head and say 'very good mortal' like she was a child.

"Thank you for restraining yourself, Elya." Raphael glanced at his Rolex (a gift from some ruler or another whose feelings he didn't want to hurt by not wearing it) "I best get going. Do enjoy your meal." He paused at the door. "Oh, I almost forgot." He reached into the pocket of his dark gray suit and pulled out a small, red bag. He tossed it onto the counter in front of where Elya sat. "Enjoy."

Elya grinned. "Thanks!"

Before she could grab her favored candy, a hand snatched it away. She turned a glare on the other angel. "What gives?"

Gabriel chuckled. "If I'm going to cook you nourishment, I would prefer you did not spoil your appetite with this—" he eyed the bag in his hand "—junk. This stuff cannot be healthy for you. And what kind of name is Skittles?"

Elya sighed. "It's candy. It's not meant to be healthy. It's supposed to soothe my taste buds and rot my teeth if I don't brush them, which, lucky me, I do."

Gabriel placed the bag of skittles on top of a cabinet, far out of her reach. "Raphael should not be indulging such atrocious eating habits."

"You only say that because you've never tried them," Elya eyed the array of ingredients out on the counter: Cauliflower, broccoli, bell peppers (in seven colors – three of which she'd never seen before), carrots, onion, and a mixture of vegetables both familiar and unfamiliar to her. "What are you making anyways?"

"Haven't the slightest. My job is to listen to the ingredients and let them do the difficult work." He started chopping a bell pepper. "Would you pass me the spice rack?"

"You want to explain to me how the ingredients tell you what to make?"

"You are familiar with the Bible, correct?"

"I read it kind of thoroughly after I realized I was actually tripping into the bad place daily and, you know, here, on occasion."

She read it not out of any desire to conform to any organized religion, but out of hopes she might learn a thing or two about the places she tripped into. And while it didn't have nearly as much information as she wanted, she had learned a bit about the people she'd met since her tripping first began, namely Satan, Gabriel, and Raphael. Having Satan around was always great because he could expand upon things and answer the big questions, like whether the man Jacob wrestled was an angel or God himself.

"Yes, well, as the messenger, I have some rather unusual abilities. For some unfathomable reason, the ingredients speak to me."

"Aren't all angels considered messengers of God though?" Elya asked.

Gabriel sighed. "Technically, yes, we are all messengers, but I'm the one called upon for the most important of messages, and somehow this translates to the ingredients speaking to me."

Elya laughed. "Yeah, you're pretty weird. And I can't believe I'm trusting you to make food when you have no idea what you're making."

"It is not too late to change to go to Texas Roadhouse." Gabriel put the knife down. "In fact, I could call Azrael and you can interrogate him."

"Oh, that's tempting. I really have got to ask him how long he's been hiding Loki from me and why. I mean, I understand why – Loki is crazier than Azrael – but I have so many questions Loki didn't answer."

Gabriel coughed. "When have you met Loki?"

Elya shrugged. "He was in Hell yesterday."

Gabriel picked the knife up and resumed chopping vegetables. "Loki should not be separated from — if you will excuse me, I think I need to go have a quick discussion with Azrael, or perhaps see if I cannot convince Michael to."

"I can head home if you need," Elya suggested.

"And allow you to leave without proper nourishment? Do not move. I shall be back quickly to ensure you receive sustenance, then I shall take you home." Gabriel vanished in a shower of golden glitter.

Elya sighed. Reaching into her backpack, she grabbed Satan's reports, thinking she might as well get them done while she was waiting. Silently, she sorted the papers into the reports for the government and the ones meant to go to Heaven. She might as well get the ones due to go to Heaven done while she was here. If she could get ahold of a printer, she could fix Satan's reports, type them up properly, print them, and have Gabriel take them wherever they needed to go. She stifled a laugh at the fact she needed a printer in Heaven and tried to focus.

"There are so many better alternatives to doing Satan's paperwork, you're being left unsupervised in Heaven. Don't you want to explore?"

"No," Elya said. "Especially if the disembodied voice I keep hearing that may or may not be real is encouraging me."

"You'll come to love me, or I'll one day destroy you, personally, I'm fine either way though I suspect they'd prefer you alive."

"They being?"

The voice scoffed. *"As though, I'd ruin the surprise."*

She managed to get through three of the overdue reports before Gabriel returned. His hair was disheveled, and his shirt had become wrinkled. He offered her a tired smile as he picked the knife up and resumed cutting vegetables as though he'd never left. Elya had no idea how time worked in Heaven – sometimes she was there for what felt like hours, but when she returned home, it seemed to only have been five minutes – but based on how much work she had gotten done, he was gone a while.

"Are you okay?" Elya asked.

"Why would I not be?"

"Have you seen a mirror?" Elya asked.

"I am well, just had a little disagreement with Azrael, nothing to concern over." Gabriel dumped the vegetables into a pan. "What is it you are working on?"

Elya glanced up from the report. "Your brother's overdue reports. It's what I'm paid to do." She fixed a comma splice.

"I was not aware he paid you," Gabriel said as he stirred the vegetables in the pan.

Elya shrugged. "It's a recent development."

"I see." Gabriel silently resumed his cooking. "Would you prefer chicken, beef, or pork?"

"You pick."

Gabriel opened the fridge. "I think chicken today."

"That works for me."

Elya watched for a few moments as the angel cooked. He moved gracefully around the kitchen as though he had cooked the dish a thousand times. It was hard to believe he had no idea what he was making. Elya glanced to her Skittles; she wanted to eat them, but there was no way she'd get past the angel. The years of tripping into Heaven taught her that Gabriel was a mother hen and eating candy before her dinner would give him an aneurism.

Sighing internally, Elya resumed fixing Satan's paperwork. Her skittles would still be there after she ate whatever Gabriel was cooking. They fell into an easy silence. The intoxicating aroma of Gabriel's cooking soon overcame Elya's senses, but she wasn't going to distract Gabriel when he was clearly in the zone. Besides, if Raphael was to be believed, the wait for the food would be worth it.

It was strange how she could be friends with Satan and Gabriel, Zeerlo and Raphael. In a way, perhaps it wasn't so strange. Gabriel, Raphael, and Satan were all brothers, even if not all on speaking terms.

Not being able to tell anyone about it sucked a lot. What she wouldn't give to be able to tell everyone she traveled to Heaven and Hell, Gabriel was cooking her dinner, Satan paid her half a million dollars, and Raphael gave her Skittles. It wasn't that she wanted to brag about these things, it was just that she didn't have very many mortal friends because of it, and of the ones she did have, only Charlie knew about Afterlife – and Charlie's family came with its own large share of secrets she couldn't tell anyone.

At first it was hard because she was so young and didn't understand what was happening – not that anyone would've believed her anyway. As she got older, the difficulty came from the isolation. After a while, her high school friends gave up on inviting her places because she could never go. Satan always monopolized her time. Sometimes, Elya thought she'd give anything to be normal, but she wouldn't trade her current life for anything. It could be isolating, but most of her best friends were in Afterlife, and if not for her tripping problem, she'd have never met Charlie.

"I do believe it is finished," Gabriel said. He opened a cabinet and grabbed two plates. Very carefully he divided his dish evenly on the two plates, he opened a drawer and grabbed two forks. "What would you like to drink?"

Elya eyed the chicken on the plates. "What do you suggest?"

Gabriel drummed his fingers on the counter. He opened a cabinet and pulled down two stem wine glasses. Wordlessly, he moved to the fridge and pulled out a bottle of white wine. "I feel that a nice white Chenin Blanc would go well with this meal." He opened the bottle and poured a little into each glass.

Elya eyed the glass as he handed it to her. "Is this for real? There's alcohol in Heaven? I thought that was a big no with you guys?"

"There is wine, yes." Gabriel placed a plate in front of Elya. "That is not to say drinking it is encouraged, and we do not drink enough to get drunk, but the occasional glass of wine with a meal is perfectly acceptable."

"What do you know? Learn something new every day."

Gabriel smiled. "It is important you learn."

Elya took a bite of her meal. As an array of flavors burst across her taste buds, her fork slipped from her grip. "OH MY—" Gabriel raised a brow. "This is so amazing."

Gabriel took a bite. "It is adequate."

"Dude, stop being humble for a minute and just say you're an amazing chef."

Gabriel shrugged as he silently ate his food. Elya rolled her eyes. It was too amazing to call it adequate. All too soon, her plate was empty. Gabriel took her plate and placed it in the sink. He moved to the cabinet and grabbed her bag of Skittles.

"Yes!"

Gabriel sighed. "I will never understand your delight with consuming such junk."

"Don't knock it 'til you try it." Elya ripped open her bag of skittles.

He shook his head. "I will allow it this once in congratulations, as I understand graduating from college is a rather significant milestone in the lives of some mortals."

Elya smiled. "Thanks! I'm so stoked. I mean, Commencement is what I've been working toward for four years!"

"Shall I return you home now?"

Elya laughed. "Please and thank you?"

Gabriel smiled. He placed a hand on her shoulder, and a familiar warm feeling overcame Elya. She closed her eyes as a blinding light consumed them. As it died down, she found herself alone in her room with the only sign Gabriel had been there: a pile of golden glitter on her carpet. She sighed. She needed to start having him drop her off outside. Moving to the corner of the room, Elya grabbed the vacuum. She always needed to clean up glitter.

From the silence alone, she could tell her roommates were all out again, which was fine by her – the less she saw of Cathy and Laurel, the better. It wasn't that she didn't try to get along with them, it was just that they were the worst. And in all honesty, while she wasn't always a fan of the solitude, it did have its moments, like when she was exhausted and trying to come to terms with the fact that, as of tomorrow, she would no longer be a college student.

"*Congratulations on that by the way,*" the voice said.

Elya groaned. "Go away."

"*I will soon, but I need to make a determination first.*"

"What kind of determination?"

"*Whether I want you dead or alive.*"

Elya decided against responding. The more she talked to the odd disembodied voice the more she worried she was going insane. And she did not get this far in life to be locked in a padded room.

Eight

She liked to think of herself as smart, but now she questioned that. Clearly, she hadn't been thinking. She couldn't do this. Hundreds, if not thousands, of people were watching, her mother and grandparents included. A single wrong move, one misstep, a sneeze, too many nerves, something jumping out and scaring her, and she'd vanish in front of them all, landing in Hell, maybe Heaven.

If that weren't bad enough, she'd have to worry about the entire Lucifer family being in the audience. And where there was Kalael, there was the Reaper family. There was no way they'd make it through the entire commencement ceremony without someone either dying or getting arrested—both, probably. Or would Kalael be there? Wasn't there something about her being anywhere near her portal to Hell being too dangerous?

"Oh relax," the voice said. *"You'll be fine…probably. And if not, your Celestial companions will fix things. As for Kalael's presence, she'll likely show. While she can't be within a 50 miles radius without losing control normally, there is a loophole around that. The one the mortals call God Almighty."*

Elya ignored him. She had enough to worry about without addressing the mysterious voice that seemed to be becoming more present within her life. That she hoped wasn't her going crazy. Whose brilliant idea was it to dress graduating students in gowns anyways? Did they not realize how much of a tripping hazard they were? Never mind the fact it didn't cover her feet; she'd tripped over air before. This was going to end in absolute disaster.

It didn't take long, even in the large crowd, to spot Léana's shock of emerald green hair rising above many of the students (she was over six feet tall – a fact that Elya was continually grateful for). Weaving through the crowd, Elya made her way to her friend.

"Are you ready?" Elya asked. "Because I'm not sure I'm ready. Like, I know it's no big deal, but you know how clumsy I am. I mean, what if I trip and someone trips over me?"

"You need to breathe," Léana said.

"I'm breathing," Elya said.

"No, you're not."

Léana scoffed. "You look like you're a half-second away from a panic attack. It's just commencement! It's not like you're giving a speech."

"What if I trip?" She asked again.

Léana smiled. "Then I'll catch you. Nobody will see you trip. I mean, maybe a few people – hard not to with literally thousands here – but you know."

"Thanks." Elya evened her breathing "I'm glad I have at least one friend."

Léana snorted. "You have plenty of friends, even if you hate two of your roommates and disappear for hours at a time." She ticked off on her fingers. "Not to mention, you're almost never available for social events and when you are there, you disappear halfway through. And there's the whole fact you work some internship I know nothing about. It's a wonder you have time for homework and classes! Sometimes you spread yourself too thin."

"Sometimes I wonder how you haven't been expelled," Elya countered.

"The key to causing trouble, Elya, is to not get caught," Léana grinned. "And darling, I never get caught."

Elya laughed. "I can't argue with that. You probably hold the record for the craziest things done without getting expelled or arrested."

Léana's eyes glinted with mischief. "I'm gifted! Smuggling drugs into our dorm freshman year was the mere first step into the chaos I would cause."

"And never once in all the mischief you've caused over the years has one person suspected you of being the culprit. Not even when you disassembled the dean's car and put it on the roof of Wescoe Hall!" Elya laughed. "Or remember the time you bought a whole bunch of inflatable pools and put them on the roof because the school refuses to 'listen to the people'?"

"What can I say?" Léana said. "If I wasn't already planning to be a business tycoon like the world's never seen, I'd make an *excellent* criminal mastermind."

"It's such a good thing you're more concerned with prestige than being a criminal."

"The last name Kaos suits me," Léana shrugged. "We've had some wild times, Elya, and I hope the party doesn't stop just because we're graduating."

Elya smiled. "Of course not."

She wouldn't trade the girl for anything. It was nice having a friend who wasn't angelic or devilish; someone who hadn't been around for thousands of years or someone who was raised to be weapons of war. There was something relieving about having a human friend. Gabriel and Raphael were great, Satan was alright, and she could live with Zeerlo and his brothers, but Léana made her feel *normal*.

"Just think," Léana said. "After today, our problems of classes and homework are gone. Just the worries of cheating boyfriends, work, paying rent, and buying groceries and gas will remain!"

"Yeah," Elya said without nearly the excitement.

That was… Léana had simple problems. Normal problems that normal people had. They were problems angels and devils didn't have. What she wouldn't give to have only normal problems – on top of those, she had her tripping problem, and she had to deal with Satan's problems because he made them hers, and Zeerlo's, and Fiend's. It was strange to think how different she was. Normally, she didn't feel different – at least not until moments like this, when Léana talked about normal problems, or when others were out partying while she was in Hell training or doing Satan's paperwork or getting lectured by Gabriel. Or the latest issue of the mysterious man that was apparently targeting. Things normal people didn't do.

All too soon, it was time to line up and make the walk. Elya linked arms with Léana, it was her only chance at making it through commencement without tripping. Sure, there was a chance nobody would notice her disappear, but the chances were equally high that somebody would. And she could not have that happen.

The walk was crowded (unsurprising). Parents, friends, and other relatives were all lined up to watch as they walked down the hill. For the first time in her entire undergrad career, she would walk beneath the campanile (campus superstition said anyone who went through early wouldn't graduate on time). She was nervous about the possibility of tripping, yet at the same time, she was excited. It was exhilarating to know she would be graduating, but it was kind of bittersweet. This would be her last walk on campus as a student. She had met so many people over the years, and she had so many great professors, and four years of amazing memories.

As she walked through the campanile, she was careful to watch for any possible cracks she might be unaware of. Her vision had grown slightly blurred with tears of mixed emotions, and she almost went tumbling down the stairs, only to find Léana placing a hand on her shoulder to balance her when she stumbled.

It was weird how Léana could keep her from vanishing. She had never noticed it until that moment, and, curious as she was, Elya wasn't about to complain. Someone that could anchor her to earth was nice to have, even if Léana had no idea what she was doing.

Thankfully, they made it to the end of the walk without further incidents, the rest of commencement passed in a kind of blur, up until she got to the stage. Not that she minded. She was too busy waiting for the inevitable screams caused by Zeerlo and his brothers or Satan himself, the echoing shouts of Satan arguing with Gabriel and Raphael, the embarrassment of Azrael chasing squirrels through the crowd… Something. But they never came. She wasn't complaining, but she knew this must be the calm before the storm.

She half wondered if her celestial friends weren't in the crowd after all, until she was on the stage and spotted Satan dressed casually in a pair of jeans and a white t-shirt. She didn't think anything of it, until she saw him a second time dressed in his usual black suit alongside the Deadly Sins, Azrael, and two archangels. That was when she about tripped – she did a double take, but the first Satan wasn't there. She turned back to the other second Satan stood next to Kalael, who had a firm hold on Azrael, and noted that Fiend and Twist appeared to be doing their best to restrain Zeerlo while Satan and Gabriel glared at them in disapproval. Elya was certain they'd both be horrified to know they were reacting the same as the other.

Before she knew it, it was time to leave. It didn't take long to find her mother and grandparents. They exchanged a few brief words and took a few photos before they parted ways. She'd meet them later to celebrate. In the meantime, she had excused herself to go say goodbye to her friends – or, at least, that was what she claimed. It was more like she needed to go make sure Satan hadn't let his sons kill anyone, and to make sure everyone was behaving themselves, because Heaven forbid any immortal know how to act in a crowd. That said, she was endlessly grateful they were there. It was amazing seeing all her celestial friends supporting her.

It was in the parking lot next to the Union that Elya found everyone else. They were stood next to their respective cars, aside from Gabriel and Raphael, who stood by an empty parking space because neither of them knew how to drive, and Satan stood in front of a limo because of course he couldn't drive himself when he had his five sons with him. That would be absurd – they might damage the car.

And how weird was it she knew why Satan brought a limo instead of a car?

"Congrats, Elya," Kalael said, pulling her into a hug. "You did well."

"*Eh-hem*." Fiend grabbed Elya from Kalael and put an arm over her shoulder. "We did well. And thanks to Dad pulling a few strings, I have actual documentation of me being a student and taking classes, so I get an actual degree as well."

Satan elbowed Fiend. "This is Elya's moment. Don't ruin it."

"Yeah, well, she's not the one that had to take the MCAT, then apply to a bunch of medical schools in the fall." Fiend crossed his arms. "By the way, I got accepted into thirteen different medical schools, so I can take my pick." He grinned. "I'm going to go be a doctor and then you guys will have to call me Dr. Fiend Lucifer when I tell you to."

Elya snorted. "You know you have to take the Hippocratic Oath, right?"

Fiend shrugged. "Yeah, so?"

"It's like an oath to do no harm," Elya said. "Your job of a mercenary seems kind of like a major breakage of that oath."

Satan placed a hand on Fiend's shoulder. "Now leave that to me."

Zeerlo shook his head. "Why you'd want to help anyone's injuries is beyond me. The way I see it, if you get hurt in the line of duty, then you deserve it."

"Well that's truly both horrifying and disgusting," Elya said.

Twist raised a brow, ignoring Elya's input. "And if you end up with a missing arm, are you going to just walk it off or let Fiend get whatever potions will fix it?"

"Excuse me?" Shredder cut in. "I'm the one that makes the potions."

"Still rather have Fiend administer them over you," Hellas muttered.

"Maybe we should send you to be a lawyer, Zeerlo," Kalael suggested.

Zeerlo raised a brow. "Now why would I want to go and do a thing like that?"

Kalael grinned. "Think of it this way: You learned negotiation and contracts from the best. Dad is likely better than any other lawyer you'll get. Unless you intend to go to trial, he's not a trial attorney. Sure, there's the whole swearing to uphold the law, but I'm sure Dad can find you a way around that as well."

Satan frowned. "That might be a bit more difficult, but I've got thousands of years under my belt, which the mortals who wrote the oath do not. If there's a way around it, I'll find it. And if not," he shrugged, "I'm sure we'll think of something."

Zeerlo sighed. "I'll consider it, but I make no promises."

Gabriel frowned. "I do not like the idea of anyone breaking sworn oaths. Even if they are your sons, brother. Besides, I thought you never break your word."

"Loopholes aren't breaking," Satan said.

"Think of it this way," Kalael said, placing a hand on each of her eldest younger brothers. "A career where the goal is to help people might be good for them."

Gabriel shifted uneasily. "I suppose."

Raphael smiled. "Worry not over these things, brother." He turned his attention to Elya. "Now, would you like to see your gift?"

Elya grinned. "What is it?"

"So, a few of us pitched in." Raphael said.

"And we got you something we thought you would like," Gabriel added.

"Thought?" Satan scoffed. "I know people's innermost desires. I know she'll like our gift – love it, really."

"Anyways, the five of us—" Gabriel gestured to himself, Raphael, Satan, Kalael, and Azrael "—and your Guardian Angels got you a gift."

"Wait. Hold on," Elya gaped. "I have guardian angels? As in plural?"

"You didn't know?"

Raphael shrugged. "It happens, and *no,* you can't meet them."

Elya sighed. "Fine. I'll hold off on interrogating you over that in exchange for my present. What is it?"

Gabriel reached into his pocket and pulled out a small wooden box. Elya frowned. There was no physical way a box that size could possibly fit in his pockets, especially without ripping them or showing. What was with immortals and their tendency to basically deny everything high school physics and common sense had taught her? But her questions about that could wait until another time – at least until after she opened her present. Her curiosity over her gift far outweighed her curiosity over their defiance of the laws of physics.

Elya took the box into her hands and flipped the lid open. "Car keys? You guys got me a car?" She looked at the keys. "But I don't recognize this logo. Is it as good as Toyota?"

"You're embarrassing. Maybe I should kill you instead of making you my queen after all."

"Even better," Raphael grinned. He snapped his fingers and behind where he and Gabriel stood was a shiny dark green car, the word *Bugatti* spelled out on the grille.

"Whoa." She hugged Gabriel, then Raphael, and, lastly, Satan. "I can't believe you guys got me this."

"The Bugatti Chiron Super Sport? I thought we were getting her a practical car." Kalael frowned. "Dad, that's a nice car but I'm not sure Elya's experienced enough to handle that kind of speed."

Gabriel nodded. "That is precisely what I said, but somebody—" he turned his gaze to Satan "—persisted that Elya would be much happier with this."

"How fast does it go?" Elya asked.

"Fast enough to kill you," the voice said.

Satan shrugged. "I believe this one tops out at 304 mph or something along those lines."

Elya gaped. "That's insane!"

"And much too dangerous!" Gabriel's eyes became panicked. "What if she wrecks? She could die!"

"I assumed she'd follow the speed limits displayed along the roads. And if not," he shrugged. "Zeerlo, Fiend, or Kalael would be sufficient for teaching her to drive it. Besides, you agreed I could pick the car."

"Yeah, let's have me do that," Kalael said before either of her brothers could lay a claim. "I learned to drive while street racing. I'm the least likely to get her killed."

"Can't argue that," Zeerlo said.

Fiend gestured to Elya. "She's all yours."

"Speaking of Elya, we—" Hellas gestured to himself and his brothers "—also pooled together to get you a gift."

"By that, he means our powers," Shredder said. "Nothing in the universe has the power to make Greed part with his money."

"Anyways," Zeerlo cut in, shooting his youngest brothers a glare, "we got you this."

He held out a box wrapped in solid dark green paper with a matching bow on top. Elya carefully took it into her hands, a little nervous to open it – one could never be too careful when it came to the deadly sins, especially Zeerlo. Tenderly, Elya began to undo the wrapping paper until she was holding a cardboard box. Bracing herself for the worst, she pulled open the lid and peered inside.

It was a tiny metal silver dragon with glowing green eyes. Elya couldn't believe the detail: Every scale, the spikes along the tail, even the teeth seemed to be made with the utmost care and detail. It was surprisingly light – hollow, most likely – but it was beautiful.

Elya smiled at the younger five deadly sins. "Thanks, guys. I mean it – it's lovely."

Twist grinned. "It's far more than lovely. Like Shredder said, we combined our powers to create it, and this little guy is far more than some fancy paperweight."

"He's a guardian," Fiend said. "He creates a forcefield that blocks out any hackers or viruses from your electronics, like the ultimate firewall."

"Speaking of fire," Zeerlo grinned. "Should anyone unauthorized enter your room, he emits smoke from his nostrils as a warning. Should they linger, he'll blast them with fire with precision aim so as not to accidentally set anything on fire."

"More importantly," Shredder said, "if you're injured or in danger, it sends an alert to all of Afterlife."

"There's one other feature on him," Hellas's gaze lit with mischief, "but we'll leave that as a surprise."

"You guys are the best," Elya said, eyes stinging with tears.

The Sons of Satan could be vicious, cruel, and vile, but at times like this, she was glad she knew them. After her visit from that mysterious Satan lookalike, it was exactly what she needed. The little dragon really was a wonderful gift, even if she didn't know everything it did – and, in all honesty, she wasn't sure she wanted to know what the feature they weren't telling her was. Knowing them, it could probably grow in size enough to eat someone, and she'd really rather not know.

"Why don't I take the Bugatti and park it in our garage?" Azrael suggested. "That way it stays safe from scratches and the elements until you get a chance to learn to drive it. And it'll be able to make itself a nice home with other cars of similar caliber."

"That's a good idea," Kalael said, "but you're not driving."

Azrael crossed his arms. "And why should you get to drive?"

Kalael raised a brow. "You remember we came in your car, right? Do you really want me driving REAPER1?"

His eyes widened. "Absolutely not! I gave you REAPER2. 1 is my baby and nobody drives it but me. I don't care how experienced you are or if you literally have the same car."

"That's what I thought." Kalael snatched the keys from Zeerlo. "I'll get this put away safely for you, Elya, then I'll make sure the keys are put where nobody can find them, and when you're ready to learn how to drive it, let me know."

Elya nodded as Kalael climbed inside the car. The engine roared to life, and Elya wanted nothing more than to be in it, but practicality stopped her. She had her old car and she needed to go meet her mom and grandparents before they grew worried… and it'd probably be best if she showed up in the car she left the house in that morning, at least for the time being. She hugged Gabriel and Raphael one more time, telling them goodbye, hugged the Reaper family, and gave a respectful nod to Satan and the sins.

"Congratulations, Elya. You worked hard for this. I'm proud of you," Satan said, climbing into the limo.

Elya smiled. "Thanks."

She decided not to think about how weird it was that Satan being proud of her made her eyes fill with tears.

"Don't you still need to go meet up with your family for lunch?"

Elya groaned inwardly. Now the disembodied voice kept track of her schedule. Worse, he was right, she did need to get to meet with her family for their celebratory lunch.

Nine

Lunch with her family had been nice, unfortunately they couldn't stay in town for more than a few hours, but she was okay with that. At least she got a nice calm celebration of her graduation without the chaos that was the Celestial world.

"Your family is rather normal, which you are not my dear."

Being alone without the worst roommates in the history of the universe was peaceful. Wherever Cathy and Laurel were, she was glad they were gone. As for Jules, while she was a lovely roommate, Elya knew she was out having dinner with her parents. Though, it'd be nicer if she didn't still have a disembodied voice in her head.

"Harsh, you'll miss me when I leave you my darling."

"I really won't," Elya said.

It was strange being done with school—no homework, no fall classes, and if she could get Satan to leave her alone, she could get a real job. Thanks to him, she'd be debt free, able to buy a house, and she had a brand-new car! She'd probably still have a lot of money left over after taxes. If not, her only spending would be necessities, which any job she chose could probably cover. Financial security was *amazing.*

"As my queen you'd never have need for money."

"Are you seriously going out in *that?*" Twist asked from behind her.

Elya turned to see Sloth with his arms crossed, disapproval in his gaze.

"What are you doing here?" Elya asked.

"I got the short straw," he shrugged. "You realize we're going out in celebration of your graduating and your clothes are so—" he eyed her up and down "—dull."

"No, thanks," Elya walked past him to the bedroom. "Last time I let your dad take me out was my 21st birthday and I don't remember anything past seven."

She did remember waking up on the couch in Mercenary Mansion, Zeerlo passed out in a chair while Fiend was on the floor with two cheerleaders, and the horrifying image of Satan passed out on the other couch in only his boxers. She had no idea of what drugs and alcohol they had partaken in, but she did know it had to be strong stuff to do that to Satan.

How she didn't die was beyond her.

She also remembered a raging hangover and a hundred dollars missing from her wallet. The last thing she wanted or needed was a repeat occurrence, curtesy of Satan.

Twist chuckled. "I have it all on security footage if you're ever feeling daring enough to know. And don't worry, we are *never* giving you the heavy drugs again. You can stick with alcohol and occasionally getting high."

"I have never done either of those things," Elya lied.

Twist snorted. "You're lying to one of the deadly sins, remember? We don't judge anyone for trying to have some fun."

"No, but your uncles might," Elya said.

"True, but they're the forgiving sort," he shrugged. "You know, practice what Granddad tells them to preach and all. But if you're that worried, we're just going out to an expensive dinner, then getting some drinks. We even got Hellas and Shredder a babysitter for the night."

Elya laughed. "What poor sap has to babysit them?"

"Azrael." He grinned a twisted grin. "He owed my dad for the time he took Kalael and got her wasted when she was at risk of dying because of her powers." His expression dropped. "Not exactly the time to be partying it up."

"You're fifteen, Fiend's sixteen, and Zeerlo's seventeen—" she crossed her arms "—not even a college bar is about to let the three of you in."

"I'll be sixteen in November," he shrugged. "Besides, we're going to Italy! Legal drinking age there is sixteen if it's a fermented drink and not distilled. And we all know Italian is your favorite food group."

Elya rolled her eyes. "Italian isn't a food group."

Twist raised a brow. "Do I look like I care? Shredder is the foodie. Me, I'm just the tech guy. As far as I'm concerned it is."

Elya sighed. "I'm not getting out of this, am I?"

"You know my dad."

"Fine, just give me an hour to get ready."

"An hour?" He glanced at the clock. "What, do you need to charge your phone?"

"No but I need a shower, to find an outfit, do my hair, put on makeup—"

"Please, with your skin, you don't need makeup." He came up behind her, breathing in deeply. "You don't smell, and if we're going to be drinking, there's a possibility of you getting sweaty anyways." He tilted his head toward the closet. "Go pick out an outfit and let's go."

"Stop sniffing me!" She shooed him away with a look of disgust on her face. "When did you get so bossy?"

Twist raised a brow. "Would you rather I let Fiend or Zeerlo in here?"

"No! No, I'm good." The last thing she needed was one of them bossing her around in her bedroom. They had short tempers. "I'd like to live to see tomorrow."

"As though I'd let them harm you my queen, say the word and I shall make them suffer."

"Your internet here sucks by the way," Twist said.

Elya turned to see what he was sitting on her bed on her laptop. "Dude! That's my laptop."

"I'm fixing your internet connection to something more tolerable," he said simply as he typed at a speed that couldn't be humanly possible. "You'll thank me later."

"Why do I bother?" Elya asked aloud.

"Because you, like the rest of humanity, like the delusion of having control," Twist said, not looking up from the computer. "Nothing wrong with that, it's in your nature. Embrace it."

"Right. Why don't you go do that on the couch—" she gestured to the open door "—while I get changed."

"Why? It's not like I'm going to peek." He glanced up from the laptop screen. "You're not even remotely interesting to me."

"Why am I friends with any of you?" Elya asked.

"Because you love us." Twist smiled as his fingers glided across her keyboard. "Except Shredder, of course – we all know you hate him. Not that I could possibly blame you," he stood up, laptop in hand. "You wouldn't happen to have any milk in the fridge by chance?" Twist walked out of the bedroom. "I need to flush some poison out of my system."

"Top shelf," Elya said.

"Right." He moved to the fridge.

Maybe she should've been more concerned about the fact Twist had been poisoned, but even the most lethal of poisons only caused minor stomach problems in the deadly sins. If she remembered Fiend's explanation correctly, it had something to do with how their internal temperatures were so high that no poison, virus, or bacteria could survive, essentially, giving them the ultimate immune system.

Pulling herself from her thoughts, Elya shut her bedroom door, locking it to be safe. (Not that it could keep Twist or any of his brothers out if they wanted in, but it felt good to establish a boundary, even if it was a feeble one. At the least it would give her a warning someone was about to bust the door down.)

As she got ready for the night, she contemplated Twist's bizarre nature. She wasn't even going to ask why Shredder had poisoned Twist this time. Sloth wasn't like his other brothers; he was relaxed, no tenseness. No overwhelming desire to have blood on his hands at every moment of every day like Fiend and Zeerlo, not constantly brewing poisons like Shredder or taking everything he could from others like Hellas. Out of the five of them, he was perhaps the most normal, and that's what made him strange. It was also a crazy thought that any of Satan's sons could remotely resemble anything normal – then again, Twist didn't have a sin that was quite as prone to becoming dangerous like the others.

Satan had trained each of his sons to have a specialty; for Zeerlo, that was warfare, for Fiend it was healing, for Twist it was hacking. Shredder's specialty was poison, and Hellas – well, she didn't know what Hellas was trained in. He wasn't quite thirteen yet, so Satan wouldn't share Greed's specialty.

In the end, she only needed ten minutes to find something to wear and get changed. She was proud of herself – she managed to find a cute outfit that would be perfect for Italy, though she wasn't entirely sure it was good for drinking in Italy.

In her mind, she laid out her boundaries: She was not going to be partying, a few drinks with dinner, maybe after, but if Satan ordered so much as a shot of the hard stuff, she would demand to be brought home. It wasn't that she couldn't handle her liquor – she could down a shot of vodka no problem – it was just that Satan would keep them coming until she was at risk of alcohol poisoning.

"Elya, are you ready yet?" Zeerlo called.

"Yes."

The door opened as though she hadn't had it locked. She didn't know why she bothered. She took in Zeerlo's appearance, and was surprised to see that he was dressed in a maroon suit with his black hair gelled back. It made him look less like a teenager and more like a young adult.

Fiend stood behind him in a similar suit, only his was a dark purple. From what she knew of the color wheel, that suit with his hair was a *bold* move.

Twist stood next to his brother, no longer in the t-shirt and jeans he was wearing earlier; instead, he was dressed in a simple black suit that resembled the one Satan wore. It really highlighted Satan's features in him – the sharp angles, high cheekbones, and the Devil's smile. His light brown skin came from Lilith.

Elya smiled. "You guys clean up well."

"We were raised to be gentlemen," Fiend said, smiling easily.

"You were raised to be killers," Kalael said, stepping into view.

As always, Kalael looked beautiful. No matter what Pride wore, she tended to be the most beautiful person in the room. How could she not be when she had divine blood giving her all the best features, a beauty that was simultaneously classical and exotic? But Kalael's dress was gorgeous. It was short, black with lace sleeves, and just the slightest hint of sapphire sparkles. Simple, yet elegant. And as always, there seemed to be the faintest glow around her.

"I didn't know you were coming," Elya said.

Kalael laughed. It was airy, musical. "And miss a chance to go to Italy? I may have been adopted, but I still consider it a part of my heritage," she smiled. "Besides, I wouldn't leave you to deal with my dad and brothers alone."

"Is that an insult?" Satan asked.

"It might be," Kalael said, eyes glinting, "but not this time. All I'm saying is last time I let you take Elya out, she blacked out. I know it's supposed to be just dinner and maybe a couple drinks after, but when you get the Devil involved, things turn sinful *fast*."

Satan smiled softly. "I can't argue." He looked to Elya. "And you look lovely as ever."

Elya smiled. "Thanks."

Satan clicked his tongue. "You really must have more confidence in yourself Elya."

"I have self-confidence," Elya said simply, "but I'm the only human in a group that has divine blood. All of you have an ethereal appearance I lack."

"That doesn't make you any less beautiful," Kalael said. "You're one of the prettiest girls I know, Elya. You are absolutely beautiful."

"Seconded," Fiend said.

Twist grinned. "Total ten."

Elya snorted. "That's going too far. Appreciate the attempt at a confidence boost, though."

"No my dear, they're correct, you're absolutely stunning."

"Keep the smile," Zeerlo said. "It suits you." He walked to the door. "And remember, while we can lie, we don't tell them. It's a point of pride in this family." He held the door open. "And Lucifer men don't pay compliments lightly." He vanished in a blur.

One by one, the Deadly Sins vanished. Soon, all that remained were Elya, Kalael, and Satan himself. The two seemed to be having a silent conversation as they stood there – probably deciding which of them would go ahead with the boys and which would be dragging her to Italy because she was the only one in the group who couldn't travel there alone. Sure, she could trip into Heaven or Hell (other realms on occasion as well, but those instances were few, far between, and always brief, with someone showing up to take her to Earth shortly after her arrival). But using her traveling abilities to her will to travel the world? That she couldn't do. Finally, Kalael disappeared into the shadows, leaving her alone with the Devil himself.

"I just want to make one thing clear before we pop off to Italy for the night," Satan said.

"Don't worry, I won't embarrass you," Elya teased.

He scoffed. "I'm hardly concerned about that. The only person who would embarrass me is currently babysitting my youngest sons – not that we'll use the term babysitting in front of either of them. They'll make life a living Hell for all of us. No, I'm talking about something else. Something far more important."

"I'm listening," Elya said.

"No, I don't think you are. But you will." Satan grabbed her chin, forcing her to look him in the eye. "Believe what you will about me, about my sons and my daughter, about yourself, but never *for one second* doubt that you are important to my family. Not just my brothers who see you in Heaven, not my brothers that act in capacity as your guardian angels, and not just my father. You hold importance to my daughter. She adores you, and not many get such an honor. While it may seem irrelevant when I say this, Fiend, Zeerlo, and Twist would kill for you. I know you and Shredder have your grievances with each other, but even Shredder would kill in cold blood if it meant keeping you safe and happy. Hellas would as well, even if he hasn't even had his ceremonies yet."

"Alright," Elya said.

"No, not alright." His eyes flashed red briefly. "You must understand, Elya. You may not always like our methods, but we will do everything in our power to keep you safe and happy, and right now, you're not seeing yourself with the value you have. You think because you don't have the blood of angels in your veins that you're of any lesser value to Kalael? Of Zeerlo, Fiend, Twist, Shredder, Hellas, Gabriel, Raphael? You have more value, Elya, than any of us. I will live for eternity. My children – well, it's uncertain what lifespans they will have. But you, Elya, your human blood makes you valuable. My father loves you for that blood alone."

"I feel like I'm missing something here," Elya said.

"You are. You're missing the fact that we do notice when you're unhappy – and I promise you I'm reserving a special place in Hell for Cathy and Laurel. I just might place Fiend and Zeerlo in charge of their torture." He shrugged. "Whatever they said to you, ignore it. You know better than to let them get to you."

Elya smiled sincerely and hoped he could see the genuine appreciation there. "Thanks."

"Yes well. Just don't go spreading it around." He straightened his suit. "I do have a reputation to uphold, after all."

"I know," Elya said.

He offered her an arm. "Shall we?"

Elya took it. "Let's go."

Kalael and the boys were already waiting for them outside some restaurant that she had no doubt was expensive and needed advanced reservations. She had no idea what was with Satan, or what he was trying to get at, but that didn't mean she minded. Sometimes it was nice to have a reminder that she had friends who would literally kill for her. Disturbing, but nice. Maybe she should double check to make sure they weren't murdering her ex-boyfriends or ex-girlfriends. She didn't have a string of them or anything, but there were a few, and all of them had broken up with her due to something Zeerlo or Fiend had done (she admitted that definitely took the sting out of the rejection). Then again, surely they wouldn't kill someone over things they had technically done.

Maybe she should just focus on her celebratory dinner.

Ten

As great as celebrating her graduation had been, that didn't mean Satan didn't ensure she was back in Hell the following Monday to do his paperwork. Heaven, forbid him to give her an actual break. Even when she'd gone on family vacation she was dragged into Hell at some point. On the bright side, Kalael had given her a brief driving lesson in her new car over the weekend, which was amazing. Still sucked being dragged back into Hell.

Though, this was the first time she was there alone.

Being alone in the throne room was… odd. No Satan, no Deadly Sins. It was *weird*. It wasn't like them to leave her unsupervised, not when demons could enter the room any moment. And without Satan to hold them back? Maybe she should've been more concerned than she was. Sure, Satan was down the hall, but when it came to demons – well, screaming wouldn't get her anywhere. If she screamed, it'd be lost in the screams of the damned.

"I'm here my darling," the voice said.

Well, she was physically alone inside the throne room. More than likely, Satan had someone stood guarding the door. But if he did, it had to be someone he'd trust to follow orders without question. It couldn't be one of the Deadly Sins, which left the question of who would Satan trust not to enter the room? It had to be a demon, didn't it? But what demon would possibly leave her alone, even with him gone? From what she understood, the demons rarely obeyed when Satan wasn't around. They did their own thing.

Great. Now she was curious. Luckily, this once, her self-preservation outweighed her curiosity. No need to risk going in search of a demon and finding the wrong one. She didn't want to be killed or to end up tormented because the demons viewed her as weaker. Not that it wasn't true; in the battle between celestials and humans, humans always lost.

Clearing her head, Elya grabbed the next piece of paperwork, only to see an envelope at the top of the pile. Odd. Letters belonged in the mail pile, not in her never-ending pile of paperwork. And it *was* never-ending.

She glanced to the crack in the floor. She had taken a flashlight to it once, and she couldn't see the bottom, but she did know that as soon as she grabbed something from the top, the next thing popped through the crack. Heaving a sigh, Elya grabbed the envelope to take it to the mail pile.

The address gave her pause. Hell. Nothing else, just Hell. Strange. She had never once seen an envelope simply addressed as Hell. She shifted. It wasn't addressed to a single individual, so technically it shouldn't hurt anything to open it. It was like the mail that got sent to 'current resident.' Right? Fighting against her better judgement, Elya opened the envelope, pulling the single piece of paper out.

Gather your army. There's no time to waste. Hell's destruction is coming.

That was it. No explanation of what would cause the destruction, just a warning to gather an army.

"That's interesting," the voice said.

Satan needed to see this.

Thankfully, she'd taken enough trips from the throne room to his office to know the way. So long as she didn't run into any demons during the quick trip down the hall, she'd be fine. She hoped. Really, what were the chances she'd run into a demon anyways? She knew most would be off torturing the souls of the damned. Even if she did run into a demon, she'd claim she had an urgent matter to discuss with Satan and hope for the best. If that didn't work, well she'd hope the alarm system worked in Hell.

Pulling the door open, she staggered back in surprise. She expected one of the grotesque demons, but instead there was a man. He was tall, just slightly shorter than Satan. His skin was tanned, his cheek bones high, his eyes looked like pure onyx, and his silver hair was pulled back into a ponytail that came down between his shoulder blades. He bore a strange resemblance to Twist. The man was dressed in a pair of jeans, combat boots, a black shirt, and a leather vest. A sword was strapped to his waist, and knives were strapped to his arms, but that wasn't the most dangerous thing about him. His wings were exposed – large and feathery like Satan's, like the angels. The feathers were an unnatural charred black. His wings weren't full; feathers were missing and some appeared tattered.

"Oh—" she honestly hadn't expected to see anyone "—um, hi?"

"I've been told you're not to leave the throne room unless it's an emergency," he said.

Elya scoffed. "You think I'd attempt leaving what little safety the throne room offers if it weren't urgent?" She crossed her arms. "I need to see Satan. Now."

He frowned. "It's really not allowed."

"You said I can leave if it's an emergency—" Elya glared "—and I think Satan will qualify this as an emergency."

The demon scoffed. "If you believe that, then you don't know my brother well."

Elya gaped. "You're one of his brothers? But that means you're one of the original demons. One of the fallen angels cast from Heaven."

He gave a bow. "Asbeel, at your service."

She offered a smile. "Nice to meet you, Asbeel. Could you please take me to your brother? Even if he dismisses what I have to say at first, I know I can convince him to take this seriously." She hoped.

He raised a brow. "What could possibly be so urgent?"

Elya shifted. She had no idea if she could trust him. She didn't know anything about him. She wanted to trust him, but how could she? He wasn't just a demon; he was a *fallen angel*. Yes, that meant he was Satan's brother and had been in Hell just as long, but that also meant there was plenty of time for

Asbeel to have developed resentment for Satan. For all she knew, whatever brotherly loyalty existed when the rebellion happened might be nonexistent now.

"I think someone's going to try and destroy Hell."

He laughed. "Nobody in their right mind would attempt destruction on Hell, and any foolish enough to try would be in for a very harsh reality. Hell's army is not to be taken lightly. We were severely outnumbered during the rebellion and still we nearly took the throne of Heaven. Now our numbers are more than triple that, thanks to Lilith and her spawn."

Elya refrained from commenting about how she heard otherwise. Instead, she said: "Not a fan of Lilith, I take it?"

"Trust me, the only time anyone down here wants anything to do with Lilith is when they want to take her to their bed. She thinks herself above everyone down here, Satan included. But after the stunt she pulled with Adam, she's not exactly allowed in Heaven." He crossed his arms. "I'd know. I hate them, but I tried to make a deal for them to take Lilith. But no, she's not welcome in Heaven. I also tried dropping her back off with Adam. That ended poorly."

"Adam didn't take it well?" Elya asked.

"He was thrilled," Asbeel's brows rose. "As much as he thought he wanted someone submissive all the time, Eve probably got boring after a while." He sighed. "Lilith was a welcome sight. To Adam, at least. Eve went ballistic. It's surprising, really – she was tiny, and probably the most nauseatingly nice person I ever had the displeasure of meeting, but the second she laid eyes on Lilith... well, let's just say Lilith still has scars from the encounter."

"This was after the forbidden fruit thing, right?" Elya asked.

"Yes." Asbeel rolled his eyes. "Not that it matters."

"Sorry, just curious," Elya said.

He chuckled. "I know."

She frowned. "You know?"

"You've been tripping into Hell since you were six, Elya. After sixteen years, word gets around." He shrugged. "Your curiosity is dangerous, and unrivaled. Yet, for some reason, Satan and his sons still protect you. I never understood why until now."

"Well, someone has to do his paperwork," Elya said.

"I admit it is nice not having my despicable holier-than-thou brothers constantly popping in because the paperwork hasn't been turned in. The less I see of them, the better." Asbeel shook his head. "But that's certainly not the reason."

"And what precisely do you think is the reason? That I juggle torches for him?"

He laughed. "Not what I meant. It's that stupid little feeling you give off. It's utterly revolting."

"Okay, you're going to have to explain." She crossed her arms defiantly. "I give off an utterly revolting feeling, and for some reason Satan keeps me around because of it?"

"I didn't say it'd be revolting to him." Asbeel shrugged. "What's revolting about it is the power it gives you. Over him, the deadly sins, the angels, all of Afterlife, probably."

"Riiiight." She needed to get away from this guy.

"Oh, don't go getting in a panic. I won't hurt you over it." He crossed his arms. "But I don't like it."

"Look, will you take me to Satan or not?" Elya asked.

For once, she didn't want the answer. Whatever Asbeel had meant, it was probably for the best that she didn't know. At least – yeah, she probably didn't want to know. Handsome or not, he was still a fallen angel, and for him to have his wings exposed the way he did, he wasn't weak either. Even she knew the wings were the most vulnerable point on an immortal's body. From what she had seen, not even the angels in Heaven left their wings on display. In fact, the only times she really saw wings were if someone used them to take flight or if they came out in a moment of rage. It said all she needed to know:

She didn't want to be on Asbeel's bad side. Not with the amount of sheer strength he had to be harboring.

Or he was just insane. Either way, this was a new friend she did *not* want to make.

Asbeel groaned. "Fine, I'll take you to Satan, but you take full responsibility for the blame. You never spoke to me. If he asks where I was, I was having a talk with one of Lilith's spawns, shouting about staying away from the throne room or something."

"Seriously?" Elya asked.

"Don't make me regret it," Asbeel muttered.

Elya rolled her eyes. "Dude, it's a two-minute walk."

"Two minutes in which you could talk my ear off," Asbeel said.

"Well, harsh," Elya said.

He chuckled. "What part of fallen did you miss?"

"Not a reason to be a jerk."

Asbeel grinned. "Never insinuated I was nice. I'm the deserter of God. He forsakes me, so I forsake him and all those who live in Heaven. Loki may have been his right hand during the rebellion, but look around you. Loki isn't here. The coward is with his brother pretending to be a prisoner. Down here, I'm Satan's right hand. I'm someone to be feared and revered."

"Now who's talking whose ear off?" she quipped, then fell silent at his scathing look.

Now was probably not the time to mention that she had seen Loki in the throne room not long ago. Nor was it the time for her to point out that Asbeel, apparently, had an ego. And for someone who was supposed to be Satan's trusted right hand, it was odd this was the first time she was even hearing about him.

No, best she didn't mention any of those things. There was a glint in his eye that spoke of madness. He seemed composed, acted friendly, albeit grumpy, but something about Asbeel was most definitely off. Maybe slightly unhinged.

Definitely a good idea to befriend him.

"Is that why you leave your wings out?" Elya asked.

"I leave them exposed because I do not fear the demons that are Lilith's spawn," he said simply, "nor do I fear my other fallen brothers."

"Not even Satan?" Elya asked.

"I have nothing to fear from him," Asbeel said.

Nothing but Satan's wrath should she be interrupting Satan with something unimportant. Not that she was, though she was sure Asbeel thought it was a waste of time. Yet, he was still escorting her. Rough around the edges, and potentially insane. Overall, Elya liked him.

Yes, Asbeel would be her friend, whether he liked it or not. He wouldn't be great at friendship, but then again, neither was Satan. Even still, the Devil was one of her best friends, so what harm was there in befriending one of his fallen brothers?

"Fine. Ask," Asbeel snapped.

Elya frowned. "What?"

"You're just radiating curiosity. It's no wonder Satan went to his office." Asbeel crossed his arms. "You're impossible to think around. So, whatever questions are plaguing you, ask."

"But I wasn't."

"Whatever." He rolled his eyes. "If you're not going to ask, then tone it down."

"Sorry?"

That was strange. She hadn't been thinking about that many questions, had she? And how had been able to tell she had a question on her mind, even if for a brief second? How was that even possible? Satan had certainly never indicated an ability to tell when she had a question on her mind. Yes, he knew when she was bursting with questions, but, then again, almost everyone did. This wasn't a multitude of questions, though. It was a single question.

"You're doing it again," Asbeel said.

"Sorry! Just – how could you tell I had thought of a question?" She asked. "It wasn't a multitude, which is usually how people know I have questions. It was just one."

He shrugged. "You had that glint your eye."

Elya frowned. "What glint?"

"It's the glint of curiosity. The same glint I've seen a thousand times when — well, it doesn't matter where I've seen the glint." Asbeel crossed his arms. "Just know I know how to recognize it."

Elya sighed. "You did that on purpose, didn't you?"

Abseel grinned. "Gave you an answer without giving you answer? It's possible. It could've been pure coincidence. You'll never know." He tilted his head to the door next to them.

"Thanks," Elya said. "You're not a half-bad friend."

Asbeel frowned. "Never a friend. I don't do those." He turned to walk back in the direction they came.

She wasn't going to bother arguing. She'd spent enough time with Satan to know Asbeel wouldn't willingly confess that he didn't despise her very existence. Hell, it took sixteen years of her tripping into Hell every day, sometimes multiple times a day, for Satan to finally admit he didn't hate her existence. Though, with the news she was about to bring the Devil, he wasn't likely going to be too pleased with her. Doubtless, he'd be furious, and if he didn't take it seriously… Well, she'd convince him to. Even if that meant he went full devil. So long as he didn't shoot the messenger, it was no big deal.

"If he tries to harm a hair on your head, he'll meet my wrath," the voice said as though he could do anything.

"You'd be surprised."

This was it. The moment of truth. The moment she found out if Satan had any trust in her – real trust. She'd have to be vulnerable. Exhaling, she pushed the door open.

Eleven

Satan sat at the fireplace watching the fires dance, a bottle of whisky on his side table and a glass in hand. He looked haggard—his hair in disarray, he looked as though he hadn't shaved in days, and he was pale. Completely unlike himself. In the sixteen years she'd known him, she'd never seen him let his appearance falter. Not unless he was fighting, and even then he was quick to straighten his appearance. This wasn't him. It wasn't the right time for bad news.

"Are you alright?" Elya asked.

Satan startled and dropped his glass. Whiskey splattered across the floor as the glass shattered and ice fell into a pile. "Shit!" He waved a hand and the whiskey stain left the carpet, the ice vanished, and the shards of glass collected until they once again formed his glass.

"Sorry," Elya said.

"Not your fault—" he grabbed the bottle "—I should've noticed you come in." He refilled his glass, ice appearing as he went. "How did you get in?"

"Not important," Elya said.

He raised a brow. "I've taught you well." Satan sipped from his glass. "Did you need something or are you going to make it a habit of coming into my office uninvited?"

Elya shifted. "There was something in your paperwork."

He waved a dismissive hand. "I don't care about the paperwork." He cradled his glass. "Do with it what you will."

"Not what I meant," Elya sighed – this was going to take a while. "I found something that didn't belong, at least not with your paperwork. It was an envelope, so it should've been in your mail pile."

"I have a mail pile?" Satan asked.

"Yes. The fact you don't know about it tells me I'm going to have to sort your mail sometime as well." She crossed her arms. "Anyway, the envelope was addressed to Hell."

"Nothing odd about that," Satan said.

"But it is. Most of the letters are addressed Satan Lucifer, 666 Castle Street, Hell, Afterlife. This was just addressed Hell."

He straightened. "You're right, that is odd. How did it get through the postal system?"

"Satan, focus," Elya snapped.

He frowned. "I am focused."

Elya raised a brow. "Are you?"

"Yes? What do you want from me?"

"The letter inside was dated just this morning," Elya said. "It was a warning that someone is out to destroy Hell."

"That's ridiculous—" he downed his drink "—the only people capable of destroying Hell are — well, nobody is going to destroy Hell. And who in their right mind would send me a warning? And what were you doing opening my mail?"

"It wasn't specifically addressed to anyone, and it was in my pile of paperwork to do for you," she shrugged. "It felt necessary."

He grinned. "Opening other people's mail is definitely a step in the right direction for becoming corrupt. We should celebrate."

Elya frowned. "No. This is serious."

"Is it though?" He asked. "Because I feel like you're trying to tell me a random envelope contained legitimate information. It could easily be a prank, a gag. If you didn't know, Elya, we're in Hell. Malicious lies are a normal occurrence."

"Will you at least look at it?" Elya asked.

Satan huffed. "Fine. I'll look at it." He took the offered envelope. "But I swear, if you're wasting my time, there will be dire consequences."

"I'm not," Elya said.

He sighed, taking the letter into his hand and sat back in his chair. His expression darkened as his eyes went down the paper.

Elya struggled to keep from looking smug – she loved proving anyone in the Lucifer family wrong. Some more than others. The most satisfaction came from proving Satan and Zeerlo wrong. It was a rare day in Hell when she managed it. This was a moment she was going to remember forever, if possible.

Satan ran a hand through his hair. "You're never letting me live this one down, are you?"

Elya grinned. "Nope."

"I was afraid you'd say that." He stood. "We're going to have to do something about this. Verify its legitimacy. I hope you're happy now. You've created more work for all of us."

"Hey, I'm just the bearer of bad news," Elya said.

"Well, I don't like bad news!" Satan snarled.

Flames consumed his gaze. His skin tinged the slightest red. He paced the office rapidly. She could barely keep up with his movement – if you could call barely spotting a blur as keeping up. She had to give him credit – he knew how to keep his anger in check, especially when others were near who could get hurt.

He must have learned from the Zeerlo incident after all.

She'd only been tripping into Hell for about four years when it happened. Satan had been rather persistent in his pursuit to keep her away from others back then, but she still heard about what had been termed the incident. Secrets weren't easily kept in Afterlife. Demons gossiped; Azrael was vocal about his outrage. The other sins whispered. And Zeerlo himself – well, he didn't keep quiet about it either. While nobody had ever outright said what happened, there was always a challenge when it came to his disobedience. A dare. The words "do it again" had often been uttered.

Not that Satan tried to hide it either. Always talking about how he stole Zeerlo back to life. Nobody mentioned how that life was lost, but everybody who had anything to do with Afterlife knew the truth: Satan had killed his son at the mere age of five in a fit of rage, unleashing all Hell on a defenseless child. Well, as defenseless as you could get when Zeerlo was involved.

It was what placed Zeerlo on a pedestal above his brothers. He had Hell literally thrown at him. It killed him, sure, but he came back. Can't keep a good devil down, as it were. Zeerlo had already endured the worst. There was nothing left for him to fear.

"We're going to need to take care of this." Satan drew her from her thoughts. "Immediately. The slightest hesitation and we might fail."

"Right," Elya said. "And what could I possibly do? I'm only human."

He raised a brow. "Are you? You trip into Hell daily. It doesn't matter what you were born as, Elya. At this point, you're just as much a resident of the Afterlife as the rest of us. If we go down, you go down as well."

"He has a good point," the voice said.

She shrugged. "I can't help nearly as much as you seem to be thinking. I don't have powers, I *trip*. I have enough curiosity to do things that could get me into trouble, but I've reached my limit."

"You've reached your limit?" He asked.

"Yes," Elya said.

"You really going to deny me?" He asked.

"You probably should." The voice said.

"Yes." She really needed to get home and start — well, maybe not looking for employment. As much as she wanted a job outside of Hell, she had enough money now that she was set for a long time to come. But she wouldn't mind looking into getting an apartment far away from her roommates from wherever was worse than Hell.

"Fine," he shrugged. "Though, I was hoping you could do me the favor of getting into Heaven for me. Verify if this threat is in fact something I should be worried about. Maybe see if it originated in Heaven." He waved a dismissive hand. "But I understand entirely if you're too busy. I'm sure Zeerlo could do it. Azrael used to smuggle him into the palace all the time; he'd know what to do and how to do it."

"See? You don't even need me," Elya said.

"You're right," he said. "Of course, on the off chance Zeerlo is caught, I'm afraid it's game over for him. I mean, one of the deadly sins sneaking into Heaven… they'd bring him home and lock him up. Could you imagine? An eternity in Hell, being tortured by your own father! But I understand completely."

Elya groaned. "You're a manipulative bastard."

"Manipulative, yes. Bastard, I'm afraid not," he grinned. "You see, to be a bastard as you claim, I would've had to have been conceived out of wedlock, and, well, I was not conceived in the traditional sense. Perhaps as an idea, but if that were the case, every thought we have would be bastard thoughts. Besides, it could be argued I wasn't conceived at all. Father simply decided one day to create me. That same day he created the Heavens, the earth, and all the rest of the universe as well."

"Whatever," Elya huffed. "Just tell me what I need to do."

"No need for sass. I only need you to infiltrate the palace and verify the validity of this threat of yours. Maybe ensure it's not Heavenly in origin."

"I somehow doubt it," Elya said.

"Oh, you'd be surprised. After all, didn't I and a third of my brothers fall from Heaven's grace?"

Elya shrugged. "That's what humanity claims, and admittedly Gabriel and Raphael seem to have lacking opinions of you, but I've yet to hear from the horse's mouth."

He chuckled darkly. "It's quite the tale. Not the one humanity knows – there are some discrepancies there. I daresay not even Azrael knows the full story, and he was there for quite a bit. How could he not be when he was in on the plotting until he turned to my Father and offered his services in any way possible?"

Elya raised a brow. "You don't think Loki would've told him?"

"Loki was only my second in command," he shrugged. "One of my best friends at the time, sure, but even he didn't know *everything*."

"Care to share?" Elya asked.

"You know I won't."

"But it sounds interesting."

His gaze glinted. "Oh, it's quite the tale of scandal. Why, if I didn't think my Father already knew – just from the sheer fact he knows everything – oh, I'd think Father would be surprised. The thing is, as much as I loathe him, he does know everything."

"Oh, a scandal? And you won't tell me? I mean, to hear the story of your rebellion is one thing, but to hear it straight from the Devil himself? It's unheard of."

"It's unwanted memories for everyone involved."

"Come on, you know you want to tell me!" Elya said.

"It's a juicy secret, I'll give you that, but sorry, but not going to happen. If I confess what I've done that wasn't stated in the courts, then who knows? It might be brought back. And I simply refuse to go on trial again."

"Not like I'd tell."

"No, you wouldn't," Satan said, his gaze darkening. "But this is a matter of — well, it doesn't matter. You're not finding out and that's final. Now, are you going to help me by infiltrating the palace or not?"

Elya pouted. "Please? With a hot fudge sundae and a cherry on top?"

"Not happening." He sat back at his desk. "You're just going to have to take no for an answer, and that's final."

"I'll buy you Dairy Queen," Elya tried.

He smiled. "Tempting, but no. But good work – keep that up and we'll make a temptress out of you yet."

"You're more than welcome to practice on me darling."

Satan was smart, she'd give him that. They both knew if he gave her a little, he'd tell it all. And she would ask questions. She couldn't help it – it was who she was. She had to have all the facts. Her curiosity, her desire for proper answers, had gotten her in more than a few sticky situations over the years. Once, Satan had come to her rescue because she stumbled onto what would've been the biggest scandal in known history, only Satan refused to let her submit the story to the news. She had recordings of it even, but no, her phone ended up smashed under Satan's heel.

Elya huffed. "Fine. What do I need to do?"

"What indeed?" Satan muttered.

He paced. Slower this time, as though he were thinking of a plan. They needed to get her into Heaven and back without her being seen and given there seemed to be an alert system for when she arrived there, they'd need to find a way to circumvent it.

She was smart, but she wasn't Satan. He was intelligent, cunning, and ruthless. If anyone could get her in and out of Heaven unnoticed, it was him. He plotted a rebellion, led it into action, and, if stories were to be believed, nearly won. That didn't come from brute strength alone – it took intelligence, strategy, cunning, tactics, and probably some manipulation.

Elya knew one thing with certainty: whatever plan he had, she'd be at its center.

Twelve

Satan pulled a long, thin wooden box from the shelf behind his desk. He laid it out on the desk, and his eyes flicked to the office door. The deadbolt turned to the lock position.

Elya shifted uneasily. She trusted Satan not to hurt her, but sometimes she worried he'd fall over the edge and kill her along with everyone else.

"I was waiting to give you these once you've finished your training," He unlocked the box. "But all things considered, if this threat is real, you'll be needing them far sooner." He flipped the lid open. "They should help you if you run into trouble – in Heaven or otherwise." He slid the box toward her.

Elya glanced inside and found two daggers, a sword, and a necklace.

One dagger was encrusted with dark green emeralds and a silver hilt. The other was different: The blade was a glowing green, the hilt was a sleek, shiny black, and silver dragons adorned the front and back. The sword wasn't encrusted with jewels, there was no strange glow, and the hilt was plain black. The necklace was an emerald shaped into a circle about the size of a quarter, and the left and bottom edges held the body of a small dragon made entirely from diamonds, with the head coming toward the center of the emerald from the right. She reached to touch the contents of the box, only for Satan to slap her hand away.

"Do not take these lightly. The sword may look unassuming, but it's deadly. The emerald encrusted dagger is Hell forged. I'm certain you know the dangers that come with that. The other dagger as you can likely tell from its color, is enchanted." He picked up the necklace. "This is much like the pendants my sons wear and the necklace Kalael wears. It contains all the same properties, such as storage. It is keyed to your energy, which means nobody can touch it unless you allow it."

Elya stared at the weapons. "Do I need a sheath or something for the daggers and sword? Or do I just keep them in the necklace?"

He smiled. "While you're in Heaven, I suggest you keep them in the necklace. After that, I suggest wearing them unless you're in human populated areas." He pulled three sheathes from beneath his desk. "The sword you'll have to carry at your waist, and the daggers you can attach to your legs, your arms, or to your belt."

Elya frowned. "I'm not wearing a belt."

Satan raised a brow. "The sheath for your sword is strapped around your waist like a belt." He sighed. "Honestly, Elya, you're smarter than this."

She blushed. "Sorry, I totally forgot that part."

He chuckled. "Understandable in the circumstance." He pulled a large, folded piece of paper from inside his desk. "Now, pay attention. I need to give you the layout of the palace."

"Wait, what?" Elya asked.

Satan rolled his eyes. "I told you we need to verify this threat with Heaven."

"Yeah got that part, but why would I need the layout of the palace?" Elya asked.

He ran a hand down his face. "Nobody, not even Raphael and Gabriel are just going to tell you the information," He unfolded the map. "Or take you where it's going to be."

Elya frowned. "Where is it going to be?"

Satan's gaze hardened. "The War Room."

Elya blinked. "I'm sorry, did you just say war room? As in a room for war? Making plans, strategizing, and it's in Heaven?"

"It's not used by many, mainly Michael. He practically lives there, anything and everything of importance is in there," Satan leaned against his desk. "If there's any indication of the legitimacy of this threat in Heaven, it'll be somewhere in that room."

Elya frowned. "If that's where he spends most of his time, then how exactly am I supposed to get in and search?"

"It's Monday," Satan said as though it explained everything.

"And?"

He huffed. "My brother will be in meetings with my Father until four o'clock. He'll then head to his room to get changed, stop by his actual office to ensure his papers there are organized before he returns to the war room. It's one o'clock. That gives us a four-hour window of opportunity. You should be able to get in, get out, and find what you need in an hour."

"If something goes wrong?" Elya asked.

"Let's hope it doesn't," Satan said. "But so long as you're not caught, you should have time on your side."

"Right," Elya exhaled. "Alright what do I need to do?"

He pointed to the map of the palace. "From my understanding, this is where you typically land when you trip into Heaven. It's right across from the throne room." He traced his finger down the halls. "This is the war room. To get there, you need to go from your landing point down the hall toward the left. At the end of the hall, you'll need to take a left. It's crucial you're unseen down this hall – it's where the archangels' rooms are. At the end of this hall, swing a right, and the third door on the right is the war room."

"But Gabriel or Raphael is always there to greet me when I land. I've never landed in Heaven and not had someone there to greet me," Elya said.

Satan frowned. "Then we'll find a way to distract them."

Elya raised a brow. "Both of them?"

"Leave that to me. I have a trick or two up my sleeve."

"Alright, so you distract them so nobody's there to greet me when I land, then I make my way to the war room."

"Yes. Do you remember the directions?"

Elya nodded. "Left from the landing point to the end of the hall, take a left, stay unseen, hang a right at the end of that hall and go through the third door on the right." She smiled. "I think I can handle that."

He scoffed. "Don't get cocky. The war room will be locked and the only people with access inside are my Father and Michael," he pulled a small silver key from his pocket. "Thankfully, Zeerlo managed to snatch a mold of the key ages ago."

"How?" Elya asked.

Satan shrugged. "Azrael and Zeerlo used to play chess in Azrael's palace bedroom."

"Okay, so I use the key you gave me and hope the locks haven't been changed," Elya frowned. "Anything else I should concern over?"

"Escape routes. Ideally, you'll trip out and land back in Hell, if not return to your landing point. But, if something goes wrong, you need to know where to go." His fingers traced the map. "If for some reason you can't go back the way you came, it's ideal if you continue down the hall, take a right, and follow the hall to its end. There'll be a replica of "The Creation of Adam" on the wall. Tap the bottom left corner three times and it'll open a secret passage out of the palace. The tunnel lets out in the middle of the city."

"How do I get out of the city?" Elya asked.

Here, he frowned. "You'll need to be careful to avoid being seen. Anyone who isn't an angel won't recognize you for a living human, but angels are everywhere. One sees you, they'll instantly know you don't belong and take you to my father. Thankfully, it'll be simple enough to get you out of the city. The main road from the gates to the palace is paved in gold and lined with diamond-encrusted streetlamps. It's the only one that has both. You'll be let out in an alleyway right next to this road."

"Heaven has alleys?" Elya asked.

Satan rolled his eyes. "Yes."

"Don't judge," Elya crossed her arms. "I've never stepped foot outside the palace."

Satan snorted. "You know there is a far larger number of people who have lived in Heaven for thousands of years who've yet to step foot inside?"

Elya shrugged. "Not like I've seen much of the palace."

He chuckled. "Well, you'll get to see a bit more of it today."

The two of them went over the plan again from the beginning, coming up with alternative escape routes in case the first failed, ideas for what to do if Satan's plan to distract Gabriel and Raphael failed, memorizing every detail of every plan, and every detail of the map. There wasn't room for mistakes, but they needed to be prepared for anything and everything to go wrong. She glanced to the clock, the hours slowly ticking by as they went over the plan again and again until she could recite it in her sleep – including every contingency plan Satan could think of.

"Anything else I need to know before I go?" Elya asked.

Satan sighed. "If you're found, I cannot help you. If they realize you were around the war room, you better lie and lie good, because if you're not taken to Gabriel or Raphael, you'll likely be taken to Michael, and that *cannot* happen."

Her brows drew together. "Why? What happens if I'm taken to Michael?"

"Chances are, he'll take you to our father." His tone darkened. "And, despite your status of living, if you're not forthcoming with information, you will be judged and sentenced then and there. Odds are that even if you are honest, they won't like the answer you give."

"Isn't that a little harsh?" Elya asked.

"You forget, Elya—" Satan sat back at his desk "—over the last sixteen years, you've become associated with me." He kicked his feet up on his desk. "And nobody associated with me is considered as being harmless."

"Gabriel and Raphael are still two of my best friends," Elya said.

"They are." Satan leaned back. "Doesn't matter. Believe me, gossip may be a sin, but Heaven is a place *filled* with it." He chuckled. "You wouldn't believe what's on the rumor mill sometimes."

Elya raised a brow. "Do I want to know?"

"Probably not," he grinned. "But because we both know how not knowing things annoys you, I'll tell you the top votes on the betting pool for why I tolerate your presence are as follows: we're having an illicit affair, you're my child from an illicit affair with a mortal, you're the result of an affair with Loki, I'm using you for a scheme of some shape or form, or I'm just tolerating your presence to mess with people."

Elya snorted. "So, either we're having an affair or I'm the result of one of your affairs, or you're up to something. Not very creative, and certainly not flattering to either of us."

He chuckled. "I never insinuated they were intelligent. The last time I had what might be considered an affair with anyone – mortal or otherwise – was when Kalael wasn't quite yet three. As such, you're far too young for the numbers to add up."

Elya laughed. "Not to mention you're way too old for me."

Satan bristled. "Excuse me? I am not old. My human equivalent age is twenty-four."

Elya raised a brow. "You don't find it weird that you're 24 when your daughter is almost 29? Because that's weird."

He shrugged. "My eldest grandson and granddaughter are 33. Time travel and different rates of aging make things complicated. Besides, nobody in this family ages past the age of 25. Well, except my Father. Point being, I still haven't maxed out my age yet."

"How do you know you won't age past 25 then?" Elya asked.

Satan's feet hit the floor. "My Father and I may no longer get along, but there was a time he and I were on good terms." He shuddered. "This sort of thing was discussed. I still have a few thousand years before I reach twenty-five."

Elya raised a brow. "Seriously?"

Satan shrugged. "Something like that. It's been thousands of years – billions depending on how you count." He waved a hand. "I try to block out most of the memories from back then, so between that and the passage of time, things become a blur."

"Right." Elya shifted. "You know, if word gets out you gave me a Hell forged dagger, another enchanted dagger, a sword and a necklace similar to what you've given your kids, it's going to do nothing for the rumors."

He sighed. "I'm aware, but it's a risk I'm willing to take."

Elya smiled. "I've always wanted my own dagger." She grabbed them both carefully by the hilt and held them over her new necklace still laid on the table, which promptly sucked them in. "That's badass." She glanced to the sword. "You know I'm not good with swords, right?"

He chuckled. "You'll be surprised at what you can do. You just need more practice, though I confess daggers are your weapon."

Elya grabbed the sword, it glowed briefly as she allowed it to be sucked into the necklace. "So, any other warnings before I try to trip my way into Heaven?" She pulled the necklace to her neck, struggling briefly to get it to clasp. "Ha. Got it."

He chuckled. "You'll be alright." Satan pulled her into a hug. "Just promise me you'll be careful and try to stay safe. The rumors may be wrong, but you're still important to me."

"If anyone tries anything, they'll have me to deal with."

Elya smiled. "Thanks."

Taking a breath, Elya did something she never thought she'd do. She tripped on purpose. The sensation of rushing water surrounding her, but as she landed on soft ground, she found something was very wrong. She wasn't in the palace.

Wherever she was, though, it was breathtaking. There didn't seem to be a sun; the light instead seemed to come from everywhere. The grass was greener than anything she'd ever seen, the sky bluer, and there were flowers in colors she'd never seen in her life. It didn't matter that she'd never been outside the palace, Elya recognized where she was. How could she not? The air felt cleaner than anywhere she'd ever been, and her landing hadn't hurt in the least. She was in Heaven. Where in Heaven she had no idea, but if the beauty wasn't a dead giveaway, the lack of physical sun was.

The only problem was there weren't any roads nearby and Satan hadn't mapped out all of Heaven for her. Hadn't even mentioned there were areas without roads in sight. Why would he? Neither of them expected her to get into Heaven any way but through her usual landing point. Sixteen years, and the one day she needed to get in and out as fast as possible, she didn't land outside the throne room of the palace.

How was she supposed to find a place she'd only found through tripping? Was it even possible? All she knew was the golden road lined with diamond streetlamps, which didn't even make sense. What use was there for streetlamps when she had been told by several people and witnessed the light streaming in through the windows at all hours that there's no actual nighttime in Heaven, which *really* didn't make sense.

Elya huffed. She was lost, had a time limit, and now she had a million new questions that she had no answer for. She'd have to remember as many as possible and ask Satan later. Or, since they were questions related to Heaven, maybe she'd be better off asking Gabriel or Raphael… just not when she was on a mission for Satan.

But first, she needed to figure out how to get to the palace, infiltrate the war room, verify the threat to Afterlife, and avoid detection while at it. It shouldn't be too hard. Just her typical Tuesday, only it was Monday and there was nothing typical about it. Though, if she pulled it off, she could brag about successfully breaking into Heaven – even if it was only around Satan and the sins.

"You always have me my queen."

Elya ignored him.

Thirteen

Over the years, she had managed to get into numerous sticky situations. This, by far, was the worst. The safest, sure, but if she were caught, like Satan said, it wouldn't be good. Somehow, she needed to find the city and the proper road so she could find her way into the palace. Theoretically, it was easy, but implementing it would be messy.

"Just stay calm," she muttered to herself. "You're only trying to sneak into the palace. Just look like you belong, and it'll be good."

And if one angel spotted her, she'd give them a partial truth: she didn't land right when she tripped, which was true, the only difference was this time her arrival wasn't unplanned. Though, getting caught would likely ruin any chance she had of getting the job done. She hoped she wasn't caught because, partial truth or not, being dishonest with an angel didn't seem like something that'd go over well on her judgment day.

"Are you lost?" a small voice asked.

"And that's my cue to ditch out," the voice said. *"I'll return for you in a few months my darling queen."*

She wasn't sure whether to be worried or relieved. She supposed it depended on who it was that had finally scared her disembodied voice away.

Elya turned to see a small Arabic boy stood there, not more than five or six. He had dark brown hair, his face was a little thin, his nose was bridged, and he was dressed in a white t-shirt that read *Jesus Loves You* in black lettering and a pair of torn jeans. He also wore a pair of navy-blue Velcro strap-on shoes. He was covered head to toe in mud. If he weren't in Heaven Elya would assume his shirt would never be its proper white again. His joy-filled eyes were a shade of blue she couldn't quite name and didn't think she'd ever seen on a person. He didn't look like an angel, and as far as she knew, Gabriel was the youngest angel, but something about this little boy *felt* like the angels. Maybe even purer. Which was surprising… How was it even possible for someone to be purer than Gabriel?

Realizing she was staring, Elya said something. "Oh no, I'm good."

He frowned. "You're lying, but I forgive you. After all, you don't recognize me."

Elya frowned. She raked through her memory, trying to find some recollection of the small boy in front of her. Did she know him? A child she met by accident in the palace once? Or maybe someone she passed on Earth while he was living? There was something about this child that made her feel she should know him, but for the life of her, she couldn't think of anyone she knew who looked like that. She'd remember those unnaturally blue eyes. They were a perfect match for Heaven's sky.

"Should I know you?" Elya asked finally.

"Yes and no," he said simply.

Elya raised a brow. "What?"

"I'll show you the way to the palace if you like." He offered her a small, mud-covered hand, but even through the mud, Elya could make out an odd, round hole through his wrist, as if a nail had gone through it…

She gasped. "Jesus?"

He grinned. "Hello, Elya."

"Hi?" Elya managed.

"Walk with me?" He asked, blue eyes shining with warmth.

"Uh—yeah—um—yeah—of course." She had never sounded so ineloquent in her life. She could practically hear Satan's monologue about the importance of speaking with a degree of refinement, or Gabriel's lengthy lecture – loss of words seemed to be a shared pet peeve of the angels.

It was crazy. She was in the presence of Jesus and he wanted her to walk with him? It was something she'd never thought possible so long as she lived. Maybe after she died and was lucky enough to get into Heaven and not sent to Hell. She wouldn't be surprised if she ended up in Hell, if the frequency she tripped into Satan's throne room was any indication. Satan, she could deal with for an eternity. Doing his paperwork and living on dialup, though… that, she would not be able to handle. That and the demons. And while she didn't know for sure what Satan would assign her for her personalized torture, she had an idea. But despite her constant trips to Hell, she still made a lot of trips into Heaven, and Gabriel and Raphael could vouch for her. Well, maybe. Raphael probably would. Gabriel wasn't the type to speak up for what he wanted… Though, who knew? Maybe when it came to her spending eternity in Hell with his brother, he'd say something.

"Take my hand," He urged.

"Right," She took the offered hand a little too quickly.

"Are you hungry, perhaps thirsty?" He asked.

"I'm good honestly." Elya said.

He nodded. "Let's go."

It was bizarre. She was about to break into Heaven's war room and Jesus of all people was going to walk her there.

Though she had some questions about why he was a child, she wrote off his mature speaking abilities to the fact he was Jesus. But in all her Bible reading she'd done, never once had she come across something that indicated he'd be running around Heaven as a child. Of course, she learned long ago that the Bible was written for the faith-based system they operated on, which was why it was often unclear. Even to those who studied it endlessly.

"You can ask questions." He said suddenly.

"Huh?" Elya startled. "Um. Wow." Her mind raced. "I guess I'll start easy. Why are you a child?"

"Why not be a child?" He asked. "Child, adolescent, adult, they are all me." His smile seemed to widen. "Sometimes, though, someone needs to see the innocence of a child."

She fidgeted. "You could tell me if the threat to destroy Hell is real and where it originated from, couldn't you?"

He was silent a moment. "Yes. But I believe it is best to let you determine that for yourself."

Elya sighed. "I was afraid you'd say that."

Nobody ever simply gave her the answers, but now was when she really wished someone, *anyone* would come through and tell her what she needed to know. Infiltrating the palace, breaking into the war room, not getting caught… again. It was going to be difficult. And God (the Father) likely knew she was there, because Jesus clearly knew, which meant she was in trouble already. She'd much rather just have the answer given to her and head back to Hell. Alas.

His eyes glinted knowingly. "Don't fear. I will stand before my Father for you."

"You will?" Elya asked, stunned.

Why vouch for someone who worked for Satan, even if as his unwilling recently paid intern and maybe a grudging friend?

"You are overthinking." He said, releasing her hand to pet a lilac-colored rabbit. "It is a simple matter, Elya."

She frowned. "It is?"

"Yes." He scooped the rabbit into his arms.

Elya watched him curiously. He was so calm, at peace with the world. He held none of the curiosity normal children did, which made sense, she supposed. Even still, he stood there as though nothing in the world could ever go wrong. Granted, they were in Heaven, so in the current world they were occupying, that was likely true. It was also strange how calm the rabbit was in his arms, and it was a little funny because the rabbit almost seemed to be as big as he was. He placed the rabbit back down. He didn't bother brushing the fur from his shirt. His shirt which was staring Elya in the face with the answer: unconditional love.

He offered her a hand. "You're smart, Elya. Smarter than you sometimes give yourself credit for. Whether you do the right thing is your decision, though."

Elya frowned, taking his hand. What was that supposed to mean? Yes, it was probably wrong to be breaking into Heaven's war room, but it was for the right reasons. Wasn't it? She groaned inwardly. Now was *not* the time for her to be developing doubts about this, to suddenly question if her current goal was right or wrong. Moral questions were never quick or easy.

They fell into silence as they walked. She was too lost in thought to ask questions, struggling with an internal battle of morality, though that didn't stop her from appreciating the beauty of Heaven. There were so many colors, plants, animals she'd never seen or heard of before. It was like something out of a fantasy novel. Stunning. And all too soon, they reached the pathway Satan had told her about, spanning from within the palace to the gates of Heaven. The path really was gold, and there were diamond street lights. They appeared to be purely decorative, which made sense. From her understanding, there was no night in Heaven, though that left some questions about how anyone got any sleep, even if they held no need for it. Satan mentioned the archangels had bedrooms, which implied they slept, though it was entirely possible their rooms were more for the purpose of giving them their own personal space than anything else.

And now she had questions again.

Sometimes she wondered if the meme about God accidentally spilling things when creating people was accurate. It would explain her admittedly endless curiosity.

It wasn't long before Elya could make out a city if you could call it that. Yes, it had a large population, but the thing was, it wasn't crowded. Even though this was the first time she had been in Heaven outside the palace walls, she could tell the city lacked the hustle and bustle, the urgency that was found on Earth. Everyone here had an eternity – there was no need to rush. It was amazing what a little time could do for the betterment of humanity.

"Once we reach the city, I can no longer walk with you without drawing attention," He said suddenly.

Elya nodded. "Makes sense. Thanks for helping me."

He smiled a big toothy smile. "You still have a long journey ahead of you."

She frowned. Did he mean that literally? Or metaphorically? Spiritually? She sighed. What was with immortals and leaving her with more questions than answers? She turned to ask him what he meant only to find he had disappeared altogether. Elya sighed. She was on her own, both getting through the city and getting into the palace.

She had to be out of her mind. It was the only logical conclusion for why she would take this kind of risk. She was about to enter the main city, and Satan had warned her angels are on every corner. Unlike the archangels, they would have no golden wings pinned to their clothes to show off who they were. The only good news in this was she was no longer lost, and Jesus gave no indication that he'd do anything to stop her…

Which created its own set of questions. Dang it! Why anyone would think it was a good idea to give her such an endless curiosity was beyond her. She loved having the answers, but this was — maybe she should focus less on the questions and more on the answers.

That was a good idea. Heaven had a war room. Why? Who other than Michael used it? Was it guarded? What secrets laid inside? If she focused on the questions like this, on getting the answers, maybe she'd be able to break into the palace and get into the war room to find whatever Satan thought she'd find there. Probably not plans from Heaven to destroy Hell – at least not plans for anytime soon – but that still left so many possibilities and questions. She really should've gotten a job as an investigative journalist after college. She had the curiosity for it. Of course, doing that would have required

Satan to stop sending his sons to force her into Hell, and probably would've led to her having no idea about the threat to Hell, which would mean Satan would be in the dark, and maybe there was a reason for everything.

Taking a breath, Elya continued toward the city. She could do this. She just needed to get through the city until she reached the tunnel. From there, she'd just have to reverse Satan's directions until she reached the war room. It was possible. Wasn't it?

"Okay, Elya," she muttered to herself. "We've got this. You've made it this far. Michael should still be in his meeting with God, so you don't have to worry about him finding you. You just got to get in, get out, and make it back to Hell. Verify with Satan whether this threat is legit and head home."

So that was that. She was going to walk into the city, find the tunnel and infiltrate the palace so she could break into the war room. Yet, if it was so cut and dry, why was she hesitating? She had an alibi if she got caught, Michael was supposed to be meeting with God, at least according to Satan, and Raphael and Gabriel wouldn't say anything about her having a mis-landing despite all the years she landed in the same spot. Sure, it'd ruin her chances of getting into the war room, but at least she'd be able to get out of Heaven without getting into trouble. Or was that her problem? She didn't want to get into trouble, but she had a safety net if she found it. She always did.

Fourteen

Once she got into the city, finding the hidden tunnel to the palace was surprisingly easy. Most people wouldn't think twice about a manhole in the middle of the road, but Elya had used the palace bathrooms enough to know the toilets didn't flush, everything in them just vanished. She never questioned it, as it wasn't the type of thing she wanted to linger on. But she'd also noticed how the sinks had no drains, and while she'd never used them, she assumed the showers were the same.

Though she knew all of that, when she opened the cover, she was careful to check for any scent or signs of sewage beneath. Finding none, she carefully climbed down and was relieved to discover that, yes, it was just a tunnel. No signs of rats, mice, snakes, or sewage. Just a long tunnel lit by torchlight.

From there, it was simple matter of following the tunnel to its end. The walk felt like it took half an hour, but at its end was a flight of stairs made of gold. Careful to step slowly on the off chance it was possible for golden stairs to squeak, Elya climbed, counting the stairs as she went. At the top of the thirty-two steps was a door. This was it. She cracked the door open, searching for any signs of angels. Seeing none, she pushed it open wide enough for her to squeeze through before silently shutting it.

Elya stepped back. Sure enough, the door was just as Satan had said, hidden by a replica of the "The Creation of Adam." Now, all she had to do was avoid being seen and reverse the directions Satan had given her to get to the painting from the war room – continue down the hall, take a right and follow the hall to its end – which meant she needed to go down the hall, then take a left, and continue down the hall until she got to the third from last door on what would be her left. As always, it seemed simple enough to pull off in theory, only this would be easier than everything else, so long as she managed to avoid people, at least until she reached the war room. Then, she had to hope Zeerlo's mold made an exact replica for a key only Michael and God had. She'd also have to hope the locks hadn't been changed, otherwise she'd have the difficult task of picking the lock to one of the most secured rooms in all of the palace. Satan was so lucky she considered him a friend.

Following the reversed directions to the letter, Elya found herself outside what could only be the war room. The door was unassuming, and didn't stand out from any of the other doors in the hall, but the fact the door was locked was her first clue that it was the right room. The second was the ease with which her borrowed key opened the door.

She wasn't sure what she expected with the prospect of Heaven's war room, but the scene in front of her certainly wasn't it. There were maps *everywhere*. World maps, not just of Earth, but of planets Elya had never even heard of. And there was a map of Heaven, and one of Hell. That honestly wasn't overly surprising; it made sense to have maps. There was room for meetings of maybe ten people, more if needed, but those extras would be left standing. The room still looked comfortable, chill, just a place to hang out and relax. Sure, the desk was cluttered and surely brimming with all kinds of strategies. There were filing cabinets that most definitely were full and organized, unless Michael was like Satan and everything was a disaster. But if that was the case, he was much better at hiding it. Then again, Satan did say Michael would stop by his office to make sure it was organized before heading here.

In all, the room looked like it saw plenty of use, but she wasn't so sure it looked like someone was spending enough time there that it was their second bedroom. A second office, sure, if the state of the desk was any indication, but it didn't seem like the second bedroom type of location.

An old painting seemed to be hidden behind the bookshelf. Carefully Elya pulled it out. Whatever she expected, a painting of Heaven's gates wasn't it. Why would anyone who lived in

Heaven want it as a painting? A small leather-bound notebook fell from behind the case. Picking it up Elya flipped it open.

For Michael, so you may organize your thoughts and feelings. With love, your Father.

Her first instinct was to snap the notebook shut and put it back where she found it. But, if she were going to hide something, what better place than to hide it than with something that was already hidden? Especially if it managed to stay hidden for who knew how long…

Elya opened it to the first page.

Day 6

Father says today shall be the last day of Creation, and tomorrow He shall rest. He has asked Sam and I to watch over our many brothers to ensure they let him rest in peace. He never seems to have time for us lately. I couldn't even guess at the last time we sat as a family and enjoyed something. Sam's locked himself in his room. He said he won't come out for anyone and he won't let anyone in. I know I could get him to let me in if I tried, just as I know Uri could easily get him to come out. I worry, though. This isn't like him.

Elya frowned. Was the Sam Michael wrote about… *Satan?* His original name had been Samael, hadn't it? And Uri, that had to be Uriel. She wanted to read more, but doing so would be an invasion of privacy, and while at times the others would disagree, she did have some control over curiosity. Maybe just one more entry wouldn't hurt? The next one was short; it couldn't be too personal, could it?

Day 7

We were given the delight of yet another brother today. Gabriel, our Father called him. The last piece of creation. The youngest of the angels. I don't want another brother. I'd much prefer to see my Father. He is all knowing, he should understand that.

She knew Gabriel was the youngest of the angels – it was hard not to pick up on with the way Satan called him the baby of the family or the way Raphael said he was still young and had much to learn. She didn't think six days could be that big of a difference for aging and maturity, though it was hard to say. Apparently, Michael was writing with some of the best penmanship she'd ever seen by the time he was six days old. Tearing herself away from reading more entries, Elya flipped through the pages until she found something stuck inside. But no, it wasn't what she was looking for, just a bookmark.

Day 372

Humans are strange creatures. I dislike them, but Father asks that we care for them. I'm not sure what there is to care for. Sam pointed out I had the same problem when Uri was born, but Uriel has existed for hundreds of years now – and also for just over a year. Time between Heaven and Eden is strange. I want them gone.

Whoa. That didn't sound like the angel she'd read about in the Bible. Michael was supposed to be obedient, but this made it sound like he was the one that would lead a rebellion. What had happened? She skimmed to the next bookmark.

Day 400

Samael fell. I failed him.

That was the entire entry. Two sentences. No explanation for how it had been Samael that fell, no details of how he fell, just a statement of fact followed by his opinion.

Day 401

Heaven is no longer the same. I was the oldest, yet I failed to see what was happening before me. Who could have, aside from Father? Samael was always the perfect child. The good child. Pure, good, just. He was following in the footsteps of our Father. He was obedient, kind. He never tried to rebel. Not until he fell. I wish I could blame the influence of Death and Sin, but Azrael sided with us. And Loki may be persuasive, but Samael would never allow anyone to force him into something he didn't want. His actions were his own, and it was a choice he made of his own free will. He led a third of our brothers down his path, and now they are to be judged and cast out of Heaven.

If she had been hoping to find a secret confession that Satan was innocent and Michael had framed him for the rebellion, she'd have been sorely disappointed. As it was, she knew Satan had no qualms with admitting he rebelled against God. His only issue was that he failed, and the aftermath was less than desirable. But that would have been *quite* the scandal.

Day 402

I pled with Father to spare Satan. That is Samael's new name. Satan Lucifer. Azrael seemed to have had the same idea – the only difference is Azrael is the favorite. Not even our Father's creation, but resultant of the acts of humanity, and he chooses to favor Death above all others. Azrael's plea on behalf of Sin worked, to an extent. Loki is to be Azrael's prisoner, and he, his warden. My plea resulted in nothing. My brother was renamed and cast from his home, tasked with ruling over the humans who sin.

That was… she didn't even know how to process it. Michael had pled on behalf of Satan and been denied, while Loki was granted mercy because of Azrael. Maybe they were all right after all. Maybe Azrael really was the favorite.

Day 403

It feels as though an eternity has passed without my brother by my side. After everything we've been through, this is what it has come to. He sits in Hell, while I remain here alone in Heaven. It's a cruel fate. I wish I could have done more to change our Father's mind. But the punishment was set. Satan will serve out his in Hell, and I shall serve my own here. I will spend eternity knowing I failed him. I'll forever miss my brother.

That was the last journal entry.

She returned the journal and painting back behind the bookshelf, hopefully in a way that wouldn't be noticed. She had no idea how the journal was positioned before it fell with the removal of the painting, but she did know enough to know that it needed to be replaced in a way that, should someone else remove the painting, it would have the same result as when she had done it. But that was the best she could do.

"Okay Elya, enough snooping. Time to get serious. If I were a seemingly unimportant envelope containing drastic information inside, where would I hide?"

The problem was, she didn't know Michael. She could search the whole room top to bottom, and it might still be hidden in the end. He could've already removed it from the room, had it on his person... She had no idea what he'd do when presented the information, since her knowledge of him came from others, and it wasn't much to begin with. She supposed the most logical place to look was on the desk, then maybe the filing cabinets. It felt like it'd be the logical choice, though she could have been entirely wrong. For all she knew, it could have been under the couch cushions, which she would check if she didn't find it anywhere else. If it even existed.

"Why do I let Satan talk me into these things?" she asked aloud.

As much as she liked him, he was the type of friend with no regard for rules who could find dangerous situations, even when he sometimes held the best of intentions. She learned that early on. He was likable, yes, but his tendency to do wrong was never ending. But what could she say? He was the Devil. She was just lucky she had Gabriel and Raphael to help her out of the bad situations Satan had gotten her into over the years – not to say she hadn't gotten herself in a fair bit more. And Zeerlo, Fiend and Twist certainly all helped. Thankfully.

Elya began scouring the room, checking first the desk, then the cabinets. She looked in the couch cushions, under the couch. Under the desk, behind the bookcase, behind paintings on the walls, behind the maps, but there was no sign of anything indicating Heaven was planning an attack on Hell. No evidence they knew Hell had ever received such a threat. Nothing. But she wasn't going to give up until she was certain.

Finally, Elya decided to check one last place. It was a long shot, but she had to know for sure. She pulled the painting back out. Ignoring the journal this time, she checked the seams of the frame.

And there it was. An envelope just like the one she'd found in Hell, only with a different address. Heaven. There was no 777 Palace Avenue, Heaven, Afterlife, like she'd seen on the mail occasionally in the hands of Raphael or Gabriel. It was still unopened.

It'd have to do for now. Whatever was inside likely was the same as what she received in Hell, or at least similar. Right now, she needed to get out of Heaven and back to Hell so she could show Satan that this threat was very much real.

Pocketing the letter, Elya cracked open the door, looking for signs of people. All she had to do now was make it safely to either her landing point or back into the tunnel, though the landing point was preferable. And if she ran into anyone, she was just the poor, lost human that landed in the wrong spot. Hopefully, though, her natural clumsiness would come through and she'd trip before even getting to that point. She stepped into the hall, shutting the door behind her.

Fifteen

It shouldn't have been so difficult. All she needed to do was trip and boom, she'd be in Hell. Well, most likely. There was always a chance she'd return to Heaven or end up elsewhere in Afterlife, which was fine since most celestials would take her home. Or she could land on Earth, which would be great because she always landed in her bedroom. After that, she just needed to trip her way into Hell. But you couldn't trip in Heaven, and she forgot her emergency sneezing powder. She had nearly made it to the end of the hall, when—

"Stop right there," a voice called behind her.

Elya pivoted. She cringed inwardly as she came face to face with an unknown angel. This was just *not* her day. She observed the unknown angel, looking for any hint of who he might be. He wore a suit with a golden pin on the lapel, so he was definitely one of the archangels. His hair was dark brown, but his eyes were a vibrant green.

"Um, hi, you wouldn't happen to know where I could find Gabriel or maybe Raphael?"

"Follow me," the angel said.

Elya waited a moment, weighing her options. If he was taking her to Gabriel or Raphael, she wasn't going to complain. But what if he took her to someone else? Like, she was not where she was supposed to be, *and* she was a living human. She was certain if people were aware she showed up to Heaven about once a week, they'd know she landed in the same spot usually. And oh, this was so bad.

They made their way through white-walled, marble-floored halls, but nothing seemed familiar. All too soon, they came to a stop outside an unfamiliar door. The angel knocked before leading her into the room, and Elya hesitantly walked inside. She gulped as she took in the figure of the angel in front of her. He was tall, taller than Gabriel and Raphael. His shoulders were broad, his hair was dark, his eyes a cold, dark brown. His features were sharp, and he bore an *uncanny* resemblance to Satan. Sure, she knew all the angels were related, but it was almost terrifying seeing how much this angel in the casual human attire of jeans and a t-shirt with a sword at his waist resembled Satan. And the strange golden-eyed man that had shown at Léana's.

The only major difference was that this angel's gaze seemed to pass judgment on her, whereas Satan's only ever seemed to be trying to determine whether he should offer her drugs or torture her. And the strange man had made her feel like she might be murdered. The three of them could have been twins, or stunt doubles at the least.

"I found her snooping around the war room," the unknown angel who brought her said.

"Thank you, Uriel. You've done the right thing bringing her here," the Satan look alike said. "Ensure no others are lurking about, if you'd please."

The other angel, Uriel, left wordlessly. Elya shifted uncomfortably under the gaze of the unknown angel. "I swear I wasn't snooping," Elya lied.

He raised a brow. "You weren't? Because it seems to be the case. You were found not far from the war room." His gaze hardened. "I know who you are, Elya. You work for my brother and, by my understanding, you do not usually land near the war room. If anything, you tend to land outside the garden."

"Do you mean the Garden of Eden?" Elya asked.

The angel crossed his arms. "You do not help your case."

Oh, she was *definitely* in trouble. Maybe if she mentioned Jesus helped her find her way to the city she'd be less in trouble. Was that allowed? Like…salvation through Jesus was usually more in terms of receiving eternal paradise rather than damnation, but he had helped her.

Elya was about to respond when the doors burst open. Gabriel and Raphael rushed in, both looked surprisingly out of breath. The two brothers slowed their pace and moved to stand between Elya and the still-yet-to-be-named angel. Raphael held out a hand, and a bag of red skittles appeared in his palm. He handed it to Elya with a soft smile and she grinned in return. She was nervous – terrified, really – but she was glad to know Raphael and Gabriel had her back, and who was she to turn down free skittles?

"She should not be here," the angel said, his gaze hard.

"I'm sure she wasn't trying to hurt anything," Raphael said.

The angel raised his brow. "She was outside the war room."

The other two angels spun on her. Raphael's eyes were filled with curiosity, but Gabriel's swam with disappointment. Elya's stomach knotted. Being looked at with disappointment by an angel wasn't comfortable, and she shifted under their gazes. She was in big trouble; she couldn't tell them why she was there, but there was no way any of them would believe her if she lied.

Satan didn't give her an escape plan for this one.

"Why were you outside the war room?" Gabriel asked softly.

Elya shuffled under his gaze. "I didn't land inside the palace." She tried to look innocent. "I knew you guys wouldn't be there, so I went looking for you and Raphael."

Raphael nodded, accepting her answer. "See, a simple case of mistaken location due to an improper landing."

"Except she would've walked past her landing point in order to get to the war room. She should have stayed there and awaited you," the unknown angel said. "She is beneath Satan's payroll – she cannot be trusted."

Gabriel stepped forward. "Michael."

Elya internally winced. This wasn't bad, it was far worse than she thought. This wasn't a random angel, this was *Michael*. The angel who, from what she read, oversaw leading the angels into battle, and here she was caught snooping outside the war room when it was known she was on Satan's payroll. Oh, it looked *bad*.

"I'm sorry, Gabriel, but she cannot be trusted." Michael didn't look apologetic. "I need to take her to Father."

Elya gulped. Oh, she was in so much trouble. There was no way she'd be able to lie to God. He probably already knew what she had done. She was probably going to be sentenced to Hell before she even died. She couldn't spend eternity using dial-up! And the heat was awful outside Satan's throne room, and personalized tortures – she knew what that meant.

Gabriel came to stand beside her. "She does not mean any harm to us, Michael."

"You are vouching for her?" Michael asked.

Gabriel straightened. "I am."

Michael's gaze flicked to Raphael. "And you?"

"Yes," Raphael said.

Michael sighed. "Very well. I'll allow you to escort her home." His gaze flicked to Elya. "But let me make myself clear. I understand she cannot help her arrival, but if in future she is not immediately returned home, I will take her to Father. Humans are not meant to enter Heaven whilst living. She is not welcome here and I expect the two of you to stop indulging her presence."

Gabriel frowned. "I trust her."

"Then you are a fool," Michael snapped.

Gabriel winced. "I will do as you ask, brother, but know I disagree."

"It's noted," Michael said.

Silently, they left the room. Raphael offered her a second bag of skittles and an encouraging smile before he walked away, but Elya's stomach churned. He looked so disappointed. She turned toward Gabriel and saw his eyes revealed the same disappointment he held earlier. He placed a hand on her shoulder and she closed her eyes in preparation for her journey home. There was a familiar flash of light before it vanished.

When she opened her eyes, Gabriel was still there, his arms crossed as he leaned against her door.

"What were you thinking?" he asked icily.

"I got lost looking for you and Raphael."

"Elya, you were caught outside the war room." He stood straighter. "Michael has banned you from entering Heaven again so long as you are living."

Elya looked to the ground. "Can he do that?" She asked, refusing to meet his gaze.

Gabriel sighed. "As the one charged with protecting Heaven and leading angels into war should the need arise? Yes, he can."

Elya's eyes snapped to Gabriel. "I wasn't trying—"

"Enough, Elya!" he shouted. "I am not a fool. I know you are lying about your reasoning for being outside the war room. I trust you have no ill intentions toward us, but you do not stand in a good position. I spoke on your behalf *knowing* you had lied. Do you have any idea what position it puts me in?"

"I didn't ask you to stand up for me." Her gaze hardened. "And what makes you sure I was lying?"

"Elya, I am known as the guardian of truth." He folded his arms. "I cannot be lied to."

She winced internally. That hadn't come up in her readings of the Bible… maybe she should've done more research into Gabriel and the other angels. If she had, maybe she would've known lying to Gabriel was literally impossible. In the past, she just assumed she had an obvious tell – not that she tried lying to the angel often. Maybe two or three times in the beginning before it became obvious that she was better off telling him the truth.

She didn't know what to say. Lying would get her nowhere, but telling the truth wasn't an option. "I only did what needed done."

Gabriel ran a hand through his hair. "Unless my Father states otherwise, you are banned from entering Heaven."

Elya scoffed. "I can't help tripping."

"And it is being taken into account." Gabriel sighed. He looked tired and defeated. "As Michael said, you will be returned home immediately upon your arrival."

"That's so not fair," Elya argued.

Gabriel shrugged. "I hope whatever my brother asked of you was worth it, Elya. I do not see anything being worth all this trouble."

"What makes you so sure I was there on his orders?"

"Had you not been there on his orders, you would have confessed your reasoning for being outside the war room."

"That's not even fair!" Elya snapped. "I didn't even know you guys had a war room until today. Seriously, who would think Heaven has a war room? Why do you even need it?"

"The prophecies foretold in the book of revelation will come to pass, Elya," he sighed. "Michael, as the one who leads the angels, must prepare for when that day comes. He spends hours upon hours changing his tactics and plans, revising the plans. He does not share them with any but our Father. You are lucky he has only banned you from Heaven for being anywhere near there. You see our brother, our enemy, every day, Elya. Michael has no reason to trust you."

"I told you," Elya said. "I did what needed done."

"And I pray it was what is for the best and worth this trouble." He vanished in a shower of golden glitter.

Elya rubbed her temple. This was so much worse than she had thought. She reached into her pocket for the scrap of paper she had found inside the war room. Maybe she should have told Gabriel the truth, told him why she was there and what she found. It wasn't like he could accuse her of lying. But he could lecture her, and if she had learned anything over the years it was being on the receiving end of one of Gabriel's lectures was not fun. He had this way of invoking guilt in his victims… lecturing was like his superpower.

Her stomach growled and Elya glanced at the clock. 9:00 pm. She had spent hours in Hell talking with Satan, planning for when she got to Heaven. Then, she lost time by not landing in the hall of the palace for once in her life and landing out in the city. And to top it all off, she had gotten caught. She was tired, she was frustrated, and she was hungry. And she might have hurt her friendship with Gabriel. Flopping onto her bed, Elya opened one of the bags of skittles Raphael had given her. Hopefully they wouldn't be the last bags, but it wasn't looking good. Not when she was banned from Heaven and Gabriel had brought her home without feeding her. He *never* let her leave Heaven without feeding her. He or Raphael… they always were going on about ensuring she got proper nourishment. Remembering that just made her feel worse.

Elya sighed. She needed to tell Satan what she found, only she didn't have the energy now. It could wait until the morning. Elya eyed the pile of golden glitter on her carpet. Sighing, she got off the bed and went to plug in the vacuum. Satan could wait just one night, but the glitter could not. Otherwise, it would serve as a constant reminder of the awful day she was having.

Making quick work of the glitter, Elya decided to get something more than skittles to eat. Quiet so as not to disturb her roommates she wasn't in the mood to deal with, Elya made her way into the kitchen. Ignoring the cabinets, Elya opened the fridge and her eyes browsed over various Tupperware containers before lingering on one she had never seen. She pulled it out and found a note taped to the lid with her name written in neat script. Elya peeked into the container to see spaghetti and her stomach growled greedily.

Putting the spaghetti in the microwave, Elya opened the note.

Elya,

As I was uncertain when you last received proper nourishment, I chose to leave this in the refrigerator for you. It would be improper of me to leave you alone with nothing of nutritional value, and the candy Raphael gives you is certainly not nutritional.

It is uncertain when I will see you next. Michael has ordered neither Raphael nor I maintain contact with you. Father has agreed with his decision, though he has allowed Raphael and I to say our goodbyes. I am unsure who will be there to greet you the next time you trip into Heaven, but I do hope you find them to your liking.

Raphael asks that I remind you to enjoy your Skittles and do not allow this to bring you undue upset.

Best wishes,

Gabriel

P.S. We shall keep you in both our thoughts and our prayers. And do not drink all your wine in a single night. It is not healthy.

The microwave beeped. Elya opened the fridge, her eyes immediately going to the bottle of Pinot Grigio. She was curious if Gabriel grabbed random wines or handpicked the wine to go with the meal. Given the way he said he listened to the ingredients, she leaned toward the latter. Grabbing a wine glass from the cabinet, Elya poured herself a glass, replaced the bottle in the fridge, and grabbed her plate of spaghetti from the microwave. Tonight was an eat alone in her room kind of night.

Sixteen

Satan awaited her return to Hell, eager mischief in his eye. She wanted to wipe the smugness from his face. It was a tempting thought, and Satan always told her to embrace her desires and act on the temptations, but the problem was, just because the Deadly Sins didn't appear to be present didn't mean they weren't lurking. And there were still demons he could call to attack her if she tried to assault his person. But it was his fault she'd never see Gabriel or Raphael again. Would never witness as Raphael pulled a bag of skittles from thin air or hear one of Gabriel's lengthy, guilt-inducing lectures. Never again would she see Raphael attempt to keep a straight face as Gabriel panicked over the nutritional value of food. All because Satan talked her into infiltrating Heaven's war room.

She'd had an entire night to stew on this feeling, and seeing that smug look on his face pushed her over the edge.

Without registering what she was doing, her hand was balled into a fist, her arm cocked back, and with all the force she could muster, she pushed forward. Her fist collided with his nose in an oddly satisfying crunch. Satan recoiled, hands going to his face instinctually.

"What the Hell was that for?" he asked, cupping his nose.

"You and your stupid—*I've been banned from Heaven for the rest of my living life!* Can't talk to or see Gabriel and Raphael ever again." She crossed her arms. "And I'll probably spend eternity down here with you on dialup. So, thanks."

He pulled his hand away, his nose gushing blood. "That hurt." He poked at his nose. "And I'll have you know, I would give you access to my personal Wi-Fi router." He conjured a wet washcloth. "Or at least I would've. Now I'm not sure I feel so generous." He wiped his nose. "Damn! Did you get lessons from Michael on punching while you were up there?"

"Don't be a baby." Elya rolled her eyes. "I've never even punched anyone before."

"Are you telling me in all those lessons I've had you endure over the years—" he tilted his head back "—we never went over something as simple as punching?"

"No, we covered it," she shrugged. "How else would I know how to avoid hurting myself? But you never let me off the training dummies. Something about how punching Zeerlo, Fiend, or Twist would break every bone in my hand and maybe my arm."

"Well now that you've had the satisfaction of assaulting me—" he examined the blood on his rag "—did you at least verify the threat? Did it come from Heaven?"

"Here." She thrust the envelope into his chest. "I didn't bother reading it, but it was addressed the same way as the one to Hell."

Satan took the envelope in his slightly bloodied hands. He turned it over to unseal it from the back, his blood staining the white envelope with the shape of fingers (without any print left behind, of course). That was probably what scared her most about Satan and his sons. In a way, they didn't exist. They left no visible marks. No fingerprints. They didn't lose hair or skin cells. They could commit all the crime they wanted, and it didn't matter. They'd never leave any evidence at the scene of the crime. How could they? The world was at their mercy and they knew it. Enjoyed it as well, she was sure. The only thing hindering them was the archangels. So long as they existed, Satan would tread carefully and ensure his sons did as well. At least, she wanted to say it was all the archangels, but even she had her doubts. It was more likely *one* angel in particular. Humanity told stories of it, and the immortal world gossiped about it. A fight between Michael and Satan. Brothers turned enemies. Both powerful, fast, strong, intelligent, but only one could prevail. Michael was faster. Michael was stronger. Michael had more raw power. And, in the end, Michael likely proved himself more intelligent as well. Elya had never been certain of any of that before, but now that she'd seen Michael herself, she'd believe it.

"Well, that's it then." Satan wiped the last of the blood from his face. "This is a real threat to Afterlife. Someone is out to destroy Heaven and Hell."

"What happens now?" Elya asked.

"What happens now indeed," he said.

Once again, the Devil paced. He seemed to do that a lot lately. Not that she could blame him. Hell, whether he claimed to like it or not, had been his home for thousands of years now. Many of the demons were his fallen brothers – the others, the children of Lilith. Though, what she heard from Satan, the woman wasn't very motherly. But Elya knew he and Lilith were friends, at least to an extent. She had only met Lilith once when she was seven, and if she could help it, she'd never meet the woman again. People imagined Lilith as being someone who stood for women's rights, a feminist. Lilith was neither of those things. She focused far more on seducing men. She could have been wrong – her memory of Lilith was brief – but it's hard not to remember a woman stood only in her underwear asking Satan to come play with her. That had been disturbing and maybe she should have gone to therapy for it at some point.

"I've got it!" Satan exclaimed suddenly.

"What?" Elya asked.

"We'll gather an army," he grinned.

"How?"

His expression dropped. "How indeed?"

Satan's pacing continued. Elya sighed, taking a seat in the beanbag chair she had Zeerlo sneak in for her a little over two years ago. This could take a while. Good at thinking on his feet or not, Satan tended to take his time when it came to things that weren't deemed an immediate threat. And unless this threat was literally on their doorstep at the gates of Hell, wherever those were, he wouldn't consider it an immediate threat.

The additional problem with that was he tended to think of every possible scenario, but not the ones they needed to account for. No, he'd be thinking of what would happen if Loki showed up with green skin versus yellow. It was ridiculous.

She hated sitting in silence, especially when Satan seemed to be having an internal struggle. You never knew when he'd suddenly lash out, and odds were, he wouldn't lash out at the bookshelf or the desk. No if he decided to lash out, he'd lash out at her. So long as the fires in the fireplace weren't reacting to him though, she should be fine. If those fires didn't react, it meant he had himself under control.

"I suppose we could — no, far too risky," Satan muttered to himself. "What if? No. Someone's liable to get killed."

He continued to mutter to himself. Elya knew better than to attempt contributing while he was in the middle of thinking. If you threw him off his thoughts with so much as a sneeze when he was in this state, you were liable to get killed. Satan was currently hanging onto the last threads of his control. So long as he wasn't disturbed, he should stay that way – if he didn't manage to work himself up into a frenzy, which was possible. At least, she thought it was possible. They'd never been in this situation before, so it was a little hard to judge.

Elya would do the wise thing. She would sit, and she'd wait. Either for him to come up with some brilliant plan, for him to calm himself down, or for the signs of his inevitable loss of temper. Of course, it was only inevitable if she saw the signs, a reminder that this wasn't a man pacing the room. This was the Devil, and he was powerful and dangerous. She just wished she had the Wi-Fi password to the network named Welcome to Hell. It was his personal network and the only one in all of Hell. But if Twist, who could hack into government files like he was googling cat photos couldn't hack his way in, she didn't stand a chance.

If he were a typical parent, she'd just try all his children's birthdays. She might still try that, except she learned the hard way that three wrong attempts and his network unleashed a virus that would absolutely destroy her cell phone. Maybe she could risk it.

"How long's the Wi-Fi password?" Elya asked.

"Twenty-four characters," he said without pause.

That was long. Or least it felt like it was long. Maybe it wasn't. She thought over her own passwords for various things over the years, but never had she had anything that was up to twenty-four characters long. It must have been a phrase of some sort. That, or he was using a lot of numbers, probably a bunch of random numbers and letters. It was the kind of thing he'd do.

"How many numbers, how many letters?"

"12 and 12," he said.

Elya frowned. She wasn't ever going to figure this out. Though, with him in his current state and his current willingness to answer, she just might be able to get it in three attempts. That is, if she could manage just enough questions worded carefully enough that he'd be willing to share. It'd be difficult, but it wouldn't necessarily be impossible.

"Is that all letters then numbers?"

"Letter number letter, follow the pattern."

Elya opened a blank note on her phone. 24 characters. Odds were letters, evens were numbers. The numbers would be easier, as there were only 10 options there. But the letters, that would be more difficult. There were more than twice as many options for letters as there were numbers.

"Any important dates?" she asked.

It was a wild guess. But if she was right, she'd have to only narrow it down to the dates which held significance to him. Good and bad. The Ides of March, Christmas, Easter, Halloween – well, maybe Halloween. Whenever he celebrated his birthday. She had options if there were dates somehow incorporated into his password. She hoped there was. It'd make it that much easier to figure out. And if she hacked

Satan's Wi-Fi, she'd never let Twist live it down. Though she wished she could say that it meant she was capable of hacking, but going that far would be a tad bit ridiculous.

"Two of them," he said absentmindedly.

She hoped he didn't decide to lash out against her once he figured out what she was doing. He was in a mood, so it was hard to tell what he might do. She could see how he reacted and try lying, but if she couldn't lie to Gabriel, she couldn't lie to Satan. Besides, if she had learned anything in sixteen years, it was that Satan hated lies. No. It was much better to tell a terrible truth than to lie to Satan.

"Caps?" Elya asked.

"All," he muttered.

Elya frowned. She had an idea and it was crazy, but it might be crazy enough to work. She pulled open her Wi-Fi settings and selected Satan's network. Carefully, she turned on her phone's caps lock settings. Maybe she was crazy for trying, but she had three attempts before facing down a virus. She typed in K0A8L1A8E0L3Z0E8E0R6L1O4 and clicked connect. Her phone thought over her decision before connecting her. She had done and in only one try! Who said blondes weren't smart? It was unbelievable and she couldn't *wait* to share her superiority with Twist. She did what he spent years trying to do in a matter of minutes. Sure, she got the answers she needed from Satan in a moment he was distracted, but she had the Wi-Fi.

Satan stopped in his tracks. "Are you trying to figure out my Wi-Fi password?"

Elya grinned. "Already did it. I knew Kalael and Zeerlo were your favorites, and their names are both six letters long, so that fits the 12 letters thing. Then for their birthdays, using the years they were born wouldn't have worked, at least not for Kalael, so the only option was to put in zeroes before their birth month and in Zeerlo's case, day. Then, I just used the last two numbers of the year. Kalael's was a given, Zeerlo's was a gamble because you could've used the year on him, but I took a chance that it'd be the same, and it was."

"You took advantage of my being in an unfocused state," he said.

"I did." Elya said.

He grinned. "Well done, though I am surprised you figured it out."

"It was knowing how many numbers and letters and the pattern that really helped." She shrugged. "And knowing it was all caps."

"Well, as part of my deal, every time I update the password you get the new one, as you earned it through finding this one," he chuckled. "Twist is going to hate you."

She grinned. "I know."

"Yes, well," he resumed his pacing. "As impressive as your feat is, I really must get back to thinking of a plan."

Elya nodded returning to her phone. It was nice having internet. Now she could play any game she wanted, or do all the browsing she pleased. And as far as she could tell, if Michael had any say, she'd be sentenced to Hell when she died. So, she already had one way of lessening the torture of the place. Yes, she knew it was supposed to be an eternity of torture, an individualized cell of solitude, but Elya also knew Satan allowed one hour of recreation a day where people could use their phones and computers, write letters, read, watch tv. A lot of what was used during free time was dependent on the period people were from. Now, whether it was allowed she wasn't sure. Personally, she thought it might be crueler to give people a reprieve from the torment only to take it away and send them back. But, then again, this was why it was Satan running things and not her. Punishing the damned was his area of expertise.

Seventeen

For the first time, the fires no longer danced in the fireplace. Instead, they raged.

Tendrils of fire whipped out of the fireplace, the crackling logs echoing throughout the room. The flames were brighter than any fire she'd seen, the coloring different from normal fires: the bottom was a strong black followed by red, then orange, yellow, blue, and finally white. The black wasn't found in normal fires, and it was what distinguished this from the fires of humankind. These were clearly the flames of Hell. Capable of burning through anything, hotter than the sun. Though she did not plan to get close to the fireplace while Satan was in a mood.

Watching Satan pace was nerve-wracking. Irritation and nerves seemed to roll off him in literal waves, if the steam coming from him was any indication. Flames traced his steps, his pale skin had taken on the slightest tinge of red, and his wings sprouted as he muttered under his breath. He was dangerous in this state – just barely keeping his temper in check. From what she heard, Satan's barely concealed rage was the deadliest of all. She'd only ever seen him this way once, and while she trusted he wouldn't hurt her on purpose, she was still nervous.

Satan sat abruptly. Yanking his desk drawer open, he pulled out a sheet of paper and grabbed a pen from his penholder. Elya stayed quiet as he wrote furiously.

(She didn't have to worry about deciphering his chicken scratch – his handwriting on most days was stunningly beautiful and the last time she saw his frenzied handwriting, it was thankfully still legible. It was more than she could say for Gabriel, his script was so illegible the first time she saw it she asked him to translate it into English. She was still baffled that it *was* English.)

Hesitant to leave, Elya waited for him to finish his frenzied writing. She shifted uneasily, unable stand still when the rage was so obviously bubbling beneath Satan's surface. She could practically feel Hell stirring outside his office and she didn't even have powers connecting her to it! It was worrisome. If she could feel the disturbance then it had to be *big*, and that only happened when Satan was about to lose control.

When it was contained, Hell was miserable and unpleasant, but when Satan lost control, it usually meant a volcano erupted somewhere on Earth.

(How the two were related, she'd yet to figure out. From her understanding, despite the basic childish concepts of Heaven being in the sky and Hell being below the Earth's surface, they weren't on Earth. Their connection had been described to her as three separate locations connected through threads, like putting beads on a bracelet. It wasn't to say every volcanic eruption on Earth was the result of when he lost his temper but a fair number. Actually, from her understanding, every planet in the universe was affected.)

As Satan jumped from his chair, it rolled back, colliding into the wall with a thud. He grabbed the papers and walked around the desk, coming to a stop just in front of her. He grabbed her arm and placed his paper into her hands.

"What's this?" Elya asked.

He rolled his eyes in annoyance. "That is a list of everyone you're going to need to get ahold of to fight off this threat."

Her brows furrowed. "Why me?"

He huffed. "Because you're equally connected to Heaven and Hell. If I were trying to do it, over half of them wouldn't so much as let me come to the door. The same could be said for my sons. Nobody would follow any of us into battle. But you, they might be willing. At the very least, they'll be willing to listen to you, and this threat needs to be assessed. The best way to do that is to gather everyone on this list."

"Right." She couldn't argue that logic. "But isn't someone – *anyone* – else more qualified than me?"

"Doesn't matter. There are only a few people who can travel between Heaven and Hell, and nobody would take

Azrael seriously." He crossed his arms. "As it is, the only other options are Dimitri and Kalael. As it stands, you're the one who is available, and unlike Kalael, you probably won't offend my brothers' delicate sensibilities. And there's miniscule chance you'll invoke unwanted memories. This is not the case with Dimitri. You're the only one for the job. There's too much history with any Celestial."

Elya fidgeted for a moment, digesting this new information. "How am I supposed to get help from Heaven?" Elya asked.

"You ask," Satan said.

Elya shifted. "Yeah, but there's the whole issue of my being banned, by *Michael* no less. I'm no expert, but I'm pretty sure that means me in Heaven is a no-no."

He scoffed. "Believe me, they'll get over it, even if they were to never lift your so-called ban. But, if it truly bothers you so much, you're more than welcome to obtain help from there last. I couldn't blame you; I try avoiding the place like the plague."

Elya raised a brow. "Avoiding plagues? Humanity proved it's not good at that in 2020."

Satan raised an unamused eyebrow.

"Fine, I'll do it," Elya frowned. "But don't think this means I'm happy about it. For one, I don't know where half these places are, so I'm going to need a list of addresses to go with it. Otherwise, GPS will be useless. I'd ask for gas and hotel money as well, but you basically covered that when you decided to pay me."

He huffed. "Fine—" he grabbed the paper from her "—you could have said something sooner, you know." He scribbled across the paper and handed it back to her.

"In my defense, I had no idea what you were doing," Elya said.

"I suppose." Satan ran a hand through his hair. "Just do me a favor: don't hesitate to give me a call if you need help with anything. No need to lose you in the process."

Elya smiled ruefully. "Wouldn't want to lose your unwilling intern, would you?"

He grinned. "Never." His expression was suddenly one of concern. "You have my contact information?"

"Cell-phone, office phone, throne phone, mansion phone, pager – not that I have any idea how that works – all three of your emails, and an unspecified number you said I needed. And if for some reason I can't get ahold of you through your contact info, I have a number for Kalael, Zeerlo, Fiend, and Twist." She scrolled through her contacts. "I also have a number for Shredder for some reason, but nothing for Hellas."

"Hellas gets his phone for his birthday," Satan said.

"Didn't you get Zeerlo a cell-phone when he was nine?" Elya asked.

Satan shrugged. "Zeerlo was more mature than his brothers. Fiend got his at eleven, Twist, having his penchant for all things technology, received his at six, and Shredder got his for the Ides of March."

Elya laughed.

(Satan celebrated the most obscure holidays in place of those related to religion. Their Ides of March festivities were different, to say the least. Funeral games of Roman times, a feast, though none of the food was from ancient Rome, and in fact was just modern Italian. Satan also had a penchant to get everyone a gift. If there was one thing he was talented at, it was gift giving. One of the benefits of reading people's desires, probably.)

Elya shifted. "I guess that's everything but a way out of here."

He smiled. "I think I can help with that."

He walked to the bookshelf and pulled one suddenly out of place. The entire shelf moved aside to reveal black metal doors, which slid open to reveal a molten interior.

"You have an elevator!" She gaped. "Unbelievable! Sixteen years and you're *just now* offering to let me to use it."

Elya stepped inside taking in the full interior of the elevator, the roof was unusually high, a chandelier of flames hung overhead. The edges were lined with dark black rock which only made the glowing molten metal seem brighter. It should have been hotter than an oven, but it was surprisingly cool inside. The elevator buttons unsurprisingly numbered 666.

"It's only this once—" he said "—nobody's allowed to use it except me. Not even Zeerlo and Kalael."

That was surprising.

"Where does it let out at?" Elya asked.

He grinned. "It lets out at any of my properties or the portals to Hell—" he pressed a one the button igniting in flames "—as it so happens, one such portal is in Lawrence. Just don't get in trouble."

She didn't get a chance to ask what he meant by that. The elevator doors closed before she could get a word out. The ride was smooth and surprisingly quick, given it was traversing between Hell and earth.

When the doors opened, her jaw dropped and eyes widened in a comical look of shock. The portal Satan mentioned wasn't just in Lawrence. It wasn't even just on the university's campus. No, the elevator had let her out in the *center court of Allen Fieldhouse*. She didn't even have time to think about how offended she was that the greatest venue in college basketball was also a portal to Hell. She had a job to do.

Quietly, she stepped out of the elevator. As soon as her feet met the court, the doors closed, and the elevator lowered into the ground. As the elevator sealed into the floor, Elya glanced around. She needed out. There was no way she was allowed here.

She pulled her phone from her pocket and checked the time. It was late. Three hours had passed since she had gone to Hell, but she hadn't been there for long. It hadn't felt nearly that long – thirty minutes tops!

(The difference in time between Heaven, Hell, and Earth never made sense to her. Today it had been three hours, and the other day in Heaven, she had been gone five minutes. Maybe one day she'd figure it out.)

She glanced at the list of people she was supposed to get. It was alphabetized, which was strange considering how rapidly he had written it. Aurelius, Bernard, Camael, Conquest, Dimitri, Erika, Fiend… the list went on, twenty-eight names in all, but only seven listed addresses: The Coffee Shop, Silverwoods, Heaven, Apocalypse Horse Ranch, Mercenary Mansion, The Realm of Thought, and The Clock Tower.

Satan hadn't left her with a short list, she noted, starting to feel overwhelmed. She'd start with Mercenary Mansion, she decided. There, she could get five of the deadly sins at once, though there was no guarantee they'd agree to help. They were, unfortunately, the Sons of Satan, and if there was one thing she learned in the last sixteen years, it was that, like their father, the Sons of Satan did nothing for free.

Elya grabbed her keys from her desk, thankful again for the Bugatti as her incredible graduation gift. It was like the dream car she hadn't even realized she wanted until she had it. It'd be perfect for her journey to gather troops for Satan.

Eighteen

Mercenary Mansion was isolated in the countryside. To say it was big would be an understatement. Four floors and two sublevel floors (the kitchen and basement, respectively), seven wings in addition to the central part of the building, all to complete 666,666 square feet of Hellish glory. The mansion was built with a palace-style exterior done in a French Baroque (no surprise there) and made with limestone. The driveway was literally a mile long, and a large fountain sat at its end. She knew from experience that the fountain raised to reveal an elevator that could easily hold two large vehicles at a time, which then took the cars down to the garage. The grass was the lush green dads everywhere dreamed of. The whole property was 666,666 acres (she really needed to talk to Satan about his obsession) of farmland. At the start of the driveway, were two large silver gates (silver to oppose Heaven's golden gates).

The property was stunningly beautiful. The magnificence of the façade was meant to be alluring like a deadly flower… Nobody would know from first glance that everything from the gates to the plants, animals, insects, and even the front door were designed to kill.

Exiting her car, she stared at the large silver gates, heart pounding. She could wait there all day, even if one of them deigned to show, none of the Deadly Sins would let her in. No, they were too sadistic for that. She needed to find her own way in.

(If she were child of Satan, she wouldn't worry. The barriers around the mansion wouldn't activate unless someone else went into the grid and turned it on manually. Never once has she seen someone who wasn't a Celestial or the child of one get through unscathed.)

Elya wasn't a math whiz. Honestly, she was average at best. However, she had always been good at probability. It was the only time she got hundreds on her exams. And, with her calculations, her odds of getting to a safe point in the mansion were 1 in 987.64 trillion. The odds of making it inside only needing a hospital were closer to 1 in 892.73 billion. The odds of her getting in without needing a hospital were incalculable.

The most likely outcome was the odds of her dying. She might as well have arranged her funeral first. She would need a silver or gray coffin because she couldn't risk offending Satan by getting white or disappointing Gabriel with black. Most other colors were a bit outlandish, and brown was too traditional. Elya shook her head. Maybe she shouldn't be worrying about it.

Elya wracked her brain, trying to remember if there was any way to disarm Satan's security from this end, or if it was only from the mansion itself. She was almost certain it had to be from the mansion itself. But the gates… surely there was a way to get through the gates without a risk of dying. Finally, she spotted it: the emergency shutoff Satan had hidden among the trees. It'd turn off the gates but the rest of the system she'd have to go through. Brilliant.

The gates slowly swung open with a loud creak.

Taking a deep breath, Elya launched herself into the death trap that was Satan's front yard. As soon as she stepped onto the threshold, flames burst from the ground around her. Elya surveyed the ground quickly, looking for any sign of tripwires or landmines. The Devil's lawn was flawless; if there were any, she couldn't see them.

She took a hesitant step forward. An array of arrows shot from the distance. Elya screamed, tripping as she attempted to duck for cover. The sensation of rushing water surrounded her and Elya hit the cold, hard concrete with a smack. Groaning, Elya sat up to take in her new surroundings. Her eyes widened in shock as she gazed out at the blazing lawn in front of her. She had tripped onto the front porch of the Mercenary Mansion.

"Well, that's a first." Elya stood, wincing as pain shot through her.

She examined her elbows and found they were both scraped and bleeding. Her entire forearms were, in fact, and her hands stung. Despite the harsh landing, she was almost to safety. Not wanting to linger for long, Elya turned around to face the door.

Guarding the door was a large male lion with pure black coat and sapphire eyes. Next to him was an almost equally large arctic wolf with eyes of aquamarine.

Xemarius and Roma. Of all the animals, it had to be Zeerlo's pets? She didn't know much about them.; she had encountered them only a few times. She did know, however, that they only obeyed Zeerlo. And more importantly, either one of the beasts could manage to maul the other seven deadly sins without needing any help. She could only imagine the damage the two of them could do together. And against her, a human, she was dead. Forget the inevitable electrocution she knew would come from touching the doorknob. She wasn't even getting that far.

She had made it through the yard (sort of) only to meet her end here on the porch. It was just wrong. There probably wouldn't even be a body to send home to her mother, and neither Zeerlo nor Satan would be nice enough to let her mother know she was dead. If anything, they'd discard any remains she had, hide the fact they had any association with her, and inform the police they had seen a girl fitting her description halfway across the country.

"Alright Elya, you can do this," she said aloud. "Just walk slowly and don't get eaten, open the door, ignore the pain from being barbecued, and get inside. Slam the door behind you and try to not die."

Elya stepped forward.

Xemarius let out a loud, resounding roar, swiping a paw in warning.

Okay, so maybe she needed a new plan. Preferably one that didn't result in either lion or wolf pouncing on her.

"Xemarius, Roma, will you guys please let me through?" She couldn't believe she was talking to apex predators raised by Zeerlo as though they'd listen to her. "I need to talk to Zeerlo about something important for his father."

Roma rolled her eyes but stalked off in the opposite direction. Xemarius eyed her a moment longer, as though he was trying to determine the validity of her words, or if it would be worth the effort of dealing with a pissed off Satan later if he ate her. For her sake, Elya hoped Xemarius would realize it wasn't worth the effort and let her pass. His eyes seemed to glow as he moved to the side and laid down, head in his paws, tail flicking lazily behind him.

Neither lion nor wolf moved as she slowly approached the door. Taking deep breaths, Elya mentally prepared herself for the inevitable shock and placed a hand on the doorknob. A jolt of electricity coursed through her veins with enough force to feel as though a horse ran her down. She pushed the door open, released the handle, and rolled inside on the ground, pulling the door shut from the bottom. After a moment, she stood on her shaky legs.

Elya barely had time to breathe a sigh of relief before an alarm began to blare. "Intruder Alert! Intruder Alert! Intruder Alert!" Elya groaned. That *would* be her luck. By some miracle, she managed to get into the mansion relatively unscathed, and then she was faced by the siren. Odds were she'd be ambushed any minute by all five Mercenaries, and she knew better than anyone that the Sons of Satan were a 'kill first ask questions *never*' type of people.

The alarms went silent. Her muscles tensed. That wasn't a good sign. It was a sure sign she'd be dead in the next few seconds if one of the Mercenaries didn't immediately recognize her. A slight breeze hit her. If she were anyone else, she'd have assumed a window had been left open, but she knew better. One if not all of Satan's sons were near.

"Oh, it's you," a familiar voice sounded behind her.

Elya spun to see Zeerlo, clad in only a pair of black boxers. She tried not to stare, but it was hard not to. It was nothing to do with his well-defined muscles or the spiral scars which seemed to wrap around his torso. (Curious as it was, almost nothing could break his skin.) No, what held her gaze was the large pentagram branded into his chest, centered over his heart. When she had first met him, this mark was branded into his cheek. The mark of the Devil's mercenaries. Zeerlo and his brothers were all the Sons of Satan, meaning they bore the pentagram over their hearts as soon as they reached thirteen.

Elya tore her gaze from the brand. "Where's everyone else?"

Zeerlo scoffed. "Let's see. Fiend is out trying to find someone who can appease his bloodlust. Twist is giving a weapons demonstration at the Pentagon because they still have no idea he hacks them constantly. Shredder went to the grand-opening of some new gourmet restaurant, and Hellas should be breaking into the Federal Reserve right about now."

Elya blinked. "Sorry I asked."

He chuckled. "My brothers aside, I believe the real question is what are you doing here?" His eyes seemed to rove over her. "And you're unharmed, quite the impressive feat for a human."

"Oh!" Elya held her thumb and first finger a centimeter apart. "You were this close to complimenting me."

"Don't be ridiculous." He walked in the opposite direction.

"Ridiculous is the deist having religious symbols on his skin," Elya muttered, her gaze going to the upside down cross seemingly burned into Zeerlo's upper left shoulder blade.

Zeerlo stopped and his muscles tightened. Elya winced. Maybe making comments in hearing range of someone who could hear a butterfly's wing beat from a mile away wasn't her best idea. Just because she was smart didn't excuse her from doing dumb shit. He turned around slowly, blue eyes replaced with dancing flames. He took a step forward, a pair of large, red, feathery wings sprouted from his back. His fangs seemed to elongate as he moved toward her, and fire licked at his ankles.

"I do not question your religious beliefs," he seethed. "Do not question my lack thereof."

"Not religious, spiritual," Elya said before she could stop herself.

Zeerlo raised a brow. "Do you think I care for the difference?" His wings flexed. "Why are you even here?"

"The guy who, for some reason, doesn't have a pitchfork or red skin sent me." Elya said.

Seeing the different depictions of Satan was always hilarious. Her favorites were by far the ones that made him resemble a goat, if only because the only thing she had ever seen from him which remotely resembled an animal was when he lost his temper, and even then it was more akin to a dragon. The real scary thing was when it wasn't a small temper tantrum, but full rage, as it was at that point he grew in size, his wings were no longer feathery but much more dragonish, and he even developed a dragon snout.

"And that is why religious figures are dumb," Zeerlo said. He waved a hand and clothes covered his body.

"Your dad is Satan. How can you be deist?"

Zeerlo rolled his eyes. "Why did he send you here?"

Elya winced. "Almost forgot. He wanted me to tell you and your brothers to prepare for war. Someone is plotting to destroy the Afterlife."

He smirked. "Can't destroy what doesn't exist."

"Damn it, Zeerlo!" Elya snapped. "Your deistic views aside, I know you've been to Hell, so you at least consider it to be a place. And while you've never been, I have been to Heaven. There is a very real threat planning to destroy them both."

He sighed. "Alright, I'll bite. What do you know about this supposed threat? And why should I care? And side note, I have been to Heaven, I just don't care."

Elya grinned. "Because if there's no Hell, your dad will have no choice but to spend all of his time here in the mansion."

"When you put it like that, I'll help. Just know that I don't believe in the Afterlife. Heaven and Hell are not real, and my dad is just a guy who has immortality and loves to piss off my grandfather. I find neither as being worthy of something so ridiculous as worship."

"Well, I should get going," Elya said, turning toward the door. "After all, I'm sure you can inform your own brothers about the impending battle."

"I could," Zeerlo shrugged, "but I won't. You want their help, you'll need to tell them yourself. I don't do anything for free. Besides, you only just got here. Do you really want to go back out there and face the security system again?" He raised a brow. "You got lucky once, but the odds of it happening again are rather low."

Elya raised a brow. "Are you offering to take me through the security?"

He shrugged. "I might be convinced for the right price."

Elya shifted. "Fine, you can have a bag of my Skittles."

He scoffed. "You realize I have no real interest in your Skittles, right? They are junk and filled with sugar. Sugar is fattening and unhealthy. I am a machine bred for greatness. I haven't indulged in something as unhealthy as sugary snacks since I was seven, and I don't plan to resume such habits anytime soon."

Elya bristled. "Are you telling me you once broke my wrist because I wouldn't share my Skittles that you had *zero intention of eating*?"

"Well, duh." He rolled his eyes. "Honestly, Elya, you should know by now. I'll do shit just because it annoys you.

Just because I'm Wrath incarnate doesn't mean I don't take great amusement in annoying others."

Elya sighed. "Are you sure you're not Loki's kid?"

Zeerlo gasped. "How dare you?" He held a hand to his chest. "I have never been more insulted in my life!"

"For the record, you're weird enough to be his kid."

"You met him, what, once?"

"Details."

Zeerlo rolled his eyes. "So how do you want to pass the time while we wait for my brothers to arrive?" He smirked. "Personally, I can think of several ways."

"Netflix?"

"No can do. Television rots the brain and hinders proper development."

Elya huffed. "Do you do anything fun? I mean like what normal people might consider fun?"

"Definitely not. But what fun is normal anyway?"

Elya sighed "Training?"

He smirked. "Now that I can get behind."

Elya rolled her eyes but followed Wrath nonetheless, loathe as she was to train with him, her swordsmanship still needed work, and honestly, maybe the sword she'd been gifted would actually suit her and she'd prove that she'd been right all along when she said she needed a different sword to train with.

Nineteen

Hours later Elya found herself drenched in sweat but pleasantly surprised to learn that while she still wasn't great with the sword, her new gift had improved her skills greatly. She always knew it was the swords that were the problem. She followed Zeerlo onto the Elevator (simple mahogany and not nearly as opulent as the one in Hell). He naturally hadn't broken a sweat. The ride up was silent.

As the elevator came to a stop on the main floor the doors opened to the sounds of arguing echoed throughout. The younger sins were fighting again. Satan usually cut things off, and if not him, Zeerlo could do the job. The younger sins feared Wrath. Maybe Fiend held more respect for his older brother than fear, but Elya wasn't blind. She knew there was fear present in all of Zeerlo's younger brothers. She couldn't blame them – while physically they all appeared to have the same general build, with some slight variations in height attributed to age, they were not nearly as capable. Zeerlo was strong, powerful in ways his brothers weren't, and his control over his powers was unmatched. Sure, Fiend could make a fire do his bidding, Shredder could push flames out of his way, Twist could bring the flames higher, and even Hellas could summon them… but Zeerlo, he could make the flames *dance*. And not just the flames of Hell, any flame bowed to his bidding. He could calm flames into nothing. They were attuned to his breathing.

She understood where the fear came from.

They came to the main entrance of the mansion. The four younger sins were in an all-out brawl. Fiend had Shredder in a headlock while Twist had Hellas against a wall, a knife to his throat. None of them seemed to notice they had entered the room.

"Gentlemen," Zeerlo said icily.

All four younger sins paused. Fiend released Shredder while Twist dropped Hellas and pocketed his knife. All four scrambled to stand in front of their brother, backs rigid, arms to their sides. They looked like soldiers getting ready to greet their commanding officer. Technically, in Satan's throne room, they were under the Devil's protection. There, the sins had less to fear. But here, alone in the mansion, Zeerlo was in charge, and their father wasn't around to save them.

Zeerlo stepped in front of Fiend. The two were nearly the same height, Zeerlo having just the slightest edge, but it was enough. Elya could see the slightest hitch in Lust's breath as he stood rigidly in front of his brother.

(Satan had once explained to her that the order of their birth indicated the strength of the sin. He told her that, while an argument could be made for any of them as being strongest, the stage had been set when Pride was born first. She was fascinated to learn about the order of the sins: Pride gave way to Wrath, which led to Envy. In Envy came Lust – or, rather, bloodlust. From Lust came Sloth, and Elya never quite understood how he fit in there. Lastly, from Sloth came Greed. Gluttony was in the mix somewhere as well. Somehow, he fit between Sloth and Greed, but it didn't make much sense to her. Then again, most of Satan's explanation was lost to her.)

"Tell me," Zeerlo sneered, "is this any way to act in front of guests?"

"No, Zeerlo," they chorused.

"Apologize."

As one, the four younger deadly sins turned to Elya. "Our apologies."

"Apology accepted," Elya said, a little freaked out.

Zeerlo nodded, satisfied. "Good. Now that we've got that taken care of, Elya can explain why she's here."

"Right," Elya said. "Um, well I'm kind of here because I need your guys' help."

Fiend scoffed. "Hard pass. We don't do anything out of the kindness of our hearts, and somehow I don't think you'd be willing to pay the price any of us would ask."

"You'll listen to what she says," Zeerlo said.

"Why should we?" Shredder asked.

Zeerlo smirked. "How about if you don't listen, you join me for my morning training session for a month."

Shredder gulped. "On second thought… lovely to see you again Elya, how can we be of a service to you?"

"Right, so as I've already told Zeerlo, the guy without a pitchfork sent me," Elya began.

Fiend perked up. "Please tell me he sent you because there's a riot in Hell and we get to bash some heads in."

"Oh, that'd give me the perfect opportunity to test my new weapons. And I've been meaning to convince him to let me install a new security system I've been working on in Hell," Twist grinned. "Please tell me it's a riot."

"I've got some new poisons I'd love to try out," Shredder added.

Hellas nodded. "A few of those idiots owe me money. I haven't had time or an excuse, but this would be the perfect opportunity."

Elya sighed. "No riot."

Fiend huffed. "Then what did he send you for?"

"Someone's out to destroy Heaven and Hell, and Satan tasked me with gathering an army," Elya shrugged. "You five were at the top of his list."

"What kind of threat are we looking at?" Fiend asked.

"No idea," Elya said.

Twist sighed. "Any clue who's behind the threat or how viable of a threat this is? I mean, will this be like our dad's rebellion level of fighting? That'd be worthwhile. Or will this be like if we were to take on a bunch of second graders in a fight? That'd be an embarrassment."

"Don't know that either," Elya said.

Twist ran a hand through his hair. "So, let me see if I got this, someone's plotting to destroy Heaven and Hell and our dad sent you to gather an army even though you have no idea what this threat is or how viable it is? Yeah, no thanks. Way too much effort."

Elya sighed. "Look Twist, your dad said we need all of you and I agree."

He crossed his arms. "I'm Sloth in human form. Laziness is my specialty. There's a reason I spend my time making things to make my life easier. A few more years and I won't even have to get off the couch to cross-out everyone on my daily hitlist. So, again, no."

"A chance to kill people not on my hitlist and not get a lecture for it?" Fiend grinned, blood dripping down his chin. "I'm in. I never seem to have enough people on my list."

"I just have one question," Hellas said.

"Which is?" Elya asked.

"What's in it for me?"

Zeerlo crossed his arms. "If we don't save Heaven and Hell, then Dad is moving in with us permanently and he won't ever go to Hell for the day."

"Good enough for me," Hellas said.

Twist sat up. "Alright, I'm in. When Dad's home, he makes me do things, and I cannot have that."

"Shredder?"

"Let's see, stay home alone or go out and kill to my heart's content without fear of repercussions? And if we succeed, I don't need to worry about Dad putting a stop to all my cooking endeavors? Divine war it is."

Zeerlo nodded. "Good. Now that we're all on the same page," he rolled his shoulders back, "I'm going for some training. Don't disturb me."

Elya stared as he disappeared down the long hall of doorways. She had rarely been in the mansion, but she knew that the hall of doors was to be avoided at all costs – at least if you didn't know your way around. Even when you did, it was probably still risky.

"So, anyone willing to help me get off the property?" Elya asked.

Hellas snorted. "Not a chance."

Shredder scoffed. "Yeah right. And risk Zeerlo getting pissed we helped you get out unscathed? So not happening."

"It's my security system, I don't help anyone get past it," Twist deadpanned.

Fiend shrugged. "I would, but Zeerlo's got the right idea. I don't have time for something so frivolous."

"So, there's no convincing you to help me out through normal means?" Elya asked.

Fiend raised a brow. "What do you think?"

Elya sighed. "Do you guys have a guest room I could borrow? Preferably one where nobody can access the room once I'm in it?"

Fiend balked. "Are you kidding? There's not a room in this mansion my father or Zeerlo can't access. Well, Zeerlo can't access my dad's office. But that aside, they both have free reign of the entire mansion. I love your thinking though."

"Maybe I could just trip out," Elya mused.

Fiend laughed. "We put the same parameters around the mansion as are in Hell. Once you stepped foot inside, you became trapped here until you either A go through Twist's security protocol or B one of us is willing to help you out."

Elya huffed. "Sleepover with the five most dangerous teenagers on the planet it is."

Fiend's eyes lit as he grinned, his fangs showing. "If you were anyone else, we'd feed you to the wolves, so to speak. Unfortunately, we're not allowed to kill you. But that doesn't mean you'll have an enjoyable stay either."

"Joy," Elya deadpanned.

"Let's go." Fiend turned toward the stairs.

Elya glanced at her phone. It was getting kind of late, and she was trapped until one of them decided to take pity on her or Satan came to the rescue. Heaving a sigh, she followed

Fiend as he led her up the stairs to a landing. There were several doors to her left and right, and in front of her was also a turn to go up even more stairs. Even thinking about how many rooms there must've been was mentally exhausting.

"Don't leave this floor," Fiend said.

"I wouldn't dare. But out of curiosity, why?" Elya asked.

"Simply put?" Fiend asked. "We're in Zeerlo's wing. This floor, however, isn't used much even by him, so you're free to take one of his spare rooms. He won't say anything, and since he can't kill you, there's no safer place in the mansion."

Elya just nodded. She rather not share a wing with *any* of them, especially not Zeerlo, but she wasn't dumb. She understood what Fiend wasn't saying.

At night, the Sins were far more dangerous. Kalael had called it their predator state. Once the nighttime hit, each of the deadly sins lost all inhibition and control over their urges to act out their sins. Mercenary Mansion was the last place she wanted to spend the night, but it probably was best if she stayed on Zeerlo's floor.

"So, any tips for surviving the night?" Elya asked.

"The suite you're staying in has a bathroom, television, showers, and a small kitchen. Essentially, there's no reason you should leave the suite, unless it's on fire." Fiend came to a stop outside a door.

She nodded. "Don't worry, I've been warned. I've been told how you guys can't recognize anyone aside from each other in the middle of the night. The why has never been explained and I'm super confused by a few things. Like, I've seen a few of you in the middle night in Hell before and you all seemed fine?"

Fiend chuckled. "There's a password. If you know it, you can pull us out of that state, but it's not simple. We don't even know what the word itself is. I'm not sure who other than my father knows what it is… maybe my sister."

"Right. Okay, well, goodnight Fiend," she pushed the door open, "I guess."

"Night, Elya," he winked. "Stay safe."

Twenty

The suite she was given for the night was simply too much. The carpet was the color of blood, the walls were a dark black, the kitchen had granite countertops and pristine mahogany cabinets, there was a large television with several gaming consuls against one wall and a couch across from it, a coffee table sat between them, and that wasn't all. There were two more doors – for the bathroom and bedroom.

As she entered the bedroom, Elya thought she had accidentally left her suite. She couldn't believe its size – it was bigger than her living room at home! Though the color scheme was *so* not her. It was gloomy and it made her feel like she was going to be met by her impending doom any minute. Given she was at Mercenary Mansion for the night, in Zeerlo's wing to top it off, that wasn't off the table. If anything, she probably *would* die. Locking the bedroom door, Elya turned to the bed.

A small trumpet on a keychain and bag of skittles laid on the pillow. Carefully Elya grabbed the keychain. It was from Gabriel, she didn't know how she knew, but she did. Except the skittles, those were from Raphael. She smiled, it was like they were reminding her even though they couldn't drop in, they still had her back.

Only, their gifts while appreciated would do nothing in helping her survive a night in Mercenary Mansion. Pulling out her phone, she laid down and started scrolling through her contacts. Somehow, she didn't think Satan was the person she should call for help surviving the night.

Reaching the name she had been searching for, Elya pressed call.

She clicked her tongue at the sound of the phone ringing. After a moment, it went silent. "Hello?" A voice said.

"Kalael," Elya said.

"Elya?" Kalael asked. "What's wrong?"

"Long story, but I'm kind of stuck spending the night at Mercenary Mansion and Fiend mentioned there's a password to snap them out of the crazed state and I was hoping you might know what it is."

"Hold on, *what*?" Kalael gasped. "What the Hell are you doing at Mercenary Mansion at this time of night? At all?"

"I was actually planning to drop by and see you and Azrael tomorrow. I'll explain then. But the password, do you know it?" Elya asked.

"I'll give you the password," Kalael said "just don't let them know I'm the one who told you what it is. And please text me every hour so I know you're still unharmed. If you need anything, call for help."

"Of course."

"Stay safe."

"I will."

"No, the password," Kalael said "it's 'stay safe.'"

"That's the password?" Elya asked.

"My dad figured nobody would ever guess it."

Elya shrugged. "Well, he's not wrong. Wait a minute, do your brothers not know the password, or was Fiend just messing with me when he said he didn't?"

"They shouldn't know it, why?" Kalael asked.

"The last thing Fiend said to me before I went to my suite for the night was 'stay safe.'"

Kalael laughed. "It wouldn't surprise me if he figured it out." There was a pause. "I need to go, but seriously Elya, stay safe. None of us want to lose you. And you better have a damn good explanation when I see you tomorrow."

"I will, and thanks," Elya said.

"Of course." The line went dead.

Elya exhaled as she glanced at the time. 11:30 pm. The danger had already begun, she was sure. She just hoped Zeerlo was still in whatever intensive training he put himself through. She did not want to see them in their crazed states, especially not Zeerlo. She could only imagine what Zeerlo was like with nothing to hold him back from his murderous tendencies. Normal Zeerlo held no qualms in showing off how dangerous he could be, but a Zeerlo that wouldn't recognize her and would only see a stranger in his territory… she'd rather face off with a demon, or a werewolf. A vampire, a pack of rabid wolves, anything would be safer than Zeerlo.

Elya messaged Kalael her thanks again before turning on a mindless sitcom that, despite her best efforts against it, lulled her to sleep.

After what felt like no time at all, a crash from outside her door startled her awake. Elya winced, hand drifting to her newly acquired daggers. Not that they'd be much help, but maybe they'd buy her enough time to use the password and calm Zeerlo. Because that was the only thing it could have been that crashed outside the room. Zeerlo had realized someone was in his wing in one of his guest suites. No doubt he heard her shows. Silently, she cursed herself for being so stupid. She should've gone to bed and hoped he didn't hear her breathing in her sleep.

The doorknob jiggled. Elya raced from the bed, only to hit the floor. "Dammit!" Elya glanced at her feet to see she had been caught in the covers. Now was *not* the time for her excellent ability to trip to make an appearance.

The door crashed open, wood splintering across the floor. Frantic, Elya's gaze searched for her lost dagger while she tried to maneuver the blankets from around her feet. Zeerlo stood in the broken doorframe at his full height. His crimson wings spread behind him as he was engulfed in flames, his fangs glinting in the firelight. His gaze went right to her. The predator-style tracking would've been funny if it weren't so terrifying.

"You don't belong here." His voice was raspy and very unlike his own.

She continued to struggle with the blanket as Zeerlo stepped forward slowly, menacingly.

"Yes, I do," Elya said.

He paused. "You don't."

Elya jumped to her feet, hand going to her other dagger, only to find that it and her sword were gone. She backed away as Zeerlo stepped closer. This was bad. "Zeerlo, it's me! Elya! You don't want to hurt me."

He was undeterred by her plea, the flames surrounding him growing as they danced in his eyes.

Zeerlo didn't step closer. No, he rushed her using his ability to move faster than the speed of light, forcing Elya into a corner. The rage still swam in his eyes, and his crimson wings spread out behind him. His hands had turned into something more claw-like – almost like an eagle or a dragon. In a way, it was just something generally demonic. He reached out his clawed hand, clasping around her throat and pulling her off the ground.

"Stay safe!" Elya choked.

She slid down the wall, gasping for breath as Zeerlo released her. He stepped back, eyes coming into focus.

"Elya?" Zeerlo asked.

"Hey, Zeerlo," she croaked, massaging her throat. "I don't feel so good."

He knelt in front of her. "I don't imagine you would. Didn't Fiend tell you that the air around us becomes toxic at night?"

Elya frowned. "What?"

"Every poisonous gas known to mankind is essentially filling this room right now." Zeerlo slid a hand under her knees and moved the other to support her neck. "Any normal human would already be dead."

"Why aren't I dead?"

"You've been tripping into Hell since you were six. My dad is a lot of things, but dumb isn't one of them." He glanced around the room. "I'm sure he figured out some way to lessen the effects on you so you wouldn't die upon exposure." He opened the window. "That's not to say too much exposure wouldn't kill you."

"I'm going to die, aren't I?" Elya asked, already accepting her fate.

"No. At least not tonight." He maneuvered them out the window and onto the roof. "A little fresh air while your room clears out and you'll be good as new."

Elya smiled. "Thanks."

He shrugged. "Just don't go spreading it around that I went out of my way to keep you alive. I do have a reputation."

"You know it's really weird that you have a section of roof on like every floor of the mansion except the ground floor, right?"

He laughed. "My dad has the money to act like some eccentric billionaire, so he does so gladly. Whenever anyone ask him about it, he just goes on some rant muttering about Karen."

"Somehow, that makes sense," Elya said.

"Yeah," he frowned. "Who told you the password?"

"Does it matter?" Elya asked.

"Yes."

"I gave my word I wouldn't tell," Elya said.

He sighed but nodded. That was something Elya knew he and his brothers understood. When they gave their word, it was never to be broken. It was their promise, even if they'd never call it that, but it was the one time she knew whatever was being said wasn't a twisted truth.

Elya yawned. She glanced at her phone: 4:30 am. Sunrise wasn't for a while yet, and she was honestly exhausted, but she couldn't risk Zeerlo going back into his crazed state if she was inside with him, and there was no way she could risk the toxins he apparently released in the middle of the night.

"You must be exhausted," Zeerlo said.

Elya shrugged. "A little, but I'm running on adrenaline now. I'll probably be up for a few more hours."

He frowned. "I could probably put you to sleep if you want. That, or your other option is to stay late into the day tomorrow. I know humans need significant amounts of sleep."

She laughed. "Yeah, that's a way to put it. But I can run on a little less sleep. It won't be pleasant, but not impossible."

Zeerlo stood. "No, we're getting you to bed. For one, I nearly killed you, and for two, I don't want to hear any rants from my father or lectures from Gabriel over not allowing you to get proper amounts of sleep. And for three, Kalael will have my head if she finds out I didn't let someone get at least nine full hours of sleep."

Elya decided it was for the best if she didn't argue the point. He had played the lecture card. While he was referring to himself, she would also doubtlessly be on the receiving end of several lectures – at least three from Gabriel alone. One on why it was dangerous of her to go Mercenary Mansion, one about the stupidity of spending the night there, and the last about her disregard for the importance of sleep. Then, Raphael would back him on the importance of sleep and Satan would question why she didn't just call him to get her out of the mansion, which, admittedly, was dumb of her not to do. Then, she'd likely receive a lecture from Kalael on the importance of sleep because all of Afterlife knew that Kalael was not a morning person, and that when she was younger, her sleep was not to be disrupted for anything short of an emergency. Satan had claimed her need of sleep was related to her power and that he had worked that kink out by the time Zeerlo was born.

Elya bit her lip. "Is it safe for me to go to bed?"

Wrath ran a hand through his hair. "You'll be alright now. I won't go back to bed until sunrise hits and it's safe for you to be in the mansion again. Plus, none of the others would dare come into my wing no matter what state of mind they're in. Your guestroom should be aired out by now, so I'll help you back to your window, then I'll head over to my own room without reentering yours, as that would just bring the toxins back."

Elya huffed. "I can walk on my own, you know."

Zeerlo raised a brow. "With the rate you trip? I don't think we should take any risks, not while you're on the roof and one misstep could lead to your death. And I *really* do not want to deal with the fallout of that from my sister or my dad, or Gabriel and Raphael. Or worse, Michael." He shuddered.

Elya snorted. "Michael? Why would he even care? I snuck into his war room, stole things from him, and then had the audacity to lie about it. He doesn't know about the last two things, but even still he banned me from Heaven and from speaking to Raphael and Gabriel ever again."

Zeerlo frowned. "I'm sorry. I know that they are important to you–" his brows furrowed "–though I can't fathom why."

Elya raised a brow. "When did you learn to recognize when people are upset?"

He gasped. "How dare you? I can tell when people are upset. I just prefer them that way in almost all scenarios."

"Almost all?" Elya asked.

"I dislike when Kalael is upset," he shrugged. "And when you're upset, it usually leads to me having listen to long rants from my father."

"Now that sounds right," Elya said.

Zeerlo sighed. "I'm not one of the – you know me, I don't do touchy feely," he ran a hand through his hair. "What I'm trying to say is you matter to me, Elya. I don't want to see you upset, and I don't want to see you die."

She smiled. "That's the nicest thing you've ever said to me."

He chuckled. "Don't go spreading it around."

"No promises," Elya said.

He shook his head. "We should get you to bed, you've got a lot of work ahead of you."

"You could come with," Elya said.

He scoffed. "I've got four brothers to whip into shape before we potentially go to war."

"I don't pity them," Elya said.

"Sleep well," Zeerlo said as they stopped at the window.

Elya laughed. "I'll do my best."

He disappeared in a blur, leaving Elya alone. Carefully, she grabbed the sides of the window frame and slowly maneuvered herself inside. She glanced around the dimly lit room. The comforter and bed were intact, but the rest had taken some damage. Sighing, she grabbed her phone off the bed and shot Kalael a text telling her not to worry and that she'd text her again when she got up in the morning or afternoon.

Adrenaline suddenly gone, Elya crawled under the covers, pulled them tight around her, and slowly drifted into sleep, content knowing that Zeerlo would keep her safe.

Twenty-One

It was just after noon when Elya finally pulled herself out of bed. Leaving the bedroom, she saw the door to the suite was in shambles, but otherwise in pristine condition. Stomach growling, Elya rifled through the cabinets in search of some acceptable form of breakfast food. Unsurprisingly, the cabinets were fully stocked, which made it that much more difficult to decide. She was starving after her near death experience the previous night, but she also didn't feel like cooking. After a while, she settled on fixing an egg sandwich.

After her quick breakfast, Elya washed her few dishes and returned them to the cabinet. Returning to the bedroom, she searched for her missing weapons, only to find all three were laid out on the dresser. Zeerlo must have come back when it was safe to find them for her. Naturally, he would've been muttering about how he was ruining his reputation the entire time. Digging through her backpack, Elya grabbed a change of clothes before heading to the bathroom for a quick shower.

It was only as she left the shower that Elya remembered Kalael was likely worried sick about her. Grabbing her cell, she shot Pride a quick text to reassure her she was still alive and would head her way within the hour. Or at least Elya thought it'd be an hour. There wasn't much left for her to do at Mercenary Mansion aside from convince one of its occupants to have pity on her and get her safely off the property.

Ensuring her laces were double-knotted, Elya grabbed her daggers and strapped them to her sides, along with her sword.

(Despite how dire the circumstances were, she kind of felt badass walking around with daggers and a sword on her side never mind the fact her skills with a sword were clearly lacking and the daggers, while her best weapon to date, weren't the best weapon unless you wanted to get real close to the enemy. Honestly, she probably needed to look at getting a long-distance weapon.)

Silently, Elya left the room only to bump into Fiend at the hall's end. His bright red hair was unkempt, his eyes were bright, and his million-dollar smile was from ear to ear.

"Oh, hey Fiend," Elya said wearily. "I was just getting ready to find Zeerlo so I can get out of your guys' hair."

Fiend snorted. "Yeah, don't disrupt his sleep. You won't live to tell the tale."

(After last night's close call, she thought she might actually be able to survive an encounter with a tired Zeerlo. Still, she only knew with certainty that the security password worked at night, and there was no need to risk finding out what might happen during the day. After all, there was nothing hindering Zeerlo's ability to control himself, and if he was half as bad as his sister when her sleep was disrupted… It was best if she let the beast rest.)

"Right," Elya eyed Zeerlo's right hand man "any chance you'd be willing to help me off the property?"

Fiend stroked an imaginary beard. "I'm tempted to say no because I enjoy watching people suffer as much as the next sin," he mused, clicking his tongue, "but at the same time, my father will have a conniption if you get hurt – not to mention you went through all the effort of surviving the night, which couldn't have been an easy task. Also, you're in the middle of gathering an army, so I guess this once I'll help."

"Gee, thanks," Elya snarked. "You really know how to make a girl feel special."

He winked. "I try."

"So, can we go now?" Elya asked.

"Actually," he shifted, "I have something to give you first."

Elya's eyes lit up. "Oh, a gift? What is it? Wait, why are you giving me gifts? It's not a box that's going to explode, is it?"

Fiend shifted uneasily, rubbing his arm. "Kalael may be the one with the gift of prophecy, but I have a bad feeling."

"What sort of bad feeling?" Elya asked.

Fiend's expression dropped. His brows furrowed as though he were attempting to decide how to put into words what he meant.

(Bad feelings were never a good sign when it came to immortals and their family. If she had learned anything over the years, it was that those who had divine blood somewhere in their family lineage should always trust their guts. Whenever they had a bad feeling, something always followed. It was like a sixth sense for them. She remembered when she was thirteen and Zeerlo had a bad feeling. A swarm of demons managed to swarm them moments later, and it was only thanks to Zeerlo's sheer strength and Satan's control that she got out unscathed.)

"I'm not entirely sure what it is exactly." Fiend ran a hand through his hair. "All I know is this war is going to cost more than any of us are ready to sacrifice."

Elya winced. "That's not ominous or anything."

He shrugged. "I'm practical."

"So," Elya said, "what are you giving me, and do I actually want it?"

He laughed. "You know me well, but in this instance, you're going to want this," Fiend reached within his necklace and pulled out a small blue gemstone on a silver chain.

Elya raised a brow. "A bracelet?"

"It's an Arthenian gemstone," he said as though it explained everything. It probably did. "They come from the royal family of Arthenia. They have the power to heal anything." He held it out for her to see. "There's only three on Earth and I happen to possess two of them. I want you to have this one."

She frowned. "When you say anything?"

"Any injury, any illness. It's very powerful but that doesn't mean you should use it for minor injuries." He put it in her palm. "Save it for when circumstances are dire."

"Alright, emergencies only." Elya watched as he fidgeted. "Fiend, just how bad is this feeling you have?"

"Bad," he said softly.

"We'll pull through." Elya offered an encouraging smile. "We're strong."

His gaze softened. "I hope you're right, Elya." His voice cracked. "But I don't – we're going to lose someone and–" His eyes watered slightly. "I don't want to."

"I promise Fiend, we're going to get through this."

He shook his head. "I'm not sure we can. Just promise me you'll hold onto the bracelet. I'll keep mine on me, but just in case."

"I will," Elya said softly. "How did you get two of them in the first place, especially if there's only three on Earth?"

"Gifts from my father–" he waved a dismissive hand "–he got them from some shady deals." He chuckled. "And I mean shady for him."

"I have so many questions about that," Elya said.

Fiend laughed. "Trust me Elya, the less you know about my dad's shady deals, the better."

She pouted. "You know I like knowing things. You've pulled me out of a number of dangerous situations I got in over my curiosity. Why would you do this to me?"

He smirked. "Like I said, I enjoy watching people suffer. Psychological suffering is no less satisfying than the physical, at least for me."

Elya huffed. "I hate you."

Fiend chuckled, the light returning to his eye. "No you don't. If you did, we wouldn't be having this discussion. Now let's get you out of here before you end up hurt. Mercenary Mansion is unforgiving to the best of us. There's a reason Zeerlo hates Door 13 and believe me, I never in my life want to find out why that is. I suggest we get you gone before you have an encounter with a room you'd best avoid at all costs."

"What is behind Door 13 though?" Elya asked.

Fiend shrugged. "The only people with any idea are my father and Zeerlo, and neither of them are inclined to share. Whatever it is, I'm sure it's dangerous and I'm just waiting for the day one of them slips so I can find out."

When she just looked shocked, he shrugged.

"What? You don't have exclusive rights on being curious."

Elya laughed. "Fair enough. Now about getting me safely out of here?"

Fiend sighed. "Very well. We'll do the boring thing and let get you off the property safely." He shuddered. "Ugh, it's disgusting."

"You'll live," Elya deadpanned.

"Debatable."

"Seriously?"

"Fine." He rolled his eyes. "I'll disarm the security system. From there you'll have one minute to get from the porch back to the outside gate."

"A minute? Are you insane?" Elya stared at him, gaping. Surely he was kidding? "There is literally no way I could make that. Your driveway is like a mile long."

"A mile?" His face contorted as he gazed out the nearby window. "Are you sure?"

Elya frowned. "Yes, and you know it."

"Humans are so boring," Fiend muttered, typing a series of numbers into the keypad against the wall. "Am I dragging you or carrying you?"

"I think I'd prefer riding piggyback. When Zeerlo drags me when he runs, it sometimes dislocates my shoulder." Her shoulder ached just thinking about it.

Fiend pouted. "Fine, hop on."

Elya grinned, hopping onto his back. "Mush!"

He laughed. "You might want to hold on tighter. Don't forget – I run faster than the speed of light and we've got 32 seconds before the security system reboots."

Elya tightened her grip. If he weren't one of Satan's mercenaries, she'd worry about choking him, but the Deadly Sins were practically indestructible. Hell, not even bullets could break through their skin, so, it wasn't as though she was going to hurt him. She glanced to the keypad, where a countdown timer ticked down the seconds. Ten. Fiend threw open the door. Nine. Cold wind rushed past Elya for only a brief second before they were still again.

As soon as they were safely off the property, Fiend dropped her. Elya, with all the grace of a drunk, crashed to the ground, a sharp, piercing fiery pain shooting through her ankle with a resounding *crack.* She grimaced as she sat collapsed on the ground, clutching her ankle. She fought back tears of pain – she'd broken enough bones over the years to know Fiend's carelessness broke her ankle. She also knew that without adrenaline, the pain would be worse than it currently was.

"Seriously?" Elya asked.

He shrugged. "I like watching people suffer."

Elya removed her shoe to see her ankle was already purple and swelling. She poked it. Fractured, maybe a clean break. She didn't know much about injuries, but she had enough broken bones in the past to have a vague idea of what it was.

"You know I'm visiting your sister next, right?" Elya asked through clenched teeth.

Fiend cringed. "Way to ruin my fun." He knelt next to her on the ground. "Let's see what the damage is." He gently grabbed her ankle. "Well, the good news, it's nothing you haven't suffered before. The bad news is if my father finds out about this, I'm going to be in major trouble. Better news, though: with my abilities, what would normally never heal properly can be fixed in a few seconds." His eyes lit with mischief. "Lucky you."

"So, it's broken?" Elya asked.

"Shattered like an eggshell crushed in a hand," Fiend said.

Elya cringed. "Please tell me somewhere in your Fiend-to-English translation book that means it won't be painful."

He grinned. "Oh, it's going to be agonizing. Probably somewhere between childbirth and having your wings touched. Since you don't have wings, it'll be the most painful thing you'll ever experience."

Elya raised a brow. "I was told by a high-school anatomy teacher that childbirth feels like breaking every bone in your body at once. Are you sure about that?"

"Yes," he shrugged. "For this, it feels like you're on fire. 3rd degree burns. Granted, it's isolated to your ankle, but additionally it'll feel as though you're enduring five thousand pounds of pressure."

"Any way to numb the pain?" Elya asked.

"Dozens. However, I won't. As we've discussed–"

"Yeah, yeah, you like to see people suffer." Elya shot him a glare. "You're an asshole, Fiend." She wished for the millionth time that Satan didn't raise his sons to be so ruthless.

He grinned. "That may be so, but I'm the only one you've got to fix your ankle, unless you want to go clear to Heaven or search out Life."

"I'm sure Kalael can fix it," Elya smirked "and when she asks how I broke it, I'll be sure to let her know it was because you threw me off your back after running at the speed of light."

Fiend raised a brow. "You're deliberately attempting to manipulate the situation in your favor." He wiped an imaginary tear. "I can honestly say I have never been so proud of you, Elya. We're finally having a bad influence on you." He grinned. "And for that, I'm willing to remove the pain of fixing your ankle. At least this once."

Elya smiled as Fiend placed a hand around her ankle – all she felt was a warmth entering her injury as a soft, yellow flame surrounded both her ankle and Fiend's hand.

(It wasn't her first time being healed by Fiend, but it was the first time he was doing so without a direct order from Satan. It always fascinated her that he could heal using fire, especially when fire usually burned and caused pain. Though she could have done without all of Fiend's ways of diagnosing injuries. she swore if she had chicken pox, he'd diagnose her with an itching and scratching disease which causes blisters commonly found in children and was evidence she wasn't mature. Or something like that. He tended to go out of his way to make things complicated and confusing, but he was good at what he did.)

"There!" Fiend stood up proudly. "Good as new."

"Thanks," Elya said.

He offered her a hand. "Yeah, well, don't mention it."

Elya took it. "Of course. Can't have you ruining your reputation."

Fiend pulled her to her feet. "I'm violent and cruel. I take joy in ripping people apart. I get a rush when I see blood. I'm not a good person. So, no, I don't like that I healed you. But I am good at healing, I admit."

Elya smiled. "Dr. Fiend Lucifer."

He grinned. "That's right. That'll be $5,000."

Elya scoffed. "You broke it in the first place."

Fiend cackled. "Get going."

He vanished in a blur. Suddenly alone after the shock of sustaining a horrible injury that was miraculously healed, Elya huffed. Turning from the gates of the mansion, she walked back to her new car.

(It was still unbelievable she had an amazing car. But she was glad she had it – it'd make the long drive to the coffee shop comfortable. Plus, thanks to Satan, she had more than enough money in the bank for gas and road trips snacks. It was nice not being broke for once.)

Twenty-Two

Something about the clanging bell of the Coffee Shop was comforting. She hadn't spent much time there over the years, but every time she did and heard the bell ring, a wave of tranquility washed over her. This moment was no different. Glancing around the empty coffee shop, Elya startled as she found herself wrapped in a hug.

"You have no idea how worried I was about you," Kalael said.

"I'm fine!"

"You went hours without responding."

"I fell asleep!"

Kalael raised a brow. "You owe me an explanation, and I want the full story."

"Can we wait for Azrael then?" Elya asked. "It's a long story."

"I almost went to Mercenary Mansion myself last night," Kalael said.

"But you didn't."

"Only because I love my brothers dearly, and Zeerlo may be many things, most of which aren't positive, but he is smart. Smarter than all of us." Kalael stroked Elya's hair. "I knew he'd put you on his floor and as long as you had the password, you'd be able to get through to him. And after that, he'd ensure nobody came near you. Not that there was much risk of anyone else going near his floor anyways, but…what can I say? I know my family."

"So, will you please let me go now?" Elya asked.

"Only if you promise never to stay the night alone with my brothers in Mercenary Mansion again," Kalael said sternly. "With my father, sure. He could find you a place to sleep where there's no risk of my brothers getting nearby. But never with just them, okay?"

Elya nodded, having no desire to repeat the experience anyway. "Deal."

Kalael stepped back, leaving a hand on either of Elya's shoulders. "Do you need anything? Food? Water? Anything you need, it's yours."

"I'm alright," Elya said.

Kalael frowned. "You're sure?"

"Yeah, I kind of just want to sit and wait for the others so I can explain what's going on."

Kalael nodded, sitting on the couch and grabbing a sketchpad. If she was honest, Elya was surprised. Kalael wasn't one to let things go, especially when it was information that had been kept from her. Really it was one of the most dangerous things you could do, hide things from Kalael…

Time passed in silence, Kalael drew quietly while Elya played on her phone. It was nice knowing the two of them could just fall into an easy and comfortable silence. (It was more than she could do with her roommates. Of course, Cathy and Laurel were awful and there was a reason she avoided them as much as possible.) A half hour passed before the bell clanged, announcing the arrival of the sons of Death and Pride, Dimitri (the virtue of Charity) and Zeke (the virtue of Temperance).

"Hey, Elya," Zeke said.

"What happened?" Dimitri asked.

"Hello to you too, Dimitri," Elya said pointedly. "Hi, Zeke."

Dimitri crossed his arms. "Seriously Elya, did something happen?" His eyes darkened. "Say the word – I'll take care of it."

Elya held up a hand. "No need to go full Reaper on someone."

Kalael snorted. "You have no idea how terrifying he can be. Given the choice between a pissed Dimitri and a pissed Zeerlo, I'd take Zeerlo every time."

"That's because no sane person would piss him off," Zeke said.

Elya raised a brow. "How bad is it?"

"Bad," Kalael and Zeke replied.

Dimitri scoffed. "I'm not that bad."

"No," Kalael said. "He's worse. You saw Zeerlo crazed last night, Elya. Imagine that on steroids. The only benefit is Dimitri will still recognize you."

"Hold up." Dimitri turned to Elya. "You did what last night? Were you trying to get yourself killed?"

"No, your grandfather sent me," Elya said.

Zeke coughed. "He did what?"

"Look, I promised Kalael I'd explain after everyone's here so I only have to explain once."

Zeke nodded, signaling his acceptance. Dimitri shifted from foot to foot, glanced to Kalael, then ran a hand through his hair.

(Elya wasn't dumb – she knew if Dimitri demanded it, she'd be giving answers twice, because while his moral compass was a bit ambiguous, nobody knew for certain what he was and wasn't willing to do.)

"Fine," Dimitri said at last.

Elya exhaled slowly. That was good. She really didn't want to find out just how little of a moral compass Dimitri had.

Another hour passed in silence. It wasn't as comfortable as the previous silence. Kalael continued her drawing, but now Zeke also sat tapping his fingers, trying to fill the silence with some form of noise while Dimitri remained silent. Staring. Elya attempted to ignore this by playing on her phone, to no avail. Finally, a familiar fog rolled through the door as the bell clanged. Azrael appeared with Simone not far behind him.

"Oooh—" Azrael's eyes lit up "—please tell me we're throwing a party."

Simone rolled her eyes. "Don't be stupid." She hopped over the couch, landing in the empty seat between Zeke and

Kalael. "Elya's probably here for something." She peered at Kalael's sketchbook. "Who's that?"

Kalael's eyes snapped up. "Kasta James."

Azrael frowned. "Never heard of her."

Kalael rolled her eyes. "She hasn't been born yet. She's very beautiful though, like her mother." Kalael smiled softly. "Kasta will have very big footsteps to follow."

(Elya had almost forgotten about Kalael's gift: her ability to see past and future. Kalael tended to be quiet about it. She had once described her visions as invading memories: The room around her disappeared and in their place was whatever past or future event she had found herself in. Sometimes they weren't quite as powerful, sometimes Kalael expressed her visions through drawings, and while each one was skillfully done, they didn't share many details.)

"She looks annoying," Simone commented.

Dimitri snorted. "Everyone looks annoying to you."

"I can't help if people annoy me," Simone shrugged. "So, Elya, what brought you?"

Elya sat up straighter, pocketing her phone. "I found something indicating someone was out to destroy Hell. My first instinct was it wasn't a threat, but then it kept bothering me, so I took it to Satan, and he, of course, took it very seriously. So seriously, in fact, he sent me to Heaven to break into the war room I didn't even know they had to find out if the threat originated from there. Instead, I found the same note addressed to Heaven. Someone or something is out to destroy Afterlife," Elya said grimly as they all tensed. "So, after reporting it to Satan, he gave me a list of people to gather and sent me on my way, and that's how I ended up spending the night at Mercenary Mansion."

Kalael frowned. "Why send you? You're fully capable, yes, but despite tripping into it since you were six, you're still new to the Celestial world. My dad and uncles tended to shelter you, despite your constant back and forth between Heaven, Hell, and Earth."

Elya smiled bitterly. "Apparently he couldn't because half the people on this list wouldn't let him at the door. Also, only a few people can travel between Heaven and Hell. Of those few, Azrael apparently wouldn't be taken seriously."

"It's Thanatos—" the Reaper corrected "—and I take offense."

"Anyway," Elya cut in quickly, "he also said Zeke and Simone don't know how to travel into Heaven, leaving Dimitri and Kalael." She shrugged. "The problem there was I was available and didn't run as high of a risk of offending one of the angels as Kalael. And Dimitri apparently risked invoking unwanted memories."

"Can I see this list?" Kalael asked.

"Sure." Elya pulled it out. "I've never even met most of the people on it, but I guess I'll figure out how to get to them somehow."

Kalael hummed as she pursued the list. "It's not bad. War, Conquest, and Famine won't agree easily. They have a very personal and more recent grudge against my father." She handed the list back. "Aurelius, Marco, and Bernard won't be fun for you, but they should be manageable. It's a good list, though I would add one more person on."

Elya raised a brow. "You would?"

Kalael nodded. "Charlie may be human, but he's skilled with a gun. I'd know – Papa raised him. And unlike me, there was no deal involved where he was meant to give him back. And you know mob rules: Charlie's expected to take over the business someday."

Elya snorted. "While I know Charlie is capable, I have sincere doubts he'd be able to stick to the dress code of being a mob boss."

Kalael grinned. "He'll get there eventually. Maybe."

Simone frowned. "Am I missing something? Because the Uncle Charlie from the timeline I left didn't have any fashion issues."

"It's an issue of pants," Kalael said.

Azrael frowned. "You people are so weird."

"Anyway," Kalael said, reigning in the conversation. "Charlie would definitely be useful in a fight, especially one where most of the people have little to no experience with guns."

Elya frowned. "Assuming the people out to destroy Afterlife don't know how to use them. We have *no idea* where this threat originated, and honestly, I'm a little concerned with how seriously Satan is taking this. Who could possibly be powerful enough to destroy Heaven and Hell?"

Azrael frowned. "I can think of a few with the means and motivation. Alex for one, Cain for another." He sat on the arm of the couch.

"Who's Alex?" Elya asked.

"Michael's best friend who went unhinged some several millennia ago," Dimitri said. "Loathe as I am to say it, Cain is a viable suspect."

"Welp—" Azrael stretched "—as fascinating as this is, we can't do anything now. Who's up for squirrel hunting?"

Kalael frowned. "This is serious Thanatos."

"I didn't say it wasn't, but there's little we can do about it right now. Why bother stressing over something beyond our control?" He grinned at his wife. "Come on darling, you know you want to."

"I really don't," Kalael said.

"Dimitri, you in?" Azrael asked.

"Couldn't if I wanted to – and I don't – but I have a meeting to attend that nobody ever seems to let me get out of."

Azrael cringed. "I don't envy you. Makes me glad I was banned from the meetings early on,"

Dimitri sighed. "You make it sound so easy. I showed up naked once and they still make me go."

"Start a riot, that's how the rest of us were banned." Azrael turned to the others. "Zeke? Simone?"

"It's childish," Simone said.

"I'm in," Zeke grinned.

"Excellent!" He turned to Elya. "What about you? We can do teams! You and Zeke against me and Speckers." Said squirrel climbed from Azrael's pocket, up his arm, onto his shoulder, and on top of the Reaper's head.

"No thanks," Elya said.

"Oh come on, you know you want to," Azrael said.

Elya shook her head. "I should probably get going."

"With your tripping problem? And the night you had last night?" Kalael scoffed. "Absolutely not. You're going to stay here for a few days, make sure you're well rested before you go back out."

"I'll be fine," Elya said.

Kalael's eyes burned. "You're staying and I won't hear any arguments," she said, smiling sweetly. "If you need anything, let me know, and I'll get it."

Elya sighed, defeated. "Fine, but only because I know it'd be pointless to argue." Not that she minded – something about the place made her feel at home. "But I'm still not going squirrel killing."

Azrael shrugged, pulling out his paintball gun. "Ready Speckers?"

"…"

"Agreed!" He looked to his youngest. "Speckers wants to do a free for all. First to a hundred wins."

Zeke scoffed. "Only a hundred? I'll have those before you even make it outside, old man. Make it a thousand."

"Who you calling old?" Azrael asked.

Zeke smirked. "The guy born in the Garden of Eden."

"Oh, it's on!" Azrael ran out the door, Speckers jumping from his shoulder.

Zeke laughed, following his dad outside. Kalael shook her head, watching her youngest and husband leave. Dimitri soon followed with a look of complete disdain.

(Whatever meeting he was going to must have been awful to get such a bad reaction. She was kind of curious to know, and since she'd be staying for a few days, she could probably ask him when he got back – or if he was back late, she'd be able to ask in the morning. If it was a meeting that angels, demons, fallen angels, Keepers, *and* Riders were banned from, it had to be interesting. That was only all the categories of celestials she knew of – excluding God, considering He was his own category. But who could possibly ban celestials from a meeting? And why? And why did the thought of the meeting make Dimitri miserable?)

And maybe during her short stay, she could get Azrael to teach her how to talk to animals (assuming such a thing could be taught) because it was totally unfair that he could. Maybe she'd even get a chance to learn about Loki and the rebellion and what really went down because humanity seemed to be lacking a complete account of that. While most of Afterlife was very hush, hush about such things, Azrael was never good at keeping secrets that weren't life altering. And who knew about Loki…

Mentally making a list of all the things she wanted to try to learn in her brief stay, Elya made her way back into the kitchen of the coffee shop and up the increasingly creaky stairs. The apartment above the coffee shop should've been small, but celestials defied all laws of physics (or at least a good portion of them) and so there were dozens of bedrooms down one hallway. Remnants from Elya's childhood when, due to Satan's meddling, children across the globe began to develop Death's powers.

Like so many others, she had been given a guest room, but whereas a vast majority of those children had their powers removed, Elya's ability to trip into Afterlife wasn't resultant of Satan's meddling, and couldn't be removed. Consequently, while she wasn't there often, they left one guest room for her.

Twenty-Three

She didn't recall tripping. But it was the only explanation for the scene in front of her. A purple and blue sky, hills in the distance. A dove. A cross almost seemed to be hidden in the sun. It should have been beautiful, but it was tainted by the lake in front of her. Red as blood, and strangely enough with small flames on the water. It defied logic.

"You are preparing for war," a voice said.

Elya turned to see a strange woman. She was ethereal, beautiful in a way. She looked familiar yet Elya knew she'd never met this woman. And yet, something inside her felt as though this woman was a lifelong friend. How strange.

"Life is often strange," the woman said.

"Who are you?"

"A lifelong friend," she replied.

Elya huffed. "Helpful."

"You need not worry about who I am Elya," the woman's gaze went to the water. "You have a war ahead of you."

"I know, which is why I'm preparing, gathering an army."

"No," the woman shook her head. "I do not merely mean the physical war you will soon face. There is an internal war which will occur. This war for Afterlife is to take place in the spiritual realm, not the physical but it will not be without cost."

"What do you mean?"

"Secrets will be revealed, lies shall unravel. The balance between good and evil, Heaven and Hell. It will come down to you Elya Tempest Adams."

Elya frowned. "Why me? Who are you?"

"As I said…a lifelong friend. As for why you, who else but the very one who was created for this day. All of your life Elya has been leading to this war."

"What happens if I lose?"

"You cannot lose Elya," the woman smiled sadly. "You are the determiner of who wins however. This war for Afterlife has been set since before Creation. It has always been known you would be made to end it. Free will, however, means that the outcome is made by you."

"But—" Elya frowned. "That doesn't make sense. God is supposed to be all knowing and all powerful. How could I determine the outcome of this war. Why would I choose anything but to save Afterlife? You don't make sense."

The woman shook her head. "You will understand when it is time little one."

"I couldn't be further from understanding!"

"That's where you are wrong Elya. You will soon understand everything. You have three paths in front of you. But you may choose but one."

A splash in the water drew Elya's attention away from the woman. The air rippled, heat shimmering from the blood lake. Something moved beneath the surface. A pair of dark horns and a skeletal hand rose from the lake's depths. Elya turned to ask the woman what it meant only to find her gone.

Elya drew her sword as the figure continued to rise from the water.

It stepped onto the shore, water, or maybe blood dripped off the skeletal figure. Her grip tightened as she fell into a familiar defensive stance. Sword wasn't her best weapon but she didn't want to get quite as close and personal to this creature as her daggers might require.

Its jaw dropped open breaking cobwebs. A spider crawled out of its eye socket. It shut its jaw before opening it again. It repeated this. Once. Twice. And then.

"El-y-a," Its voice was haunting.

"What—"

"Elya," It said more confident.

"Who are you?"

"You killed me," the skeletal figure morphed growing skin and taking on a familiar face.

"Satan?" Elya asked.

It shook its head slowly.

She frowned. If it wasn't Satan, then that meant it had to be either the mysterious man or…

"Michael?"

It nodded. "You killed me, Elya."

Fire immersed him. The flames consumed his very being his flesh melted away until once again all that stood in front of her was the skeletal figure. "You destroyed me."

He lunged toward her.

Elya screamed. Breathing rapidly. Drenched in sweat. She took in some calming breaths as she checked her surroundings. She was in her guestroom at the Coffee Shop. It had just been a dream. Well, nightmare really.

"The decision is yours Elya," the woman's voice echoed.

Elya's pulse pounded in her ears. The echo of the woman's voice lingered like smoke.

The door to her room burst open. Kalael, rushed in scythe drawn. Her gaze searched frantically before she vanished her scythe. Kalael's gaze seemed to be searching for hidden threats before landing on her.

"You, okay?" Kalael asked.

"Just a nightmare…" Elya remembered the voice she heard after she woke. "At least I think it was."

Kalael pulled the chair from the desk taking a seat. "You think?"

"I mean…it had to be right?" Elya asked. "I was asleep…it's just—after I had woken up I heard a voice speak to me. It belonged to the woman from my dream."

Kalael frowned. "Who was the woman?"

"I don't know," Elya said.

"What did she say that had you so scared?" Kalael asked softly.

"She's not what scared me."

Kalael frowned. "Then what happened?"

Elya pulled her knees to her chest. "Michael was in my dream. Only he wasn't Michael. He was a skeleton. And he said I killed him."

"You killed him?" Kalael asked.

"It's what he said."

"That's—" Kalael ran a hand through her hair "—Elya in the Celestial world dreams aren't always just that. Sometimes they're visions of the future. Or warnings."

"What do you think it means?" Elya asked.

Kalael sighed. "I don't know." She stood suddenly leaving the room.

A moment passed. Then two. At the third Kalael returned with Azrael in tow. The Reaper was dressed in black pajama pants with skulls on them. His lack of shirt showcased his well-defined abs and biceps. And unsurprisingly, Speckers sat on his shoulders. Elya didn't let her gaze linger long. She wasn't going to ogle Kalael's husband.

"Kamille said you had a nightmare vision?"

"Nightmare vision is a good word for it," Elya muttered.

"Can you describe it?" Azrael asked. "In detail."

Elya explained her dream recalling every detail that she could. Unfortunately, it was a lot. She remembered it vividly. The Reaper listened with rapt attention to every detail and word she spoke of the dream. He did an impressive job of keeping his expression unreadable as she ended her description of the dream with how the woman's voice had echoed after she had awoken.

"I see," Azrael said.

"Do you know who the woman was?" Elya asked.

"I do," Azrael said.

"And?" Kalael asked.

"I won't disclose her identity. There's a reason it was kept from you Elya, and I trust her judgement on the matter. Just know that a lifelong friend is likely a very apt descriptor for her identity and leave it at that."

"But—"

"I'm sorry Elya, I know this whole thing is frustrating, and that you have a lot of questions but it's not my place to identify her."

Eyla sighed. "Fine. But what about the rest of the dream?"

"Definitely a warning," Azrael said. "The good news, however, is that you can avoid the future in your dream. Michael's death is preventable."

"How?" Elya asked.

The Reaper frowned. "How indeed?" He paced. "We don't even know how Michael ends up dead." He split himself in two. "Not really."

"Okay Thanatos," Kalael grabbed her husband's shoulders (identifiable by Speckers on his shoulder). "Let's not duplicate into dozens of you."

"Huh?" He looked at his duplicate. "Oh," the clone vanished. "Sorry, bad habit."

"You should try to get some rest," Kalael said to her. "Come on Than, you can do your thinking and pacing in our room so Elya can sleep."

Azrael nodded. "We'll solve this, Elya."

Kalael shook her head. "Try to get some sleep Elya, if you need anything you know where our room is. Zeke and Simone are home as well. Unfortunately, Dimitri, king of level-headed-decision-making, isn't back from the Mystic Summit yet."

"I have so many questions about that," Elya said without her usual enthusiasm. "I'll have to ask him when he's back."

"A good plan," Kalael said as she turned off the lights. "Goodnight," the door shut with a soft click.

Elya took a few calming breaths. She was fine. Everything was okay. It had been…well she wasn't sure if it was just a dream but whatever it was. It hadn't happened yet. And Azrael said it himself, Michael's death, if possible is preventable. They'd just have to figure out how. Or more aptly try to ensure she makes the right decisions.

She laid back under the cover, mind drifting to her nightmare. Elya had the distinct feeling she wouldn't be falling back asleep anytime soon. She didn't know the archangel well, and he had banned her from Heaven and seeing her best friends, but that didn't mean Elya wanted him dead. How was she, a mere mortal with a Celestial level tripping problem, supposed to prevent the death of Michael? Heaven's mightiest warrior?

Twenty-Four

While Elya loved the Reaper family, they could be a bit much sometimes. Especially given her dream the night before. She needed a break from the walking on eggshells Kalael was doing. And the constant pacing of Azrael. In addition to that, she just needed to clear her head. And the best solution for that was taking a walk for some solitude. In all honesty, she wasn't sure where she was… The Coffee Shop was between realms. She knew she managed to enter through Kansas City, but Kalael first entered through New York City.

The place didn't look big enough to be New York, but it was certainly bigger than Kansas City. Maybe it wasn't wise of her to wander alone through a city she didn't know, but it wasn't the first time she did something Gabriel considered reckless, and it likely would be far from the last.

Over the years, she'd certainly found her fair share of trouble. If not for the Deadly Sins, she'd probably be dead a thousand times over, if not more, and that wasn't even counting all the times Satan, Gabriel, or Raphael came to her rescue.

(Practically growing up in Hell meant she had to keep secrets. It meant that, from a young age, she had to be careful of things like spending the night with her friends, lest she trip into Hell. Her only friends growing up were Raphael, Satan, and Gabriel until she was eleven. That was when she first met Zeerlo and befriended him – not that he'd admit it. After Zeerlo, she met Charlie, and knowing Charlie made all the difference in her life. Elya smiled, remembering the eight-year-old blond who could speak languages long considered dead. Back then, he was essentially a goofy kid, and now he was the same goofball with a mastery in torture, blackmail, and lying.)

Only now, she didn't think it would be so simple to get out of trouble. A Celestial war was brewing and somehow, she'd come to be at the center of it all. And if the woman in the dream was telling the truth, her decisions would have an impact on how that war ended. And on whether Michael lived or died. No pressure.

Snap.

Glancing around her, Elya searched for the source of the noise and spotted a solid black cat walking down an alleyway. A solid black cat with familiar silver eyes and a bright red collar... Dread settled in the pit of her stomach as she hoped against hope it wasn't the cat she thought it was. But as it moved, the shadows seemed to dance, and when it leaped onto a dumpster, flames followed its trail.

Elya turned around. She needed to get back to the Coffee Shop.

"Meow."

Elya quickened her pace slightly, trying desperately to remember what it was that made Kalael's cat so dangerous. She knew the cat, Midnight, was a bad omen. She just couldn't for the life of her remember if it was seeing the cat or if had something to do with his meows.

Step, step, step. Soft footsteps sounded behind her. Elya turned, but nobody was there. Just Midnight, his tail waving behind him as his eyes glowed an eerie silver.

"Meow."

Elya continued, telling herself she was just being paranoid. She kept walking, telling herself that now was not the time to run. If she ran, she'd trip, and if she tripped, there was no telling what would happen. Not when she had seen Hell's black cat. Normally, she didn't mind black cats – all cats were angels in her opinion, just like all dogs – but Midnight was different. Midnight belonged to Pride, lived in Hell, and over it's 27 years in Hell, became its own type of celestial entity. No one knows how.

A shadow fell over her.

"Meow."

Elya ran.

If she tripped, then so be it. If she managed to land in Heaven or Hell, then she could tell someone what happened – about Midnight, the footsteps, and the shadow that fell over her. Everything grew quiet and still. Maybe she was just being paranoid after seeing Midnight… still, she kept running.

Her feet pounded against the pavement, her eyes searching for any indication the Coffee Shop was open to her, but it was nowhere in sight. Had she gone so far? Had it left? Was it possible for it to have disappeared when she had intentions of returning from where she left? What if she was trapped here? Was this the day she died? Question after question plagued her mind as she continued running.

"Meow."

She risked glancing behind her to see Midnight was following her. She was so focused on the cat that she didn't notice the man in front of her until she collided with him. Elya went sprawling backwards, only for a pair of arms to catch her, wrapping themselves under shoulders tightly. Elya squirmed. The arms holding her dragged her backward while the man in front of her just leered at her, as yet another man stepped out of the alleyway.

"Gabriel!" Elya screamed. "Raphael!" Her eyes watered, and her breathing quickened. "Michael, please—" a hand covered her mouth, muffling her screams for help.

"Meow."

As she continued to squirm, attempting to kick them, she managed to bite the hand over her mouth. Her mouth was freed, but the overall grips on her were solid. This was it. Her breathing became rapid. She couldn't get away, couldn't trip her way out of it. No Satan, no angels, no sins could rescue her this time. After everything, she was going to die, and with the poor impression she left on Michael, she was more than likely going to take up a residence in Hell with Satan. And she could *not* spend an eternity there.

As Elya continued to fight, her attempts growing weaker as she used more of her energy, she felt the temperature drop.

It was as though a cold front rolled in, the temperature in the alley dropping by 20 degrees. The shadows danced.

"Meow."

A breeze blew in, carrying with it a familiar sound: the flapping of large wings. The kind on the backs of the angels, or Satan and his sons. Elya glanced to the sky, searching hopefully, but there was no sign of any of them. The skies were empty. Her gaze dropped, taking her heart and her hope with it. As she began to lose all hope, she noticed a single gray feather flutter down, landing at the feet of the man not holding her.

"I suggest you put her down," a familiar voice said.

Relief flooded her. She had been so sure she was going to die, but he came to save her. Maybe she had panicked too soon. Elya calmed her breathing – she didn't know what was going to happen now, but It didn't matter. She knew one thing with certainty: she would live.

"And if we don't?" One of the men holding her asked.

A figure stepped out of the shadows, bright blue flames trailing his steps. "Then we'll have a problem." There was a familiar glint in Satan's gaze, the kind that promised suffering.

"Fine by me," one of the men said, aiming a gun to Satan's forehead. Where it touched his skin, the end of the pistol began to sizzle.

The Devil stepped forward and a shot rang out. He was undeterred, continuing to move forward. Gunshot after gunshot was fired, but the bullets merely bounced off their target. Human metals couldn't penetrate the skin of celestials – it was why they favored weapons forged in the fires of Hell.

The gun dropped. "What are you?"

"Ever wondered what the Devil looks like?" He gestured to himself, grinning devilishly. "Take a good look."

"What–" The man holding her dropped her to the ground.

Elya hissed as her knee hit the hard pavement. That was going to leave a bruise. She had never gotten into this situation before – well, not this close to dying. She'd been in plenty of sticky situations, but in the past, nobody had managed to ever hurt her. Even if it was a banged knee, usually the sins or angels interfered before that could happen. Maybe she was too reliant on them…. Sure, they had taught her fighting, but if her first instinct was to yell for help instead of grabbing one of the daggers she had spent years mastering, then something was wrong with this situation, and she needed to fix it.

Satan rolled his shoulders, the fires around him growing, trapping them all. The men screamed. Tilting his head to the side, Satan opened a small doorway in the fires. The man that had stepped in front of her tried to move, but the shadows came rushing toward him, dragging him back into the flames. He screamed, clawing at the ground, and vanished.

"Are you alright, Elya?"

She pulled her gaze from the morbid scene. "I've been better."

"Mind telling me what happened?" Satan asked.

"I took a walk, and then I heard a twig snap," Elya said. "Then I saw a cat, Midnight. He meowed at me, so I turned around."

Satan's eyes widened. "You saw Midnight? He was here?"

"Yeah," Elya shifted uncomfortably.

"And he meowed at you? How many times?"

"I don't know. Five, I think," Elya said.

His gaze searched hers. "Are you certain?"

"Yes."

He placed his hands on her shoulders. "Elya, it's important you be right about this. If Midnight gets to the sixth meow, the results are disastrous. Are you sure it was only five?"

Elya went silent. She thought back to the cat. The first time had been after she turned around, then again when she heard the footsteps. The third time was when the shadow fell over her. The fourth was when she was running, and the last time was when she called out for Gabriel and Raphael, so it was only five. She wracked her brain, trying to recall if it had meowed another time, but she came up short.

"Yes," Elya said at last, "only five."

Relief flooded his gaze. "Good." He released her shoulders. "Come on, let's get you back to Kalael."

Before Elya could ask questions, he steered her through the gateway he had created in his blue flames. She had never seen these flames before. Hell's fires tended to be blacker than these, with only the slightest hint of blue.

"How did you know I needed help?" Elya asked.

"My Father may be all knowing, but I have my ways," he shrugged. "And might I say, I was tempted to leave you—" he crossed his arms "—not calling for my help."

"Sorry, but it might seem weird to yell for Satan's help," Elya said.

"You need more training," he said. "Have Simone and Dimitri teach you hand to hand combat and see about getting Kalael to teach you to use a gun."

"A gun?" Elya frowned. "You're telling me that I should get a gun? The guy who says guns are for the weak – and Kalael because she likes them?"

"I will not compromise your safety," he said.

Elya nodded in acceptance.

(For all his talk, she knew Satan wouldn't let anything happen to her. Not something so mundane as murder, at least. He refused to let Zeerlo behead and gut her; he wasn't about to let mortals harm her. Especially not when he knew if something happened to her, it'd upset Kalael. That was one of the most important rules in the Afterlife: don't upset Kalael. Not simply because the woman herself could be terrifying – she could be – but because she was favored by Satan and married to Azrael and the archangels were her uncles. Elya knew Michael favored her too, which was quite an accomplishment, in Elya's opinion.)

"Come along," Satan said, turning in the direction of the coffee shop. "We best get you back to Kalael."

Elya frowned. It wasn't like Satan to willingly walk somewhere. He popped in and out of places constantly. Sure, he walked around Hell, but that was different. There, he was the king; nobody would think twice about him walking around. They'd still cower before him, and steer clear. But here, on Earth, he was nobody. Just a person. At least, as far as most people could tell. He tended to avoid being seen by people who couldn't respect him for his power. Unless, of course, he was making deals and getting people to trap themselves in Hell for eternity because they made the mistake of trusting the Devil.

Then again, maybe he didn't want to give Azrael the satisfaction he was bound to get out of seeing Satan pop in. Nobody was free of Azrael's spell, or whatever it was that announced their arrivals and departures.

Completely lost in thought, Elya didn't even realize they had made it back until she heard the familiar clang of the bell above the door announcing their arrival. She was barely through the door when she was assaulted with a hug from Kalael.

"Elya!" Kalael hugged her tighter. "Where were you?"

Elya frowned. "I wasn't gone that long, was I?"

"Two hours," Kalael said.

Elya's eyes widened. She hadn't been expecting that. How had she lost that much time? She wasn't even that far down the road – or was she?

"I went for a walk and ran into some trouble," she shrugged. "Luckily, your dad came to the rescue."

Kalael looked past Elya to Satan. "He did?"

"Yes, I did," Satan said pointedly.

Kalael released Elya and hugged the Devil. "Thanks for bringing her back."

Satan smiled. It seemed a little off, genuine without the lingering darkness beneath. It was the kind of smile you wouldn't expect from Satan, though Elya supposed that was what Kalael did to her father. It wasn't surprising, not really. He had always made himself clear when saying Kalael came first. If Kalael asked it of him, he'd give up his throne in Hell and lived under a park bench, and no one in Afterlife would even blink Whether Kalael realized the power she held over her father, that was another matter.

"Yes, well," Satan straightened his suit. "I best be going."

Kalael smiled. "Bye, dad."

"Yes, I shall see you another time, princess," Satan said.

Elya frowned. Something was off with Satan's behavior. Was this threat to destroy Hell bothering him that much? It could be, she supposed. Hell may have been his punishment, but he was brothers with the demons, or at least some of them, and there was the reality that if he didn't have Hell, he'd probably go insane spending all his time with the Mercenaries. No sane person could spend extended periods of time with Zeerlo and his brothers without facing repercussions for it.

"So, you needed rescuing?" Kalael asked teasingly.

"Unfortunately," Elya said.

Kalael laughed. "Been there." She pulled out a metal box. "I had been planning to save this for a Christmas present," she flipped the lid open, "but I think it's needed." She turned the box around to show Elya.

"A handgun?" Elya asked.

"I had it custom made," Kalael explained. "It can fire regular bullets and the special bullets Thanatos and I've worked on developing. It's nothing overly fancy because it's practical, but it's a got a few touches. It's got your name engraved, of course, and we made it so no one but you can pick it up without getting burnt, unless you grant them permission to grab it, of course."

Elya took the gun in her hand carefully, like it could explode at any second; it was simultaneously exhilarating and terrifying. Kalael just held the gun with such ease, like she was born with one in her hand.

"Legally, you're old enough, and you should buy your own gun," Kalael said, passing her the box, "but since this wasn't exactly made by humans, we'll circumvent the rules a little. I know a guy who can get the gun registered properly, they'll run a background check, and we'll get you a carry permit," Kalael grinned. "So, it'll be legal, just a little unorthodox. We'll also get you some proper instruction."

Elya smiled. "Thanks."

"Anytime," Kalael said.

"Ooh," Azrael popped into the room, "what rules are we bending?"

"None," Elya said quickly.

With no warning, Azrael's body split, a near exact replica emerging from himself. The only indication this wasn't one of his clones and was, in fact, his twin was his coloring. Loki never seemed content with human skin tones. He wore them on occasion, but he preferred colors like his current turquoise with pink hair and eyes.

"Give a guy a warning next time!" Azrael rubbed his arms, disgruntled.

Loki frowned. "There isn't time for such frivolous and unimportant things as warnings." He turned to Elya. "You're lying skills are grossly inadequate."

Elya startled. "What? I'm totally a great liar."

Loki scoffed. "Maybe for an amateur. By the time I could talk, I could weave lies so sweet even the best of liars believed my words."

Elya rolled her eyes at this ridiculous standard. "Sorry, we can't all be the Norse *god of lies*."

"No need to take offense," Loki said. "I can easily correct this."

She raised a brow. "You're going to teach me to lie?"

Loki snorted. "No. I will simply pass to you my ability to lie. Teaching you to lie would be a waste of time and effort," he shuddered, "especially when transferring my lying capabilities would be far simpler."

Elya raised a brow. "And how are you planning to do that?"

Loki placed a hand to his throat and pulled it away slowly, a silver string of light coming with it. "With this," he said dangling the glowing string. "I have an extra vocal cord that is purely for lying. It allows me to tell any lie convincingly to anyone, unless they can't be lied to like Michael, Satan, Gabriel, the Boss and myself, of course. As much as Satan would like to make you think his sons can detect any lie, their abilities do not extend to me, just as my abilities don't extend to Thanatos. He has an obvious tell."

"Are you saying that string is your extra vocal cord?" Elya asked.

"Yes," Loki said simply.

"We're immortal," Azrael shrugged. "It'll grow back in a few minutes."

Elya's stomach churned. "That's disgusting."

"That may be so, but in your position, you cannot afford to wait for anything else. You must be able to lie, Elya, and lie well," Loki grinned. "Now, say goodbye to your honesty and say hello to having a silver tongue."

"Looks more like a silver vocal cord," Elya said.

"Both, actually." Loki stuck his tongue out, and sure enough, there was a silver sheen when it caught the light. "The vocal cord just coincides, but honestly that doesn't sound nearly as good."

"Right. So how exactly are you planning on transferring that vocal cord to me, and is it gross?" Elya asked.

"Not at all," Loki grinned. "You merely take the vocal cord like so—" he moved it in front of Elya's throat "—and insert it same as it was removed."

Before Elya could get the chance to protest, Loki placed the glowing stringy muscle against her throat. It was cold and felt oddly slimy. She really didn't want to know why that was. Her throat itched and burned – it felt like something was crawling through her skin, being pulled into her throat. She reached for her throat, only for Loki to grab her wrist. Clearly, she wasn't getting out of whatever weird thing this was. A moment passed, then two. Finally, the scratching feeling subsided. Her throat no longer burned. Instead, the burning sensation was replaced by a cool feeling, as though she just downed a cold water.

"There! Not so bad," Loki said.

Elya scoffed. "Speak for yourself."

Loki shrugged. "That may be so. But now you can do something you never could: lie like you're a goddess."

"Loki!" Azrael snapped.

"What?" Loki bristled, spinning to face his twin. "I'm Sin incarnate. Blasphemy is under my jurisdiction."

Azrael shook his head. "You never learn."

Loki shrugged. "I'm Sin, I am Freedom, I am Mischief, and I am Chaos. If you can't accept that, then the Boss will gladly take your feelings into account and assign me elsewhere." He huffed, turning back to Elya. "Now lie, And make it a whopper."

"I robbed the national treasury," Elya said.

Loki nodded. "Beautiful. Not a hint of a tell remains in you. Your voice remains calm. Your eyes don't go searching to make up a lie. It's delectable! The lies you can tell!" He became misty-eyed with possibility.

"Okay," Kalael cut in, "enough of that." She placed a hand on Elya's shoulder. "We're going to go practice our shooting, and you, Loki, are going to get that glint in your eye under control."

Elya didn't get a chance to ask what Kalael meant before she was being steered from the room. She could've asked in the hall, but something told her she didn't want to know what Kalael meant by the 'glint' in Loki's eye.

Twenty-Five

There was something unnerving about Loki. For someone who just lazed on the couch with a book, he seemed scarily like he knew things he shouldn't. And he likely did. There was intelligence hidden in his gaze, along with mischief and a desire for fun, but there was no malice. Nothing that indicated that this was Sin incarnate, that this entity had stood as Satan's right hand in the rebellion. At least, as far as she could tell.

"Alright," Loki announced to the room at large. "I've made my decision."

Azrael gasped. "You made a decision without me?"

"I made a decision which has little effect on you," Loki said. "Therefore, I was perfectly within my grounds."

"What decision?" Kalael asked.

"I'm going to do what should have been done long ago and teach this poor child how to sky travel properly." He gestured to Elya. "She is an embarrassment, and she needs to learn it properly before she falls through the wrong crack and ends up somewhere she'll get hurt."

Elya frowned. "What do you mean by sky travel?" She chose to ignore the comment about her being an embarrassment for now.

"This is precisely what I mean. Sky traveling, Elya, is an art and a form of transportation far superior to the shadow travel my brother does, or the teleportation done by the angels. Azrael is limited to shadows, the angels can easily block each other out, but sky travelers like us, Elya, are not bound by such pitiful limitations. If you want to waltz into the Mystic Summit, not even their barriers capable of keeping the angels and Satan and his demons out will prevent your entrance. Enter uninvited into meetings of the Intergalactic Space Confederation! I dare them to try and stop you. You are limited by *nothing*." Loki paused, then frowned. "Or at least you will be once you master the technique. You have an innate gift for it, so it'll speed the process along."

"You mean you can teach me not to trip into Heaven and Hell?"

Loki frowned. "I'm afraid that wording is a bit difficult to answer. I can teach you how to keep from traveling elsewhere when you trip, so long as you are not in the middle of sky traveling when you do so. As it is, tripping while sky traveling can land you in different times, dimensions, places, and leave you injured."

Elya frowned. "Maybe I should stick with tripping into Hell – and sneezing, and startling, and, well, the list goes on for a while."

Loki scoffed in disgust, pity, embarrassment… it was hard to tell. "Absolutely not. We are doing this lesson. Sky traveling is supposed to be skillful and graceful, neither of which you are. We, unfortunately, do not have the time to help you become graceful on your feet, but we will get there eventually. For now, I will help you to stay put when you trip, or whatever else causes you to accidentally walk." He clasped his hands behind his back. "Furthermore, we will be teaching you to actually *use* the ability. Once you have basic understanding, it'll be easier to control. And as I said, with time, we can teach you how to be a picture of grace as you walk."

Zeke snorted. "A picture of grace? Are we still talking about Elya? Next to Fiend, she's the clumsiest person I know. No offense."

Elya shrugged. "I mean, you're not wrong."

"Only because she's yet to learn to properly sky travel. She's not meant for the ground – she's meant to be walking the back doors of the universe. To travel galaxies in minutes." Loki's eyes glinted. "Sky traveling is a rare skill, and I shall not stand by and let her gift go to waste a moment longer. Elya will learn, and that's that."

"You seem to walk fine on the ground," Simone said.

Loki ignored Simone. "You're a natural sky traveler, Elya. By default, that means I have to like you, but I dislike your attitude." He crossed his arms. "You should have more confidence in yourself. You can do what few others can. Plus, sky traveling is easy. Believe me, I learned to sky travel before I learned to walk on the ground."

Azrael shrugged. "He's right. His balance was so bad we often just absorbed him into me, and I walked us everywhere. That was before he discovered he could sky travel. Then, I learned shadow travel," he laughed. "It was a nightmare for the Boss trying to reign us in once we could fly, sky travel, and shadow travel."

Loki chuckled. "An understatement." He clasped his hands together. "Enough reminiscing about the past, though. I have a pupil to teach."

Elya shifted. "Why do I get the feeling I should be concerned?"

Loki grinned devilishly. "Because you should be. Now everyone else: out. My pupil and I must begin lessons."

Kalael raised a brow. "A please wouldn't kill you."

"Out!" Loki gestured to the kitchen door. "Or I swear, I'll teach her on the roof."

"Please no roof," Elya said.

"Whatever." Azrael rolled his eyes. "We're going to head out for squirrel hunting. Be back whenever."

"I think I'll stay, help out if I can," Dimitri said. "I may not be able to sky travel, but I know a thing or two about mastering difficult powers."

Loki huffed. "Ugh, fine."

"See you later, if you're gone before we're back," Azrael said.

"Bye guys," Elya smiled.

Pride pulled her in for a hug. "Be careful. I know Loki can be odd, but you've just gained a lifelong ally in him by accepting his lessons."

"I'll be fine. Promise."

Azrael ushered out his family (minus Loki and Dimitri) leaving the three of them alone in the dining area of the coffee shop. If you could call it that. Yes, there were tables, but there was also a large plasma screen on the wall, six game consoles hooked up to it, a nice couch across from it, and a couple of recliners. Then again, when you ran a coffee shop that never had any human customers, she supposed you could run and decorate it however you liked.

"Now, sky traveling is easy to grasp a basic concept of. You were born with an innate ability, so I believe we can have you mastering this within the year," he conjured a whiteboard from thin air, "even with the inevitable delays gathering an army and the eventual fighting will cause."

Elya frowned. "A whole year?"

"Be thankful you have talent for it and I'm a promising teacher." He wrote Sky traveling 101 across the board. "Others would take years to be able to do what you do."

"Oh."

He smiled. "You have a gift, Elya. That's the most important thing for you to understand. It is not a curse. You can transverse the universe."

"So, how do I control it?" Elya asked.

"Focus." He wrote it across the board. "It's the key to everything related to sky traveling. Focus on your current surrounding. If you don't lose control, what usually makes you accidentally walk won't trigger that response anymore. Focus on an image of the location you wish to go, and you can transport yourself there. With time, you will be able to do this without even an image of your destination; you'll learn to travel with only a general idea of where you're going. And once you've truly mastered it, you'll be able to travel to places in the universe without so much as an idea of where you're going."

Elya frowned. "That sounds sketchy."

Loki chuckled. "Maybe. Now, no better time to learn than the present! I want you to picture a location you know well. Make sure it's a clear image."

"Maybe we should have her picture the cemetery across the road," Dimitri suggested. "That way, if something goes wrong, it'll be easier for you to find her."

Loki raised a brow. "I can focus on people's energy signatures to find them, but fine." He crossed his arms. "As you are just starting, I suggest you close your eyes as you picture the location you're going to."

"Right." Elya closed her eyes, picturing the cemetery across the road. A familiar sensation of rushing water engulfed her. Quite soon, her feet felt as though they were on solid ground. She opened her eyes to see Dimitri and Loki still staring at her.

"You're trying too hard," Loki said.

"Maybe relax a little when you walk," Dimitri suggested. "If you're too tense, your energy won't be able to flow. If it can't flow, it'll be incapable of surrounding you and transporting you to your desired location."

Loki nodded. "He's essentially correct. Sky traveling is in your nature; it's as much a part of you as your blonde hair. Keep calm, don't try to force it, and allow it to happen naturally."

"I can do that," Elya said.

Again, she shut her eyes. This time, she took deep breaths to calm herself, an image of the cemetery across the road at the forefront of her mind. Again, she felt the water consume her, and her feet hit ground. Elya opened her eyes to see she had made it to just outside the coffee shop doors.

"I suppose it's a start," Loki said from behind her, Dimitri next to him.

Elya spun around. "How did–? Never mind."

Dimitri smiled. "You did well, Elya."

She frowned. "I didn't make it to the cemetery."

"No," Loki said. "But you've at least managed to will yourself to sky travel, and that is the first step in mastering it."

"He's right," Dimitri grinned. "You've got a start, now let's finish this."

"Focus, Elya," Loki said softly, "on the cemetery. Remain calm, and as soon as you feel that watery sensation, embrace it. Step *into* it, and before you know it, you'll be able to take a step forward on land and walk the waters of the sky."

Elya nodded, taking in Loki's every word. She could do this – she knew she could. She had been sky traveling into Heaven and Hell since she was six by accident. Had just teleported from inside to outside (no she didn't travel to her desired destination, but it gave her the reassurance she needed).

Mustering her determination, she took a deep breath and once again closed her eyes, focusing on the image of the cemetery across the road. Water engulfed her and she tried to take Loki's advice and step with it… Her feet hit the ground. She opened her eyes, the metal gates of the cemetery in front of her.

"I did it!" Elya gasped.

"You did."

Elya spun on her heel to see Dimitri and Loki stood behind her, both grinning. Loki stepped forward, placing his hands on her shoulders. He nodded, a hint of pride in his gaze, before he stepped back.

"Tell me, were you aiming for the entrance of the cemetery or did you not focus on somewhere specific? Either way it is fine, as I did not specify. I'm merely curious," Loki said.

"I was sort of picturing the whole cemetery," Elya said.

Loki nodded. "Good. Now I want you to picture the coffee shop kitchen. The spot just in front of the refrigerator."

Elya shrugged, repeating the earlier process, only this time with the kitchen in mind. When the feel of rushing water vanished, she found herself in the exact spot she had envisioned. She grinned, turning around to see both Loki and Dimitri nodding their approval.

"Nice," Dimitri said.

"It is sufficient for now. I suspect if you can get a point so narrowed down, then it will be a simple matter when it comes time for you to do long distance." Loki's hair and eyes turned green. "Yes, you've done well. I would prefer we could work on this until you master it, but unfortunately, your mission interferes." He smiled. "Just know that once this threat is taken care of, you and I are going to be having lessons three hours a day every day until you master the ability."

Dimitri snorted. "You sure you could handle that much effort?"

Loki rolled his eyes. "Whatever." He turned to Elya. "I want you to go to *Starbucks* and get me a latte. I don't care what kind, so long as it's a grande."

"Excuse me?" Dimitri raised a brow. "Did you forget I run a coffee shop?"

Loki snorted. "That may be so, but you are not Starbucks, and I desire to see if Elya can make it there and back."

Dimitri shrugged. "By all means."

Elya frowned. She didn't have the slightest clue where the nearest Starbucks was, though she supposed she could theoretically envision the drive thru in Lawrence or maybe another one she'd been to. She just hoped it'd be enough. She didn't want to fail, and who knew what'd happen to her if she tripped? Loki had said it himself; she could end up anywhere. That thought alone was terrifying. Combined with the fact she was prone to tripping, she was half tempted to just pretend she tried and stay put. Only, she couldn't do that. Her mother didn't teach her to quit, and Satan sure as Hell would never allow it. Closing her eyes, she focused on the image of Starbucks, and the rushing water engulfed her once more. When it stopped, she opened her eyes to find herself outside a Starbucks she had been to a couple of times in college.

Smiling, Elya walked inside. There wasn't a line, so getting a hot chocolate for herself and coffee for Loki was quick. Once she left, two scalding drinks in hand, she walked carefully out of sight before allowing the watery feeling – one that she was becoming surprisingly accustomed to – to rush over her. She was still worried she'd fail, terrified to know what would happen if she tripped, but somehow, she was a little more at ease. She gained a slight confidence in her ability as she replaced the image of one coffee shop with another. Again, she was consumed with the feel of water.

"Well done," Loki's voice said smoothly.

Elya's eyes snapped open. "I did it?"

Loki chuckled. "Yes. Congratulations Elya, you are now officially a sky traveler in training." He took his latte. "Keep at this rate, and you'll be a master in no time."

Elya grinned. "Thanks." She hoped he was right, but she wasn't so sure. There was no saying her recent walks weren't a fluke. She could still fail.

Loki set his coffee down. "Now that we've done a practical lesson and gone over the basic knowledge, let's go over some theory." He handed Elya a notebook. "Take notes, there will be a quiz at the end and a test after a few more lessons."

Elya sighed. She just finished school and yet he wanted her to study like she was still in college. At least it was only one class, sort of. Flipping open the notebook, Elya sat on the couch and listened as Loki went into full professor mode. He began a lengthy lecture on the ins and outs of sky traveling. He was a good teacher, which was surprising, but she wasn't going to complain. Who knew? Maybe by the time the lessons were over, she'd be capable of walking without tripping. That'd be nice, not tripping into Hell constantly – well, it'd be nice to stop tripping in general, though she sincerely doubted she'd ever become the picture of grace Loki seemed to envision.

It was weird if she thought about it, that she had an ability that Loki had. He was the embodiment of chaos, Sin incarnate.

As far as she knew, none of the other immortals she had met had the ability… Shadow travel and teleportation, sure, but sky traveling, that was something only they possessed. So, what did it mean for her that she could sky travel? Was she destined to cause chaos wherever she went like he did? What was it about her and Loki that allowed them to sky travel? What commonality could they possibly have that didn't overlap with anyone else in Afterlife? That had to be it, didn't it? They had something in common, a singular trait no other in Afterlife possessed which allowed them to sky travel. Only she had no clue as to what, and if she was honest, she wasn't sure Loki knew either.

Twenty-Six

Her short break at The Coffee Shop had been nice, she certainly felt re-energized and she'd learned to get a little control over her tripping. But after three days, Elya was more than ready to continue her journey to gather an army. She rose at dawn and put her next destination into the GPS and she was off.

Driving through the country was both relaxing and nerve-wracking. She had only a vague idea where she was going, GPS wasn't always reliable, and she felt as though she'd been driving far longer than she was supposed to be. Frustrated, Elya pulled into an open field as soon as she saw a turn into one. Climbing out of the car, she began searching her surroundings. The property included several large barns, and a long, white picket fence seemed to run along the edge and through various portions of it. Acre after acre of land, with what appeared to be hundreds of horses grazing in the grass.

Even from the distance, those horses appeared bigger than any she'd seen before. Not like Clydesdales, but more like impressive thoroughbreds with a little more height than most, and far more muscle than even the most muscular of racehorses. Her gaze fell on a metal sign above a gate that told her everything she need to know. *Apocalypse Horse Ranch.* This was the home to Azrael's brothers, the other three riders of the apocalypse.

Slowly, her gaze drifted toward her car as realization sank in. She wasn't trespassing on just anyone's land, she was trespassing on War and Conquest's territory. And Famine's, he'd be there as well. Elya's hand drifted to her side where her Hell-forged dagger rested. Hopefully, she wouldn't need it, but just in case.

The sound of thundering hooves came pounding toward her, and Elya turned to see three figures advancing quickly on horseback – white, red and black. By far the biggest horses she'd seen since arriving. The horses circled her, closing in around her until they came to a stop, each horse turned broadside, surrounding her. The men dismounted.

"What are you doing here?" The rider of the black horse asked. His eyes were a dark forest green, his hair a sandy blond; his jaw was square, and his nose was a little thin.

"I'm here to ask for your help," Elya said.

"With what?" The rider of the red horse asked, arms crossed. His eyes were honey brown, his hair light brown, and his face was more angular than the first rider's.

Elya exhaled. "There's a threat to the Afterlife. Someone has set out to destroy Heaven and Hell. Satan sent me to gather as many people as possible to help."

The first rider frowned. "Get out. We want nothing to do with Satan and his ilk."

"Agreed," the second rider said. "The last time Satan came 'round here ended in death for my nephew."

The third and final rider frowned. "Now is not the time to be petty." He glared at his brothers. "If there is a threat to Afterlife, then it is our duty to help."

"I'm not helping no city girl, especially one that works for Satan," the first rider snarled.

"So that's it?" Elya said. "You won't even hear me out?"

The first rider crossed his arms. "We won't."

"Famine!" The third rider warned, his blue eyes going from warm to cold. "Put your personal issues aside for a minute."

The first rider – well, third if the Bible was correct, frowned. "Whatever."

"I suppose you're right, Conquest," the second rider, War said.

"So, you'll help? Elya asked.

"We absolutely will not!" Famine snarled.

Conquest grabbed Famine's shoulder. "Listen here, *brother—*" he spit the word as though it were poison in his mouth. "We are going to at least give her a chance."

Famine's eyes turned black. "Satan killed MY son!"

"We know," Conquest said softly. "Believe me, I know. And Satan deserves to rot in one of those cells in Hell for it, but we can't change the past. Afterlife needs us, and we never turn our backs on it when called."

Famine frowned. "The Boss hasn't called us forth, *Satan* has through this–" he eyed her critically "–child."

"Afterlife needs your help," Elya pled.

"Very well," War rolled his shoulders back. "You want our help? Then prove you deserve it."

"What?" Elya asked.

"I only fight alongside those who are worthy," War shrugged. "Prove to me your worth on the battlefield – a duel between you and myself. You won't win, but manage to impress me and you'll have myself and my brothers at your side in this so-called battle for Afterlife."

"What?" Famine bristled. "Hell no! I am not doing anything that helps Satan. It's thanks to him and his children I no longer have a son!"

"If she proves worthwhile, you will join in the fight," War said matter-of-factly. "We fight as four, Famine, whether you like it or not."

Famine glared. "It wasn't your son who was killed!"

"It wasn't," War said simply.

Famine muttered under his breath, his frustration evident. Elya couldn't blame him, not really. If she had lost a child because of Satan, she'd probably be acting the same way. And while she could sympathize with Famine, she couldn't let it cloud her judgment. Afterlife was in danger, and they'd need all four horsemen to save it.

"So, I need to beat War to get your help?" Elya asked.

Famine scoffed. "Don't flatter yourself, only Michael has ever bested War with the sword, and few others have even come close to matching him."

Conquest grinned. "If you last five minutes, then we'll help."

"Don't worry," War chuckled. "I'll hold back."

If she wasn't aware of how bad she was with the sword, Elya would've been offended. As it stood, she knew she was bad with it, and if they were willing to give her increased odds, miniscule as they were, she'd take them. She wanted to do well, after all. To earn their respect – even Famine's – and get them to help against the threat to Afterlife willingly. Not because Conquest or War was forcing him.

"Do you have a sword?" Conquest asked.

Elya nodded, drawing her sword as she stepped in front of War. He regarded her quietly before drawing his own. Their gazes locked as they assumed high guard.

War was quick to take the offensive and advance; Elya stepped back, moving into a guard. Her breathing evened as her continuous lessons with Satan and Zeerlo came rushing back. The corner of War's mouth twitched into a smirk. His eyes darkened. He lunged, and Elya pivoted, barely avoiding War's blade. War didn't seem impressed as he made a diagonal cut. Elya deflected, the sound of clashing metal ringing around them. She passed back only for War to thrust his blade toward her again. She tried to dodge, only for the tip of his sword to hit her in the shin.

Elya winced, reaching down to her shin – she pulled her hand away to see blood. Gritting her teeth, she stood, tightening her grip on the hilt of her sword. She was not going to throw the sword around randomly like she did with Zeerlo. The entire afterlife, the fate of existence depended on this fight. They couldn't win without War and Conquest. Their back and forth continued in silence, Elya constantly on the defensive.

She was doing surprisingly well – at least, she was until she nearly tripped and found her side meeting the sharpened edge of War's sword. Elya grimaced, clutching her side. Blood seeped through her fingers.

"Yield," War ordered.

"No," Elya gritted through her teeth.

"Very well." War resumed his stance.

Elya took a breath and went on the offensive this time; she lunged toward War, and he pivoted. Their swords once again clashed. He had the advantage of greater strength – he knocked Elya's sword from her hands. As the sword went flying, he caught it in his free hand. Before she could get away, Elya found her neck trapped between two sharpened blades.

"Do you yield now?" War asked.

Elya huffed. "I yield."

War grinned. "Good." Flipping both swords, he placed his own back in its sheath. He maneuvered her own a little more, getting a feel for it. "It's a very well-balanced sword. And you fought valiantly. You are surprisingly skilled, and for that you will have our aid."

"*What?*" Famine gaped.

"She held her own," War said.

"Unbelievable," Famine muttered, storming off.

War sighed. "I'll go talk to him." He handed Elya her sword, following silently after his brother.

"That was awful," Elya said.

Conquest chuckled. "No sane person would willingly go on the wrong end of War's blade. But you clearly were desperate."

Elya grimaced. "Understatement."

He gestured to a bale of straw. "Have a seat, I'll get you stitched up."

"You know first aid?" Elya asked.

Conquest shrugged. "Well enough."

She studied the horseman silently. He was quiet and methodical as he pulled out a first aid kit, preparing to stich her wounds. There was something in his gaze that spoke of a dark past – of pain, suffering, and loss. But there was also something else, the tiniest hint of hope.

He pushed his Stetson hat back just a tad, and Elya got lost in thought. Conquest was the only reason she had been able to convince War to help, and hopefully, between the two of them, they'd convince Famine as well. They needed all the help they could get to face this unknown threat. She was glad he was willing to help her out, both then and now. He didn't know her, so he had no reason to… Though, he felt oddly familiar, as though she should know him. Like she *did* know him.

"You did really well," Conquest said pulling out a needle, thread, and peroxide.

Elya scoffed. "I didn't land a single hit."

"You still held your own against War. Not many can." Conquest dipped the needle into the peroxide. "Especially someone as young as you." Elya hissed at the sting of peroxide as Conquest poured it onto her wounds. "You should be proud of yourself, Elya."

Elya smiled. "Thanks."

Conquest smiled. "You've earned War's respect today and mine as well." He threaded the needle and worked it through her skin, stitching it together in neat, even rows. "Not many can." He tied off the thread and snipped it.

Elya grimaced as Conquest moved to her shin. "Ahh."

"Sorry," Conquest cringed. "Unfortunately, I don't have my sister's healing talents." Conquest stitched her shin together. "But thankfully, I do know a thing or two about first aid."

Elya laughed. "Good thing or I'd be in trouble."

"War knows it as well," Conquest said, eyes not leaving his line of stitching. "And while he may act cold, he would never let anyone in need of help go unaided." His eyes flicked to her as he finished her shin. "Not anyone as innocent as yourself."

"Well, he definitely had no problems hurting me," Elya muttered.

"Sometimes my brother forgets his own strength," Conquest sighed, grabbing a cloth to clean her forehead. "He is War, just as I am Conquest. Satan's sons are Wrath and Lust… I'm certain you have an idea of how it goes."

"Zeerlo did break my wrist once over me not sharing my skittles," Elya said.

Conquest snorted. "That's a little aggressive."

"Oh yeah," Elya laughed. "You should have seen Satan. He absolutely freaked."

"He cares for you," Conquest said.

Elya snorted. "I wouldn't go that far."

"I would." Conquest put his sewing supplies back in the first aid kit. "Satan is complicated, but when it comes to those he cares about, he's not as good at hiding it as he thinks," he smirked. "We may have our problems, but I'm willing to admit he has his good qualities. For Kalael, he swallowed his pride, went to Heaven and, before his Father and before his brothers, he got on his knees and begged to keep her safe."

"What is it about Kalael?" Elya asked. "I mean, I like her well enough, but the way everyone talks about her," she sighed, trailing off. "I've known her since I was eleven and I feel like I'm missing something."

"As exposed to the supernatural world as you are Elya, you still have a disconnect. One the rest of us do not. Kalael is pure in ways no child of Satan has right to be. She wasn't planned for – not by Satan, at least. But Consequence decided enough was enough, and she went to their Father, and so Kalael was born. Pride incarnate, only pure and good. When I first met her, she was broken and too stubborn to realize. Satan's greatest fear is that Kalael won't be able to defend herself and will be used as a weapon. This resulted in him breaking her."

"I remember," Elya grimaced. "Sometimes I have nightmares." Her tone darkened. "All I hear are Kalael's screams."

"He doesn't understand love," Conquest said. "He understands power. He should never have left her to the demons – Kalael was too pure for them. She came out of it stronger physically, but emotionally, Kalael's never been the same." He shook his head. "You should have seen her when Azrael first brought her here to heal. The horses wouldn't go near her, she was constantly threatening to kill us, and the poor girl didn't have a clue just how broken she was until it was too late. Once my nephew died, the dam broke and she was able to feel again."

Elya raised a brow. "So, because of Kalael, Zeerlo and co. attacked your ranch and killed Famine's son? Which is why you, War, and Famine were against working alongside him?"

"There is far more to the story than you know," Conquest forced a smile, "but you needn't worry. Kalael is not your concern. Your job is gathering an army to save Afterlife."

"It's not exactly easy." Elya clicked her tongue. "I'm Satan's unwilling intern."

Conquest snorted. "That doesn't mean you can't convince people to help you. You convinced War you're worthwhile on the battlefield, and you've got me on your side for this."

"Yeah, and Famine still wants me dead," Elya said.

"He's bitter about the loss of his son," Conquest shrugged. "But that doesn't mean you should give up." His eyes glinted knowingly. "You have no idea of the power you hold, Elya."

"Power?" Elya scoffed. "I'm just some girl who keeps tripping into Satan's throne room, so he decided to make use out of her."

"You're more than that. Satan willingly humbled himself for Kalael's sake; he went to great lengths to bring Zeerlo back from the dead; for Fiend, he learned more than basic first aid; for Twist, he pays the mortal government millions to look the other way when they catch him in their systems; for Shredder, he went through the efforts to reduce the risk of the Mansion burning down and even bought his own construction company so the boy could continue his cooking endeavors. Hellas is the reason he learned to drive; the boy wouldn't sleep unless he was in a car. He sent one son away to be raised by humans who would be capable of loving and caring for him because he didn't believe himself to be capable."

Elya raised her brow. "What does any of that have to do with me?"

"I'm getting there," Conquest chuckled. "Satan loves each of his children and he shows it in the little things. He'll do whatever it takes to protect Kalael, to keep his sons alive and free of confinement. To give them their best life."

"They work for him as mercenaries," Elya deadpanned.

"They love to kill," Conquest countered.

"Can't deny that," Elya laughed.

"Good. Then hopefully you'll realize that your tripping problem could put you anywhere in the world, the *universe*. Mortal plain, immortal… far more places than just Heaven and Hell. Satan interferes with your ability. Using his own powers to redirect you, he closed off all locations except Heaven and Hell until you could control your powers. Sure, on occasion you'd slip through the cracks, but you didn't ever fall anywhere dangerous."

"Satan did that?" Elya's brows drew together. "But why?"

"You're no less important to him than any of his children, Elya." Conquest offered a smile. "You'll never be Kalael or Zeerlo, but neither will you ever be Envy, Shredder, Twist, Fiend or Hellas. He cares for each of them in his own way and I have it on good authority he cares for you equally."

"How do you know?" Elya asked.

"He gave you two daggers and a sword," Conquest said. "One dagger forged in Hell, and the other was enchanted, along with your sword by the looks of things."

"Wait," her eyes grew, "they're enchanted? With what? By who?"

"The sword? I'd recognize that work anywhere." Conquest frowned. "It's been spelled by Alex. What it does, though, I can't get a reading on. You'd have to ask either Satan himself, or someone a little more familiar with Alex's work. That won't be easy. Alex has been imprisoned for millennia, and is insane to top it off. In fact, other than his prison warden, the only one who really knows anything about Alex is Michael."

Elya straightened up, interested. "Michael?"

"He and Michael fought alongside each other in more than a few battles, back when Alex was still sane. Every Tyver crown royal gets an angel guardian for their first battle. As it so happens, Michael usually volunteers because the Tyver warriors were one of the three peoples who originally taught him war, alongside the Arthenians and humans."

"Arthenians?"

"An alien people of the planet Arthenia. They have a complicated history with humanity," Conquest cringed. "And a bloody one at that."

"And Tyvers, what are they exactly?"

Conquest frowned. "To be honest, few people actually know. From what I understand – and bear in mind a lot of this is hearsay – but, supposedly, they originated from humans, then were taken by Mother Nature and altered to have powers, along with the Tyver spirit they were given. Tyvers were given the purpose of guarding humanity and their planet."

"What's the Tyver spirit?"

Conquest shook his head. "You're curious, Elya, and that's not a bad thing, but I'm afraid you're asking questions even I don't know the answer to."

Elya nodded. "Okay, then what about my dagger?"

He grinned. "The dagger looks to have been spelled by Hel."

"Hell? As in Hell? How could a place spell a dagger?"

"No, one 'L'. Hel as in Loki's daughter of Norse myth," Conquest said.

"Oh, I guess that makes sense."

"Yes," Conquest chuckled. "My niece. Loki is not currently aware that she's more than a myth."

"How would he–"

"His memories were taken out of necessity," he said shortly. "It's a long story we do not have time for. Just be careful with the dagger. People who get cut by it are bound to turn into a zombie, and I don't know if it's a permanent or temporary transformation."

"You're saying I have a zombie dagger?"

Conquest laughed. "Yes, you have a zombie dagger."

Elya gaped. "Holy shit!"

"Language," Conquest scolded, laughing. "Come on, let's get you inside," he ran a hand through his black locks, "get you some lunch. You should rest up a while before heading back out."

"I couldn't possibly," Elya said.

"I insist," Conquest stood, walking in the direction of the house.

Elya sighed, following him nonetheless. It felt wrong, considering how clearly Famine didn't want her around, but who was she to argue with Conquest? Especially after he had just stitched her up. Not to mention she was starving, and if Gabriel found out she turned down an offer of food when she needed it, he'd have her head. She could already hear the beginnings of what would be yet another lengthy lecture. Besides, she'd been working almost endlessly to get from one location to the next, training her powers with Loki… a little break couldn't hurt. Surely, Satan wouldn't fault her that. And if he did, she could always call in Gabriel. Elya's smile dropped as she was hit with realization: She was banned from seeing Gabriel. He couldn't lecture her. At least, not yet.

Twenty-Seven

Lunch was quiet. The only sounds were the clanging and scraping of silverware against dishes. It was awkward and uncomfortable, and Elya would do just about anything to get out of it. She knew silence wasn't always good, but she had never had it ruin a perfectly good meal. Beyond good, actually. It was by far the best steak she ever had – the only thing she'd ever eaten better, Gabriel made. It was odd to think that Famine would be so good at cooking considering who he was, but in a way, she supposed it made sense.

"What do you say we go riding?" Conquest said, breaking the silence.

"No," Famine said.

"A ride sounds like just the thing I need," War said, leaning back in his chair.

"Care to join, Elya?" Conquest asked.

She swallowed. "I uh – I've never been on a horse before."

"Well now," War grinned "we'll just have to fix that, won't we?"

"I guess," Elya said.

"Good!" Conquest stood from the table, moving to grab his hat. "Let's go."

War followed suit, grabbing his own hat and following his brother out the kitchen. Famine stood and walked down the hall in the opposite direction. Elya didn't quite know what to do; she wanted to go talk to Famine, to try to make things right with him, but she hadn't done anything wrong, and she wasn't going to fight with someone for no reason. Instead, she followed outside to see War headed toward one of the stable while Conquest stood waiting for her.

"Ready to go?" He asked.

Elya exhaled. "Ready as I'll ever be."

Conquest grinned. "That's the spirit."

"Just one thing, what horse am I going to use?" Elya asked.

"Come on." He turned in the opposite direction of War. "You can use one of mine."

The barn he brought them to was white, the name Conquest shining above the doors in gold lettering. A bow was painted onto each door. With a flourish, Conquest pushed the doors open to reveal stall after stall of large horses. Most of them were white, some were light gray, others dark gray. Some were paints, and others dapple. As she stood there taking in the horses, she realized she knew little about them.

"There are so many," Elya said.

Conquest laughed. "This barn is just mares that I've retired from breeding and don't really use for riding beyond their basic exercise. They're older, gentle, and perfect for learning on. Well, most of them. I've got a couple other mares in here that just don't do well in the other barns right now."

Elya frowned. "Why not?"

Conquest shrugged. "Personality clashes with the other mares, but not bad enough to put into the barn with my more spirited mares."

"How many barns do you have?" Elya asked.

"Of just my horses?" Conquest clicked his tongue. "Ten. They're bigger on the inside than they are outside. The spirited stallions, older stallions, regular stallions, then the same three but for mares. The last four are my mares with foals, young colts, young fillies, and the ones I ride most frequently."

"How many horses is that?" Elya asked.

"We have enough horses to cover two thirds of everyone in Afterlife. The last third are covered by the horses in Heaven." He shrugged. "We keep a smaller four horse stable attached to the house for Despair, Victory, Combat and Hunger."

"How do you keep track of whose horses are whose?" Elya asked.

"The fencing," he said matter-of-factly. "My barns only let out into certain pastures, the same could be said for each of my brothers and their own. There's also a forcefield around the entire property that prevents our horses from leaving unescorted by ourselves."

Elya stepped up to one of the stalls with a white horse inside. The mare walked to the door of the stall. She had a black mane and, oddly enough, both her eyes seemed to have black stars around them. The horse nuzzled her hand. "I like her."

Conquest smiled. "That's Breeze. She doesn't take to most people. She's bred out of Victory and my mare Gloria. She's one of my prized horses and not up to your speed. Maybe when you get good at riding, you can give her a try. For now, she's in here to keep separated from the other mares."

Elya sighed. "So, who did you have in mind?"

He walked to the end of the barn and opened a stall. A lovely, light gray mare walked out. "I think you need Serenity."

"Promising name," Elya quipped, stroking the gray mare. "She's pretty. So how do I ride her?"

"Hold your horses," He chuckled stepping into the stall. "I need to get her saddled up and into a corral before you're ready to ride her."

Elya raised a brow. "A corral?"

"I'm not about to let an inexperienced girl on a horse without her being in a controlled environment," Conquest placed a blanket over the mare's back. "This way, I can keep her on the lead the entire time." He placed a halter on the horse's face. "I'll let you have the reins, but I'm not taking risks. You do everything I say."

Elya grinned. "Yes sir."

He chuckled. "You've definitely been hanging around the Lucifer family." He attached a rope to the horse's halter. "Put these on." He handed a pair of boots to her.

Quickly, she changed out of her shoes and followed silently as Conquest led her and Serenity outside the barn. It was a short walk to the nearest corral. It wasn't large – in fact, it looked big enough for the mare to take five steps in any direction. The dirt was completely flat – Elya guessed it was to make sure the horse wouldn't trip, which would be for the best, or she'd be stuck in Hell with one of Conquest's horses, and there was no way that'd end well.

"Alright, what do you know of riding?" Conquest asked.

"I know that's a horse and that's a saddle," Elya said.

Conquest huffed. "I must be out of my mind. This here is the stirrup. Put your foot here and put a hand on the saddle horn – that's the thing that sticks up – step in, swing your other leg over, and you should be fine."

Elya nodded. She lifted a foot to put in the stirrup, only to fall flat on her face. Wiping the dirt off her face, Elya turned to see Conquest shaking his head and approaching her. Elya sighed and allowed Conquest to help her. He placed her right hand on the saddle horn, then helped her get her foot in the stirrup. As she tried to lift herself to swing a leg over to the other side of the horse, she found herself slipping, landing on her backside this time.

"Alright," Conquest laughed. "Funny as this is, we should get you on the horse before you hurt yourself." Conquest walked over, put her in position, and kept a hand on her back to keep her from falling backward as she climbed onto the horse. "See? There now, that wasn't so bad."

"I'm only on the horse because you helped," Elya pouted.

"Nothing wrong with a little help," Conquest said. "Now, I want you to grab the reins. When you're ready to stop, pull gently back. She won't go fast, so there's no need for yanking. Now squeeze a little to get her to walk."

Nodding, a look of deep concentration on her face, Elya did as instructed. The horse moved forward slowly. She tightened her grip on the reins, knuckles turning white. This was a bad idea.

War rode up, coming to a stop a few feet behind the corral. "How's the lesson going?"

Conquest grimaced. "Well, we've got her on the horse."

"Arms down! You're riding a horse, not walking a balancing beam," War shouted at her. "You should keep them at hip level and loosen your grip."

Groaning, Elya adjusted her arms. Books did *not* make horseback riding seem so difficult. They always made it seem like the rider just got on the horse and went. Sure, she had seen *Spirit,* but he was a wild horse. This was entirely different. The horse wasn't trying to embarrass her – she was doing a good job of that on her own. Elya exhaled to loosen her grip, and the color slowly came back to her knuckles. Maybe she could do this.

"Don't look at Serenity, or you won't know where you're going!" Conquest called.

Or not. Elya's shoulder slumped as she pulled her head away from the horse beneath her to watch what was in front of her – not that she saw how it mattered. The horse was directing itself thus far and all she was doing was walking in circles.

"Sit up straight!" War called.

Elya stiffened. What she wouldn't give to have natural talent for riding horses. But she only fell off three times and all while trying to get on, so this was progress. She just needed to learn to sit on the horse properly and hold the reins right, and maybe Conquest would let her steer the horse instead of letting Serenity walk wherever and however she wanted. She hoped. Surely that wasn't too much to ask.

"I don't get it," War said.

"What?" Elya asked.

War dismounted Combat. "How can someone possibly be so bad on a horse?"

Elya shrugged. "I don't know how to ride."

War crossed his arms. "I've seen kids young as five get on a horse for the first time and do better."

Elya sighed. "So, horses aren't my thing."

"Understatement. Loosen up!" he shouted. "You're too stiff."

Elya rolled her shoulders in attempt to appear less stiff. How was she supposed sit up straight, but not be stiff when she had never ridden before?

"Remember to breathe!" they both called.

"Right. Breathe," Elya muttered.

She took a deep breath to try to get herself back into breathing, but it was easier said than done. There was so much that could go wrong. What if the horse bucked her off? She could be paralyzed. Or worse, die. Or what if Serenity decided to run off or jump the corral or tripped? Or – there were too many things that could go wrong, and this was *not* a good idea. Why did she think it was? Scenario after scenario of what could go wrong flashed through her mind, and Elya didn't even notice as the reins slipped from her grasp. Or when a snake moved in front of her path.

In seconds, Elya had gone from panicking about what could go wrong to flying back as the horse reared and she fell. She heard panicked shouts and suddenly a pair of arms caught her and righted her on her feet, still supporting part of her weight. Elya looked up into the cool gaze of War, while Conquest was stood in front of the panicking mare, hands held up to calm her.

Elya watched, heart racing, as Conquest got close to the horse and got a hold of the lead rope and pulled her down. He placed a hand on her nose and stroked her.

"Easy, girl," Conquest said.

"Did she ever rear before?" War asked.

"No," Conquest said.

"Hmm. Get her back in her stable and see if she's injured." War placed a hand on Elya's shoulder. "I'll get Elya inside and make sure she's alright. A horse that old shouldn't start rearing out of nowhere."

"Alright," Conquest said, leading Serenity toward the stables.

"Can you walk alright?" War asked.

Elya put weight on each foot. Her left felt fine, but when she put weight on her right leg, a searing pain shot up from her ankle. She grimaced. War sighed, and without another word, he hefted Elya into his arms and walked toward the house.

"I can walk, you know," Elya said.

"You're hurt."

"I just need a little help, not carried," she protested.

"Don't be stubborn. I've stood on every battlefield in the history of human, Tyvers, Arthenians, Angels, Zyrogs, and every other humanoid species the Boss deemed a good idea to create. And some that are less human in appearance but of equal or greater intelligence," War said matter-of-factly. "That said, I'm not taking any risks."

Elya huffed. "Whatever."

War chuckled as he opened the front door and set her down on top of a washer. He grabbed a bucket and flipped it over to sit on. His gaze flicked up to her forehead, then to her side, and lastly her left shin. "You're lucky you didn't tear open your stitches. We should probably double check to be safe. It was a bad idea to start with. Even if you knew how to ride, you shouldn't have been on one with your injuries."

"I'll be fine – Raphael can heal me." Elya shrugged.

War raised a brow. "He can doesn't mean he should. Maybe if he didn't heal your injuries so frequently, you would've been wearier about getting on a horse while so injured. Maybe Conquest and I should've used our damn common sense and kept you off."

"Accidents happen," Elya said, surprised at the shift in his tone.

"Looks like you've got a minor sprain," War switched back into doctor mode and began wrapping her ankle.

"Nothing severe. I'll get you some pain killers, then I'll get Life to come heal you up."

Elya raised a brow. "Life?"

War shrugged. "She is my sister, and she shouldn't be too difficult to get here. I could probably get her to fix your other injuries properly as well."

Elya smiled. "Thanks, but I think I'll tough it out with the stitches."

He chuckled. "If you're certain. In the meantime, you should rest up your ankle. Come on, I'll help you to the living room."

"I think I can walk a few feet and still be alright," Elya said.

He raised a brow. "And let Life kill me? Not a chance."

Elya sighed but allowed War to help her, nevertheless.

She thought through her options and saw it was the only choice. It wasn't like it was a huge deal anyway – the living room wasn't far, and he had already carried her inside. Helping her a little wouldn't be nearly as embarrassing, and if it weren't for Famine's clear dislike of her, she'd be more inclined to accept help. But one thing she had learned early on from Satan was to never show weakness to her enemies. True, Famine wasn't necessarily her enemy, but they weren't exactly friends. So, she'd take the help from War and ignore Famine if he made any comments. It'd all be fine.

She tried to ignore the fact that that's what she told herself last time, too.

Twenty-Eight

Normal people weren't comfortable spending the night with practical strangers, but nobody could claim Elya was normal. Any sane human would think her crazy for agreeing to stay with three Horsemen of the Apocalypse, especially considering she'd already needed stitches in three places, and sprained her ankle since her arrival that morning.

The decision was cemented when she laid down on the mattress. Whoever bought the beds was her hero. It was by far the most comfortable bed she'd ever slept on, and it was in a guestroom – a spacious guestroom at that, with a surprising amount of closet and dresser space. It outdid her tiny bedroom and thin mattress in Lawrence by a mile. Maybe she could get herself one with the money from Satan after she found a new place to live.

Elya yawned. Tired as she was, her throat was insanely dry. Carefully, she got off the bed and grabbed the crutches War had provided. There was no point in injuring herself further, and there was no way she'd get to sleep with her throat feeling like the Sahara. Quietly opening her door, Elya made her way down the halls to the kitchen. Laying her crutches against the counter, she pulled open the cabinet doors, using the light over the kitchen sink to help her find the glasses. It wasn't until the third cabinet she found what she was looking for. She gulped down her water hastily – far faster than she should've probably, but she was so thirsty… more than she should've been probably.

She refilled her glass, drinking it a little slower this time, and then panted, staring at the empty glass. Why was she so thirsty?

She glanced at the clock. 3:00 am. Frowning, Elya refilled her water one last time. Hobbling over to the table, she sat down, slowly drinking her water. She'd probably get up later needing to pee desperately, but if she could get rid of her thirst it'd be worth it. She didn't think she'd ever been so thirsty in her life. Hopefully she wasn't getting sick…

When she was finished, Elya made her way back to her room and laid her crutches against the wall. Suddenly, she paused at the sound of muffled voices outside her door.

She should go to bed and ignore whatever was being talked about down the hall. That was the responsible thing to do. Unfortunately, her curiosity was stronger than her self-preservation had ever been.

Eavesdropping on normal people was one thing, but now she was thinking about eavesdropping on two, maybe three immortal beings… Not just any celestials, but the riders of the apocalypse. Famine admittedly didn't seem that scary, but War and Conquest – their names alone were something to be terrified of.

Quietly, she cracked the bedroom door open and peered down the hall. Conquest and War were stood in the doorway of the former's bedroom. They seemed to be having a whispered conversation – the problem was they both seemed to have voices that carried.

"You need to tell her," War said.

"I will," Conquest said. "After all of this is over. Now's not the right time."

"Will you?" War asked.

"Yes," Conquest replied.

"That girl's good," War crossed his arms, "smart, and she doesn't deserve the short end of the stick."

Conquest sighed. "I'll tell."

"Don't wait until it's all over," War said. "If you don't want to tell her now, I get it." He ran a hand through his hair. "That's a lot to stress about. But if she dies without knowing, you'll regret it."

"What's her relationship with Raphael?" Conquest asked.

Raphael? Elya's eyes widened, struck with the realization they were talking about *her*. But what War thought his brother should tell her was beyond her – they'd only knew each other for a day! It wasn't like he could really have anything of importance to tell her. And why did he care about her friendship with Raphael? It wasn't his business.

War raised a brow. "Why would I know?"

Conquest folded his arms. "I know you meet with Michael once a week."

"Don't worry about Raphael. He feeds her skittles and heals her injuries, but other than that they're just friends. Gabriel, on the other hand…"

And now they were bringing Gabriel into it? Elya didn't know what their problem was, but Gabriel was a cinnamon roll and he did *not* need to be talked about. She had liked the two riders, but she wasn't going to be friends with people who talked about her, Raphael, and Gabriel behind their backs. Gabriel was a doll who did not deserve such behavior, and Raphael was nice too. And here they were talking about him. But why?

"Gabriel?" Conquest asked.

"Uriel caught Elya snooping around the war room and took her to Michael," War shrugged. "Gabriel and Raphael both came to her aid." He smirked. "Without hesitation, Gabriel vouched for her."

Elya winced. She hadn't expected word to get around about that. Not that she thought it was – okay, so she knew it was a huge deal. Humans weren't supposed to be in Heaven alive in the first place and she was constantly tripping there, and then she broke whatever trust she'd been given and went and snooped around the war room, stolen something (not that anyone knew about that yet aside from Satan), and had lied to Michael. In Heaven, too, which was probably a thousand times worse than lying in church.

Conquest raised a brow. "So? Gabriel is the angel of truth."

"Far as Michael could tell, she was lying," War said.

Elya covered her mouth to hide her surprise. While Michael hadn't exactly seemed keen on believing her, she hadn't realized it was because he knew she was lying. How could he? Gabriel was the angel of truth. Elya frowned, wondering if maybe he didn't know with certainty, but just felt that she was lying.

"Gabriel vouched for her despite knowing she was lying?" Conquest gaped. "When she works for Satan?"

Can nobody get past that? Elya thought indignantly. It was hardly fair that people were judging her just because she worked for Satan. It wasn't as though she willingly entered the position – she had a tripping problem and Satan took advantage.

War nodded. "Michael even banned her from seeing Raphael or Gabriel again. She's banned from Heaven so long as she's living, as well."

Conquest exhaled. "Then there's nothing to be concerned over."

War smirked. "She's still allowed in Hell."

"What does that have to do with anything?" Conquest asked.

He shrugged. "She spends a lot of time with Satan."

Elya refrained from scoffing. The whole celestial world seemed to know she hung around Satan a lot, and most of them held it against her even though it wasn't her fault. Granted, she never actually tried to leave the position but considering her only recent ability to control her inter-Afterlife travel, what was she supposed to do quit and hope Satan didn't kill her?

"As if he were anything to worry about," Conquest scoffed. "He may be a threat to us, but he's not a threat to Elya. You know how he gets ever since Milly—"

"—Kalael, really," War interjected.

"The first time he loved was his daughter, but Milly was a human," Conquest said.

War chuckled. "You know he'd kill us if he knew we knew about Milly."

Conquest snorted. "All of Afterlife knows about Milly."

Biting the inside of her cheek, Elya made a mental note to ask anyone who wasn't Satan about Milly. Something told her that'd be a soft spot for him, so probably not any of his sons… but maybe Raphael or Gabriel? Assuming she could keep her curiosity to herself that long, Satan loving a human was a foreign concept – well, Satan loving *anyone* sounded crazy. She needed to know everything, and she couldn't ask them because she wasn't supposed to be hearing the conversation. Elya cursed herself inwardly.

"Very true," War went silent for a moment. "He still loves her, you know."

"Now how do you know that?" Conquest asked.

War shrugged. "The Boss may disapprove of gossip, but Camael is a hopeless romantic."

Conquest nodded. "Makes sense. He's the angel of love and war, of course, you'd spend time gossiping."

"Hardly," War snorted. "He's the light side of war. I'm the dark side of it."

"You ever wonder why you're not one entity like Death?" Conquest asked.

War snorted. "No, and I'm glad for it."

"What are your thoughts on this threat to destroy Afterlife?"

War frowned, brows furrowing. "It's not good. There's only a handful of people who have the power, strength, and resources to even attempt something like this. To be frank, I'm not entirely sure Satan isn't in some way involved. I find it suspicious that he's sending Elya around to get people to save Heaven and Hell when he's got ill feelings toward both."

"Agreed," Conquest sighed. "For now, we'll give him benefit of the doubt, but we should keep an eye out for something. Aside from him, our most likely candidate is Alex."

"He's imprisoned, and so long as Azar has a warden, he won't get free," War said.

"We all know he'll escape with or without a warden one of these days."

"The Tyvers in general were too powerful from the day of their creation." War crossed his arms. "And Alex is powerful for even one of their kings."

"Let's just hope Alex and Satan aren't working *together*." Conquest ran a hand through his hair. "Otherwise, we're in for a rough battle."

Elya frowned. Whoever Alex was, he sounded powerful and dangerous. And from what she was told, Alex made her sword, which meant Satan had contact with this Tyver king at some point. From the sound of things, that wasn't good, not if Alex was in prison. And even worse, if Alex was involved with this whole destroying Heaven and Hell thing, then there was a high chance Satan was involved. And if Satan was involved, then the Deadly Sins were involved. Elya hoped they weren't. They were her friends, even if none of them would ever admit it.

War frowned. "How many know of Kalael's prophecy?"

Conquest sighed. "The four of us, Satan, the archangels, and very likely Satan's told Zeerlo and Fiend, maybe even Twist as well. I'm not even sure if Kalael knows of the prophecy."

"Let us hope. The fewer to know of it, the better."

Conquest snorted. "Understatement."

"And what of the other prophecy?" War asked.

"Hopefully, it won't be fulfilled, and if it is, not for a few more years." Conquest's hand made its way back to his hair. "Elya is far from ready. But at the current rate, she's going to need to be ready real soon."

"Think she's sleeping alright?" War asked.

"I'll go check," Conquest said.

Quietly, she shut the door. As the sound of footsteps grew near, Elya dove underneath the covers pulling the blanket tight over her head as she buried her head in her pillow pretending to be asleep. She tried to make her breathing light and even as she heard the doorknob turning. Light footsteps sounded, walking toward the bed. Whoever it was stopped somewhere near the bed. A hand touched her forehead lightly.

"She's asleep," Conquest whispered.

"You're certain?" War asked.

"Yes," Conquest replied.

"Kid must be exhausted," War said. "Between dueling me, getting stitches, riding and injuring herself further, she's had a long day. She's tough."

Elya fought to keep a smile off her face.

"And who knows how much else she's been doing, gathering people to fight in this war."

It was nice to be appreciated. She really should eavesdrop more often.

"She'll definitely need more riding lessons down the line. She's not exactly a natural on a horse, though I admit things could have gone worse," War said.

"Never in my life have I seen Serenity rear like that. And at her age?"

War chuckled. "The girl was cursed with clumsiness. I don't think I've seen a kid more accident prone than her."

She didn't have to fight against a smile this time, though he wasn't wrong.

"Well, aside from Satan's boy," he continued. "I don't even know how that boy does some of the things he does."

"Remember the time he knocked over sixty motorcycles and an entire motorcycle gang tried to kill him?"

War snorted. "Who could forget? Azrael complained for months about the needless slaughter, Satan was rather vocal about the mess he had to clean up too, if I recall. The boy knocked over a building and blew up a gas station as well."

Elya bit the inside of her cheek to keep quiet as the two walked away. Maybe she was cursed with clumsiness... Considering how many bones she'd broken over the years, not to mention the number of trees she had fallen out of, she wouldn't be shocked. She hadn't learned to ride a bike until she was ten because she kept falling off or getting her shoelaces caught in the peddles.

"Cursed with clumsiness…."

Well, it was accurate.

Twenty-Nine

A light tapping on the door woke Elya the next morning.

On the nightstand laid a bag of skittles, and a single tiger lily. Elya smiled. Gabriel had told her once how the lily was a flower attributed to him.

The tapping continued reminding her of why she woke in the first place.

Dragging herself out of bed, Elya walked silently across the soft carpet to the door. She pulled it open and gasped at the unexpected figure stood there. She had expected Conquest or War, Hell maybe even Famine, but not the woman stood there. She was stunning. Her hair was long, wavy, and golden, and her eyes sparkled like emeralds. She was one of the most beautiful women Elya had ever seen and she radiated a warmth that made Elya feel safe, almost as safe as she felt when she was in Heaven with Gabriel and Raphael.

"Hello dear," The woman said.

Elya tried not to gape – not only was this woman stunning even her voice was melodic and ethereal. "Um, hi. Not to sound rude, but who are you?"

She laughed. It was light, tinkling. "I'm Rosemary, but my brothers are all rather persistent on calling me Life."

"Oh, hi," Elya said.

Rosemary crossed her arms. "From my understanding, you have a sprain. You should not be on your feet. Now back to bed with you."

Elya huffed. It wasn't as though she hadn't had a thousand sprained ankles in her life. In fact, she probably had more. The swelling wasn't as bad as others she'd had and she could walk on it, even if it did hurt some. But she also knew not to argue with immortal entities over injuries – Raphael had taught her that much. Even Fiend refused to let her ignore her injuries if he deemed himself willing to look at them, which was more often than he'd ever admit aloud. After all, he had a reputation.

"Thank you for coming to fix my ankle," Elya said.

Rosemary smiled. "Healing is a part of life, which is why I do so gladly."

"Interesting… tell me more," Elya said.

"While I know your curiosity is endless, I am afraid that now is not the time. But I promise I'll tell you sometime in the future," she smiled. "Now, do you want to start with the ankle or the stitches?" Rosemary asked.

Elya frowned. "Actually, could you just do my ankle and leave the stitches?"

Rosemary raised a brow. "Are you certain? I don't usually leave my patients with their injuries. The exact opposite, really."

"I am. I won't always be able to rely on Fiend, or Raphael to heal up my injuries. Plus, they look kind of cool." Elya frowned. "Actually, could you teach me first aid? If not for War and Conquest knowing it, I wouldn't even have been able to get stitches without a hospital."

Rosemary smiled. "I think I can teach you a thing or two," She glanced at Elya's leg. "After we fix this ankle of yours, of course."

Elya nodded, watching as Rosemary placed a hand on her swollen ankle. There was the briefest flash of warm white light as the pain eased. Rosemary removed her hand to reveal the swelling had gone, along with the throbbing.

It was one of her favorite things about being friends with celestials: She was never injured long, and she got to witness what most would call miracles almost every day. This time though, she'd tough out the stitches, she wanted to prove to herself she could handle injuries.

"Thank you," Elya said.

"Of course," Rosemary said. "It is admirable what you are doing. Dangerous, yes, but very admirable. You don't have to, but you are going out of your way to aid everyone in saving both Heaven and Hell, and that demonstrates you hold strong compassion."

"I have friends in Heaven and Hell who mean everything to me. They're not just friends, they're family. It sucks I'm banned from seeing Gabriel and Raphael again, but this feels more important. I mean, it is kind of important that there's an afterlife." Elya shrugged. "Who knows what would happen without one?"

Rosemary sighed. "Nothing good, but let's not dwell on that. After all, you wanted to learn basic first aid, didn't you?"

Elya nodded. "If you don't mind teaching me."

She smiled. "Of course I don't mind. However, I am afraid we are a little short on time, so, I will not be able to teach you properly." Rosemary clicked her tongue. "I could, however, impart the knowledge to you."

"You can impart the knowledge without teaching me?" Elya asked.

"Yes. It will be a simple enough task, though I ask you remove your bracelet for the duration. I would not want any accidents."

"My bracelet? Why though? Fiend said it could heal anything. I mean, he also said not to use it for minor things," she shrugged, "but I just assumed it's power was limited."

"Arthenian gemstones are *very* powerful. They come only from the skin of the royal bloodlines. To obtain them is very rare but they are also highly dangerous. While they have the power to heal anything, they drain the power of the user. Only an Arthenian royal could possibly use such a gem without risking death. And it most certainly would be too risky for me to do what I am about to attempt while you are wearing it."

"Should I not keep it?" Elya asked.

"You may keep it, but please use it with caution." Rosemary eyed the sapphire colored hung on a silver chain. "In emergencies only. You do not yet have the strength to stand against the stone."

Elya nodded, unclasping the bracelet. Leave it to Fiend to offer her a gift that could kill her if she wasn't careful.

"So, how does this work?" Elya asked.

Rosemary moved the bracelet to the nearby dresser. "I'm going to be transferring my knowledge of healing to you. While you won't have my powers, you will know what is needed for first aid and even more difficult things. I am gifting you medical knowledge beyond what many mortals, even some doctors have. I am not saying you could go using it in practice, not beyond basics. And especially not without proper certifications and licensing. But you will be able to use the knowledge you most need."

"This won't hurt, right?" Elya asked.

"Not in the least," Rosemary said.

"How exactly will you be transferring your knowledge to me?"

"The process is simple enough, in theory," Rosemary shrugged. "You need do nothing but sit still and I shall place my hand on you and concentrate on the knowledge I wish to transfer. After, you will fall into a sleep. Once you awaken, you'll have all the knowledge you will need and more. Conquest and War will monitor your state while you sleep to ensure you are well, though I do not expect anything will go wrong. It will mainly be for peace of mind."

"Before you knock me out for a while, about this threat to the Afterlife, will you help fight against it?" Elya asked.

"I do not believe in violence; therefore, I will not fight. I will monitor over everything and step in where I can, but in something like this, there is no knowing what I'll be able to heal."

Elya sighed. "I can respect that."

"Thank you, Elya."

Elya smiled. "Alright, let's get this over with."

Rosemary chuckled. "Sit very still. You'll find yourself drifting into sleep as we do this, but don't worry. Just focus as long as you can. I will ease you back into the bed once you are asleep. You'll feel a warm sensation envelope you as I transfer the knowledge. Do you understand?"

"Seems pretty straightforward," Elya said.

"Are you ready?"

She wouldn't have minded having something for breakfast first, partially out of hunger and partially because she knew Gabriel would have a lecture ready, but Rosemary seemed to be ready to start, and she couldn't see Gabriel… And she wasn't that hungry. She was more curious than anything, Rosemary was the first celestial she had ever met that was a woman, which was bizarre now that she thought about it.

Rosemary raised a brow. "Your mind looks occupied. You need to be calm and focused when we do this."

Elya winced. "Sorry, I just got thinking and every angel I've ever seen is male. Like, why is that? I mean, isn't it a little weird most of the celestial population is male? Azrael, Loki, Conquest, War, and Famine; Time, Thought, the archangels, Satan, six of the seven deadly sins… what's with the lack of women?"

"Well, Satan had no control in the sex of his children. As for myself and my brothers, it is the way in which we each emerged into existence. I could take the form of a male just as my brothers could fully become female. However, my brothers have long since chosen to remain purely as male as I have preference to female. Beyond that, I cannot explain further to you. For that, I would ask someone more knowledgeable."

"Fair," Elya said.

"Now, are you ready?" Rosemary asked.

"Yeah… no…. yeah."

Rosemary laughed. "Very well. Count down from ten, and I'll begin."

"Alright. Ten, nine, eight…" Rosemary placed a hand on her shoulder "Seven, six, five…" Elya yawned as she was enveloped in warmth as though she were wrapped in a blanket.

"Four, three, two…" a glow surrounded Rosemary's hand. "One." Elya's eyelids grew heavy as she yawned again. She had never been so tired after having just woken up.

"You're doing wonderfully," Rosemary's melodic voice said.

Elya tried to focus on Rosemary, but she was so tired. A hand came to her other shoulder, both gently pushing her back. The warmth remained strong around her, but as tired as she felt, she couldn't bring herself to sleep. Elya pulled the blankets tight around her. She was cozy and wanted nothing more than to rest… She shifted at the sound of the door softly opening. Her eyelids were too heavy for her to see who it was.

"How's she doing?" Conquest asked.

"She's fighting the sleep," Rosemary responded.

"She's stubborn," War chuckled, "like her father."

Rosemary laughed. "You have no idea. Most people would be out already. I haven't had this much resistance in years. Since I last treated Kalael. Elya's both stubborn and powerful. Between her ability to travel through the realms and everything else, I can't say I'm surprised. Hopefully, she'll fall into sleep soon… the knowledge I'm transferring won't take root properly otherwise."

"Is there anything we can do to help her to sleep?" Conquest asked.

"Turn off the lights and close the curtains," Rosemary replied "if the room's dark enough, it should help give her the last push into sleep."

The room grew darker.

"Do we have to let her leave?" Conquest asked.

War sighed. "You know we do. Michael's given me his word he'll watch over her."

"When did that happen?" Conquest asked.

"Shortly after her birth," War said.

A light musical laugh sounded. "You only got a promise he already gave. Michael gave his Father his oath that he'd protect Elya at any cost millennia ago."

"So why ban her from Heaven?" Conquest asked.

Rosemary laughed. "You should know by now that he works like his Father. Mysteriously." The soft padding of feet across the floor sounded. "Come, let her rest. Trying times await her."

Elya wanted to say something, it felt weird with them talking about her when she was too exhausted to respond. But her eyelids were growing heavier, her ability to even listen decreasing. Snuggling into her bedding, Elya yawned, and slowly drifted into sleep.

Thirty

Despite the injuries she endured spending time with War and Conquest, Elya felt more rested than she had in a long while. Her powers were recuperated, her sprain was healed, and as much as she didn't want to, she was ready to leave. She wasn't done gathering everyone on Satan's list, and was low on time. Besides, Famine still hadn't warmed up to her, and being with them seemed to generate more questions than answers – about the prophecy they mentioned, the fact Michael had sworn an oath to protect her… and eavesdropping solved nothing.

A knock sounded at the door.

"Come in!" Elya called.

The door pushed open to reveal Conquest, a darkened glint in his blue eyes. He stepped in silently, leaving the door open behind him. He eyed her weapons she had laid out on the bed: two daggers, a sword, a handgun, and a Swiss army knife. If she was honest, it seemed obsessive, but they had been gifts.

"I know you need to get going, but I haven't had a chance to test your skills," Conquest said.

Elya frowned. "I'm better with the daggers than sword, and you saw how well that went. I haven't had a chance to use the gun yet, but you know Kalael and her guns. And I know you can't be referencing my skills on a horse because as we saw yesterday, they're lacking."

He chuckled. "You need practice, but I meant with my own weapon of choice."

"A bow?" Elya laughed. "Dude, I've never picked up a bow in my life."

He shrugged. "You never know," he said mysteriously.

"I'll almost certainly end up shooting you, someone else, or myself." Elya deadpanned.

Conquest smiled. "Only one way to find out."

Elya frowned. She needed to go, but at the same time she didn't want to. Not yet, something about Conquest put her at ease, and he had been nice to her since she arrived. She kind of wanted to know why he seemed familiar, as though she should know him better than she does… And the only way to find out more answers to her questions would be to stick around longer and stay on his good side…

Besides, he was going through the trouble of convincing Famine to help her and the others out with their upcoming war for the Afterlife. Plus, learning a new weapon couldn't hurt, especially when it wasn't for close combat, like her daggers and sword.

"Alright, I guess it wouldn't hurt to give the bow a try," she grinned, relenting. "But if you get an arrow through the eye or something, you have nobody to blame but yourself."

"I'm willing to risk it," Conquest said.

Without another word, he led Elya outside. Victory stood waiting, as though he expected Conquest to take him riding. For all she knew, he was – it wasn't like she knew their routines. Then, just as Victory had been expecting, Conquest climbed into the saddle. Elya just stared, flabbergasted.

"I am not getting on a horse again," Elya said.

Conquest laughed. "Relax, you can ride with me. All you need to worry about is holding on." Not waiting for a response, he pulled her up in front of him.

"This seems dangerous," Elya said.

"Can be," Conquest said, "but it's a way to the archery range on foot, and you don't know where it is, so you can't travel through supernatural means."

"I don't mind walking."

"Through a river?" Conquest asked.

"You guys have a river on your land?" Elya asked.

"Should we not?"

"Just odd is all."

He laughed. "I'll make sure you don't fall."

Without warning, the horse took off at a run. Elya yelped, but Conquest just steadied her as they rode.

After about fifteen minutes, they finally came to a stop. Elya couldn't help staring as she took in their surroundings. This took the term archery range to whole new levels. Rather than normal targets, bright red apples were scattered around the area. She could only assume those were meant to be the targets. A large cabinet stood under a sheltered area with a picnic table.

"Um, Conquest?" Elya eyed the tightrope and nearby river. "This doesn't look like a normal archery range."

"I would hope not. I like something that gives off the appearance of being difficult. We can have you shoot from the tree, floating down rapids, hung upside down, on horseback – sitting or standing, not that you're ready for that given your skill with horses – and, of course, one of my personal favorites: stood on the tightrope. There will also be several projectiles aimed toward you while you shoot."

"Can't I just stand on the ground and hope I shoot the arrow and hit the general direction of the target?" Elya asked.

"Nope."

"I'm going to die," Elya deadpanned. "I mean, you realize I'm one of the clumsiest people on the planet? If not in the universe! I trip into Hell *daily*!"

He grinned. "Your target is also the core of the apples that have been laid out. I also got a skeet thrower so you can aim for the clay pigeons as well."

She scoffed. "Dude, do you realize the odds of someone managing any of this are like—"

"A billion to one," he finished. "Or, for myself blindfolded, the odds of me hitting every target are 3 in 4. For you, given your clumsiness, I'd say the odds are 1 in 4 you can hit all those targets blindfolded."

"I've never shot a bow before," Elya said. "How could it be 1 in 4?"

"I'll let you in on a little secret," he winked, "I'm never wrong when it comes to figuring the odds."

"Right. And the odds that I slip and die?" Elya asked.

"1 in 15," he shrugged. "Most likely, I'll catch you or you'll land safely in Heaven or Hell – possibly Dimitri's coffeeshop or Azrael's castle."

"Right," she exhaled. "Okay, so what now?"

"Pick your bow." He opened a cabinet filled with bows in all shapes and sizes. Almost all of them were black, and a few were brown. "I'd recommend a recurve takedown bow. It's the same bow the mortals use in the Olympics and the type Odysseus himself used. I must admit a certain fondness for it. Or," he grinned, "I have a few collapsible bows of my own creation. Quicker and easier than a takedown, which is always good for when you need to access your bow quickly but don't want to be hauling it around. It's basically an improvement on takedown bows, just not found among mortals."

"Something tells me it's not the easiest."

"Not in the least, but you'll do well, I think. Let's see…" He pressed a button, rotating his display of bows. "Ah! Here we are. This looks to suitable for you. Do you mind dark green? I don't seem to have this one in another color."

"No," she grinned, "it's actually my favorite."

"Well then," he smiled. "I'll tell you what, if you impress me, I'll let you keep it."

"Really?" Elya asked.

"Yes."

"Alright, I still think this is a terrible idea, but I'll try. Where do we start?"

"How about with a demonstration?" Conquest asked.

"Please?"

"Watch and learn." Conquest climbed into Victory's saddle and tied a black blindfold over his face.

Victory took off at a run while Conquest drew his bow, aiming at apples all over his archery range. Mid-motion, he flawlessly moved from a sitting position to standing as he continued to shoot. As they neared the tree, Conquest jumped from Victory onto the tree branch, taking aim at more apples and clay pigeons that flew everywhere. Not one arrow missed as he leapt from the tree onto the tightrope. From the tightrope, he hung upside down, continuing to flawlessly hit his targets. He was completely unbothered by the arrows that were being launched toward him. Conquest let himself fall, landing on his feet on a log floating down the rapids. His arrows shot true even as he dodged and maintained balance. Finally, he leapt off the log onto the riverbank, and hit one last apple through the core. The apple centered on the arrow as it embedded itself into a tree. He pulled the blindfold off.

Elya gaped. "That was both awesome and obvious showing off."

"I know," He grinned. "Now it's your turn."

"Yeah, no, I like living," Elya said.

"You'll be fine." He handed her the bow. "Trust the odds."

Elya scoffed. *That* was easier said than done. She eyed the archery range Conquest had set up for himself. If you could call it that. It was more like a death trap. But while she couldn't get a reading on the odds, she did feel strangely like they were tipped in her favor, even if there was no way she'd hit any targets. She'd be too busy trying not to fall.

"Alright, I'm ready," Elya said.

"One more thing." Conquest held out his blindfold.

"What? No way!" she laughed.

He stepped forward. "Just trust me on this."

"Do I have to?" Elya asked.

"I won't let you get hurt." He put the blindfold over her eyes. "Besides, if you did, Life would have my head." He stepped back. "Just feel the bow in your hands, and let your instincts guide you. You'll be surprised what you can do."

"I need arrows," Elya said.

He chuckled. "Here, I'll help you strap on the quiver."

Elya stood still as he moved her arm to place the quiver onto her back, the strap falling onto her shoulder.

Well, it was finally true. She was insane. She had lost all sense. That was the explanation to why she was doing this. No sane person could possibly let someone talk them into attempting something so dangerous – blindfolded to top it off. If Gabriel saw her right now, he'd probably have a heart attack, and even Satan would probably be having an aneurism.

"You're ready," Conquest said.

Elya didn't launch into shooting blindly, instead choosing to take a few deep breaths to help calm her nerves, if only barely. Exhaling, she pulled an arrow from the quiver and knocked it in the bow. She drew back and released. Her arrow hit something with a loud thud. She reached to remove the blindfold, only for a hand to grab hers.

"Don't stop, keep going," Conquest said calmly. "Don't worry about what you hit or miss, just go."

Easier said than done. He was Conquest, the bow was his weapon of choice, and who knew how many times he had gone through his archery range blindfolded. He probably had the whole thing memorized, including the way the other arrows came shooting towards him. Her, on the other hand, she had never held a bow before today. Still, she ran through the obstacle course Conquest called his archery range as best she could. Every now and then, she would dodge or duck as something whizzed through the air. Getting into the tree was no simple task – how Conquest managed was beyond her. She only lasted a few moments when she was on the tightrope before she started to lose her balance. She braced herself to be caught in the rushing water below, only to land with a slight jolt on a piece of wood.

"You're alright, Elya—" Conquest called as she gasped in shock, "—just a little slip. Keep it up, focus on what you're doing, not on what you've already done."

Elya nodded, adrenaline coursing through her veins. Inhaling, she ducked, aimed, and fired her arrow. Repeating this five times, she paused, feeling the river picking up. Taking a breath, she jumped from her platform, praying she'd land on the riverbed. Feeling wet ground under her shoes, Elya moved forward, nearly slipping in the mud. Once she found her footing, she took aim one last time. She took a deep breath, exhaled, took another breath, and let it half out. She held her breath, released the arrow, and exhaled fully. The arrow hit something with a resounding thud. Again, she reached to remove her blindfold.

Conquest stood in front of her, blocking her view of the archery range. His expression was blank. She grimaced. That couldn't have been a good sign. Silently, he stepped aside and tilted his head toward where she had started. Elya let her eyes drift to where the arrow was supposed to go. Her jaw went slack. She had split Conquest's arrow!

"Am I seeing things?" Elya asked.

"It would seem not only was I right that you could do it, but you're a natural with a bow." Conquest gestured to the rest of his archery range. Every arrow he shot through the apples had one of hers splitting it.

"I—I did that?" Elya asked stunned.

He laughed. "You did. Not only that, but you kept your balance almost the entire time and when you nearly slipped, you found your footing."

"No, you don't understand. That's never happened before. I've never been a natural at, well, *anything*."

"Keep practicing and perhaps one of these days, you and I could have a competition. You just might give me a run for my money, if today was any indication."

Elya smiled. "Thanks."

"Of course. But, as good as you were, you still need to get going." He glanced to where the sun stood high overhead. "I'll get the case for your bow."

"What?" Elya asked.

"I did tell you if you impressed me, you could keep it." He gestured around them. "Color me impressed. You're a skilled archer, Elya. This wasn't luck, that was God-given talent. You can use daggers well, you're a fair hand with the sword, and I have no doubt if you tried, you'd shoot decently with the gun Kalael gave you. But your skills with a bow? No mortal could compare."

"Could we maybe not tell others that I went through your obstacle course of an archery range? If Gabriel finds out you let me go through this – blindfolded to top it off – he'll have a heart attack. And Satan's likely to have an aneurism."

He chuckled. "No worries, nobody knows the intensity of the archery range aside from my brothers and the Boss, of course. Not even Life has an inkling to just how dangerous it is down here. But it's special, too. This is where I come when I need to calm my temper, to relax, or just to have fun."

Elya smiled. "Thank you for letting me come down here."

"It satisfied my curiosity and was definitely more impressive than I was expecting. You did well, Elya," he smiled, "and you're welcome on my range anytime."

"Thanks," Elya said.

He nodded. Taking the bow from her, he pressed a little switch and the bow collapsed in on itself, string and all, until all that remained visible was the handle of the bow. Conquest further surprised her by pushing this together until all that remained was the spot where she put her hand. He then put that in a small case only a few inches high and wide.

"It took me a while to get it to where it wouldn't need to be restrung every time I used it, but the whole bow collapses down into the grip of your riser. A flick of a switch and you have a working weapon in seconds. Just remember to hold it in front of you so you don't get hit in the face. I set it off by accident once when I was designing it – trust me, it's not a fun experience."

Elya smiled. "I'll remember."

He nodded. "You best get going now."

"Thanks, Conquest. And tell War and Famine I said thanks as well."

He chuckled. "Anytime, kid." There was the slightest glint of pride in his eye.

Taking a deep breath, Elya focused her power like Loki had taught her. Closing her eyes she pictured her next destination carefully. She was due to report back to Satan on her progress, so she pictured his throne room. She had seen it so often, the image she had of it couldn't be much clearer. Soon, she was consumed by the feel of rushing water. When it came to a stop, she opened her eyes to see Satan curled up on his throne, asleep.

He looked so peaceful… it was easier to see how he had once been one of Heaven's angels now. Asleep, he looked innocent. Silently, she pulled out her cellphone. This was a picture opportunity she was *not* going to miss.

Thirty-One

After reporting to Satan, Elya was given a condescending pat on the head along with a cookie. While she was off gathering an army he was searching for the perfect meeting point in neutral ground and putting together plans he refused to share. She didn't get much reprieve before he summoned a door which opened to a swirling blue portal and she was shoved into the Realm of Thought.

Unusual didn't surprise her anymore. Growing up with Satan and his children, she'd seen her fair share of crazy. And all the time she'd spent with Azrael over the years, what was left to surprise her? That's what she'd thought until now. She wondered if she was high – she could totally be tripping right now. Any one of the Deadly Sins would drug her for shits and giggles.

Whatever the case, this was an experience.

The realm of Thought was like *Alice in Wonderland* on steroids. The sky was a swirling vortex, or was that the ground? The trees were above her, with tops coming down toward her. Electricity crackled everywhere, the screams of what she could only assume was a banshee sounding every third step she took. Weirder yet was the water that flowed only at waist level – above and below her hip bone there was none. It didn't matter if she stood on the tips of her toes or crouched low, wherever her waist was the water was. But as strange as all that was, it was nothing to the way the whole place flashed like white strobe lights. Keeping her balance as she walked wasn't an option, and she was a bit dizzy, but if she didn't go into a seizure, she'd be alright. For the most part.

The place was utter chaos and somewhere in it all was the next person on her list: Time's brother, Thought. Or Muse, depending which entity you asked. Apparently, he didn't care what you called him, so long as you respected him and his realm. She could totally do that if she managed to find him in his chaotic realm. Satan had warned her Thought's realm wasn't like most places she'd go, that the realm was designed to reflect humanity, that the most depraved thoughts in human history could be found manifested within. Honestly, she didn't like the idea of it, and the odds were not in her favor.

Something fell from a tree, landing in front of her. Elya stepped back as she took in the strange creature. It was tall, easily the size of a full-grown demon. It was scaley, its tail feathered. It bore seven heads with a set of horns and a lion's mane on each, and it held 13 sets of eyes. The large beak opened, revealing three sets of razor-sharp teeth. Gills were visible on its neck, while two sets of wings sprouted from its back. In place of ears were two fins; its large feet and hands webbed, but with talons on their ends.

Elya was not ashamed of what happened next. In fact, she would be the first to admit that not only did she scream at a frequency she didn't know she was capable of, but she also ran away without looking back. Or at least she did until she managed to trip. She wanted to embrace the rushing water, to get out of there, but getting to the Realm of Thought hadn't been easy and Satan had been clear when he said the door into the realm could be opened only once for her, meaning now was her only chance at speaking with the entity about getting his help. She glanced at the hulking creature as it grew closer. Maybe she'd be better off asking someone else to speak to Thought in her place…

"Freddie, heel!" A voice shouted from all around.

The creature halted. A figure appeared in front of it, wearing a long cloak of gray. The figure was tall – shorter than the creature, but easily on par with Michael and Satan. It turned around to reveal a man with long turquoise hair coming to his shoulder. A scar dragged across his left eye. His cheekbones were high, his eyes silver. His face looked as though the frown etched upon it was a permanent fixture. A pair of wings jutted from his back, gradual in their color change. Starting at the bottom of his wings, there was just the slightest tinge of gold, followed by white, just slightly larger than the gold. Next came the gray and, lastly, black taking over most of his wings.

"Hello, Elya," the man said.

"How do you know who I am?" Elya asked.

The man laughed. Not a warm laugh, but a cold laugh. A chilling laugh that made Satan's occasional cackling sound like giggling children. "I am one who knows all that has been, all that is, and some of what could be. All knowing? No. But quite knowledgeable, certainly. I know you, Elya." He stepped closer to her and she fought the urge to take many steps back. "Quite intimately." He grinned – it was twisted and depraved. "I know you and all humanity. Many, yourself included, better than themselves." His wings flexed. "I am Thought."

"Then you know why I'm here," Elya said.

He nodded. "I do."

"Will you help?" Elya asked.

"No," Thought said.

Elya frowned. "You won't?"

He crossed his arms. "No."

"But why?" Elya asked.

He gestured widely. "Look around you. This realm is filled with the thoughts of humanity. Most are rather dangerous, depraved." He gestured to the creature. "Some are dangerous monsters," Thought chuckled darkly. "And Freddie there is *far* from the worst of creatures within here. So, no, I will not help. I do not have time to help. I must be here, maintaining order in this chaos." His eyes glowed. "If even one creature creates a tear in the realm, all of it could leak into Earth, Arthenia, the remainder of Eden… all the universe would be vulnerable to exposure from the realm."

Elya eyed the creature. Freddie. "Okay, that would be bad."

He nodded. "It would. The realm of Thought, as you likely have noticed, is filled with chaos, destruction."

Elya shifted. "Is there anything we could do? To, you know, prevent that while you're gone?"

"I appreciate your offer of help, Elya," the smile reached his eyes this time "but this realm cannot stand without me."

Elya frowned. "Satan wanted me to come here for a reason. He had to know you couldn't leave, so why would he ask for your help?"

Thought chuckled. "You are limiting yourself, Elya."

"I am?"

"In what way could I possibly help?"

Somehow, she didn't think it was rhetorical question. Her brows drew together in thought. A second later, her eyes widened, realization dawning on her. If *anyone* could help it would be Thought! If he knew the thoughts of everyone, then logically, he would know the plans of whoever was out to destroy Afterlife. He could be the spy that never goes near the enemy, nor steps on a battlefield.

He smiled. "Now you've got it."

"Okay, that's super creepy," Elya said.

"I'd suggest you speak with Azrael or Kalael about blocking your thoughts, but it won't work on me anyway. My ability to read thoughts is without limit." He rolled his shoulders powerfully. "But, yes, I am willing to play the spy for the army you are gathering."

"Thanks," Elya said, relieved.

"Walk with me, Elya."

"Where are we going?"

"The castle."

She flicked her gaze across the realm, but there was no sign of a castle. There was no sign of any buildings. But if all the thoughts of humanity, and whatever species were in the universe were here, then that would imply there were not only castles, but entire Utopias and dystopias – cities floating in the sky. She looked up (or was it down?) and spotted it – there, floating in what Elya assumed was the sky was a large, hulking castle with a long winding staircase connecting it to the ground. There had to have been at least a thousand steps to the entrance.

"I am not taking the stairs."

Thought chuckled. "I think I can take care of that." He placed a hand on her shoulder, and in a flash, they were stood in a large, ceilinged room. It was like Satan's paperwork closet, only there were filing cabinets, it looked organized, and was three times the size.

"Where are we?" Elya asked.

"Certain beings are assigned an actual room filled with filing cabinets to keep record of their thoughts. It prevents their thoughts from running amok in the chaos of the realm." He shrugged. "The archangels, Satan and his children, Azrael and the other riders, Kazira, Tess, Dimitri and his siblings, and yourself."

"Wait. Who's Tess? And why do *I* have a room?" Elya asked.

"Tess is short for Quintessence, daughter of War. The Arthenian people tend to worship her. As for your room, given the life you lead, I would think it obvious why you were deemed important enough to have your own room."

"This is my room, isn't it?" Elya asked.

He nodded. "It is."

"I have a lot of thoughts."

"A lot of questions."

Elya glanced at all the cabinets containing her thoughts: they were all tall and identical except for one. It was black. Somehow, she didn't think it contained her darkest thoughts. She wasn't naïve enough to think she'd had that few in her life. She'd like to, but given how much time she spent in Hell, she knew that was wishful thinking.

"That cabinet actually isn't your thoughts," Thought said.

Elya frowned. "Then why is it here?"

"They are dark thoughts, directed toward you. About you," Thought said simply. "Thoughts of people who wish you ill, of other types of impureness."

"That's disturbing and yet… I want to know," Elya said.

"You don't," Thought said. "Knowing what others think about you, it can alter your relationship forever. Destroy friendships, create rifts."

"How bad could it be?" Elya asked.

"There are a lot of plans in there to kill you. Complete strangers and people you know," he said. "There are also some thoughts of the impure nature that would align with Fiend's sin. Believe me, those are best left unseen."

"What about other thoughts people have about me. Why are there only bad thoughts in a cabinet? Or is there a good-thoughts filing cabinet?" She looked around for one.

"Those cabinets are in the rooms of their respected owners, assuming they have such rooms," Thought said.

"Can I see the other rooms?" Elya asked.

Thought tilted his head. "It is not typically allowed, but I will allow you into the thought room of one individual and only one. I suggest you choose wisely."

Elya frowned. "Does it matter? It's not like I'm going to be scouring through their thoughts. I don't mind picking people's brains, but usually I have their consent."

He chuckled. "The cabinets can tell a surprising amount. And look at it this way: the cabinets in this room are from your short existence," he smirked. "Imagine the expansiveness of their rooms. Michael and Satan were the first beings ever created."

Elya glanced at her room. It was big, but theirs their rooms had to be huge. Bigger than a gymnasium, probably. How was she supposed to pass up on seeing at least one of them? And it wasn't like she was hurting anything… She was only going to peek into the room itself, just to see the expansiveness. How could she not?

"Okay," Elya said, "let's see Michael's room."

Thought raised a brow. "Not Satan?"

"We both know I'd be too tempted to snoop," Elya said.

Thought shrugged. "I can't argue with that." He turned to the door. "Come along. Michael's room is down the hall."

Elya followed Thought from her room into the hall. It was long, and lined with doors going both directions. On both sides of her, there was no end in sight. Of course, there was probably an exit somewhere, but the doors seemed endless. Thought wasn't taking time to tour her around or answer her questions, though – he seemed to be on a straight path down the endless hall left of her door. Somewhere down that hall was the room filled with Michael's thoughts. They passed several doors as they walked, all unlabeled, but Thought knew where he was going. The walk felt like eternity, but finally they came to a stop at the end of the hall. There was no door on the end wall, but one on the left and right of it. Somehow, even without labels, Elya knew these were the doors of Satan and Michael.

Thought opened the door on the left and gestured for Elya to go inside.

The room was much like her own, only, as she predicted, huge. Bigger than she had imagined. There were also cabinets in far more colors than the white and black that occupied her filing room.

"Wow," Elya said.

Thought chuckled. "It is rather large."

Elya scoffed. "I could fit my high school in here. Not just the building – football field as well." She glanced around. "And the cabinets have so many different colors."

Thought shrugged. "When one has lived as long as Michael, it is best to have a slightly more organized filing system than simply alphabetized. White cabinets are his general thoughts, gray are for people he's met in passing, red are thoughts of his closest brothers – not by age. Well, I *did* order the drawers by age, but those contain thoughts pertaining to Satan and the archangels."

Elya glanced around. There were a lot of red – almost as many as there were white. There were several gray ones, as well as green, blue, orange, and yellow. Michael's cabinets seemed to come in every color. "What do they mean?"

"The black you already know, of course." Thought gestured to the cabinets "Then we have the gray; those are the cabinets containing thoughts of people he's passed in his lifetime. Fleeting little moments, but on the whole I would say unimportant."

"What are the green cabinets?" There weren't a lot of them. Only three. "Are those his bad thoughts or something?"

"No," Thought sighed. "Those are the thoughts he's had regarding you," He shrugged. "You're important to three of his brothers, so by default you invade his mind far more than he'd like. And before you decide you want to see, I will remind you that you'd really rather not."

Elya nodded. "Can I walk around?"

"So long as you leave the cabinets shut," Thought said.

Elya nodded. Curious as she was, especially after what she learned from the Riders, she wasn't about to invade Michael's privacy. Not without him there to stop her. Were he there to answer questions, that would be fair game in her eyes. But as it was, she didn't know him well.

If she cared less about the privacy of others, in a room like this she could learn more about a person than they know of themselves. She reached a hand to touch one of the white cabinets. It wasn't the cold metal she expected, but soft and squishy like cotton candy. She turned to ask Thought what it meant, only to trip over the cabinet as she did so. A sudden familiar sensation hit her. Focusing on where she was, Elya kept the water from sending her elsewhere. In doing so, her shoulder hit a different cabinet as she hit the floor. The cabinet dropped with a *clang*.

"Shit," Thought said.

Elya stared as a cloud of smoke seeped from the cabinet. Now she'd done it. She probably lost some of the thoughts stored inside or something else equally as destructive. Slowly, the cloud filled the room, morphing it. The cabinets disappeared, replaced by white walls and marble floors. Suddenly, she was in a familiar hall.

Elya glanced around and jumped. Two identical little boys with the same bright brown eyes, dark black hair and pure white wings ran through the familiar palace walls. They laughed as they chased after each other. It was strange – Elya had never seen an angel younger than Gabriel. She supposed they weren't necessarily angels, though, since all immortals had wings. But something about the boys screamed angels. They were familiar, in a way.

"Michael, Samael," a voice halted the boys in their tracks, "would you like to meet your little brother?"

Elya gasped. These children were Michael and Satan? They looked so young, innocent. Happy. She had never seen either of them interact with each other, but what she had seen of Michael was stern, serious. And Satan, well she had seen him happy and angry, but his main expression tended to be amused over the misfortunes of others.

Michael and Satan turned around, and Elya followed their gaze. A man who appeared to be of Arabian descent with kind unnatural blue eyes stood in a doorway, a warm smile on his face. The twins looked at each other then back to the man at the door. God?

"We have a little brother?" The twin on the left asked.

"Where did he come from?" The other asked.

The man chuckled. "I created him."

"Does he have a name?" They asked.

"Uriel," God replied.

The twins frowned. "Can he play with us?"

God smiled. "Not yet, but soon. If you'd like you may hold him."

Their eyes widened. "Now?"

"Yes," God said, "but only one at a time."

"I want to go first!" The right twin said.

"I'm older, I go first!" The left twin, Michael, said.

God held up a palm. "Peace, my sons. You will each have a turn, and whoever goes first this time goes second next."

The twins looked at each other. "Okay."

Michael stepped forward. "Sammy can go first."

God raised a brow. "You are certain?"

Michael nodded. "I'm the big brother, so I should let him go first."

Satan — *Samael*, she reminded herself. He wasn't the Devil yet – wrapped Michael in a hug. "You're the best, Mickey!"

Michael smiled. "Let's go!"

The twins raced past God through the open door. Elya followed quietly. Both were leaning over a crib to see the baby angel laid inside. Uriel's eyes even then were the intense vibrant green she recognized. His wings weren't visible yet, which caused Elya to question how angel wings worked. She refocused.

"He's so tiny," Samael said.

"And ugly," Michael added.

God chuckled behind them. "You two didn't look much better after your creation. It was a few hours before you looked less squished."

"But why is he so squished?" Michael asked.

"This is how the babies of humans, Tyvers, Arthenians, and several other species will be after they come into existence. Squished." God said.

"Can I hold him?" Samael asked.

"I said you may, just let me get him for you." God reached into the crib, grabbing the cooing baby angel. Carefully, he set baby Uriel into Samael's arms. "Remember, be gentle and support his head."

Samael grinned, looking at the baby. "Hi Uri. I'm Samael, but you can call me Sammy since I'm your big brother. The person who gave you to me is our dad. You'll like him, he knows a lot of cool tricks."

"He looks fragile," Michael said.

"For a little while he will be, but he'll be running around with the two of you in no time," God smiled. "Then I'll have three little angels constantly asking for cookies."

Michael nodded. "Good."

Samael was engrossed with the little child. "That's Mickey, he's my twin. We look the same but he's older, so he's both our older brother." His smile seemed to widen. "He's the best big brother ever, and I hope I'm as good of a big brother to you as he is to me."

The smoke returned, Michael, Samael, and baby Uriel vanishing. But instead of the filing cabinets Elya was expecting, the room was being replaced with another familiar setting. She'd recognize the high ceilings and dark throne anywhere: Satan's throne room. She sighed.

Thought must have sent her away, and she couldn't blame him, she did knock over a filing cabinet that wasn't hers. But at least the memory that was inside didn't seem to be too invasive. Yes, it was a family moment, but there was no fighting – nothing more than two little boys meeting their baby brother for the first time. In fact, it was actually quite sweet.

Satan would be repulsed to know she had seen him acting so childishly, of course, but it was what it was. Michael and Satan had been adorable children. Briefly, Elya wondered at their age in the memory. They were young – physically, at least. Perhaps five or six. Unfortunately, she couldn't ask anyone.

Sighing Elya glanced at her list she'd transferred to her phone. The next stop was Time's Clocktower where she'd hopefully be able to recruit both Time and his daughter Erika to their gathering army. She glanced to the address given. Like The Coffee Shop, Time's Clocktower tended to move, but not as frequently. According to Satan's notes, it would be in Egypt for another month. She had no idea how she was going to get to Egypt; her sky traveling was still far from ready for that kind of travel. Of course, if she got lost she could always call Kalael to send Loki for help.

On second thought…Elya texted Kalael explaining her dilemma. The response was instant. A purple and pink Loki bowing with a flourish and an eye roll.

"I hear you need help getting to Egypt."

"Yes please," Elya said.

"Fine, this once," he put a hand on her shoulder. "Only because you're still learning and I don't want to have to track you down if you get lost. I'll drop you right outside the Clocktower."

Elya barely had time to register his words before a familiar sensation of rushing water engulfed her. As soon as it had arrived it had vanished, and Loki along with it.

Thirty-Two

Elya couldn't help but admire the tall, imposing clocktower in front of her. It had to be taller than the Empire State building, but dark, gothic, elegant. She took a breath, grabbed the knocker, and knocked three times.

The door swung open to reveal a girl with light brown hair and more freckles than anyone she'd ever seen. There was something ethereal about the girl's smile – her eyes spoke of wisdom far greater than her appearance allowed. Standing in front of her felt strange, though not in the way that her soul seemed to be laid bare like with the angels. It wasn't the urgency she might die any moment as with the Reaper family. It was as though she had all the time in the world, yet had few precious seconds remaining.

"Hello Elya Tempest," the girl said. "Daddy and I have been expecting you."

Elya blinked. "You have?" This was what she got for dealing with Time and his daughter.

"Of course, we always know when to expect guests," Erika smiled. "Would you like a drink? Tea, water, milk, coffee, juice?"

"Just water's fine." Elya said.

She followed Erika as she led her through the halls. The walls were covered in clocks, in all different styles and sizes. A myriad of ticking filled the otherwise silent halls. Erika led them into a kitchen, and Elya was shocked to see clocks painted onto the cabinets, each seeming to work. Not all were set to the same time, probably showing different time zones, though the big clock above the stove had several strange symbols on it.

"That clock was gifted to me by the first Arthenian king," a new, soothing voice said. It was a man's voice that you could fall asleep to. The type you could have narrate movies and tv shows and everyone would be okay with it. The kind of voice people could easily listen to all day.

Elya turned around to see a tall, imposing man dressed in golden Roman armor. His eyes were a dark brown, his skin just a couple shades lighter. His arms were covered in watches – several name brands that Hellas would recognize, but an overwhelming number were Rolex. A watch hung from his neck. His face held a manicured beard. He looked nothing like Erika.

"Hello, sir," Elya said.

"Elya." He crossed his arms. "I presume you are here to ask for assistance from my daughter and myself."

"You Celestials seem to know everything," Elya said.

"I thought as much." Time checked the watches on his right arm. "You do not have much time left here before the tower throws you out."

"Daddy," Erika said. "Can't we help them?"

Time frowned. "You know my opinion of sky travelers, Erika. Like Loki, this girl is an unnatural abomination. The only reason I don't smite her where she stands is because Michael would smite me in turn."

"Daddy," Erika said softly.

"I stand by what I said," Time said.

"And what exactly is wrong with sky travelers?" Elya asked. She couldn't decide if she was offended by Time's comments or not.

"You have zero regard for the natural order of things! Sky travelers transverse timelines and dimensions without care to the risk."

Elya frowned. "I have no idea how to do any of that, but what I do know is that Afterlife is in danger and we need all the help we can get to save it. We need to work together, despite any grievances we may have with each other."

"Well spoken, but no," Time said.

Elya's gaze hardened. "So that's it? You'll let all of Afterlife be destroyed because you have a grudge against me for an ability I *never asked for*?"

"If my aid is needed, then I will be called upon by those of higher authority than me." Time narrowed his gaze. "That is not you."

"Fine." Her gaze drifted to a black wooden clock at the end of the counter. The intricate carvings of an unfamiliar language ran down the side. "What language is this?"

"Don't touch it!" Time shouted.

Elya cringed, noting her hand already on the clock. She moved to pull away, but it was as though someone had superglued her skin to the side of the clock. The room around her began to spin, the speed increasing to the point she felt as though she were on one of those rides at a theme park where they spin you so fast you stick to the walls. Just as quickly as the spinning began, it stopped, and she found herself plummeting to the ground.

After tripping into Hell from ages six to twenty-two, she had learned a thing or two about falling and hard landings. Thankfully, she had mastered the art of not tensing her body, so when she fell, she was less likely to break something. If only just barely. Despite this, she wasn't prepared for her landing to feel as though she hit the water from fifty feet above. Everything ached, but nothing felt broken... at the worst, she probably had a concussion, which really wasn't good either, but if she didn't sleep or overexert herself anytime soon, she'd be fine. Probably.

Staggering to her feet, Elya gaped at her surroundings. Her stomach churned. It looked as though she landed in the middle of a post-apocalyptic world. The sky was heavy with smog, and her lungs felt as though they were on fire. The grass was a burnt brown color, and the trees were all dead. The only indication she was still on planet Earth was the vague familiarity, and the trash littering the place, worse than anything she'd ever seen in the past. She tried not to breathe too much, not just because the air hurt her lungs, but because it had a distinct smell of raw sewage.

"Hey!" An unfamiliar voice called. "Are you alright?"

"I'm fine," Elya turned quickly, not knowing what to expect.

As her gaze landed on the figure behind her Elya stood, stunned. The boy in front of her couldn't have been any older than seventeen. His cerulean hair came past his ears, and sharp bangs hung just above familiar unnatural blue eyes. He wore khaki-colored cargo pants, a black jacket with pockets on each sleeve, each side of the chest and at the bottom on either side of the zipper. Above the left chest pocket was a red BA encased in a navy circle. A gray quiver of arrows was strapped to his back with a matching belt around his waist, and a sword hung from him. He bore a strong resemblance to Satan and the Deadly Sins, only the nose was off, and the shape of his eyes were wrong. Features from his mother, probably. If she had to guess, this boy was Envy.

"Mom?" The boy staggered back, eyes wide.

"Uh, no," Elya said.

He frowned. "Sorry, it's just you bear an uncanny resemblance to my mother. Of course, you can't be her. She's dead."

"Oh, um, I'm sorry."

He shrugged. "It's not your fault."

There was no time for her to comment further: a familiar face materialized between her and the boy. One she'd recognized anywhere. It was the face of the Devil. Only, based on the clothes he was wearing, Elya would go out on a limb and say it wasn't the Devil, but Michael who materialized. That, and she had never once known Satan to pass up on the opportunity to make a dramatic entrance.

"Miles, what are you doing out here?" Maybe Michael asked.

"I felt an energy surge," the boy, Miles, said.

Maybe Michael groaned. "And you thought you'd come check it out? You can't continue to be this reckless, Miles. I've already lost your mother and siblings. I won't lose you to Gabriel as well."

"Gabriel?" Elya said aloud.

Maybe... well, really, she was almost certain it was Michael, spun on his heel to face her. Any doubt she had vanished as his gaze landed on her. It wasn't the gaze of the Devil, but the gaze of an archangel, looking through her into her soul, and judging her for every wrong she ever committed.

"Elya," Michael said, stunned. "How?"

Before she could answer, another figure arrived, this one an unfamiliar blond with haunting blue eyes. Everyone had always described Zeerlo's eyes as being soulless, and she knew that look well, but this man's eyes... they were dead.

"Did you—" he cut himself off, his deadened gaze turning to her. "Well, this is a surprise." The blond smiled, the tiniest spark of life hitting his gaze. "How are you here?"

"I uh, touched a clock in Time's clocktower."

Michael snorted. "Of course you did. You just couldn't resist your curiosity, could you?"

"How was I supposed to know the clocks transport you — uh, where are we?"

"Each clock in the tower leads to a different timeline," the blond said. "I don't suppose you've been taught how to sky travel through timelines?"

"I have no idea about any of that," Elya said.

They exchanged a worried look. "Can we get her home?"

"Should be able to, but we'll definitely have to smuggle her into the clocktower," the blond replied.

"Hey!" Elya snapped. "I don't like being talked over."

The angel and the unknown man exchanged a grin. "That's Elya alright."

Elya frowned. "I know you," she gestured to Michael. "But who are they?"

Michael's grin vanished. "This—" he placed a hand on the blond's shoulder "—is my longtime best friend, Alex."

"Alex?" Elya staggered back. "As in *the* Alex, the Tyver king?"

The blond raised a brow. "Yes. You're familiar with my counterpart?"

"I've heard of him, but never met him. Still not clear on what a Tyver is either."

The blond nodded. "I suspected as much." He placed a hand on her shoulder. "Yes, I see now. You come from a very different world than our own."

"What?"

Alex huffed. "I have the ability to read through anyone's memories, so long as they have Tyver blood somewhere in their ancestry. It appears a vast majority of humanity in your timeline does. To be honest, I'd have never thought Gabriel could be so — sickeningly nice."

Michael snorted. "Did you just imply Gabriel is nice in her world?"

"Excuse me?" Elya crossed her arms. "Gabriel is a doll, and you shouldn't make fun of him. At least he's nice to me, which is more than I can say for some people."

Miles shook his head. "This is too weird. Next you'll be telling me Raphael isn't a monster."

"But Raphael's a healer, he'd never hurt anyone."

Miles's eyes flashed gold. "Tell that to my mother and older siblings who met their deaths at his hands."

Michael placed a hand on Miles's shoulder. "Enough."

"But, Dad—"

The archangel's eyes darkened. "I said enough. She is not from this timeline." He turned his gaze to Alex. "What can you tell me of her timeline?"

Alex sighed. "Best as I can tell, the key difference is in that in her world, you and Samael were the firstborns, Gabriel was the last creation, Samael led a rebellion, lost, and was cast into Hell where he became it's king and known to humanity as the Devil. Not very evil either, just sinful, I would say. Gabriel and Raphael, on the other hand, are kind, benevolent angels. Your Father, were he still alive in our own world, would be proud."

"Anything else?" Michael asked.

"I went insane, but honestly who can be surprised? But that means I did not raise Elya as I did here… in fact, her mother raised her. As for you, well, not much is different."

Miles stepped forward. "We need to get her home. If her timeline truly is a better place, she needs to be there where she'll be safe from Gabriel's rule."

Elya held up a hand. "Hold on. Not that I'm not following along, but I just want to clarify: Gabriel and Raphael are evil here, rebelled against God, and actually won?"

Alex nodded. "Those seem to be the essentials."

"So, to get to my own timeline, I need to go to the Clocktower?"

"Yes," Alex said.

"I'll take her," Miles said.

"Absolutely not," Michael argued.

"While I hate to disagree with you, Michael, Miles may be our best shot at getting Elya into that Clocktower. He is top of his class at Braidwood, and that's hardly a small feat."

"Please, Dad," Miles said. "I need to do this."

Elya wasn't sure what was going on. She recognized the way the two fell into an unspoken conversation, and it was fine with her. She needed time to process anyway. Gabriel in this world wasn't — how could *any* world exist where Gabriel wasn't an absolute cinnamon roll? And Alex… her gaze shifted to the legendary Tyver king. Never had it occurred to her she'd meet the king everyone whispered about. He was supposed to be powerful, second in strength only to God. But looking at him, the Tyver king didn't seem any more powerful than a human or other Celestial.

"The Tyver sovereign's strength comes from his people," Alex said.

Elya balked. "Are you—"

"Your thoughts aren't exactly silent, and as the Tyver king, I can hear them," he shrugged. "As for what a Tyver is, we are not much different than humans. Shortly after creation, Mother Nature had to protect Eden. She took some humans and instilled within them a connection with magic and nature itself. But that would leave us no different than sorcerers, wizards, witches, elementals… you get the point. And so, Mother Nature went to Noaket, the most powerful being the Creator ever made. Together, they altered a select handful of her experiments further, and the Tyver people were born. A people created to live alongside humanity, to protect them and Eden, then later Earth. The special thing about Tyvers is that they have more than one soul. Everyone carries an individual soul, but we carry a collective one as well. Noaket."

Elya's brows drew together. "But how—"

Miles cut her off. "If we're going to get you to the Clocktower, we need to leave now."

Elya turned from Alex to Michael. "He's taking me?"

Michael sighed. "Against my better judgment, yes."

She smiled. "Thanks. And for what it's worth, you don't seem to be a jerk like your counterpart."

The archangel shrugged. "Not sure I should take that as a compliment."

Miles placed a hand on her shoulder. "We need to go."

"Right," Elya said.

Michael looked between them, face unreadable. "Take care of each other."

Miles nodded. "Don't worry, Dad. I'll get her home safe."

Michael grinned. "I know you will."

"So, how are we getting there?" Elya asked.

"How's your sky traveling?" Miles asked.

Elya's eyes widened. He was a sky traveler too? That was… unexpected. In her own timeline, it was just her and

Loki that could sky travel. It was strange to think another sky traveler existed.

"Elya?" Miles asked.

Elya startled. "Sorry, I zoned out for a minute. I'm no master, but I'm decent."

He nodded placing a hand on her shoulder. Before Elya could say anything, the ever-familiar presence of water consumed her as she was pulled through space. When her feet touched ground, she found herself outside a familiar Clocktower.

"That was anticlimactic," Elya said.

Miles chuckled. "Getting here is the easy part. The hard part will be sneaking around inside undetected long enough to find the clock to your timeline."

Elya frowned. "How will we know which one is mine?"

He smiled. "You'll know it when you see it. Sky travelers are drawn to their natural timeline, so which ever clock draws you in, that's yours."

She shrugged. "Makes as much sense as anything else around here."

Miles chuckled, opening the door, and leading them inside the Clocktower. It was quiet, strangely so. The one she left had a constant ticking, but this was just dead silence. There was no sign of Time or Erika.

"I have a bad feeling about this," Elya said.

Miles nodded. "We'll be alright, so long as we stick together."

A laugh sounded in the distance. "Is that so?"

Elya spun on her heel to see Time stood there with Erika next to him, only it wasn't Erika. Her hair was black with neon green on its ends, her eyes glowed green, and her ever-present smile was absent. Next to them was another familiar figure – tall, blond, and instead of the warm eyes she was used to, this being's eyes were cold and calculating. All the same, she'd recognize Raphael anywhere.

"It was nice of you to drop by," Erika said.

"And Miles," Raphael grinned, "you brought me a gift."

Time chuckled. "You really should have given us more warning though."

Elya reached for her daggers, ready for a fight, only to find herself unable to move. Her eyes widened, heart racing, as panic coursed through her. She couldn't move. Her gaze searched out Miles, only to find him in a similar state. Time walked forward.

"Like it, Sky traveler?" Time asked. "It prohibits your ability to move. No sky traveling, no fighting, and no escaping."

"Which means we're in for a fun night," Raphael grinned. "Now sleep."

The room began to spin, her vision blurring. She barely made out the image of Miles collapsing to the floor. As she lost her balance, a strong pair of arms caught her, preventing her hitting the floor.

"Chain them in the dungeons and go alert Gabriel. He's going to want to know about this." Raphael's words were the last thing she heard as she fell into oblivion.

Thirty-Three

When she finally came to, it was to find herself in a small room made of bricks that gave off the smell of must. Her hands were chained to the wall, and Miles was chained beside her. Across from her stood Raphael, playing with a dagger between his fingers. Her first instinct upon seeing him was relief, until she remembered where she was. This wasn't her timeline, and if what Miles, Michael, and Alex had said was true, then she was in a lot of danger. This Raphael wasn't her friend. He was cruel, dangerous, and her counterpart's *murderer*. God, this was weird.

Raphael smirked. "You know, Elya, I'm going to take a lot of joy in the fact I get to kill you not once, but *twice*!" he chuckled. "I only wish Michael were here to see me rip you away from him again." Raphael turned to Miles. "And my dear nephew, little Miles," he conjured a dagger. "I'm going to enjoy killing her in front of you, and then I'm going to carve out your intestines."

Miles's gaze flashed gold. "If you hurt her—"

"You'll what?" Raphael asked mockingly. "Your mother couldn't stop me, nor could your sister. And your brother? He had the heart of a warrior like your parents, I admit, but he was born human. And when I killed him," Raphael chuckled, "he screamed like one too."

Miles spit at Raphael's feet. "Fuck you."

"Now, now." Gabriel walked out of the shadows. "There's no need for such hostility."

Only he wasn't Gabriel. This one carried himself differently. The Gabriel she knew walked with confidence and ease; this one's muscles were tense. Whereas her Gabriel's face was unblemished, this one wore countless scars, as though he were constantly in battle. And from what little she knew of him, Elya would believe it. Her Gabriel was well put together, relaxed most of the time, when he wasn't worrying about injuries, or nutrition, or violence. Not to mention, her

Gabriel would never use contractions. The Gabriel she knew would never be able to hurt a fly, let alone kill someone. And rebelling against God? Gabriel wouldn't even defy *Michael*, let alone God.

"Tell me, Miles," Raphael said. "You were only three when I killed your mother. Do you even remember her?" He chuckled. "You must. Michael has been so protective of you… the only way he would've let you talk him into letting you be here is if you did." Raphael pulled out a dagger, stepping toward Elya. "I'm going to enjoy carving into your pretty little face."

"You don't want to do that." Elya said surprised at how level her voice was.

A small part of her hoped Michael would come bursting through the doors, because she had the feeling he was at least on friendly terms with her counterpart, or he was before she died. And really, he had seemed reluctant to let Miles go – surely he'd have followed at a distance to keep his son safe. She hoped.

"And why not?" Raphael asked, holding the blade against her cheek.

The air shifted as the room cooled slightly. Raphael was ripped away from Elya as a figure stepped between them. He was tall, athletic, his hair was dark black, and his gaze burned with rage, but his face betrayed his amusement. Elya didn't know how he had gotten there, he shouldn't have been there, it was impossible for him to be there, and yet, there he was. He radiated calm. She may have been in danger, but him? He was completely within his element.

"Nobody touches Elya," Zeerlo's tone was low. Fire raged in his gaze.

Gabriel chuckled. "And just who do you think you are to tell me what to do?" He crossed his arms. "You should bow before your emperor."

Zeerlo raised a brow. "I don't bow to my father, nor do I bow to my grandfather, and if you think I'm about to bow down before some pathetic wannabee angel," flames flickered at Zeerlo's feet, "you have another thing coming."

Gabriel observed Zeerlo. "You're confident and defiant." He crossed his arms. "You remind me of a younger me." He turned his attention to Raphael. "Kill him."

Raphael grinned twistedly. "With pleasure."

As Raphael drew his blades, Zeerlo drew his own. Zeerlo made the first move – quick, deliberate, and powerful. His first move sent a message, warning of his power and his strength. Zeerlo may not have been a full-blooded celestial (how much divine blood he held was often debated) but he was no easier to kill than one, if it was even possible. He might have been *more* difficult to kill, if anything. Zeerlo had only one weakness: the pendant hung from his neck. And Elya didn't think anything short of the power of God could get it off him.

Raphael maneuvered with his daggers easily enough; he was light on his feet as he attempted to dodge Zeerlo, and he did manage to. Occasionally, Zeerlo would manage a cut on the angel, just as here and there the angel would cut Wrath. They were evenly matched.

Elya eyed Zeerlo carefully, and noticed a glint in his gaze. *Amusement.* She shouldn't have been surprised: Zeerlo loved violence, and nothing thrilled him more than a good fight and bloodshed. And while he hadn't killed Raphael, he had managed to draw the golden liquid celestial blood – a reminder that, unlike Zeerlo, Raphael was pure cosmic energy. Raphael looked a little worn, but Zeerlo was calm, at ease. He was completely in his element, and looked like he could keep going for hours.

Zeerlo got close to Raphael – close enough to make a long gash across the celestial's throat – but the angel was undeterred. His skin carefully wove itself back together, until not so much as a scar remained of the injury Zeerlo had inflicted.

"Hasn't anyone ever told you full blooded celestials are immortal?" Raphael mocked.

Zeerlo sneered. "You have no Hell here, which means you don't know there's an easy way to destroy celestials." His eyes glinted. "Unfortunately for you, I know it."

His gaze hardened as the fighting resumed. Zeerlo moved with ease, the grace of a dancer and the deadly force of an army. Hell, Zeerlo *was* an army. That was Satan's main goal in creating his sons, to make each nigh indestructible soldiers of war, that could go toe-to-toe with even the most powerful of celestial beings and hold their own. Apparently, it paid off.

And still yet, Zeerlo appeared to be just on par with Raphael. Which didn't make sense, how could it? She had seen Zeerlo train. Yes, this was a different Raphael, but aside from his evilness, something about him seemed different from his counterpart. Weaker. After she spent sixteen of her twenty-two years in the angel's presence, she was able to pick up a few things. Like how the power radiating from this Raphael didn't seem to be half of what radiated from the one she knew.

Zeerlo and Raphael locked in battle, Raphael pressing his dagger toward Zeerlo's chest as the sin seemed to struggle to keep the tip of the blades away from his skin.

The room went silent as Raphael's dagger went through Zeerlo's heart. Gabriel chuckled, satisfaction in his gaze. Miles's eyes widened in horror. And Raphael, he looked smug as he stood above Wrath, his blade embedded deep in the sin's chest.

Zeerlo just laughed. It was the kind of laugh that sent chills through anyone who heard it. It was crazed. Delusional. It was the laugh you'd expect in a horror movie, or to be emitted from an insane person. It wasn't the laugh of someone dying – no, it was a laugh that made hearts stop.

"Is that the best you have?" Zeerlo scoffed. "You're going to have to up your game if you want to win a fight against me." He removed the dagger. "Points for managing to break my skin, I suppose."

Raphael spit on the ground, blood mixing with his saliva. "Who are you?"

Zeerlo grinned devilishly. "I am Zeerlo Adolf Heinrich Vladimir Satan Lucifer, first son of the Devil himself." He unleashed his wings. "I am Wrath incarnate, a trained and perfected killer," his fangs elongated, "and I will destroy you."

Miles gasped beside Elya. "His wings are red!"

"Well, yeah," Elya said. "He's Wrath and has an incredible amount of blood on his hands," she smirked. "And they made a fatal mistake."

Miles looked back to Zeerlo, who moved forward at a snail's pace. Flames traced his every step. Fires danced in his eyes as smoke billowed around him. The lights flickered with his every step toward Raphael and Gabriel. The latter looked amused, but Raphael had tensed. He understood Zeerlo was powerful, and had quite possibly realized that, next to Zeerlo, he didn't stand a chance. This Raphael may have been ruthless, coldhearted, and a killer, but he was weaker than the one she knew. But how?

"He's been easily matched with Raphael this entire time," Miles said.

"No," Elya smirked, "he's been *toying* with Raphael this entire time."

"I grow bored," Zeerlo said as he grabbed Raphael by the throat. His fires flared until they consumed both he and Raphael. "Let's end this." Suddenly, he threw Raphael into the wall, drawing his sword. In one fluid motion, Zeerlo moved with his sword to where Raphael sat collapsed against the wall, and plunged it into the corrupt angel's heart. There was a burst of golden light, then nothing. No light, no body. Raphael was just gone.

Clap. Clap. Clap. Gabriel walked forward, grinning. "I have to say, you're quite impressive," Gabriel smirked. "If you're interested, I seem to have an opening for the place of my right hand."

Zeerlo chuckled. "I don't work for people weaker than me. It's a generous offer, but I already have a life I enjoy." He held out a hand, and his sword flew into it. "And I must admit, I don't take well to people who hurt those under my protection. I won't tolerate you attempting to hurt Elya."

Gabriel scoffed. "Oh, don't hurt Elya?" His eyes flashed gold. "You're pathetic and weak."

Despite the situation, Elya burst into laughter. Miles looked at her, shocked, questioning her sanity.

"I'm sorry," she said between chuckles, "but pathetic and weak? After what we just witnessed? The Gabriel I know is smart. That was just embarrassing."

"What you don't understand," Zeerlo said, ignoring Elya, "is my strength only grows as people threaten those under my protection – unfortunate as it is to have to protect anyone. Disgusting, really."

"If you're certain," Gabriel shrugged, "then so be it. I'll simply have to kill you too."

Zeerlo laughed manically. "You're going to kill me?" He sheathed his sword. "I had all of Hell thrown at me when I was five and I'm still here." The edges of his wings caught fire. "There is only one way to kill me, and I promise you will never know how."

Gabriel rolled his eyes. "You got lucky against Raphael, I admit, but I promise you," he smirked, "you're no match for me."

Zeerlo grinned sinisterly. "Normally I like to toy with my prey before killing it, but for you, I'll make an exception."

Gabriel scoffed. "Don't flatter yourself."

When faced with Raphael, Zeerlo had taken his time, enjoyed combat with his opponent, but Gabriel had made a fatal mistake: he invoked Zeerlo's wrath. While the sin incarnate had an ironclad grip over his rage, Elya knew he had no qualms with releasing it, especially in battle or when he was tasked with killing someone.

Zeerlo cracked his neck. "You have no idea how much pleasure I'm going to take in killing you," he chuckled. "Killing Raphael, well it was like a dream come true. Someone was finally letting me kill an archangel!" He tsked. "Shame, you're not nearly as powerful as your counterpart from my timeline. If you were, I might have a modicum of respect for you."

Gabriel glared. "You're confident, but you shouldn't be. Raphael wasn't a match for myself. You won't be either."

Zeerlo cackled. "Oh, uncle," he emitted a deep, guttural growl. "When will you learn?" His gaze danced with the flames of Hell. "I am impossible to kill," Zeerlo inhaled. "I am Wrath incarnate." His eyes seemed to glow. "I was designed to be a ruthless killing machine. And you? You were designed to be *good*."

He vanished in a blur. Gabriel's eyes searched frantically to no avail. Elya closed her eyes, knowing whatever was about to happen wouldn't be pretty. The sound of Miles gasping beside her the only confirmation she needed.

"Open your eyes, I cleaned up the mess already," Zeerlo said.

Elya peeked an eye open to see only Zeerlo, a pool of blood, and Miles already unchained next to him. Miles was pale, more so than Azrael, and he looked nauseous. She raised a brow at Zeerlo, but Wrath merely shrugged. Normally, she'd want to know what happened, but Zeerlo was gruesome at the best of times. For sanity's sake, she probably didn't want to know what happened.

"Well, that was boring. Can we go now?" Zeerlo said.

"Boring?" Miles gaped. "You just killed Raphael *and* Gabriel as though it were nothing."

"It *was* nothing," Zeerlo shrugged. "So, you're my alternate timeline cousin?" He eyed Miles critically. "Bow, sword, a Tyver Blessing, and a Braidwood education… if you're any good, that's not bad."

"My mom taught me bow, my dad the sword, and I'm top of my class at Braidwood."

Zeerlo raised a brow. "Impressive. Who's your Tyver master?"

"The Tyver king himself."

Zeerlo nodded. "If your counterpart can manage this in my own timeline, I might train him myself."

Miles smiled. "Thanks, I think."

Zeerlo turned his attention to her. "We need to go."

She glanced to Miles. "Will you guys be alright?"

"We'll be fine. We're free now," Miles's grin took up his entire face. "Alex and my dad have been working toward this since long before I was born. This," his eyes watered, "you have no idea what you've done for us."

Zeerlo recoiled. "Don't get sappy. I don't do sappy." He placed a hand on her shoulder. "Ready to go?"

"How exactly are we going?" Elya asked. "I was told the only way to get me back was through the clocktower."

Zeerlo snorted. "Maybe if our timeline was like this one," he smirked. "But luckily for you, it's not. As much as I loathe it, I was able to travel here from Mercenary Mansion. I know how to get us home."

Elya smiled. "Great!" She turned to Miles. "It was great getting to know you, even if our little adventure didn't end well. Tell your dad and Alex I made it home safe, and—" Elya didn't get a chance to finish as she was pulled away by a burning darkness.

When the light finally returned and the temperature cooled, Elya found herself stood once again outside Time's Clocktower, thankfully in her own timeline. Zeerlo stood across from her, arms crossed, leaning lazily against the door as though Time wouldn't throw a fit or threaten him if he found the sin like that. Not that Zeerlo would be afraid of Time. Why should he be?

Elya glared at Wrath. "I wasn't done saying goodbye."

He scoffed. "Like Hell I was letting you finish. I know you, Elya." His eyes glinted. "You were just getting started on your goodbye. You're too emotional. Stop growing attached to people. Attachments will only get you hurt."

"I just wanted to say goodbye. Miles seems to have had a rough life," Elya said.

Zeerlo rolled his eyes. "He'll be fine. He's Michael's son."

Elya frowned. "How did you—" her eyes widened. "Does Miles exist in this timeline?"

He chuckled. "No." He crossed his arms. "Not yet, at least. I mean, he was your son."

Elya startled. "I'm sorry, I thought you said Miles was my son. As in *mine*. Meaning me and Michael have a kid in another timeline. As in Michael and me and a kid."

"Three kids, technically," Zeerlo said. "The first two were killed by Raphael."

Elya staggered back. "What in the world would give you the idea that Michael and I—"

"He has your nose, and you share the same eye shape. His smile is definitely yours." Zeerlo shrugged. "Michael and my dad are identical, meaning Miles could pass for my own brother. I know how to recognize the features that belong to Michael, because they belong to me. Anything foreign has to belong to his mother. I've seen you almost every day for eleven years. I think I'd know how to pick out your features in someone else."

"But— that can't even be—" she stammered.

"Can't it?"

"Michael hates me!"

"Maybe in this timeline, but in that one, you and he definitely had kids together." He shrugged. "I need to go. Don't forget to talk to Time. We still need him."

Before Elya could even process what he said, Zeerlo vanished. She stood staring at the Clocktower door, reeling from this information.

Was Zeerlo right, was Miles her son? Hers and Michael's? If so, how had that happened? Was her counterpart so different from herself or was there something she was missing? Had her counterpart seen something in Michael she hadn't, or couldn't? Or was there something fundamentally different about that Michael? Aside from the fact he seemed nicer and less intimidating. She supposed that could explain a lot.

Elya groaned inwardly. She wanted answers and the only person who could possibly give them to her was in another timeline – one she absolutely did *not* want to return to.

Sighing in defeat, Elya once again knocked on the door. Almost immediately, it was opened by Time, his expression dark, and his eyes filled with disapproval. She gulped. If she thought convincing Time would be hard earlier, now she had gone and touched a timeline. He was probably never going to agree now.

"Before you say anything, I just wanted to apologize," Elya said. "I shouldn't have touched the clock, though in my defense, I had no idea they were portals to other timelines. But still, I should have shown more respect. I'm sorry."

Time frowned. "Very well," he leaned against the doorframe. "Tell Satan I shall attend his meeting and hear him out, but I make no promises that you will have our aid beyond that." He conjured a glass of water. "I will not use my powers to turn the tide of the war. I will help where I am able, but I will fight fairly. If Satan convinces me it is worth my time, that is. I dislike it to be wasted."

Elya startled. "Really?"

Time nodded. "I dislike wasted effort, so I prefer to be honest and upfront."

"Thanks," Elya said, "but why?"

"I may not be all knowing, but I am Time. I know how this conversation would end. Mine is precious and I do not like to waste it."

"Oh," she said.

Time looked to the watches on his other wrist. "You don't carry a time piece, do you?"

"I have my phone," Elya said.

Time frowned. "No." He reached into his pocket, pulling out a small box. "This should suffice." He opened the box, revealing a white Bulova with rose-gold accents and hands. Diamonds were in place of the numbers, and the strap was white leather.

"Wow, thanks." Elya took the offered watch. "It's so pretty."

Time chuckled. "It's nothing extravagant, but I suspect it will do its job."

"Seriously though," Elya smiled, "thanks."

"You're welcome." Time said, eyes flicking to the clock over the stove. "You should get going. You have much left to do."

"Right." Elya downed the rest of her water. "Thanks again for the watch and agreeing to at least talk with Satan."

Time vanished. Elya frowned as the door shut in front of her. If he didn't like to waste time, why had he been so adamant about not helping when she arrived? Unless had he wanted her to touch the clock? Was there something he wanted her to see in that timeline? Or do? It didn't make sense, why would he agree out of nowhere?

Elya shook her head. The only logical explanation was that he wanted her to go into the other timeline for some unknown reason. But as much as she'd like to contemplate it further, she had to get Aurelius, Marco, and Bernard in some town called Silverwoods, Kansas.

Thirty-Four

As Elya drove down the long, winding gravel driveway, she couldn't help admiring the large colonial style house surrounded by forest land. A white picket fence lined the road; it was beautiful. The shiny For Sale sign and large oak tree stood proudly behind the house, beckoning buyers in search of their dream home. She checked her phone for the address Satan texted her: 00666 Trego Road, Silverwoods, Kansas, 66666. Her eyes drifted to the number on the mailbox. This was it.

A house so picturesque nobody would suspect the horrors it contained inside. Namely, three ghosts and one demon.

Steeling herself, Elya walked to the porch. The last step creaked ominously as she walked up. Exhaling, she knocked. A moment passed and then the door opened to nothing. Elya rolled her eyes – she'd never understand why ghosts tried so hard to be dramatic. If she were honest, ghosts could be just as bad, if not worse, than immortals in that department.

"Why do you think she's here?" A voice spoke.

Elya's gaze snapped up. Two figures stood against the back wall, observing her. If she ever said ghosts couldn't be attractive, she took it back now. The first ghost's black hair was disheveled, his clothes were tattered, his features were sharp, and there was something dark in his blue gaze. He looked to be around Zeerlo's age, though he was around the same height as Satan.

The other was slightly tanned without the pale skin of the first boy. His hair and eyes were brown, and where the first boy looked like he had been lost in the woods, this guy looked put together. Though there was a crazed look in his eye, he was handsome.

"Hmm. She's too young to afford to live here, isn't she?" The older of the two asked.

The younger nodded.

Elya exhaled. "I'm here for your help."

"Oh, she can see us." The older grinned; there was something unnerving about it.

The younger grimaced. "Great."

"Oh Aurelius, you need to liven up a little." He turned his attention back to Elya. "Now, what was this about needing help?"

"There's a threat to the Afterlife," Elya explained. "Someone's planning to destroy Heaven and Hell. Satan asked me to gather the troops, and he thinks you guys should be able to help out."

The older raised a brow. "I don't exactly see what's in it for us." He crossed his arms defiantly. "Not to mention that, if you didn't get the memo, we're all bound to the house. Aurelius can be freed easily enough, but as a demon, only an angel or Satan can remove my binds to the land. And let me tell you, Kalael knows her stuff." He chuckled darkly. "She's Satan's little girl without a doubt, binding me to herself on a temporary basis. But the Reaper never did let us have any *real* fun."

Elya stepped back. "You're a demon?"

The demon laughed, revealing fangs. "Of course I am."

"Ignore him," the younger said. "Marco's a shameless flirt."

Marco's eyes flashed red. "Now there's no need for such unflattering words, *Reli*."

Aurelius huffed. "Don't call me that!"

Marco rolled his eyes. "Whatever."

"Um, so is that a no?" Elya asked.

Marco huffed. "If you can figure out how to release myself and Aurelius and, considering Satan sent you, I assume Bernard is wanted as well… Release us from our binds and we're in. Otherwise, I regret to inform you that we must decline."

Aurelius smiled. "I can help you undo my own binding; I don't need anything more than that. I'm always willing to help."

Marco scoffed. "This is what happens when we kill the son of Life." He crossed his arms. "You're absolutely useless, Aurelius! When will you learn to accept the darkness?"

"Whoa, wait," Elya gaped, "you're Life's son? But that means you're Azrael's nephew! That's crazy."

Aurelius laughed. "You have no idea. Now, could I offer you something to drink? Water, tea, lemonade? It'd be improper not to offer."

"Oh, I'm good. Thanks though," Elya said.

"Very well then – at least allow me to introduce myself properly." He offered her a hand. "Aurelius Leben. You've met Marco already."

"Aurelius!" A small voice called. A little girl materialized behind him, wearing a bright red dress and matching shoes. Her brunette hair was pulled to the sides in a pair of pig tails, and her emerald eyes swam with tears.

The older ghost knelt in front of the girls. "What's wrong?"

"Bernard depaciaked my teddy!"

"He decapitated your teddy?" Aurelius asked.

"Yes!"

Aurelius sighed. "Wait here." He stood, turning to Elya. "You'll have to excuse me; it would seem I have to take care of something."

Marco scoffed. "Just leave it. The brat doesn't need a stupid bear anyway."

As Aurelius disappeared with the little ghost, Elya glanced to the demon. "I'm just going to go make a phone call." She rushed outside before Marco could respond. Pulling her cell out, Elya searched through her contacts until she found the devil emoji. She hit call and waited as the phone on the other end rang.

"Elya, what's wrong?" Satan rushed out.

"You didn't exactly give me a lesson on releasing ghosts and demons from their binds! Or how to get them to do what I want." Elya said.

Satan huffed. "Do you have the dagger I gave you? Not the dark green one, the emerald encrusted one."

"Yeah?"

"Good. You'll need that. Now first things first, you won't be releasing Marco from his binds. Now for Aurelius and Bernard, it's a simple task. Literally just tell them you bind them to you until you release them. Marco will be a bit more difficult."

"How difficult?" Elya asked.

"To bind his will to yours, you must first prove yourself stronger than him. He's not full grown, so you'll have that to your advantage. You'll need to use your Hell dagger to your advantage if you're going to prove your worth. Don't be afraid to play dirty."

"Whoa! Wait what?"

"If you don't assert dominance over him, you'll bind yourself to his will, and believe me you do *not* want that."

"Right. And how do I bind him to me?" Elya asked.

"Slice his right palm with the Hell blade. Since you're not of my blood this will substitute. Using his blood, you'll need to draw a pentagram on him—"

"Where?"

"His palm! You use the line of the cut as part of the pentagram, and you use the blood on the blade to draw the pentagram. Then you cut your own palm, clasp your hands together, and say the words 'Demon, I bind your will to me until the time I release you' in Latin. If you don't know the words, ask Aurelius."

"Right," Elya rolled her eyes. "Sounds simple enough."

"It's that or you do a typical mortal binding ritual, but chances are, he'd break free by the end of the day. Were he full grown, it'd take an hour, but this bind will hold up to a year."

Before Elya could ask more questions, the line went dead. Sighing, she pocketed the phone. She had already faced War in a fight – granted she lost and was still stitched up, but if she needed to prove herself stronger than Marco, then she didn't have much choice. She needed to fight Marco, to prove herself stronger. Taking a breath, Elya reentered the house and spotted Marco leaning against the wall.

He pushed off the wall. "Can we get this over with? I have a busy schedule to keep."

Elya blanched. "Yeah, sure."

She was not ready to face off with a demon. Not like this. But if she didn't do it now, she never would. Elya took a breath, readying herself. She needed to assert her dominance. She needed to channel Zeerlo or maybe Kalael… She had at least seen the latter change from being disrespected to standing tall over the demons as they knelt before her. Elya needed to make this demon bow to her will. It wouldn't be easy, but it needed to be done.

"Excellent," Marco grinned.

Brow furrowed, Elya calculated the odds of her winning against a demon. Before she had started on this journey to save the Afterlife, she would say the odds were 1 in 3 million, but now, after everything she had learned, they weren't so bad. Yes, Marco was a demon and she had never fought one before, but she had fought Zeerlo and lost, she had fought War and lost, received fighting tips from the entire Reaper family, and while she had yet to win a fight, she had *learned*. She was getting better. If the chances of her winning were only 1 in 3, she'd take those odds gladly.

He lunged toward her; Elya dropped and rolled behind him. She sprang to her feet, but Marco pivoted, and before she could react, Elya found herself shoved into a wall. Instincts kicking in, she elbowed low and stomped on his foot. As she was released, Elya ducked underneath his arms. Marco spun back to her; she sidestepped. It wasn't so difficult – it was like training with Twist and Fiend or getting her butt kicked by Zeerlo. Even a bit like the sword fight she had with War.

Thumb on the outside of the fist so it doesn't break. Use your opponent's size against them. Find their weaknesses and exploit them. Every lesson she ever had under Satan's tutelage, the additional lessons from Simone, Dimitri, Kalael, War and Conquest… They had all been leading up to this.

Elya delivered quick, precise jabs to the pressure points Dimitri taught her. Marco seemed to slow as she gained momentum. She may not have been half devil like the Deadly Sins, or half Reaper like Simone, Dimitri, and Zeke, but it didn't matter. She wasn't useless. She was learning and she would prove herself stronger than Marco – there wasn't a choice. They needed all the manpower they could get against this unknown threat. After all, only someone powerful would even think to destroy Heaven and Hell.

"Nicely done, Elya!" Aurelius suddenly called.

Elya refused to be distracted, instead focusing as Marco moved to shove her into the wall again. She ducked beneath his outstretched hands, grabbing his arm as she moved, and spun herself behind him. Never letting go, using all her remaining momentum, she shoved Marco into the wall. He struggled to break free, but she refused to let him budge. Her breathing was ragged, but she had done it. By some twist of fate, she had outmaneuvered a demon. Holding tightly to Marco's wrist, Elya used her free hand to pull out her Hell dagger. Marco yanked her closer, but she didn't let go. Biting the inside of her cheek, she sliced her blade across his palm. Quickly, she used the blood on the blade to draw a pentagram as directed.

His eyes burned a brighter red, and he snarled. Elya maneuvered the blade to her own palm and cut it open with a hiss. Why she had to use blood from her palm was beyond her. It was one of the most sensitive places. Her thigh wouldn't hurt this much, since there weren't as many nerves. Even the back of her hand wouldn't have hurt as much! Sheathing her dagger, Elya turned her attention back to the demon.

"Aurelius!" Elya called, "How do I say 'Demon I bind your will to me until the time I release you' in Latin?"

"You're asking me?" Aurelius gaped. "I haven't used my Latin skills beyond rudimentary readings in years!"

"Well, I don't know any Latin!"

"Okay! Um," Aurelius frowned, brows drawn together, "*Daemon voluntas tua alligo usque ad tempus dimittere.*"

"Are you sure?" Elya asked.

"No, but it might be close enough to suffice!" Aurelius said.

"Demon—" Elya began.

"*No!*" Aurelius called "*Daemon voluntas tua alligo usque ad tempus dimittere.* You have to get the pronunciation right in a binding ritual!"

"But it doesn't matter if the translation is wrong?" Elya asked.

Aurelius sighed. "It just — repeat the phrase and pray it works."

Elya winced as she tightened her grip on Marco's hand. This was insanity. "*Daemon voluntas—*" she bit her lip "*—tua alligo usque—*" she cursed inwardly as she tried to remember the words "*—ad tempus dimittere,*" Elya rushed out.

A jolt of electricity or something rushed through Elya, as she and Marco were surrounded by a golden light. She hoped that meant it worked. She released Marco and looked toward Aurelius. "How do we know if it worked?"

Aurelius frowned. "You're not of Satan's blood – it'll take a week for the bond to settle. And you don't have that time to waste. If he can leave the property after a week, we'll at least know it did something, but we won't know what until we meet next."

Elya sighed. "Not what I wanted to hear, but honestly I'm too exhausted to care."

Aurelius nodded. "I understand. You should get some rest. We have plenty of bedrooms. Feel free to take one for yourself."

"Uh, thanks."

Marco groaned, staggering to his feet. "You fought well." He took a step forward. "I at least don't have to be embarrassed to have lost to you."

Elya smiled. "You're not bad yourself."

"I can see why my uncle admires your strength," Marco said.

Elya scoffed. "Satan doesn't admire—"

"Not Satan, Michael."

Elya's brows rose. "Michael? He doesn't— he—"

"Respects you as a warrior. He was trained in war from a young age, so to have his respect as a fighter, well, it's quite the accomplishment. Of course, we all thought he was insane when he told us the girl who kept tripping into Hell would grow into a mighty warrioress capable of bringing Afterlife to its knees. But now, I see the beginnings of the warrior my uncle spoke of."

"But how would Michael—"

Marco smirked. "You think like a mortal. You shouldn't."

The demon vanished, not giving Elya the opportunity to ask further questions. She turned to see if Aurelius would, but he vanished as well.

It seemed the more she learned of Michael, the more confused she became. He banned her from Heaven, from communicating with Raphael and Gabriel, and yet according to War, he had sworn an oath to protect her. He had given her no indication he ever held any trust or care for Satan, but the memory she saw spoke volumes. And now Marco – who, admittedly, wasn't the best source – was saying Michael admired her strength, that he respected her as a warrior. She wasn't exactly much of a fighter when she broke into Heaven, so how could Michael possibly know if she'd become a warrior? God was supposed to be omniscient, but from what she understood, that ability wasn't supposed to extend to the angels… But humanity had gotten so many other things wrong, it was possible they had been wrong about that as well. Or was she missing something else? Nothing she knew of Michael made sense. Why would he ban her from Heaven, remove her angelic friends from her life when he had an oath to protect her?

Stifling a yawn, Elya made her way up the stairs. She walked down the hall, opening a random door, she flicked on a light. Relief flooded through her. It was a bedroom, and surprisingly enough, it was in pristine condition. She stepped into the royal blue room, her gaze drifting to the furniture. The dresser, desk, and bedframe were all made of mahogany. She laughed internally.

"What is so amusing?" A familiar voice asked.

Elya spun on her heel, heart quickening. She had to be hallucinating in her exhausted state – surely, he wasn't real. Gabriel would never disobey a direct order. (Not this Gabriel, who was good and didn't disobey orders. He wasn't *that* Gabriel, the one who had tried to kill her.) But then, he had already disobeyed orders so by sending her little trinkets… No words were spoken, but each trinket sent relayed his message loud and clear. He was the messenger angel, after all. She stared at Gabriel stood in front of her; there was an odd glint in his gaze she hadn't seen before.

"Gabriel?" Elya asked.

He smiled. "Yes."

"But how – why are you here?"

The archangel grinned. "Did you truly believe I would allow Michael to keep me from you? You are one of the most important people in my life."

Elya frowned. "You never break the rules."

He shrugged. "I will make an exception for you, Elya. I will always make an exception for you. Michael has been called away to Arthenia, so I am taking advantage."

"Aren't you afraid you'll be in trouble?" Elya asked.

"Michael will understand, and I have no doubt my Father does." He ran a hand through his hair. "That said, I cannot stay long. I just – I wanted to see—" Gabriel's eyes drifted to the side of her jaw. "Are those stitches?"

"Huh? Oh yeah. War, Famine and Conquest weren't all that up for the idea of battling it out with someone out to destroy the Afterlife, especially if it meant working with Sa– your brother." Elya winced, knowing what was coming. "War decided I needed to prove myself a worthy adversary in battle, which was terrifying. I fought against War."

"You did what?" Gabriel grabbed her by the shoulders. His eyes seemed to search across her for any signs of injury. "Are you hurt elsewhere?"

"I'm fine!" Elya squirmed from his grip. "He definitely went easy on me."

"You have stitches!"

"Yeah, but only in three places." He didn't need to know she had sixteen in her side alone. "For a girl that goes to he– I mean, the *bad place* – every single time she trips, I thought I did great."

"And you are certain you are alright?" His voice calmed. "War is not an easy opponent, even if he was not fighting with his full strength. He is fearsome in battle."

Elya nodded. "I'm fine."

"I should call Raphael or Life to have you healed properly." His gaze lingered on her stitches.

"I'm not dying."

"There is no guarantee those wounds are not infected." His eyes turned gold. "Who knows when War last cleaned his sword?! How could you do something so foolish?"

"It's not like I planned on it." The exact opposite, really. "It just happened."

"That does not make the situation better. You could have been killed!" A pair of large wings sprouted from his back.

They were white, specked with gold, and bore the slightest tinge of gray at the bottom, with black tips. "Do you have any idea how important you are, Elya?" He placed a hand on either of her shoulders. "You are *not* allowed to die on me."

"Gabriel—"

"I cannot believe my brother would be so irresponsible with you! I would have thought he of all people would have ensured your safety. And now you show up here with stitches because he was careless, and you had to fight War." He began to hyperventilate.

Elya grabbed his wrist, shocked. "Gabriel, you need to breathe."

He pulled his arm free. "I have no need to breathe!"

"Well, it might help you calm down!"

"I am calm!"

Elya sighed. "Gabriel, you're shouting."

He winced. "My— I— I offer my apologies." He ran a hand through his hair. "I should not have allowed myself to lose my temper."

"It's fine," Elya lied. "Just please don't do it again."

"It is not fine, or you would not have lied to me just now. Furthermore, I have not lost my temper like this since—"

"Since—" Elya prompted.

"Since the day my brother—" his voice broke "—my siblings were cast from Heaven for their rebellion, while Loki had been protected by Azrael. The reasoning was sound. Putting Loki with my brother... well, they would have succeeded had they convinced Azrael to side with them. The fighting was long and hard, and when it was over, I lost a third of my family." His eyes watered. "I refuse to lose anyone else I care for." Golden tears escaped from his eyes. "This includes you."

"Don't get me wrong," Elya offered him a smile, "it's nice to know you care for my well-being." Or it was when he wasn't being overbearing. "But sometimes your reactions are just a little much."

His brow furrowed. "You mean because I yelled?"

"No," Elya sighed, "I mean because you panic over every little scrape and bruise I get." She folded her arms. "You act like I'm some little kid and can't take care of myself. I've been tripping into Hell every day since I was six. I think it's time to accept that I can handle myself."

"What?" His eyes widened. "Elya, it is not because I do not believe you capable that I worry. It is because I know you are capable of so many things that even when you are fearful, you do them." Gabriel grabbed her shoulders. "You befriended my brother, as well as his children." He smiled despite the golden tears streaming down his face. "You are strong and confident because the circumstances of your life have led you to be." He sighed. "But you are still human. I fear one day you will face impossible odds and not come out on top."

"You're an angel." Elya raised a brow. "Shouldn't you of all people be encouraging me not to fear dying?"

He bit his lip. "I know not where you will spend your afterlife, Elya."

Elya startled. "Wouldn't I get into Heaven?"

"You were given definitive proof of divinity when you were six, Elya." He ran a hand through his hair. "It has never been a matter of faith for you. You are a unique individual."

"But Kalael, Dimitri, Zeke, Simone, Zeerlo and his brothers, all of them—"

"Must lead their lives choosing their own path and meet the judgement of my Father when the time comes." His expression dropped. "However, the Sins will likely remain with their father when their time comes. Perhaps Pride may find herself being welcomed into Heaven," he mused, "but it is uncertain."

Elya sighed. "I guess I never really thought about it. I've been to He– the bad place – every day for sixteen years, but

I've been going to Heaven frequently as well. Even with the ban Michael gave me, I just thought of it as temporary. You know, while I'm living."

Gabriel sighed. "The day you tripped into Afterlife and it became evident you would return was the day all of Afterlife knew you would stand trial. When one has definitive proof of Afterlife, they stand trial before my Father. Michael will be your prosecutor."

"He's *what*?"

Gabriel opened his mouth to say something, only for the pin on his suit jacket to glow a bright gold. "I am sorry, Elya. I must go."

He vanished suddenly, leaving her alone. The room looked colder without him in it. Falling back on the surprisingly soft bed, Elya pulled the blankets around her. She was uncertain how to respond to this visit. Gabriel was a comfort, but learning Michael would be her prosecutor – it was just another thing about the archangel for her to puzzle out. Snuggling into her blankets, Elya drifted to sleep, thoughts of Michael plaguing her mind.

Thirty-Five

It seemed her life was getting weirder by the day. One day she's visiting a demon and ghosts, and the next she's visiting the Mafia. Surprisingly, spending the night in a haunted house wasn't as bad as she anticipated. Jamie and Aurelius kept to themselves, and Bernard was busy hiding from Marco (Marco was taking his anger over losing to her in battle out on the teenage ghost). Yes, the entire night had been filled with strange sounds and even stranger dreams, but it had been manageable. What was most surprising had been how Aurelius cooked her an actual breakfast. It had been a relaxed morning after everything, but she had been glad to leave, especially since she was going to visit Charlie.

Visiting Charlie was always a strange experience. There was just something about having thirty guns trained on her as though she were a threat that weirded her out. Sure, she could hold her own against War and had defeated a demon.... now that she thought about it, maybe she was a threat. Conquest had shown her how dangerous she was with a bow – deadly, even. It gave her a sense of balance, physically and metaphorically speaking. Really, knowing she could be viewed as a threat felt pretty badass. No wonder Kalael was always so confident. Being badass was *awesome*.

Still, she'd prefer to just transport herself to the door, but Alfonso Romano's properties had tighter security than the entrance to Heaven's palace. There, she could sneak right in, but here? She couldn't come within thirty miles without being noticed.

It was either a blatant oversight on Heaven's part or a deliberate thing to make people feel God was more accessible. She couldn't even step out of Satan's throne room without running into a demon. She had successfully evaded an army, and a large one at that, of angels. And yet, she couldn't evade Romano's men.

Alfonso Romano was the most intimidating man in the world stood there in his black suit, his hair peppered with gray, his arms crossed, his gaze cold (it almost always was).

"Elya!" Alfonso grinned. "I have not seen you here in months."

"Oh, you know, college and life keep me busy," Elya said.

He chuckled. "I cannot deny that. Have you thought of what you'll be doing now that you have graduated?"

"I'm still working for Kalael's other father," Elya said.

Alfonso sighed. "He is wasting your talents. If you need, I'm certain my daughter would be willing to have a discussion with him. You should be on top of the world, not forced to mere paperwork, even if in the supernatural world."

"Thanks, but I actually need to talk to Charlie—" Elya fidgeted under his cold gaze "—that is, if he's not too busy."

"He's in his office, although you may wish to knock first." He chuckled mysteriously.

"Still refusing to wear pants?"

Alfonso groaned. "When is he not?"

"Charlie's weird," Elya said.

He chuckled. "You are not wrong, but he is still my son and I love him." He shook his head. "Charlie should not be too busy, so you are free to go up, just promise me you will not leave until after we've had lunch."

She frowned. "I'm not sure. Afterlife is kind of in the middle of a crisis."

Alfonso shrugged. "All the more reason to join us."

Elya shifted uneasily. "Sure."

"Excellent!" He clasped his hands together. "Now, go see Charlie."

Elya smiled. "Thanks."

Not giving him a chance to change his mind, Elya took off at a brisk walk toward the long spiral stairs. She probably shouldn't know her way around as well as she did. But while Alfonso hadn't been aware, between Kalael and Charlie, she had spent her fair share of unauthorized time in Romano's mansion, and most his other properties at that. Though there had been numerous visits that Alfonso was aware of.

Reaching the top of the stairs, Elya walked down the white painted hall, counting the doors one by one until she reached the fifth door on the left. Heeding Alfonso's warning, she rapped quickly on the door, letting Charlie know she was there.

"What is it?" Charlie's voice called.

"Put on your pants, Charlie," Elya called.

"Elya?" Charlie asked.

She rolled her eyes. "No, it's Trina."

The door opened to reveal a tall blond figure. His skin was covered in sweat, his hair mussed, and his pants were unbuttoned. Had it been anyone else, she might have struggled to keep her eyes away from the six pack, but she and Charlie had been through too much over the years. He was one of her best friends (though she did have several of them between Satan and Gabriel and Léana).

"Did you get shorter?" Charlie asked.

Elya huffed. "I'm not short, you're just freakishly tall. Do you have a minute? I need to talk to you about something important."

"Who do I need to kill?" Charlie asked.

"Not that kind of important, but thanks for the offer. Not that I'd ever need it. Believe me, your sister's other brothers would solve that problem before I even knew it was one. Not to mention their father." Elya said.

"Is this relating to her other family?" Charlie asked.

"Yes."

Charlie nodded. He stepped inside his office, gesturing for Elya to follow. Elya looked around curiously. His office wasn't huge, but that wasn't surprising. Despite being the son of a mob boss, Charlie tended to be modest, and currently he wasn't that essential to the business. He was the next leader, sure, but Alfonso, Donnie, and Luca took care of almost everything. That's not to say that Charlie didn't do his fair share, she was sure he did – after all, if he didn't know what he was doing, he wouldn't be able to take over some day.

"So, what trouble has your nosiness caused this time?" Charlie asked.

Elya smiled. "You have no idea what it's gotten me into lately. That's why I'm here. But you know Kalael's biological family."

"You know, I think more people call her Kalael than Kamille anymore," Charlie said.

"Sorry. But Charlie, as much as I would love to catch up," Elya fidgeted, "now's really not a good time."

He pulled on his white dress shirt and worked on his buttons. "So, what's this about?" Charlie asked.

"You know how I've got that internship I didn't want and can't get out of?" Elya asked.

Charlie nodded. "Yes."

"Well, shortly after my graduation, there was this note I found. A warning of sorts about a plot to destroy the place completely. Not just there, but Heaven as well."

Charlie held up a hand. "You got a warning about someone threating to destroy Heaven and Hell?"

"Yes. Naturally, Satan was skeptical, and he sent me to Heaven to see if they got a similar warning. So, I broke into Michael's war room and found the same warning and swiped it. Got caught while sneaking out, lied to Michael, Gabriel, and Raphael. And it turns out Gabriel and Michael can't be lied to, but Gabriel vouched for me despite that, and anyways long story short, Michael banned me from Heaven, the threat is very real, Satan sent me to gather an army, and Kalael recommended I talk to you."

Charlie laughed. "You never do anything halfway, do you?"

"Guess not," Elya said.

Charlie sat back at his desk, kicking his feet up. "I'll help, Elya, but I'm not all that sure what I can do. I may still have my power, but the only thing I was granted was the ability to speak any language fluently. I'm not all that sure what that'll do in way of helping. I can't vanish in the shadows, replicate, cause decay, force my will on others, or levitate things. Not much good in a war of immortals."

Elya's smile softened. "Maybe you can't do those things, but I know Kalael didn't request I get your help for nothing. You're still one of Death's Reapers, technically. Those guys would follow you anywhere, Charlie, and more importantly, you can shoot a gun. I guarantee you there won't be many of *those* in this fight. You and Kalael are about the only people I know who understands that they're useful."

Charlie huffed. "Alright, you've convinced me. I'll help out, but first you have to admit that I'm the best."

"Charlie, you put everyone else to shame," Elya said.

He preened. "I know, I just like hearing it."

Elya shook her head. "Now that we got that solved, I really need to get going. As much as I'd love to hang out, I can't. Still got to finish gathering an army and people for this meeting Satan wants to have to discuss what to do about the whole issue. Text or call me if you have any problems. If I don't answer, you could probably call Kalael – she'd know how to get ahold of me."

Charlie smiled. "I've got a better idea."

"You do?" Elya asked.

"You said Kamille sent you, and like you said, you need Death's Reapers. We're not the helpless little children we were ten years ago. No, we don't number the same – Thanatos took the powers from too many of us for that – but enough of us retained our powers that we're still formidable. However, you're wrong when you say they'll follow me anywhere. We need Trina's help as well. She's got the touch, so she's too valuable to leave out of the fight."

Elya bit her lip. She remembered Trina, she hadn't talked to her much in years, but the older woman was smart and a great strategist. She'd be a good person for them to have on their side. Though, from what Elya understood, nobody was allowed near headquarters unless they were one of the Reapers… but maybe, just maybe she'd be allowed in if she went with Charlie.

"Just make sure none of them kill me?" Elya asked.

"You're an honorary member of the Reapers. Nobody will hurt you. And if anyone tries anything," Charlie cracked his knuckles, "they'll be very regretful."

Elya smiled. "You're the king."

"I know." Charlie grinned. "I'm the best."

Elya laughed. "So confident."

"I have reason to be. Let's go."

"Not so fast – your dad is making me stay for lunch."

He chuckled. "Nobody tells Alfonso Romano no."

"Don't I know it," she smiled. "But seriously, your dad is awesome."

"He is, isn't he?" Charlie offered her his arm. "Shall we, little sis?"

Elya grabbed it. "We shall."

"To lunch we shall go!" Charlie shouted.

She laughed. Charlie may have been the son of a mob boss, but he didn't let that stand in the way of just being himself. Not to say Charlie couldn't be an absolute badass and completely terrifying at times, but she wouldn't trade him for anything.

Of all the friends she had made over the years, Charlie was the one she considered her brother. Aside from her mother and Satan, there was probably nobody who knew her as well as Charlie. Of course, she'd known him twelve years and he was the only person close to her age she could discuss all this supernatural stuff with without risking an involuntary psych hold.

Sure, she had the deadly sins as friends, but they wouldn't understand. They were insanely powerful. Hellas was just thirteen and he could stop a train without budging. Not to mention that, while she knew Satan, Gabriel, Raphael, and the Deadly Sins would have her back if she was in danger, Satan and his children were just as likely to be the cause. She had nothing against Gabriel and Raphael, but they were bound by rules the others weren't.

Charlie wouldn't let anything, even the law, stand in his way

Thirty-Six

After a lengthy lunch with Mr. Romano and Charlie, Elya set out to see Trina and the rest of Death's Reapers. Charlie escorted her, of course, and it had been nice to hang out with him a bit. It was nice to slow down and just take the pressure away for a moment. No, Death Reaper's weren't normal – like her, they had powers that belonged to those native to Afterlife, but they weren't born into it. It made her feel normal. And while she had explained the situation, Trina and Jorge made it clear she wasn't leaving without giving them all a chance to catch up. She even got to see some of the new recruits, new people popping up with supernatural powers. When it was time to go, she almost didn't want to… But she had a job to do, and nothing was going to stop her.

Naturally, Charlie refused to let her go without stopping for smoothies, which was fine by her. Strawberry banana smoothies were the best, and the one in her hand was well-deserved after all the work she had done. All that was left was a trip to Heaven to talk to Gabriel or Raphael about getting the angels to help… after she checked back in with Satan and got a short break. She had been traveling for weeks; she *needed* a break. At least for a day or two. She also had a couple questions for Satan. Nothing important exactly, just something to satisfy her curiosity, Conquest had all but said one of Satan's son had been sent away to live with humans, and if Elya had to guess, that son was Envy.

Finishing off her smoothie, Elya tossed her cup in the recycling, closed her eyes and put in the unfortunately necessary effort to enter Hell. An image of Satan's office clear in her mind, Elya allowed herself to be consumed by the sensation of rushing water. She landed hard on the ground, right in Satan's office. Sure enough, at the desk sat Satan, a ballpoint pen in one hand as he drummed his fingers with the other. On the bright side, she had made it in one piece. She definitely still needed some work on her landings though.

"I'm back," Elya said.

"Just a moment." He didn't glance up.

Elya watched Satan scribble on the papers in front of him. She wanted to know what he was doing because she knew it wasn't his paperwork. It was strange, really – he was always acting like he was busy scribbling on some form of paperwork or another, or sat on his throne pretending to be busy, but she knew he wasn't.

"What do you need?" He still didn't look from his papers.

Elya shifted. "I've talked to everyone but the angels. I even talked to Charlie and Death's Reapers; it was Kalael's idea."

"And have they all agreed?" Satan asked.

"It took some convincing here and there, but yes," Elya said.

"Good," he said.

Elya shifted uneasily. She had never seen Satan look so focused. He was quiet, his answers short. He almost seemed subdued, but she had no idea why he would be. She had seen him in a lot of moods, but never once had any of his moods left him appearing subdued. It was disturbing in ways Elya never thought she'd encounter. It couldn't bode well.

Satan slammed the pen down. "How can you expect anyone to think with your nerves screaming like that?!"

Elya flinched. "Sorry I didn't mean — actually, no. I'm sorry if I'm bugging you, but that gives you no right to yell at me. Yelling needlessly is wrong, and while I know you're all for doing wrong, I'm not letting this one slide."

He ran a hand down his face. "My apologies. I seemed to have lost my temper."

"Just a tad," Elya said.

He huffed. "I may not like the occupants of Heaven, and I loathe most of Hell, but I do not wish to see either destroyed." He chuckled ruefully. "At least not at any hand aside from my own. But through all my calculations, at no point do we come out of this on top, or without sustaining heavy losses to ourselves."

"And did your calculations factor in Charlie and Death's Reapers? Or that all your sons are trained and capable killers with an insane love of violence and every desire to keep you from spending more time at the mansion than you do already? Or that your daughter – your daughter is so powerful it's scary. She's not just your daughter, she's Pride Incarnate, Death's Apprentice-turned-wife, blessed by Alex—"

Satan scoffed. "You don't even know what that means."

"I know the people with this blessing are more powerful. And Kalael is powerful, and Marco didn't exactly go down easy, and Thought, have you seen his realm? What he's capable of? Don't forget Azrael and Loki; they're nothing to be scoffed at. You've all said it, if Azrael had sided with you and Loki, you might have had the power to make the last push to winning your rebellion. That doesn't spell defeat to me. It doesn't even spell loss of others."

He sighed. "You're far too optimistic for one in your position."

"It's because of my position I'm so optimistic," Elya said. "I'm human, but I've seen Heaven, and I've seen Hell, and I've seen realms — plains of existence humankind only dreams of. At the start of this, I never would've dreamed I could do half the things I have."

Satan gazed at her. "Do you have stitches?"

Elya shrugged. "I tripped."

He laughed. "You and Fiend are perhaps the two clumsiest people I have ever met." His eyes lingered on her forehead. "Are those ready to come out?"

"Not for a day or two, I think." She honestly had no idea.

He frowned. "I see."

"Feel better?" Elya asked.

"If only slightly."

He seemed down and she didn't like it, but she had no idea how to fix it. Violence might help, but that wasn't exactly Elya's forte. Surely she knew something Satan liked enough to cheer him up, something that wasn't violent or requiring a visit from his daughter or breaking more laws than she could possibly count.

An idea struck. "Want to go get IHOP?"

Satan startled. "Why—"

"You'll feel better." Elya said

He frowned. "I do like pancakes."

Elya smiled. "Good. Let's go."

Not giving him the chance to protest, Elya put a hand on his shoulder and pictured her local IHOP. She felt a rush of water consuming them and she wobbled, only for an arm to catch her and keep her on her feet. Elya turned to Satan to see a hint of mirth in his gaze, but it wasn't strong enough. Not for him. Together, they walked around the corner to the restaurant's entrance. Thankfully, the wait for a table was short, and they were quickly presented with their menus. Satan immediately ordered himself six large glasses of chocolate milk.

The server looked between the two of them. "Are there more to your party coming?"

"No." Satan said curtly. "Six chocolate milks."

"Don't you think that's a little much?" Elya asked.

"Should I have asked for two glasses for you as well?" Satan asked

Elya addressed the server. "I'll have a hot chocolate, please."

"I'll get those right out to you, darlings." The server said. "Just take a few minutes to look over your menus and decide what you want."

Satan held up a hand. "Not necessary. I'll have a full stack of buttermilk, the harvest grain 'n nuts, the Mexican Leches, the cupcake, the New York Cheesecake, double blueberry, the strawberry banana, and the chocolate-chocolate chip pancakes."

The server raised a brow. "Sir, the full stack of buttermilk has five pancakes, and all the other stacks have four."

"It will be sufficient for now," Satan said shortly. "If I require more, I shall let you know. Elya, what shall you be having?"

"Strawberry crepes please." Elya said, offering the woman a smile.

"I'll get right on it."

Elya waited for the waitress to disappear around the corner before turning her gaze back to Satan. He was drumming his fingers on the table, his leg shaking, as he held his phone, flipping it around but never once looking at it. She wasn't going to say anything, not until she had his attention.

Finally, he paused. "What?"

"Be nice to the servers," Elya said.

He frowned. "I was nice."

"No, you were short with her." Elya said.

He sighed. "My apologies. I hadn't realized."

"You're really feeling out of it, aren't you?"

"Is it that obvious?"

"You ordered all the pancakes and six glasses of chocolate milk," Elya deadpanned.

"Oh."

Elya nodded, allowing Satan to think to himself. She could tell from his jittering he had a lot on his mind and need the time to his thoughts. She'd just have to convince him they needed to leave a large tip to make up for his poor manners.

Thankfully, after the incident with ordering, the rest of their meal went off without a hitch, and an apology from Satan. Despite this, it wasn't until his third order of all the pancakes on the menu and the server's increasing expressions of concern that a smile finally broke across his face. Amid this were, of course, several stares of confusion as people whispered about the sheer number of pancakes Satan had eaten. While she wasn't the best at math, she was smart enough to know he had eaten more than a couple hundred dollars in pancakes, and a total of ten glasses of chocolate milk.

When Elya glimpsed the bill's total, she couldn't say she was surprised it came to $595.12, and that was before adding in the tip, which had to be somewhere around 90 dollars itself, meaning overall their bill was probably about $680, give or take. Not that she was worried about it – while the server looked concerned by the sheer cost of their two-person meal, Elya knew Satan had more money than he knew what to do with. He could have spent five thousand dollars at a restaurant and still not have batted an eye.

As the server walked off with Satan's credit card, Elya noticed his eyes drifted after her. Elya frowned. It wasn't like him to stare at people, not unless they were being obnoxious or rude or just displeased him for some reason or another.

"Sam," Elya said.

"What?" He asked.

"You're staring."

He winced. "Sorry. I just got caught reading her."

"Reading her?"

"Yes. Her soul, all the wrongs she's ever done, and everything she desires. She's a truly fascinating individual." He returned to his last glass of chocolate milk. "I think it's only fair she receives a good tip."

"That dastardly?" Elya joked.

"No, her sins are rather minor on the whole, but the secrets she keeps," he grinned, "those make her interesting. And her desires."

"Just don't go offering her a deal."

"I do actually grant one desire a year pro-bono, and as it so happens, I've yet to fulfill that self-set quota. Therefore it is perfectly reasonable for me to do so."

"That's…" Elya thought over her words "…unexpected."

"I can be nice," Satan said.

Elya smiled. "I know."

He chuckled. "Come on, I'll let you watch me work my magic."

Elya frowned. "Do you mean real magic, or magic as in you're good at what you do?"

"No real magic involved today," Satan said, "but we're going to give Nerida her deepest desire."

"Doesn't it feel invasive," Elya asked, "knowing every desire of complete strangers?"

He shrugged. "You get used to it." Satan pulled out two crisp hundred-dollar bills from his wallet. "We'll start with a good tip." He grabbed a marker from his pocket and put the bills inside a napkin.

She glanced at the note he wrote on the napkin. *My thanks for the excellent service. Spend it wisely, and remember: not every customer will treat you right, but sometimes you might be surprised.* It was simple, oddly encouraging, but in a way, it was very Satan. Maybe he knew how much of a pain he had been at the start of their meal, after all. She shouldn't have been surprised he was good at understanding others.

Retrieving his credit card, Satan led them outside and pulled out his phone. "Grab your brothers. I've got a job for you," Satan said. "Not that kind of job… The yearly one… yes, it's necessary… I'm going to need a man by the name of Oliver Maddox to meet an untimely fate, along with a secured house, a safe family vehicle, and a dying child cured of her terminal illness… I know you guys don't like saving people, but this is non-negotiable. Get Fiend and Shredder on it – between Fiend's healing abilities and Shredder's talent for mixing chemicals, I'm sure they'll figure out something. Have Hellas secure the house and Twist the car. I presume you'll be wanting to take care of Maddox." He pocketed his phone.

Elya raised a brow. "Your magic is getting your sons to do all the work?"

Satan chuckled. "That's only part of the task. There's still a lot to go."

"Aren't you worried she'll think this is, you know, God's doing?" Elya asked.

He shrugged. "I'm nasty and vile, the depth of my hatred and impureness – my devilishness, if you will – is unrivaled, but as I said, I grant desires pro-bono once a year. And while it may give my brothers a false hope, the results are well worth it… even if it leads the recipient to my father. Besides, nothing I do is free, even when I grant desires pro-bono, there's always something in it for myself. This will likely be the best day of her life. How could it not? Her rapist will finally meet a terrible fate, her ill child will be cured, she'll suddenly inherit a house and car, which will be more than ideal for her situation, and as part of this sudden inheritance, she'll receive fifty thousand dollars. And to top it off, she got a two-hundred-dollar tip today."

Elya shook her head. She didn't know what Satan was getting out of this, and she was certain she didn't want to know, but she wasn't going to complain over him doing something nice.

Whatever the case, she had achieved her goal of cheering him up. The pancakes must have been what he needed, at least if the way he was talking was any indication. He seemed more himself, less subdued. How long it would last, she didn't know; if she was being honest with herself, it probably wasn't long, but for now she'd take what she could get. Hopefully he'd stop trying to run numbers.

The only thing left to do was to get to Heaven and find either Raphael or Gabriel to get their support and the support of the angels in what could very well decide the fate of the world. Or, at least, the fate of Afterlife.

Thirty-Seven

A day off from army gathering was what she needed. And the impromptu trip to IHOP helped her more than just Satan. It had been nice, and gave her the time she needed to prepare mentally for when she returned to Heaven. Today, she was ready. Taking a deep breath, Elya focused her energy, allowing the familiar watery sensation to engulf her.

Returning to Heaven was odd, yet comforting, like coming home. In a way, she felt as though she'd been gone for years, but it had only been a few weeks – ever since Loki had offered to teach her control over her ability to teleport through the dimensions. Thankfully, she could control it now and land somewhere other than the designated landing point – otherwise, she'd never get into contact with Raphael and Gabriel. And that could *not* happen. War was coming to Afterlife, a fight for Heaven and Hell, and the only way to win was if Heaven and Hell fought side by side.

Even the vaguely familiar streets felt right. That was the thing about Heaven, it always gave her a feeling of *rightness*. Satan said it had that effect on everyone because it inhibited their ability to see that it was really a dictatorship in a pretty city. Granted, he was a little biased and bitter. Though, a much more interesting answer than the 'that is the way all things should be' Gabriel gave. Or the answer Raphael gave, which was so complex that all she could ever get out of it was that it had a calming effect and left humans at peace.

She was at home in Heaven and Hell, which was why, despite the inevitable tension, she would do everything she could to get them to work together. For the safety of Afterlife. Assuming she wasn't caught before she found Gabriel or Raphael. She was not ready for judgement…

The good news was she had memorized the streets, thanks to Satan, and she knew the faces of two of the five archangels she needed to avoid, so she stood a chance at finding them.

Ducking behind a tree to avoid being seen, Elya winced as she lost her footing. She cursed inwardly – she had tripped. Again. Trying to focus on a place to land, the sensation of rushing water surrounded her as her stomach churned. As she landed on a soft surface, Elya immediately recognized where she was: her landing point. Not wanting to be caught in Heaven, Elya scrambled to her feet and rushed down the hall and around the corner. In her hurry, she got completely turned around. Now she had no idea where she was, but so long as she wasn't in immediate view of any angels, she was fine.

Slowing to a walk, Elya wandered the halls, clueless to her location. Maybe she should have paid better attention to where she was running. But if she lingered near her landing point, there was no way she wouldn't be caught.

Rounding a corner, a door began to open. An angel stepped out of a room and headed in the direction opposite her. She stopped dead in her tracks, eyes searching for somewhere to hide. The angel in front of her looked familiar from behind, but that didn't mean much. Raphael and Gabriel were identical from behind, Satan (who wasn't even an archangel) and Michael were identical from the front. Why couldn't God decorate his palace with suits of armor? Elya ducked behind an oversized vase, bumping into its equally oversized stand. She moved to catch it, but too late – it hit the ground with a resounding shatter.

The angel turned around right as Elya ducked out of sight. She held her breath, hoping he'd think it just fell for some unknown reason, but then scoffed inwardly. There was no way an angel would think something had gone wrong in a place that was supposed to be as perfect as Heaven.

All too soon, Elya was staring at a pair of dark brown sandals. Slowly, she lifted her gaze to meet the angel stood in front of her. A breath escaped her as she took in the familiar features of the blond. While she had long ago accepted God's existence, never had she been so thankful for that as she was in that moment. It was like those moments when a class was cancelled when she hadn't studied for the test. Granted, it only happened once, but it was just as relieving to see Raphael stood there.

"Elya?" Raphael's eyes widened. "What are you doing here?"

She sighed. "It's a long story."

He looked at her contemplatively. "You shouldn't be seen." He offered her a hand and pulled her to her feet. "Come on then. I was heading to the stables. You can tell me the riveting tale of how and why you came to be in this part of the palace while I brush my horse."

Elya raised a brow. "You never told me you have a horse."

Raphael laughed. "You never asked." He reached into his pocket, producing the largest red bag of skittles she had ever seen. "To make up for your depravation of skittles in recent weeks."

Elya eyed the bag. "Do you want me to get sick?" Before Raphael could respond, she took the bag, opened it and popped some of the rainbow-colored deliciousness into her mouth. "Want some?" She offered the bag.

He smiled. "So, you have learned to share your skittles."

She smiled. "Only when it's in this large of a quantity."

"I honestly can say I'm not surprised."

"I like my skittles."

"Indeed, you do. So," he said, leading them outside, behind the palace, "what has you violating your ban from entering Heaven?" he chuckled. "Somehow I doubt it was that you missed the free skittles."

"That's not fair!" Elya smirked. "I missed those and you and Gabriel, but you're right, I am here for a reason." She bit her lip. "Someone, or maybe a group of people…" She ran a hand through her hair. "Well, I found evidence of a threat to the Afterlife. Someone wants to destroy Heaven and Hell."

Raphael raised a brow. "You're certain."

Elya sighed. "Yeah, we did some investigating to see if it was a valid threat. Then, once your brother and I determined it *is* real, he sent me to gather an army to fight it." Her shoulders dropped. "But we can't win. Not without Heaven and the angels on our side."

"And so, you came here."

"Yes."

He clicked his tongue. "What happened that you have stitches?"

"Sword fight with War," Elya shrugged. "He and the other Riders weren't too thrilled by the idea of fighting alongside Satan."

"Unsurprising. Though it is curious he didn't send Kalael."

"Why wouldn't he send me?"

"Michael raised Kalael for two years; he'd do anything for her."

"Okay, I can see how she might have been a good idea, but he didn't send her."

"No, he didn't," Raphael frowned. "Instead, he sent you, which was risky, all things considered… Though, I suspect I know why Michael is so opposed to your presence."

Elya's brow drew together. "Why?"

"Both myself and Gabriel have known you from a young age, Elya." He entered a stall, waiting for Elya before closing the door.

"What does that have to do with anything?" Her eyes flicked to the horse. "On second thought: Why is your horse periwinkle?"

Raphael laughed. "To answer your first question, it's because that makes you a weakness, and Michael *hates* weakness. As for the second, animals are not as limited in colors here as they are on Earth. Why else would Azrael have a pale green horse?"

"I always assumed it was, like, dyed or something." Elya shrugged. "It's Azrael."

"Fair."

Elya looked around the barn, taking in the other horses for the first time. Aside from Raphael's periwinkle horse, there was one that was a light blue, a horse that was purple, lavender, magenta – there seemed to be a horse in every color of the rainbow and then some. How there was room for so many horses though was another question. How they fit into a single barn defied everything she knew about physics (which, admittedly, wasn't a ton).

"Would you like to try riding?"

Elya grimaced, turning back to Raphael and his periwinkle horse. "No thanks. I tried when I was with the Riders, and I couldn't even get into the saddle without falling flat on my butt. Besides, I still have to finish gathering recruits to Save the Afterlife."

Raphael dropped the brush. "Something must be done about that." He turned to the horse. "I'll have to finish brushing you later, Dash." He turned back to Elya. "This is a serious matter. Go find Gabriel; I must gather the archangels."

Before Elya could get the chance to say anything, Raphael disappeared, trumpets sounding behind him as he left. She sighed – of course he'd disappear without giving her directions. Maybe it was for the best. Otherwise, she'd have to worry about being seen with him. She'd be able to move undetected this way. Hopefully he'd be able to find the other archangels while she searched for Gabriel.

Elya stroked Dash, gave the periwinkle horse a smile, and made her way out of the horse stall. If she didn't know how bad she was at riding, she'd see if she could get a horse like the dark green one across from Raphael's, or maybe one slightly lighter. But green, for sure. It was definitely a little strange seeing a horse that wasn't a natural color, but somehow, she liked it. Glancing at the plaque above the green horse's stall, she read the name Emerald. The name seemed to suit the mare – she was beautiful and gave off a calm vibe.

Turning from Emerald, Elya made her way outside the barn and checked it was clear before stepping outside.

Elya exhaled. The odds of her getting caught were one in three. For once they, were in her favor. The bigger issue? If she was caught, there was a nine in eleven chance that it'd be an archangel who caught her, and that was considering that Raphael had already found her once. If she was caught by an archangel, the odds were two in three that it'd be someone who would take her to Michael, one in six that it'd be Michael himself or equal odds it'd be Gabriel. Of course, that wasn't accounting for Raphael gathering his brothers, as well as knowing where they're most likely to be found.

Shaking her head free of thoughts, Elya set out in search of Gabriel, recalculating the odds as she went. Her odd ability was both a gift and a curse.

Thirty-Eight

Who would've thought finding one angel in a palace would be so difficult? She should've asked Raphael where to find him, but no, he needed to find the other archangels. Uriel, Raguel, Zadkiel, and Camael – or, at least she thought that's what he said their names were. She'd yet to find a Bible that named all seven, and the internet couldn't agree beyond Michael, Gabriel, Raphael, and Uriel. It was a sign she needed to hang around Heaven more – well if she was ever able to get her banishment lifted.

Elya sighed. "Come on Gabriel, where are you?"

A chuckle sounded over her shoulder. "Might I suggest looking behind you?"

Elya spun on her heel. Gabriel was leaned against a doorframe, the door to one of the rooms she had passed that was just slightly ajar. Elya gripped her Skittles tighter in surprise. Gabriel was standing there calm as ever, as though there wasn't a threat to destroy Heaven and Hell and she wasn't banned from Heaven. Granted, she wasn't sure how much he knew about the plot to destroy the Afterlife... She had mentioned it, but he had been focused on her stitches. Either way, he knew she wasn't supposed to be there. Yet he wasn't lecturing her. Thankfully. She could not deal with one of Gabriel's patented lectures.

"Hey," Elya said.

He laughed. "Hello, Elya." Gabriel pushed himself from the doorframe. "Not that I do not take joy in seeing you..." He pulled the door shut behind him. "But you should not be here."

Elya smiled. "Just like you weren't supposed to be visiting me or sending me gifts? You broke the rules once, what would once more hurt?"

He gaped. "Break the rules, are you insane? Once was bad enough! I wasn't able to eat or sleep afterward. I had to go to my Father and tell him what I did, then I went to Michael, and they both looked at me in disappointment. I am not Azrael, I do not like to disobey my Father or Michael. I cannot do it again! Who knows what trouble I could be in for simply talking to you?"

Elya laughed. "Raphael didn't seem all that concerned." Granted, that was after she informed him of the situation, but there was no need for Gabriel to know that.

"Unbelievable. He of all people should know better than — he should have sent you home as soon as he saw you," his eyes flicked to her hand, "and instead, he fed you more of that junk! Do neither of you realize there is no nutritional value offered by your candy? You said yourself it will rot your teeth from within your skull! And do *not* get me started on the dangers of you being here. If you are caught, there is no telling the consequences. There is no precedence for this." He was gathering steam – soon to be in full lecture mode. "Anything could happen."

"Gabriel, you need to calm down."

His eyes flashed to gold. "I am perfectly calm."

"Is that why your eyes are gold right now?" Elya challenged. "In my experience, eyes changing color is usually a sign of upset, anger, or frustration with you immortal entities."

He straightened. "My apologies." He ran a hand through his hair. "I seem to have—" he sighed. "It is of no matter." The gold cleared from his gaze. "However, you must go, Elya."

"About that," Elya started, "there is a reason I'm here. An important one."

He frowned. "You have an important reason for being here? What information are you withholding, Elya?"

"Technically, I'm not withholding it. I mentioned it the last time I saw you, but you got a little focused on my stitches."

His gaze darkened. "Stitches I see you still have."

"Right. I get them out soon. Anyways, I might have discovered someone is trying to destroy Heaven and Hell. Your brother sent me to warn you guys and ask that you attend a meeting he's holding to address the problem. He said while I do this, he'll make a suspect list."

"Of course," he muttered. "That would explain why it was I found you in the home of a demon. I thought you had heard about Aurelius and recklessly chose to go meet him with zero regard to the fact he lives with a demon!"

"That reminds me, it kind of didn't occur to me when I was there because I was so out of it after the binding ritual. But how is Marco a demon if his father is an angel, or fallen angel—"

"Marco was not born a demon, he was born a Nephilim. It is a long story and not one I feel comfortable with sharing, as it is not my place."

Elya nodded. "I understand. It's Marco's story, and he doesn't seem the type to share it."

"And who else does my brother have you visiting?" Gabriel asked.

"Oh, you know. Everyone. Or at least it seems like it. You guys were last on my list."

"Everyone?" Something dark entered the edges of his gaze. "And he sent you alone?"

Elya winced. "Yes?"

"*Unbelievable!*" His eyes returned to gold. "Is he insane? You could have been killed! That is far too dangerous a task to face alone." Gabriel paced rapidly. "And now you are here when you are not meant to be. If Michael—" He froze. "Michael."

"What about him?" Elya asked.

Gabriel straightened. "He needs to know of this threat."

"I think he already does," Elya winced. "I kind of found the information about the threat to Heaven while I was in the war room."

"This is what you were hiding?" Gabriel gaped. "Elya! Of all the—" He pinched the bridge of his nose. "I have spent eternity dealing with Azrael, and yet somehow it only ever seems to be you who drives me to insanity with worry."

"I'm sorry, okay?" Elya snapped. "I made a dumb mistake, but we already knew about a threat against Hell, and your brother wanted me to get in and out unnoticed," Elya rambled. "Then Uriel found me and took me to Michael, and I panicked."

Gabriel sighed. "Regardless, Michael needs to know."

"Do I have to?" Elya asked softly. "He's kind of terrifying."

Gabriel raised a brow. "You spend every day with my brother who has a rather fearsome reputation and a legendary temper, yet you fear Michael?"

"From what I've read, Michael is supposed to be the strongest of the angels and leads your guys' army." Elya folded her arms. "Your other brother I've known since the age of six. How would I not be terrified of Michael?"

Gabriel laughed. "It is true that none are as skilled as Michael, but I am known to be rather skilled in the art of battle as well."

Elya almost dropped her Skittles. "Really?"

He frowned. "I am incapable of lying, so I would suppose the appropriate answer to your question would be yes."

Elya laughed. "I guess I just never imagined you as the warrior type. Not with the way you seem to panic at the thought of violence."

Gabriel pouted. "While I may not like the idea, and I most certainly do not encourage it, I am capable of fighting when needed, and I most certainly do not panic at the thought of it. I simply have concerns for your safety."

"You're concerned for my safety?" Elya scoffed. "Yeah, that makes total sense. You're concerned for my safety, but you're still telling me I need to go talk to Michael. You know, the guy who banned me from Heaven and from communicating with you and Raphael."

Gabriel winced. "It is unfortunate, but it does need done. None will be able to determine the strength of this threat except for my brother. And if this threat is severe, it will take all the archangels and many of my brothers and sisters to win. Michael is the only one who would be able to rally all of them to fight alongside our cast-out siblings."

"What about you and Raphael?"

"Michael is the eldest, and with that comes the benefit of holding the most sway over my siblings." Gabriel sighed. "I fear there is no choice other than to ask his aid."

"Does it have to be Michael?" Elya pled.

Gabriel chuckled. "I do not think your last meeting with my brother went so poor as to warrant such fear. Yes, he is strict and banned you from entering Heaven–"

"A ban I'm currently breaking."

"–but he is fair and just. He will hear your reasoning for being here, so long as you are honest and give them."

Elya scoffed. "Yes, because lying to him last time will make him so willing to listen to me."

He pinched the bridge of his nose. "Believe it or not, my brother is not your enemy."

"And what happens when he finds out I talked to you and Raphael?" Elya challenged.

Gabriel huffed. "I will likely learn what it is like to be Azrael and receive a rather lengthy lecture on the wrongs I have committed. The difference between Azrael and me, of course, is that he commits these wrongs without thought to the consequence. I have thought over the consequences and my only concern is for what *you* might be met with." He crossed his arms. "This is why you must be honest with Michael. He will respect you more for being honest with him. And if you can gain his full respect, he will be a valuable ally. Not only in the coming battle, but for all the years to come. It would be unwise to lose such an opportunity."

Elya shifted. "Fine. I'll try to tell him the truth. Assuming he lets me get two words out before he sends me back to Earth."

Gabriel smiled. "You will be surprised." He glanced at his watch. "Michael will be in his office right now. I shall walk you."

Elya didn't get a chance to protest before Gabriel turned and walked in the direction of the War Room. He was serious – he wanted her to talk to Michael right then. Oh, she was so dead. Like deader than one of Azrael's squirrels dead. There was no way this could end well. Gabriel was delusional if he thought Michael would listen to her.

Thirty-Nine

Her heart was going to beat out of her chest. Her stomach churned as she stood in front of Michael. She couldn't believe Gabriel had sent her in alone… Facing War had been less terrifying.

She took a partial step forward, shutting the door behind her with a soft click. Gripping her skittles, she observed the angel bent over the desk. His brow was furrowed, his mouth turned downward as though he were trying to focus.

He was an enigma. He banned her from Heaven, only for her to learn later he had sworn an oath to *God* of all beings to protect her. He wouldn't let her speak to Raphael and Gabriel, yet if rumors were to be believed, he was the one who convinced Satan to take her under his wing when she began tripping into Hell at six. It didn't make sense. None of it did.

Not ready to face the angel, Elya observed his office instead. The walls were lined with books, and twelve photographs sat on the desk. She stepped a little closer, attempting to peek. The first one she recognized immediately – she had to be around two in the photo, but there was mistaking the toddler as anyone other than Kalael. Pride was ethereal, and from what Elya had seen, very fae-like as a child. Next to it was a photo of a little boy, his eyes a vibrant gold, his hair a fiery red. She wanted to see the others, to ask who the little boy was, but she couldn't. The other photos were turned so she couldn't see, and she wasn't on the best terms with Michael.

She cleared her throat, announcing her presence.

The angel glanced up from his desk. "You are not meant to be here." He put his quill down. "Have you no regard for rules?"

The grip on her skittles tightened; they had become her safety net, both for her conversation with Gabriel and this one. Maybe if she held them tight enough, Raphael would come to the rescue, and of course Gabriel wouldn't be far behind. She just wished she didn't have to have this discussion with Michael. Already, it was off to a bad start.

"I know I'm not supposed to be here. I get it. I do. I work for your brother; I have no right to be here. But the thing is, last time I was here, I lied. Satan did send me. Not for a plot against you or Heaven or anything, but because we — *I* discovered a plot to destroy Hell. So, he asked me to determine if it was from Heaven. You know him, he's paranoid. And then I found the same note in the War Room and I panicked. I promised Satan I wouldn't tell, and I was terrified nobody would believe me, but there is a very real threat against Heaven and Hell. Your brother is trying to help save Afterlife, but we can't win, not without the angels on our side, and you command them, so here I am."

Michael moved in front of his desk, stopping mere inches from her. Elya looked at his towering figure: he didn't dress in a suit like his brothers, instead favoring a pair of jeans and a t-shirt that hugged his muscles in all the right places. A sword hung at his waist, and he crossed his arms, his biceps bulging. Stood this close, she truly felt tiny. Insignificant. No more than a spec in the grand scheme of existence. Power radiated from him, and she knew if he wanted, he could kill her with the wave of a hand. But she wasn't going to be intimidated. Shaking off her trepidation, Elya met his gaze. She had fought and survived against War. She could do this. She had to. Even if the odds of Michael agreeing to help were one in a three thousand.

"I was wondering if you'd come to confess the truth of why you were there that day," he grinned. "I admit I was beginning to doubt."

"What?" Elya asked, dazed.

"I will need to inform my Father, but I will put out a call to arms. You will have the angels fighting alongside Hell for the good of the Afterlife. And I will be there to aid you as you lead the army you've gathered into war."

Elya spluttered. "I'm sorry, what?"

He chuckled. "For this, there can be but one commander. You are the one to have rallied people to fight for the Afterlife. It must be you who takes command." He offered her a smile. "Fear not – I shall stand behind you and advise you as needed. But the denizens of Hell will not follow myself, nor will the angels follow Satan. It must be a neutral party."

"What about Conquest? War, Azrael, Kalael, Dimitri – anyone would be better than me. I don't know anything about leading a war."

"As I said, I will be there to advise you," his gaze softened, "but the others cannot do it. You gathered this army, and you must lead them."

"No pressure."

He laughed. "You will succeed, Elya, because you are no fool."

"Well, I'm glad someone has confidence in me."

He shrugged. "It is difficult not to. You tend to defy the odds."

"Well, thanks for agreeing to help?"

He grinned, revealing perfect white teeth. "Have more confidence in yourself, Elya. You came in here and confessed to having lied. You stood your ground and made me listen. Not many would have the courage to try. For that, you have earned my respect. And very few ever get it. You have potential, Elya, to be great."

"Does that mean I'm no longer, you know, banned from Heaven?"

"No. You're a distraction. For Gabriel, for Raphael, for the other archangels, and most importantly, me. Gabriel and Raphael grew attached, and it's not healthy for angels to form attachments with humans. I apologize for my bluntness, but your lives are fleeting."

"I mean, I know I hang out with your brothers, but I wouldn't call them attached."

He raised a brow. "Do you think I'm unaware of the trinkets Gabriel sends you along with skittles from Raphael? Since you have started coming into Heaven, Raphael has more than doubled his stash of Skittles. He does not eat them himself, and the only other person who does is me. And he most certainly isn't hoarding that much candy for me."

"No way! You love Skittles too?"

"It is an unhealthy habit." He eyed her carefully. "Where do you stand on the lime vs green apple debate?"

Elya thought about it. "I always said lime, but now that you say green apple, it feels right."

He nodded. "Very well. I'll lift your restriction from communication with Raphael, and only Raphael. You're still not allowed to contact Gabriel until this threat to Afterlife has been resolved. And as long as you live, you're not permitted to linger in Heaven."

Her eyes widened. "Just like that?"

Michael raised a brow. "I can maintain the ban, if you'd rather. I thought, as you've earned my respect, the least I could do was allow you your friendship with Raphael. Just know you are both on *very* thin ice. And I won't tolerate you becoming a problem."

"What about Gabriel?" Elya asked, hopeful.

"No." His gaze hardened. "The only one to lift your communication ban with Gabriel will be my Father, and I don't honestly see it happening. He grows increasingly distracted when you're around. It's counterproductive and not conducive to the health of either of you."

Elya gripped her Skittles. "What if I traded you half of all the Skittles Raphael gives me?"

He frowned. "I can neither be bought nor bribed." He stepped forward. "As I said, only my Father may lift the communication ban between yourself and Gabriel. The same can be said for your ban from entering Heaven longer than is absolutely necessary."

Elya huffed. "Unfair! You instituted the ban in the first place."

"For the good of all involved!" Michael bit out. "Now, if you would excuse me, I need to inform my Father and gather the angels to fight. Tell my brother we shall be at his gathering."

Elya raised a brow. "When you say 'we,' do you mean your father as well?"

Michael laughed. "I do not believe Father would attend. He is far too busy and his attendance would not be necessary."

Elya pouted. "Ugh, fine. Not like it would've been super cool to meet God or anything."

Michael opened the door. "You are a very likeable person, Elya," there was something in his gaze, like a hidden meaning, "but you ask for many things which are unlikely."

"Not that many," Elya muttered.

"A matter of opinion. You desire to save Afterlife, Elya. What you're doing is admirable, but know that things may not be so easy."

"I'm prepared for a challenge," Elya said.

"Even war?" He stood inches from her. "Because that may be what we're facing, Elya. A war among celestials isn't a small matter. The last one nearly destroyed us all. Anyone, even Satan, could turn against you."

Elya staggered back. "He wouldn't. He's the one who sent me to gather everyone!"

"For your sake," his gaze softened, "I hope you're not on opposite sides." Michael left, headed toward his war room.

Stepping from his office was like a weight lifted from her shoulders. Suddenly she could breathe easier. She wondered if Michael had any idea how suffocating his presence was. If she was never in a room alone with him again, it'd be too soon. Whether it was practice or natural talent she didn't know, but he gave off the impression he knew more about her then she knew about herself. It didn't help that his gaze made her feel as though he was looking right into her soul and seeing every wrong she ever committed.

"Are you well?" a familiar voice asked.

Elya yelped. She spun around to see Gabriel stepping out of another room. "Don't scare me like that!"

"My apologies, I had not meant to frighten you." He offered a soft smile. "I simply desired to know how your conversation with my brother went. You seem unsettled."

Elya grinned. "Oh, that went great. He's agreed to help and he even agreed to lift the communication ban between Raphael and me. And I think we bonded over our love of Skittles. Did you know he liked them too? I think he's a green apple guy as well. I'm not sure because he didn't say but something about his response was like I passed a test."

Gabriel straightened. "Did he happen to mention anything of my own communication ban? It would make ensuring you are properly nourished far simpler if I could be the one to greet you as you arrive."

Elya winced. "He did, but it wasn't exactly good. He said the only one who can lift that ban is, you know, God. And Michael didn't exactly sound like it would be lifted any time soon… or ever."

His smile dropped. "I suppose that is reasonable. I shall have to content myself with knowing Raphael will be able to greet you once again. Despite his tendency to indulge your desire for junk, I shall need to trust him." He tapped his foot. "I shall simply have to design a list of menu items which shall ensure you get your proper nourishment. I'll of course need to list all your favorite foods and the locations from which you most enjoy them from. If I color code it, he will be more likely to follow it properly. Though I do fear there is nothing which will keep him from feeding you candy prior to a proper meal."

Elya laughed. "Never change, Gabriel."

"Why would I?" He asked, genuinely confused.

"It's an expression," Elya explained. "It basically means I like you best the way you are."

"Oh." He frowned. "Then I shall endeavor to never change. So long as you promise that you shall never change either."

"Deal." She smirked. "Hey Gabriel, what do you call a smart blonde?"

He frowned. "I do not understand your question."

"It's a joke."

"But what does intelligence have to do with one's hair color?"

Elya sighed. "There is so much about humanity you need to understand. First of all, blonde people are typically portrayed in books and television as being dumb, and thus came the blond jokes. They're told in jest, and half the time it's the blond in a friend group who makes the blond jokes. The point is, any other hair color is supposed to be smart."

"I do not follow." His brows drew together confusion swam in his eyes. "Would this not be upsetting to the people in question?"

"Not usually, no. Despite the jokes, they're actually not meant to be offensive. Most blondes are smarter than the jokes imply. So — I don't know, It's just a part of humanity."

Gabriel shook his head. "Humans are truly odd creatures."

"We are." Elya grinned. "But back to the joke."

"You would call it a smart blonde?" Gabriel asked.

Elya sighed. "You call it a golden retriever."

He frowned. "Explain."

"Because golden retrievers are smart dogs with blonde fur. And remember, blondes in the jokes are supposed to be dumb. I'd tell you the M&Ms joke, but you don't eat candy so I'm not sure you'd follow."

Gabriel sighed. "I apologize that I do not understand."

"Dude, it's not a big deal." Elya grinned. "I'll just have to make a habit of telling them until you do understand."

"We are still forbidden from communication, Elya." He ran a hand through his hair. "I am afraid there will not be more of these conversations."

"Technically, Michael said I'm allowed contact with you until the threat has been resolved. So, I think technically, in the meantime we're allowed to communicate."

Gabriel frowned. "I do not believe that was what he meant. I believe my brother's intention was that we not communicate any more than strictly necessary." He glanced at his watch. "We should return you home. It is getting late. Have you had your evening nourishment?"

Elya smiled. As if she was going to eat before going to Heaven. Not when she had every intention of seeing Gabriel. She wasn't going to pass on free food, especially when it was from Gabriel, who either bought her takeout from the best places or cooked the best meals she ever had. If she could afford a personal chef – which, if Satan kept paying her half as much as he did that first time, she could – then he would be her first choice.

"Not yet," Elya said.

Gabriel nodded. "We shall have to rectify that. I shall take you home. Afterwards, I will see what I can throw together for you in the kitchen. I shall send Raphael with enough for your evening meal and perhaps one or two meals tomorrow? Otherwise, you'll never be properly nourished."

"Spaghetti's my favorite food."

He grinned. "I am aware." He placed a hand on her shoulder.

Elya closed her eyes as the cool feeling of teleportation overcame her. There was a bright flash of light she knew to be from the rapid transfer between light into darkness and back into light. Opening her eyes, Elya saw she was once again alone in her room and sighed. Being friends with angels was great until they took her home and left her with her awful roommates. Maybe if she complained enough, Zeerlo or someone would do something. Then again, Zeerlo would *kill* her roommates. Maybe she could convince Raphael to help her find somewhere else to live. Thanks to Satan, she was going to be rich now. She might as well live somewhere nice. She would need a place with a big kitchen for when her communication ban with Gabriel was lifted so she could convince him to be her personal chef. She refused to accept that their communication ban may never be lifted. If she had to go to God and fight for it herself, she would.

Forty

When Satan said they'd be meeting in neutral territory, she hadn't quite imagined him bringing them to a hotel conference room. Thankfully, Kalael made all the hotel reservations, and with a maiden name like Romano – well, it carried a lot of weight around the globe. Unfortunately, for the initial meeting, Kalael wouldn't be present. How it had happened was beyond her. Kalael was the only person she knew who could keep Azrael, Satan, and Zeerlo all in check. But she wasn't here now, and this was it. Everyone was invited, and slowly gathering to the hotel.

Satan had his laptop prepared to give a presentation on everything they knew about the threat, along with ideas on how to stop it. Twist had dropped by to ensure everything was in working order – not that Satan was bad with tech, but Sloth was a mastermind. Twist made every device imaginable to lessen the amount of actual work he had to do.

With everything ready, the king of Hell lounged in his chair, feet kicked up on the table as he scrolled through his phone. Meanwhile, Zeerlo loosened the screws on various chairs in an effort to get them to collapse. There were fifteen chairs in total and only fourteen people set to come, from what she'd been told. The extra chair was apparently in case Loki decided to make an appearance. It was uncertain if he would or not, given that Michael, Raphael, and Gabriel would all be present. And from what little Elya knew of him, she was almost certain Loki would be making a grand entrance.

As Wrath moved to her chair, Elya sent him a glare. "If you tamper with my chair, I will kill you."

Zeerlo paused behind her chair, which was situated between Satan and Michael. She would've thought Satan would sit himself as far away from Michael as possible, but for some unknown reason, the Devil wanted the archangel close to him. As a result, she was to be seated between the two. Not that the rest of the seating arrangements were much better… it looked as though Satan were trying to deliberately start a fight.

Zeerlo chuckled as though her words finally registered. "She survives one little fight with a demon and suddenly she thinks she's capable of holding her own."

"Touch my chair, I'll show you just how capable I am," Elya bit out.

"Feisty!" Zeerlo stepped close to Elya. "We might just see how much fun we can have later," he chuckled. "Well, I'll be having fun. You'll probably get your ass kicked.

"Zeerlo!" Satan snapped.

Wrath spun on his heel. "What?"

"Behave yourself." Satan's gaze moved to the door. "We are expecting company soon."

Zeerlo scoffed. "And since when do their opinions matter?"

"They don't," Satan harrumphed, "I just don't care to hear the inevitable lecture from Gabriel, and I can only imagine what perfect little Michael will say."

Elya laughed. "Michael and little don't go together in a sentence. He's like a more muscular and more intimidating version of you."

"Oh?" Zeerlo smirked. "Is someone crushing on the lead angel?"

"Um, gross?" Elya frowned. "I literally just said he's like a Satan 2.0, why in the world would I find him attractive?" Aside from the fact he absolutely was.

Satan's eyes reddened. "Are you implying I am unappealing? And he is not more intimidating than me, and I will have you know—"

"Shut it, old man," Zeerlo snapped.

"Excuse me?" Satan demanded. "But I do believe you should not tell your father to shut it–"

Thankfully, at that moment, the door clicked open. Elya was flooded with relief as Azrael and Dimitri walked in. If anyone would be able to help her reign in this chaos, it was Dimitri. His father was just as bad as Zeerlo and Satan. The newly-entered father-son duo made their way to their seats. Neither sat, both checking their chairs first.

"Oh, come on!" Zeerlo groaned pinching the bridge of his nose. "I worked hard to get all those chairs set to collapse."

Azrael chuckled. "You should know better than to attempt pranking the master. And Dimitri deals far too much with Loki, Zeke, and I to be fooled by something so childish."

Zeerlo bristled. "Childish? I'll give you childish, you—"

"Sit. Both of you," Dimitri said calmly.

"Excuse me?" Zeerlo and Azrael asked.

"You heard me." Dimitri looked to Azrael. "And don't even try making the claims about how you're my father," his gaze turned to Zeerlo, "or how you're my uncle. You are both acting like toddlers."

The Grim Reaper and Wrath Incarnate sat in their respective chairs. Each sent their own glares to Dimitri. As the room descended into silence, Satan placed his laptop in front of Elya. Wordlessly, she began combing through his slideshow, correcting his grammar and spelling errors as she went. It was calming, in a weird way. Editing was something normal for her to do in the chaos that had become her life. Most of the time, Satan spoke with flawless grammar, his writing was formal, but his punctuation was – well, it could use some work. Sometimes she suspected he did it on purpose to torture her.

The door opened yet again to reveal three of the seven archangels: Michael, Gabriel, and Raphael. The three brothers sent disapproving looks toward their wayward brother, who was drumming his fingers on the table. Gabriel sent her a soft smile and Raphael didn't hesitate to toss a red bag of Skittles in front of where she was currently working.

"Thanks, Raphael." Elya tore open the bag before Zeerlo could think to snatch it. She refused to lose yet another bag of Skittles to the son of Satan.

"I should like a word, brother," Gabriel said.

Satan groaned rolling his eyes. "Can it wait?"

"No, it cannot wait!" Gabriel hissed. "You sent Elya, a *human*, to gather everyone. She fought against War!"

Satan scoffed. "She's perfectly capable of — did you say War?"

Gabriel sighed. "Surely you considered the possibility."

"No I hadn't because I would have thought Famine and Conquest would keep him from doing something as idiotic as challenging a human girl to battle!" Satan turned to Elya. "Were you hurt?"

"Only needed a few stitches in three locations," Elya grinned.

"That's a lie," Zeerlo added.

"Damn it, Zeerlo!" Elya rounded on the Mercenary.

"Elya!" Gabriel gasped. "Mind your language!"

Zeerlo smirked. "Yeah, Elya, mind your language."

"Stay out of this!" Elya snapped.

"That was a lie, though," Gabriel frowned. "Just how badly were you hurt Elya?"

She sighed. "You saw the cut to my head. I also had six stitches in my shin and sixteen in my side."

"*Sixteen?!*" Gabriel gasped.

Satan's gaze turned to fire. "I'm going to kill him."

Going back to the presentation slides, Elya drowned out the back and forth between Satan and Gabriel. She didn't doubt the two of them would put aside their differences long enough to plot against War for some imagined slight. It wasn't as though she hadn't agreed to fight against War. Sure, she had been kind of terrified at the time, but she fought better than expected and earned the Rider's respect. And how many people could say they had the respect of War himself? Her eyes widened as she came to Satan's suspect list.

Azrael: Known for doing dumb shit, has done things worse than I have, knows he's the favorite and would get off with a slap on the wrist, and Loki would help without question.

Cain: Has appropriate hatred for both. Uncertain if he could gain the allies to pull this off, but I wouldn't put it past him.

The Kyles: Self-explanatory.

Destruction: The guy has a deep hatred of all things related to religion; he's a psychopath and seems to just want to see the world burn.

Elya: Able to travel between Heaven and Hell with ease. Additionally, she seems to have no real loyalty to either. Stole my favorite pen and continues to deny it.

Atheist: There are a lot of them and they could easily build a fairly formidable army.

Zeerlo: He's an ungrateful brat with little restraint and reminds me far too much of myself. What's worse, he has the strength to pull it off if he gathers his brothers. And I dread what would happen were he to get Kalael on his side, especially if she were to bring her children.

Hitler: The guy's crazy enough for it.

Alex: Our most likely suspect, as the Tyver king is uniquely powerful and can create life from nothing, as well as resurrect the dead. Extremely powerful, and close to being on par with the guy who kicked me out of the house. If it is Alex, we may as well as give up hope and accept our new existences under his rule.

Mother Nature: Seems like the kind of thing she'd do.

That guy from the bar in Vegas: The way he kept looking at me was creepy, and not in the fun way.

Myself: This is the type of plot I would come up with, though I don't recall it.

The guy who kicked me out of the house: He's flooded the world before, who's to say he wouldn't try something like this? I mean, come on, we all know I'm right to mistrust him.

"Are you serious?" Elya asked.

Satan sighed. "What now?"

Elya turned the laptop around. "You put me on your suspect list!"

"I had good reasons for doing so!" Satan's gaze flashed gold. "You still have my pen and more importantly, what allegiance do you have to either Heaven or Hell? Michael has banned you from Heaven and you only enter Hell because I make you."

Elya huffed. "You're insane."

"Don't I know it," a familiar voice laughed.

Elya glanced up to see War had entered, along with Time, Thought and Life. Now they just needed Charlie and Trina then they could start their meeting. Finished with fixing Satan's presentation, Elya moved from his chair back to her own. Carefully, she examined it to ensure Zeerlo hadn't tampered with it.

"War, might I have a word with you?" Gabriel asked from his seat. His expression was surprisingly dark and his eyes were tinged with gold at the edges.

War crossed his arms. "Concerning?"

"You hurt Elya!" Satan snarled.

"Who hurt Elya?" Trina asked as she entered the room.

"War did," Gabriel seethed, his gaze never leaving the rider.

"Which we all know isn't allowed," Zeerlo said. His eyes had darkened to black, his fangs elongated. "Only I'm allowed to hurt her."

"Nobody is allowed to hurt her!" Gabriel snapped.

The room descended into chaos. Angels and other immortal entities shouted while Elya put her hands in her head and groaned. She knew this wouldn't end well, but she would have thought they'd at least start the meeting before a fight broke out. She should have known better. These entities had all once fought against each other, and the consequences were too great for anyone to just leave it in the past. She had hoped someone would get them under control, but Michael had joined in the arguing, as had Time. Aside from herself, the only ones not in the frays of the fighting were Dimitri and Life.

"Any chance you guys can calm them?" Elya asked.

Dimitri scoffed. "Considering the only ones in the fighting I'm not related to would be Time and Thought, I can say with certainty there's not a snowman's chance in Hell."

Life sighed. "I have already tried to calm the tempers of my brothers, but it is to no avail. Nor am I capable of soothing the angels – fallen or otherwise." Life glanced at the arguing figures. "I am afraid we will simply need to let this play out."

Elya groaned, slouching into her chair. This was going to be a long night.

Once more, the door clicked as it opened. Her eyes snapped to the entrance, fully expecting a hotel employee or guest to come complaining about the noise. Satan claimed to have sound proofed the walls, but given the levels of shouting, she wouldn't be surprised. As soon as the man entered, Elya knew one thing with certainty: he was a celestial. She didn't know who he was, but he radiated power, despite the fact he didn't have the appearance of a demon or the breathtaking features of the angels. But his power spoke for itself.

He stood tall, his clothes were casual, and his eyes held warmth greater than the sun. He glanced over the arguing celestials. Wordlessly, he walked to the conference table, his posture near perfect. Power radiated from him, yet the whole time, his face portrayed patience. The man came to a stop at the table, taking a seat in the unlabeled chair that had been meant for Loki. The entire room fell silent. Suddenly, everyone was straightening up and fixing their clothes. One by one, the entities Elya had gathered moved to their assigned seats. Satan and Zeerlo were the only ones who remained standing.

"I do not recall sending you an invitation," Satan said smoothly as he took his own seat.

Zeerlo grinned as he finally sat in his chair. He leaned back, kicking his feet up on the table. He studied the man carefully. "'Sup Gramps! Long time, never see."

The entity laughed. "You are so like your father when he was young."

Zeerlo sneered. "Glad you could make it, considering you never show to any other family event."

"Satan!" Michael shouted. "Get a handle on your son."

"He has a point," Satan shrugged. "He hasn't showed for one of my children's births or birthday parties. He didn't even come to his own granddaughter's wedding."

"He was at the wedding, actually," Azrael cut in.

"And you never invite any of us to the birthday celebrations," Gabriel added.

The room descended into chaos as Satan and the Deadly sins continued their disrespect toward — Elya froze, realization crashing into her. Zeerlo had called the new entity *gramps*, as in Satan's father. This entity with the calm demeanor, looking as though he walked in off the streets, this was God. As in God? She couldn't believe it. She had so many questions, but could she ask them? He was God and she was just Elya.

God raised a hand. "Peace, my children. This is no time for squabbles." The room once again silenced. "Samael, I understand you have your grievances with me, and you have passed them to your sons. However, at this moment, we need to focus not on the past, but on the future. On ensuring there is still a Heaven and Hell."

"I hate you, end of discussion," Satan sneered.

"I understand why you would be angry with me, my son," God said calmly, "and I forgive you for not controlling your temper today."

Satan leapt from his chair, knocking it over in the process. "You forgive me? Father, I am not the one who owes an apology!" His gaze turned golden. "You threw me out of the house! You cast me from Heaven as though I were yesterday's garbage. And you expect me to just—" He ran a hand through his hair in frustration. "In all my years, I have never—"

Michael stood, placing a hand on his brother's shoulder. "Breathe." His voice was calm. "Don't let it control you." His expression softened. "Now is not the time nor place."

Satan eyes returned to brown. "You're right." He straightened his shirt. "As usual." He grabbed his seat, returning it to its place. "I must keep my rage under control." He glared at his Father. "Would be simpler if someone I hated with every fiber of my being hadn't shown."

"I only love you, my son," God said, but he wasn't looking at Satan as he said it. He was looking toward Michael. "As I have always loved you."

"Zeerlo," Michael said suddenly, "have Elya removed from the room please."

Elya startled. "What?"

"It is apparent some things need to be discussed," Michael said without addressing her. "If you would, nephew."

Zeerlo scoffed. "I don't take orders from you."

Satan's eyes flashed gold. "Do as he says."

"What? No! This is not fair!"

Zeerlo grabbed her, throwing her over his shoulder as though she weighed little more than a small sack of potatoes. Elya struggled to free herself of the sin's grip. It was undignified being carried like this, but her efforts were futile. Zeerlo was the strongest of Satan's sons, if not of all the sins. As she was deposited in the hall, she moved to stand, only for the door to shut in her face. Elya tried the handle to no avail.

"Guys!" Elya banged on the door. "Come on! How is this fair? I gathered everyone for this meeting. I did all the hard work, and you're going to just kick me out?"

Nobody answered the door. Elya kicked it one last time for good measure before sitting on the floor in resignation. She'd find her way back in the room, she just needed to be smart about it. In the meantime, she was left to her thoughts. While she was glad to be out of the fighting, it was frustrating. She thought she and Michael might have some sort of truce – they agreed on skittles, *and* he said if things went to war, she'd lead the army. And yet he threw her out of what could be a critical meeting. And worse, Satan just let him!

She'd show them. She was going to find her way back into that meeting if it was the last thing she did, if only to chew them both out for kicking her out in the first place and to yell at Zeerlo for his methods of getting rid of her. It was undignified and rude. She'd get into that meeting or die trying. If she could break into Heaven's war room, survive an alternative timeline where Gabriel and Raphael were evil on top of winning a battle with a demon, she sure as Hell could get into that meeting. All she needed was a plan.

To Be Continued